Ballpark Blues

Ballpark
Blues

a novel

C.W. TOOKE

Doubleday

New York   London   Toronto   Sydney   Auckland

PUBLISHED BY DOUBLEDAY
a division of Random House, Inc.
1745 Broadway, New York, New York 10019

DOUBLEDAY and the portrayal of an anchor with a dolphin are trademarks of Doubleday,
a division of Random House, Inc.

BALLPARK BLUES is a work of fiction. Any references to real events, businesses,
organizations, and locales or well-known personalities are intended only to give the
fiction a sense of reality and authenticity. Any resemblance of any of the fictional
characters to actual persons, living or dead, is entirely coincidental and unintentional.

Library of Congress Cataloging-in-Publication Data

Tooke, C. W.
    Ballpark blues : a novel / by C. W. Tooke.—1st ed.
        p. cm.
    1. Baseball players—fiction. 2. Journalists—Fiction. I. Title.

PS3620.O585 B35 2003
813'.6—dc21   2002067400

ISBN 0-385-50640-6

Book design by Patrice Sheridan

PRINTED IN THE UNITED STATES OF AMERICA

April 2003

First Edition

10 9 8 7 6 5 4 3 2 1

FOR MY FAMILY, BLOOD AND OTHERWISE . . .

acknowledgments

THIS BOOK EXISTS ONLY BECAUSE MANY PATIENT AND SELF-less teachers spent their valuable time on me, especially my parents, Lorrie Pierce, Curtis Miller, Thomas Heise, John McPhee, and Jim Merritt.

Over the last few years I have spent an inordinate number of nights sleeping on couches and otherwise depending on the kindness of friends. Some even helped get this book published. You know who you are—many, many thanks.

I also owe an enormous debt of gratitude to my agent, Simon Lipskar, and my editor, Anne Merrow. This novel is far better because they chose to be part of it.

As always, the mistakes are mine, anything that remains is yours.

Thus not only does democracy make every man forget his ancestors, but it hides his descendants and separates his contemporaries from him; it throws him back forever upon himself alone and threatens in the end to confine him entirely within the solitude of his own heart.

—ALEXIS DE TOCQUEVILLE, *DEMOCRACY IN AMERICA*

Never before in history have so many been so famous for so little.

—WITH APOLOGIES TO SIR WINSTON CHURCHILL

prologue

THIS STORY, THE REAL STORY OF THE FIRST TIME I SAW CASEY
Fox play, is not the version I will someday tell my grandchildren.
Kids don't want to hear unpleasant details in their fairy tales, and
I don't think I'll be honest enough to admit that Grandpa
achieved a level of grouchy cynicism at age twenty-eight that
most octogenarians never obtain. But if I'm going to tell this story
the way it really happened, I might as well start with the unedited
truth: the only reason I was at that baseball field in Providence
was dumb luck.

In fact, I almost skipped the game entirely. The weather report
that morning showed a northeaster rolling down from the Cape,
which eroded my already minimal interest in watching two
mediocre college teams play a meaningless game. So when I arrived at the field, opened the door of my rental car, and first felt
the bite of the raw wind, I contemplated returning to my motel
room and writing my newspaper story from the box score. I don't
think too many experienced reporters would blame me. Early
spring baseball in New England is a Puritan exercise; there is no
joy or warm sunshine or that indescribable feeling of awakening
that so many young writers try to describe. No, April baseball in

New England is cold rain running in the ear hole of a batting helmet and a pitching staff riddled with dead and aching arms.

But some remaining shred of professional obligation forced me to leave my warm car, and I trudged into the tiny park for what I was certain would be a pneumonia-inducing experience. It was forty degrees when the Rhode Island pitcher threw his first flat fastball, and the drizzle began to fall in the second inning. Nobody wanted to be anywhere near a baseball field. The hitters swung their cold metal bats warily, worried that their hands might shatter if they made solid contact with the heavy ball. The pitchers were blowing incessantly on their numb hands, fielders jumping at their positions to keep warm, the few spectators huddling under umbrellas and blankets. And the poor umpire, who was more than earning his $40 game fee, was wearing so many layers of wool under his dark uniform that he looked like an overstuffed scarecrow.

Yet even amid all that chilled misery, I was the unhappiest person in the park. I was trapped in what Rhode Island College generously refers to as its "press box," which is actually a dilapidated shed with a smudged Plexiglas window that overlooks home plate. The shed smelled like rotting grass, and the only warmth that chilly night came from a portable space heater that made the noise of a jet engine yet produced the flickering energy of a tallow candle. My lone companion in the press box was Les Walters, a scout for the Red Sox. I had already decided that I hated Les, largely because he had refused to join me in railing against the weather and damning both teams to eternity in a Siberian version of hell. I suspected that Les might actually enjoy his job.

Late in the second inning I was skulking about the little room, feeling exceptionally put out that the New York Times would send one of its two hundred best reporters to a miserable game between Rhode Island College and Plymouth State, when Les tugged on my sleeve.

"I want to show you something," he said. "But you have to promise that you won't tell anyone."

A good reporter would have immediately turned on his tape

recorder and started stretching his conveniently malleable code of ethics. But by that point in my career I was the Chevrolet Corvair of journalism, so I grunted noncommittally and fiddled with the roaring, albeit impotent, heater gently vibrating on the piece of plywood that served as our desk.

Les, however, refused to give up—being a scout is often a lonely business, and he had probably spent more than his share of time talking to pencils and bags of popcorn. "You'll thank me someday," he said. "I promise." His tone was intense enough to puncture my apathy, and I warily turned. "See the catcher?"

I stared out at the dimly lit field. The catcher, who was taking a ball from the umpire, wasn't as squat as most players at his position, but even his armor couldn't conceal that he was carved like a Norse god. "Big kid," I said. When it comes to small talk, I usually rank somewhere above popcorn and below pencils.

"That's the greatest Little Leaguer I ever saw play the game," Les said. He waited for me to ask the logical question, but I ignored him and again prodded the tepid heater. He continued anyway. "It must have been eight years ago. Some regional tournament in some crappy Connecticut town. I noticed him the second he came up to the plate. This little twelve-year-old kid who had a sweeter swing than Joe D. If we'd been in the Caribbean, I would have signed him on the spot. I made a mental note, figuring that he'd show up in a couple years as a superstar at some New England high school. But he just fell off the face of the earth. Weird."

An unfamiliar prick of curiosity needled my brain, and after a short pause I asked, "How'd you find him?"

"A friend of mine," Les said. "He called and told me that some kid was hitting the crap out of the ball in Providence and that I had to come up and check it out."

I forced myself to watch the catcher play defense for the rest of the inning, and my attitude gradually shifted from begrudging attention to real interest. His talents were obvious even to an observer with my lack of professional training. The miserable pitchers on his team hurled ball after ball into the mud, and every time he would drop faster than gravity, his shin guards spraying dirty water in all directions as the ball unfailingly hit either his glove or his chest protector. Midway through the inning he threw a would-be base stealer out by ten feet—from his knees—and I let a tiny whistle escape through my front teeth.

I could tell that Les was watching me, waiting for some sort of comment, but I remained quiet. He must have thought me dimmer than a broken flashlight. When the inning ended he put his feet up on the desk and stared at me, obviously preparing himself for another charge into the teeth of my overwhelming silence. I had to admire his persistence in the face of stupefying apathy.

"So we know why I'm here," he eventually said, his tone involuntarily mimicking the kind of cheery natter you hear from insufferable strangers at cocktail parties. "But what's Mr. Russell Bryant, a big guy from the *New York Times*, doing at a little game like this?"

"You don't know?" A small smile pulled at the corner of my face. "The Plymouth State coach is about to break the New England Division III record for career losses."

An embarrassed chuckle slipped from the corner of Les's mouth before he could censor himself. "You're kidding?"

"Oh, hell no," I said. Les grunted, managing to inject the noise with enough sympathy to make me want to elaborate. "I really pissed off one of my editors."

"I didn't know people got that pissed," Les said.

I was warming to the conversation and would have continued chatting, but Les's attention abruptly shifted to the field. I followed his gaze to the catcher, who was strolling toward the plate lazily swinging a bat in front of him. When the pitcher finished warming up, the catcher casually dug into the wet gravel and sand that covered the batter's box, his lithe body so relaxed that he projected absolute confidence. The pitcher, in contrast, looked as if he would have willingly hopped on a one-way flight to Fresno if it meant that he didn't have to throw to the calm beast at the plate. I glanced at my companion. Les was focusing on the scene like a professional tennis player anticipating a serve, his concentration so intense that I don't think he would have noticed if I had reached over and jammed my pencil in his arm.

The first pitch, a fastball, flew several feet wide of the plate, so far outside that the Plymouth catcher didn't even bother lunging at it. The Plymouth coach stalked out of the dugout and yelled something unpleasant toward his pitcher—I would have thought that by this point in his career he would have been far more comfortable with losing—and the unfortunate pitcher took a short stroll around the mound to settle his nerves. By the time he stepped back onto the rubber he appeared much more relaxed, and he nodded authoritatively at the sign.

The next pitch, a sloppy curveball, was halfway to the plate when I heard Les softly mutter next to me, "Uh-oh." The catcher had already started his swing. Even my inexpert eye could see the beauty in the way his bat whipped forward on a solid plane, his weight shifting smoothly forward in a perfect fusion of hips and arms and forged graphite. A sharp metallic *ping* burst through the thin window into our booth as the ball streaked upward. I leapt to my feet, trying to keep my eye on the white blur tearing through the dark sky, my breath frozen in the back of my throat. I knew it was one of those moments when my writing ability should allow me to say something profound, something that would immortalize the moment for posterity, but instead I clutched twice before stammering "What the fuck was that?"

I stared at Les for an explanation, but he had dropped his pen, his notes forgotten. For the remaining five innings Les and I were spellbound, and when the game finally ended, and the Plymouth coach had lost his New England Division III record 813th game, we practically sprinted over to the bench to speak with the baseball prodigy. But he had disappeared. The Rhode Island College coach, who has a reputation for being spectacularly unhelpful, told us with an impassive shrug that he must have snuck away early, and Les and I wandered back to our cars, disappointed, exhilarated, and confused. If I knew then what I know now, I would have insisted that we drive the streets of Providence until we found him. But I was cold and tired and hopelessly mediocre, so Les and I instead ducked in a bar for a few drinks. We were on our third Coors when Les turned to me, his expression still befuddled.

"Did we really just see that?" he asked.

"I don't know," I said. "It doesn't seem likely." I paused, and then realized I had an unfamiliar desire to keep talking, to share my own sense of awe. "I've had this feeling once before. I was at this little club on Gilman Street in Berkeley about a decade ago, and I heard this local garage band called Green Day. I walked out of there with my head spinning . . . you just knew they were going to be huge. And it was like you were part of this secret that the rest of the world would eventually discover."

"It's my job to uncover these kinds of secrets," Les said. "But this is ridiculous." He stared down at his notes and shook his head. "I can't turn this in. Scouts who write that they've found a kid with the speed of Mays, the eye and swing of Williams, and the grace of DiMaggio have to piss in a cup to keep their jobs."

"Don't worry," I said. "I won't mention anything to my editors." Les looked at me gratefully, but I wasn't really doing him a favor. My superiors at the *Times* already considered me a flake, and if I pitched a feature story on a baseball messiah at a small college in New England who turned out to be a one-game wonder, they probably would have tossed me off the George Washington Bridge with the remains of my career tied to my feet.

"Then we'll make a pact," Les said. "We don't say a word until we see the kid play again."

I agreed, and we decided to drive up to Providence the next weekend. But there would be no next weekend. When I got the Rhode Island press notes that week, I learned that the catcher had broken his wrist in a car accident and couldn't play for the remainder of the season. I returned to the dull details of my slowly imploding life, and I soon forgot that I had witnessed Casey Fox, the greatest player I would ever see, hit the last home run of his collegiate career.

Part 1

Providence

chapter 1

IN THE SEVENTH INNING OF A TRIPLE-A BASEBALL GAME IN
Rochester, New York, I realized that my existence was completely
pointless. Maybe that sounds melodramatic, but I considered the
idea for at least five batters and decided that it was damningly
true. I had no girlfriend, a job I was beginning to actively loathe,
few close friends, and a car so ugly that no one would steal it—
not even in Newark, New Jersey. I had no more right to waste
oxygen than the denizens of the afternoon talk shows.

Perhaps a lot of people come to this sort of realization in
Rochester. It's a perfectly acceptable town if your version of a
good time includes either a six-pack of Bud Light or a visit to the
Eastman Kodak World Headquarters. Otherwise, I can't particularly recommend it. Small cities start to blend together if you
spend your life trailing after sports teams. They're just a glimpse
of a Wal-Mart and a small downtown before the Holiday Inn and
the midsize stadium, all painted concrete walls—always in the
team's colors—and the inside of a rented compact car that smells
like new plastic.

My excuse for being in Rochester is that I was covering the
Pawtucket Red Sox for the *Providence Daily Journal*, which meant

I had to follow the team on its road trips. I had spent most of my childhood dreaming about that kind of a job, but the thirty-year-old version of me was finding it impossible to endure any more baseball. I had taken to leaving the press box for long periods during the game, and my stories were beginning to feature long conversations with hot dog vendors and the small children who lurk just behind the center-field fence screaming to the outfielders for a ball. Baseball had lost its grip on me.

So after the game I headed straight for the bar in the lobby of my Holiday Inn. Eddie O'Farrell, my best friend at the newspaper, came along—partially to keep me company and partially because Eddie hasn't missed a bar in almost forty seasons of reporting. He wrote the game stories for the *Journal* while I wrote the features. I liked Eddie, respected him, and spent many of my waking hours terrified that I would become him. The cliché of the alcoholic old journalist endures due to the extraordinary number of alcoholic old journalists. And, unlike the alcoholic journalists in Hollywood, Eddie was never going to write a Pulitzer-winning story. He would never bed the beautiful girl. And although he certainly wasn't a hack—his writing could sometimes glimmer—he didn't care enough to be really good.

Usually Eddie and I would drink quietly, only breaking the silence to complain bitterly about our editors, but that night he had decided that he was going to coax me into hitting on some women. Maybe he figured it would brighten my mood. I needed a lot of convincing.

"I'm not going to make an ass of myself," I said. "Not tonight."

"Russell," Eddie said, his tone paternal, "you have an obligation to try to take one of these fine ladies home."

I glanced around the bar, my eye pausing briefly on a small cluster of women sitting alone in the corner. They appeared to be in their early twenties. "Why's that?"

"Because I need to be entertained. And, of course, because a man in your condition shouldn't spend the night alone."

"My condition? What the hell does that mean?"

Eddie ignored me, downed the dregs of his beer in one swallow, and stood. "Your moment has come," he said. "I'm going to buy another drink, and I'm not speaking to you again until you've made some sort of effort with those girls."

"What if they don't want to talk to me?"

Eddie made a vulgar noise somewhere between a moan and a belch. "You're in Rochester, for Christ's sake. They'll be happy to meet a man who doesn't want to describe his John Deere in excruciating detail."

Eddie crossed the room and plopped himself on a bar stool, his body language indicating that he was prepared to spend the rest of the night alone with his beer. Our conversation had made me unusually self-conscious, and I glanced at the table of women, then fled for the bathroom to stall for time. When I emerged, my hands more than adequately washed, I spent five minutes at the jukebox trying to appear fascinated with examining the selection of '80s pop and country—not an easy task. I kept hoping that one of the women would get up and join me for a discussion of ABBA, but they remained distressingly self-absorbed.

You would think that a thirty-year-old guy who spends plenty of time in strange bars would be better than this, right? I'd like to claim that I was having an off night, but that would be an outrageous, albeit comforting, lie. I did reasonably well with women at Yale as an undergraduate. But anyone who can't get laid in college isn't trying hard enough—anything works, even growing a scruffy goatee and wearing black wool sweaters. That was my modus operandi senior year. Bars, however, require an entirely different set of skills. I've always viewed hitting on someone as basically an audition; you present your résumé and they decide whether or not you're worth going home with.

And I don't think my résumé is that bad. I'm well educated, taller than the average guy, and have read enough women's magazines to say appropriately sensitive things. My job sounds interesting to the casual listener, and while I'm no model, I think I'm comfortably in the middle of the attractiveness spectrum for most women. My problem, therefore, isn't in the details of my résumé, but in the presentation. I make a miserable first impression. My fear of embarrassment approaches neurosis, which means I approach women as tentatively as a wild horse. But picking someone up in a bar depends completely on not caring whether you look like a moron, and in trying to avoid any potential humiliation, I end up appearing aloof, arrogant, and often a little dim.

On this particular night, however, I began well. One of the women spilled her drink, and I swept in like Cary Grant with a pile of napkins. I ended up talking to Karen, a hair stylist, and Tiffany—who worked at Wal-Mart, "but not as like a career or anything"—while their three friends heckled my efforts mercilessly in the background. I soon reverted to my usual lackluster form, and we had just finished the introductions when we experienced our first awkward pause. I toyed with a napkin until Karen finally found a question.

"You're not from here, are you?" she asked.

"No," I said. "How can you tell?"

Karen shrugged. "We know most of the people who come here regular."

Tiffany, who had abruptly become fascinated with the nail on her right index finger, glanced up. "Where do you live?"

"Providence."

"Rhode Island?"

"Yeah." I paused and everyone stared at me, perhaps curious to see if I was capable of more than monosyllables. "It's a small state." At that point the three girls in the background fled for the bar. Tiffany and Karen, however, decided to give me another chance.

"We knew a guy who moved to Providence," Tiffany said. "What was his name?"

"Terry something," Karen said with some authority.

"Do you know him?"

"No." I desperately prayed that someone would spill another drink so that I could recapture the glory of the napkin move, but the glasses remained depressingly upright. I wondered if I would help or hurt my case if I deliberately knocked one over. Tiffany glanced at Karen, an expression in her eyes that I recognized from previous failures. Her head turned back to me.

"We were just getting up to go to the bar," she said, standing. "But it was nice meeting you."

"Thanks," I said. I appreciated the kindness of her delivery if not her message.

I sat alone at the table for a couple minutes, then slunk over to the stool next to Eddie and ordered a beer. We didn't speak for half an hour. Eddie and I are friends mostly because we know how to share loneliness—he understood instinctively that any transparent effort to cheer me up would backfire miserably. As we drank our beers, I couldn't help noticing that a solidly built kid in warm-up pants and a rugby shirt was chatting happily with the same group of women that had rejected me. Not good for the ego.

"How did you drop the ball?" Eddie finally asked. "The napkin thing was really good."

"I know," I said. "It's a gift. Bars aren't my thing."

"I'm beginning to think that women aren't your thing."

"Fuck off."

Eddie shook his head ruefully. "That's the problem with your generation. You think that 'fuck off' is a really witty riposte."

I was too busy watching the guy in the rugby shirt talking with the women to reply. I couldn't shake the feeling that I'd seen him someplace before. He was built like a typical modern athlete, with supernaturally broad shoulders tapering to a thin waist, and the veins on his thick forearms stood out like the seams of a baseball. His face was arresting. If he were famous, I would probably call him attractive because his features were unique. His Greek nose and slim, curving mouth, which both suggested an outgoing Mediterranean personality, contrasted sharply with his dark eyes and forbidding eyebrows. His hair was mussed just enough to suggest that he didn't really care about things so unmanly as hair. He was perfectly at ease among the same women I'd found so unsettling, and I enviously watched as they rewarded his charm with smiles and little touches on his biceps and chest.

"I swear I've met that guy before," I finally said to Eddie. He followed my eyes and, much to my surprise, laughed.

"Jesus," he said. "You have the worst instincts of any reporter I've ever met. That's Casey Fox. He's been tearing it up at Lowell—hit fourteen homers in twenty games—and the Sox just promoted him. He'll be playing for the team tomorrow."

"Casey Fox," I said slowly. "I knew I recognized his face. I saw him play in college when I was working for the *Times*. He's incredible."

Eddie was still shaking his head, bewildered by my ignorance. "That's not exactly a secret anymore. The kid's gone from a late-round draft pick to the hottest prospect in baseball in one season."

"I never talked to him. He skipped out after the game."

"Yeah," Eddie said. "The kid's a punk. He won't talk to reporters. Period."

"Really?"

Eddie's truculent voice rose so loud that I feared the kid would hear him. "You might be able to pull that crap when you've hit forty dongs in the majors, but until then . . ." His lips narrowed. "Punk."

We drank in silence for several more beers. I had lost count, but I could roughly gauge my consumption by my drunkenness. After four beers I speak too loudly; after seven beers my coordination is shot; and after ten my cheek usually ends up resting upon cool, white porcelain. So when I swerved into a table on my way to the bathroom, I knew that I must have had at least seven.

My eyes were closed and I was leaning against the wall next to the urinal when I heard the bathroom door open. I was concentrating too hard on my zipper to notice my new companion, and I jumped when I heard his voice in my ear.

"Are you okay?" His voice was low, but authoritarian.

"Never better," I said. I pulled my eyes open. Casey Fox was standing at the next urinal, a sardonic smile on his face.

"I find that hard to believe." I ignored him, letting my eyes fall closed again, and a moment later I heard the vacuum sound of his urinal flushing. I waited, listening for the sound of the bathroom door. Instead, I felt a hand on my shoulder.

"You sure you're okay?"

I opened my eyes and turned to face him, fighting hard to keep my balance. "I'm fine. Really."

He stared into my eyes, hard enough to make me uncomfortable, then turned and walked over to the sink. I watched as he washed his hands and then smoothed the curly brown hair above his brow with a splash of water.

"Let me ask you a question," I said. He glanced at my smudged reflection in the decrepit mirror. "How did you talk to those women? I got killed."

"It's easy," he said as he reached for a paper towel. "I ask them questions. Everyone likes to talk about themselves, right? Take that girl Tiffany, for example. She wants to be a writer."

"That's it?"

He turned to me and spread his hands. "That's it. No big secret. You just balked."

"And you're going home with them?"

I regretted the question the moment it left my mouth, and I instinctively sank back into the dirty tile wall. He stared at me long enough to make me nervous, then laughed. "Not really my style," he said. "And certainly none of your business."

As he turned on his heel and grabbed the knob on the door, I realized that I wasn't ready for the conversation to end. I spoke too loudly to his retreating back. "Hey, Casey. How do you know what questions to ask?"

He turned and measured me again, and this time when he spoke the levity had disappeared from his voice. "You're a reporter. You should know."

Even drunk, I could feel the atmosphere change in the room, and I smiled as disarmingly as I could manage. "Why do you think I'm a reporter?"

"How else would you know my name?" he asked, and then pushed through the metal door.

chapter 2

WHENEVER I GET HOME, I CAN NEVER FIGURE OUT WHY I FIGHT
so hard to get away from the office. I live in Rolling Oaks, a
planned housing community on the outskirts of Providence. In
addition to our outrageously annoying name, we have a tennis
court, a swimming pool, and a labeled "Large Green Space"—all
of which are continually overrun by both the black Labradors and
the offspring of my American Dreaming neighbors. The place also
has more rules and restrictions than a Soviet gulag: no loud music, no parties, no waterbeds, no charcoal grills, and absolutely no
diving in the shallow end. Every eighth Saturday in the spring
and summer I am responsible for mowing a section of the "Large
Green Space," which I treat as an opportunity to chase both the
offspring and the black Labradors with the riding mower.

My reasonably spacious one-bedroom apartment has the character of a mobile home. Sometimes I sit in my living room, staring at the prefabricated cabinets and carpeting, and I pity the
architect who was forced to design the place to the specifications
of the lowest bid. But then I realize that he was probably taking a
break from building the numbing array of franchises and gas stations that surrounds our complex, and my sympathy swiftly ebbs.

So far I had mostly contained my own decorating efforts to covering the walls with photographs and framed posters. Most of the posters are from a company called Successories. Although the photos are usually pretty good—mountainscapes and waterfalls and photogenic animals—the company sticks completely insufferable slogans like "the early bird gets the worm" under the pictures. My parents buy the posters in vast quantities on airplane trips and distribute them to their underachieving brood at Christmas, perhaps hoping that we will internalize the fact that "a rolling stone gathers no moss." I've covered all the slogans in duct tape. Last year, in a frantic fit of creativity, I pasted a couple of my own sayings beneath the pictures. The only one that remains lies under a spectacular shot of a heron taking off from a lake: "There's no problem that can't be solved by the studious application of cheap alcohol."

On this particular afternoon I had intended to drop my travel bag in my closet and quickly take a shower before heading to the ballpark for Casey Fox's debut with the Pawtucket Red Sox. But I still wasn't completely recovered from my sojourn in Rochester, so after I got out of the shower I wandered into my living room and collapsed on the crown jewel of my apartment: an enormous massage chair that I had won by being the tenth caller to KISS in New York. That still qualifies as the luckiest moment of my life. My apartment complex was completely silent—the kids were at school, their parents at work, and even the maintenance men were taking a short break from banging aluminum garbage cans together in my front yard. I idly turned the TV on to ESPN and watched the last fifteen minutes of the same SportsCenter I had seen early that morning.

I had no energy and absolutely no desire to go to the game, and suddenly I realized that I was heading toward a repeat of my breakdown nine months earlier. I had been working for the Times sports section as a staff reporter, and after several years of paying my dues the editors were starting to assign me higher-profile stories. In August, four months after I had seen Casey play in college, the paper had sent me to the U.S. Open to cover the stunning

Anna Kournikova, who was playing some relative unknown from Belgium. Kournikova was getting thrashed in straight sets—a common event for her in major tournaments—when I heard that a qualifier was playing a tremendous match against Pete Sampras on the adjacent court. So I called my editor and asked him if I could shift the focus of the story. He refused for one reason and one reason only: he wanted to run a huge picture of Anna on the front page of the section.

It's not exactly a unique observation to say that Kournikova is a victory of style over substance. And who am I to say that style shouldn't matter in sports—after all, sports are entertainment and newspapers are in the business of selling as many copies as possible. Anna Kournikova is certainly the kind of woman who sends men rushing to their computers to download photographs from the Internet, which means that when the New York Times plasters a pinup shot on the front page of its sports section, it's probably scratching the bloated stomach of its stockholders. But it's also insulting those of us who chose to spend our lives covering sports because we think there's something valuable about the silly games. When athletes treat the press like lackeys, extensions of their own personal publicity department, you ignore them because you believe that your job is important. I don't work covering sports because I want to be a jock sniffer or to follow Anna Kournikova around New York City like a camera-toting member of the paparazzi; I got into sports because I remember how they used to make me feel.

So when my editor told me to stick with Kournikova, something broke in my brain. It was the hypocrisy that really stung me. Even after all the crap I'd been through—measuring holes that athletes kicked in walls, cajoling police officers to give me the results of drug tests, patiently listening while Bobby Knight told me that I was the single dumbest form of multicellular life on the planet—this somehow stood out. If I was just going to be another hack who wrote the fluffy words that appeared next to Kournikova (gasp) showing a peek of her underwear, I had chosen the wrong job. While I followed orders and stuck with the match, the article I turned in to my editor can kindly be described as caustic. To excerpt:

> Anna Kournikova finally proves what feminists have long suspected: that men watch women's sports the same way they watch *Beach Babes from Beyond* or *Bikini Car Wash 3* . . . And the way the mainstream media covers her is the final proof that no matter what the *New York Times* and *Sports Illustrated* would have you believe, the sporting press subscribes to the standards and ethics of *People* magazine, not some glamorous reportorial ideal.

The piece obviously never appeared in the paper. My editor called me into his office, and when he realized that the article wasn't a joke, the *Times*, which does not handle breakdowns on the part of junior reporters with any grace or dignity, decided that I should "seek alternate employment." Losing my job bothered me less than the euphemism—you can't merely be fired in America anymore, you're always "downsized" or a "casualty of unfortunate market conditions." I would much rather have been called into the editor's office and been told by him that I was the single biggest jackass they had ever made the mistake of hiring. At least then I'd feel as if a person had made the decision rather than some HR computer hidden in the basement.

I spent the next several months lounging around my outrageously expensive New York apartment in my underwear until one day I realized that my meager savings had almost completely vaporized. Late that night I decided that if I was going to continue to cover sports, I needed a complete rebirth. Obviously I had spent far too much time reading self-help books. So, sparked by an image I'd gotten from *Bull Durham*, *Field of Dreams*, and hundreds of breathless magazine articles, I headed for the hallowed sanctuary of minor league baseball—only to end up four months later sitting in an enormous lounge chair wondering what the hell I was doing in Providence, Rhode Island.

I might have sat in that chair forever if Eddie hadn't called me about half an hour before the game started.

"Why aren't you here?" he asked the moment I picked up the phone.

"I think I'm quitting."

Eddie snorted. "Don't fool yourself, buddy," he said when he got his breath. "You've got no better place to be. You get your ass down to this ballpark or I'll come over after the game and give you a real reason to stay at home in bed."

"I'll see you at the park," I said, touched in spite of myself.

Casey Fox's debut with the Paw Sox was dramatic in the way that old-fashioned train wrecks and the Clinton presidency were dramatic. Things began auspiciously: he hit a home run in the first inning and another in the fifth to make the score 9–0. He had barely settled in the dugout after his second triumphant lap when the Rochester pitcher, who was obviously both rattled and frustrated, nailed the next Sox player on the arm, bringing the entire Pawtucket team to the edge of the dugout. Although the coaches managed to contain the players before they charged out onto the field, everyone in the press box knew that Erik Fogarty, a Pawtucket pitcher who had been bouncing between triple-A and the majors for a couple years, would probably hit the first Rochester batter in the top of the sixth.

Perhaps that sounds barbaric to people not familiar with baseball's byzantine internal code, but the truth is that the most effective disciplinary force in the game is the batter's fear of getting hit—after all, the results of being struck by a pitch range from brief but intense pain to serious injury. In fact, a pitch killed a Cleveland shortstop named Ray Chapman in 1920. But pitchers in the American League—and Pawtucket plays under American League rules—don't have to come to the plate, which means that they don't have the fear of the pitched ball because nobody ever throws a ball at them. So when a pitcher in the American League deliberately beans a member of your team, you can't hit him.

Instead, you have to throw at one of his teammates in the hopes that the teammate will go back to the locker room and tell his pitcher to stop being such an ass. Maybe that's playground logic, but it's also baseball's best and only system for regulating head-hunting pitchers.

The Rochester pitcher worked his way out of the inning without giving up any more runs, and when the first Rochester batter warily approached the plate, I saw Casey make a subtle motion toward Erik that could only mean one thing: nail this guy. By the time Erik was halfway through his windup, the Rochester player was cringing, knowing that he was going to get drilled and probably hoping to take it on the shoulder or the biceps. But the first pitch split the heart of the plate for a strike. Casey, confused, flashed the sign for an inside fastball. Erik nodded, then threw another pitch over the heart of the plate. Casey called time and angrily marched out to the mound.

"What's going on?" he asked when he got to Erik's side.

"I don't want to put him on base."

"We're winning nine to nothing. Who gives a shit?"

Erik was using his glove to conceal his mouth. "My ERA."

"You won't hit this guy because of your damn statistics?" Casey's voice was so loud that the third baseman, who was staring at a pretty girl in the stands, turned back to the field.

"Statistics get you back to the bigs," Erik said, his tone unapologetic.

Casey snapped the ball into Erik's glove with a violent crack. "You better fucking hit this guy. Now."

Erik, who had five years and two inches on Casey, drew himself up to his full height. "I'll do what I want, rook."

"Well, I hope you want to hit him," Casey said. "Because otherwise I'm going to come out here and shove a baseball up your ass."

Erik might have said something else, but Casey turned and jogged back to the plate. Casey again called for the inside fastball. This time Erik threw a curve on the outside corner that the confused batter just waved at. Before the umpire could call strike three, Casey was already storming out to the mound. Erik was smiling, his hands at his sides.

"I'm sorry," he said. "I guess I just missed him."

He was still smiling when Casey's fist hit him flush on the left side of his jaw. The same frame that could throw a frozen rope to second base could obviously generate a powerful punch because Erik's knees buckled and he collapsed on the rubber. Both dugouts began to clear until the Rochester players realized that they had no reason to be fighting. Casey stood over Erik's prone body, and before the tide of Pawtucket players arrived to drag him away, he leaned down and whispered in Erik's ear: "You throw my pitches, meat. And you stand up for my team."

Up in the press box, Eddie turned to me. "This season just got a lot more interesting," he said.

McCoy Stadium, Pawtucket's home field, is one of a rash of beautiful minor league parks that have recently begun attracting families in droves. Although McCoy was originally built in the 1940s, the team completely renovated the old structure before the 1999 season. And while the revised McCoy may glimmer with the same Disney Land cheeriness of all the other cookie-cutter new parks, its amenities have already endeared it to the local press corps. When the game finally ended, we prepared to charge from the spacious press box to the locker room, but we found a cordon of local police officers barring our way. We were instead herded into a large equipment room. Larry Tubson, the team's manager, came in five minutes later. Most of the reporters like Larry because he sucks up to them, but I've always thought that he is the kind of guy who tortures his kid's pet hamsters when he thinks nobody is looking.

A few guys wanted to question Larry the instant he entered the room, but he waved them off and unfolded a small piece of paper. "Obviously," he began reading, "this is a real black eye for the organization. But I think what we've really got here is a competitive kid who got caught up in the moment."

"Can we talk to him, coach?" Eddie asked.

Larry shook his head. "We're sorry, but he's not talking to the press."

"Can't you make him?" asked a younger reporter from the Associated Press.

Larry made a helpless gesture that indicated that the situation was entirely out of his control. "No can do," he said. "The kid's got something in his contract. We're working on it."

By the time they let us in the locker room, Casey and Erik had already left. We therefore spent half an hour collecting the same quote from the remaining players: "It's an unfortunate thing. Probably just a misunderstanding. We want to keep this sort of situation in the clubhouse. This team is a big family, and sometimes even families get in fights." I'm certain that they were all repeating verbatim the party line that had been dictated to them by Tubson—most professional athletes are particularly susceptible to brainwashing.

I wrote my story back in the press box, and it took me exactly one hour. While writing a real story is as difficult as squeezing compassion from a bounty hunter, constructing a mediocre newspaper piece is an elementary and predictable process. You open with either an anecdote or unusual fact, fill the body of the story with gross generalities and unnecessary quotations, and finish with the most punchy line you can design—the easiest way to snappily close is a one-sentence, no-clause paragraph. The headline should contain either a modest pun (over-the-top puns are reserved for English tabloids) or the most controversial line from your article. The whole process requires about as much creative flair as filling out a government form. That night, however, I ignored the usual rules and wrote what amounted to an editorial. The opening two paragraphs capture the tone of the piece:

> Until tonight I didn't see any hope in the Paw Sox this season.
> Only 40 games into the year, they seemed a team destined to
> play out the string with hardly a memorable whimper. But
> everything changed this evening in the fifth inning, when

Casey Fox, the new catcher, served notice that this team would play passionate baseball.

The message was delivered via uppercut to the deserving chin of Erik Fogarty, whose crime was that he had failed to retaliate against a Rochester batter for the deliberate beaning of shortstop Alex Thomas—probably because Fogarty was concerned about his precious earned run average. Although Fox was unavailable for comment after the game, his punch seemed to say that this promising rookie will fight to make sure the Paw Sox don't just limp through their remaining games.

chapter 3

THE NEXT MORNING I DISCOVERED THAT I WAS THE ONLY RE-
porter in New England who hadn't called for Casey Fox's head.
Our paper, for example, ran the headline: "Punch Drunk" next to
a picture of Casey standing menacingly over Erik's crumpled body.
As I browsed through the hysterical articles, I couldn't decide if
Casey's larger crime had been the punch or refusing to apologize
profusely to local reporters after the game. My favorite quote
came from Todd Prestum of the *Providence Star*. "If Mr. Fox is going to last as a Paw Sock," Prestum wrote, "he better turn off the
arrogance and turn up the self-control. This town has no patience
for players who think they're bigger than the game."

Although I figured that the Paw Sox would go light on
Casey—organizations treat their top prospects with kid gloves—I
was certain that he would receive at least a token suspension. But
when Eddie and I arrived early for the evening game, Lewis
Holmes, the press coordinator for the Paw Sox, told us that he
was getting away with a $2,500 fine and an on-field apology to the
fans.

"I guess the big guys in Boston liked his passion," Lewis said.

"That apology should be a doozie," Eddie said. "The kid doesn't seem like the type to back away from a fight."

"He sure didn't yesterday," I said.

Right before the national anthem, Casey and Erik jogged to the pitcher's mound and made a big production out of shaking hands. One of the team managers emerged from the dugout with a microphone that he carefully placed on the rubber while Casey slowly unfolded a piece of yellow legal paper.

"How much you want to bet he didn't write this?" Eddie asked.

I just smiled. A moment later Casey began to slowly read. His voice, amplified by the park's new speakers, sounded as solemn and reluctant as Nixon reading his resignation. "I am here to apologize to the fans," he began. "Nobody should come to a baseball park and be forced to witness the kind of spectacle that occurred yesterday. I owe you, my teammates, and Erik Fogarty an enormous apology."

Casey paused to turn over the sheet of paper. Erik had pasted a sickly grin onto his face, and I found myself half wishing that Casey would turn and hit him again. Casey's voice rose slightly as he continued. "So the next time a Pawtucket player fails to give you the kind of effort you deserve, I promise that I'll let his self-absorbed ass get away with it. Thank you, and let's play ball."

Casey crumpled the piece of paper, tossed it on the grass next to the mound, and trotted off the field. Erik appeared stunned, and it wasn't until the organ played the first notes of the "Star-Spangled Banner" that he managed to gather himself enough to limp back to the dugout. Eddie laughed through the entire national anthem, and as the teams took the field he stuck his lips so close to my ear that I could smell the Jim Beam on his breath.

"It ain't every day that you get to see a kid flip off a whole ballpark," he whispered.

"I think he was just aiming at the reporters," I said. "And maybe Erik Fogarty."

I had figured that Casey's speech would overshadow the game

and dominate the postgame coverage. But I was dead wrong because in the eighth inning Casey hit a ball so far that it probably violated several international missile treaties. I can still remember the entire at bat. The Sox had men on first and third with two outs, and Rochester had brought in its closer, a young kid with a lively arm. On a 1–2 count he challenged Casey with a letter-high fastball over the heart of the plate. Casey began his swing just a moment too early and drove the ball about 400 feet foul down the left-field line.

"Holy shit," I said. "He sure got all of that one."

Eddie was shaking his head, his mouth hanging open. "Good god, man," he said. "I don't care if it was foul. If I smacked a ball like that, I'd run around the bases just because I hit it so damn far."

We were still laughing when the pitcher threw Casey exactly the same letter-high fastball, which was a decision even I feel comfortable second-guessing. As the ball met the bat, it made a crack so loud that Eddie spilled his glass of water. For the second time in my life I rose from my chair to watch a feat performed by Casey. The ball, moving so fast that it appeared to be a smudge rather than a sphere, appeared to be still rising as it passed the grass berm in center field, 440 feet from home plate. I strained my eyes, but the orb of the field's lights didn't reach much past the fence, and the ball vanished from sight.

"Jesus Christ," Eddie said as the ball disappeared. "Jesus Christ."

"I don't think even He could hit a ball that far," one of the AP guys said. This time no one laughed.

"What was the distance on that?" I asked nobody in particular. "A mile? Two? How far is the record?" I glanced down at the field. Casey was trotting home from third base, his stunned teammates wandering out of the dugout to meet him.

"They're going to love this kid in Boston," Eddie said.

After the game we stormed the locker room, and there was no cordon of security guards to stop us. Casey was standing in front of his locker, stripped to his jock. As we poured across the room to accost him, tape recorders already whirring, he slowly turned. His expression fixed us all in our tracks. "Sorry, gentlemen," he said. He glanced at a female reporter from the *Journal.* "And ladies. No questions." He pulled his jock off, slung his towel over his shoulder, and strolled across the locker room to his shower, his naked buttocks mooning both our personal and professional curiosity.

We scattered and began asking the other players inane questions. ("I mean, how far was it? Have you ever seen a ball hit like that? Can you describe your emotions when you saw it fly over the berm?") One of my problems as a reporter is that I've never been able to get over feeling out of place in a locker room. Why do we ask athletes to suffer the indignity of being interviewed while naked—we don't interview presidents in the shower, do we? Although I can name a few chief executives who might have enjoyed the experience if one of the cute field reporters from ESPN was the one doing the interviewing.

I was talking to Pawtucket's starting third baseman when Casey returned from his shower and began toweling himself off by his locker. Most of us tried to ignore him, but Brian Hunter, a weasely little reporter from one of the local magazines, crossed the room and stuck his tape player in Casey's face.

"Hey, Casey," he said. "Just answer me one question. How do you hit the ball so good?"

"Well," Casey said. The locker room fell silent, and we could all hear the exchange.

"Excuse me?"

Casey was pulling his tan underwear up his thick legs, his tone conversational. "Hit the ball so well. You criticize my shortstop because he makes one error. But you work for a paper, and you don't even know the difference between *well* and *good*. Words should be your life. It's pathetic."

Brian clicked his tape recorder off and slunk away to lick his wounds as the rest of us stifled laughter. I finished my interview and waited by the door for Eddie. I was standing only a few feet away from Casey's locker, and I couldn't help glancing at him. Eventually, he caught one of my stares.

"Sorry," I said.

He shrugged. Apparently staring wasn't a mockable offense. "Your article today," he said. "Did you mean that or were you trying to kiss up to get a story?"

"I meant it." I watched as he pulled a T-shirt over his head. "Are you always this angry?"

"Only when stupid people ask me stupid questions," he said. And without bothering to look at me again, he slung his athletic bag over his shoulder and stalked out of the room.

The next afternoon I was once again early to the ballpark, and I hurried up to the media office to see if the team had written a press release on the home run. What I found instead was a terse, one-page statement declaring that "in light of the unsuitable remarks made before yesterday's contest with Rochester," the Pawtucket Red Sox were suspending Casey Fox for three games. Bureaucratic organizations can ignore almost anything except intelligent ridicule. I returned to my car, drove home, and called in sick for the next three games.

During my days away from my job, I have a very predictable routine. I awake in time for the 10 A.M. *SportsCenter*, and I spend most of the show annoyed that I'm watching grown men pretend that they're still in college. At eleven I take a shower, which I follow with a trip to one of the interchangeable fast-food restaurants that surround my housing complex. I fill my early afternoon by hitting several buckets of golf balls at the local driving range. While I rarely play a round on an actual golf course—my attention span is poorly suited to an activity measured in hours—I find the rhythm of hitting balls to be relaxing.

I spend the late afternoon staring at a blank computer screen. I call this time "writing my book." The process began the year after I graduated from college when I first started feeling dissatisfied with being a newspaper reporter. The notion of writing a book felt like a way of escaping the realities of my slow-moving career, and I often dreamed of my opus perching atop the *New York Times* nonfiction list as I relaxed on a Caribbean island. I did a lot more dreaming than writing. After eight years of effort I had exactly forty-eight pages of a diatribe about the decline and fall of professional sports.

My evenings are equally predictable. Sometimes I meet Eddie and a few other guys from the office for a burger and a beer, but I spend most of the night dreading having to face my answering machine when I return. There's something so crushingly precise about having a robotic voice tell you that you have "no new messages" in a tone that seems designed to damn the solitude of your existence. So usually I order a pizza and watch television. I have a weakness for the cliché-ridden melodramas that the networks pitch toward teenagers. Perhaps I belong in that demographic: jaded yet hopeful, romantic but filled with angst stemming from a thousand humiliating failures. Late at night, when the prime-time shows have gone off the air, I flick back and forth between the sports channels. I'll watch anything—luge, power lifting, sheepdog competitions borrowed from the BBC. Sometimes, when I'm lucky, I fall asleep in my enormous lounge chair. But usually I end up staggering back to my room at 2 A.M., sick in my knowledge that I have wasted another day.

My editor yelled at me for five minutes in front of the entire newsroom the morning I returned to work. The gist of his lecture was that he had a paper to fill and wouldn't be held hostage by prima-donna former reporters from the bleeping *New York Times* who couldn't be bothered to actually show up to their goddamned jobs. Midway through his speech, he pointed across the room to Jerry Stith as an example of the kind of reporter I should be emulating. I made the mistake of laughing. Although I like Jerry—he's about my age and possesses the temperament of a golden retriever puppy—he has two fatal flaws as a reporter. First, he's far too nice to ask tough questions. I can imagine Jerry interviewing Genghis Khan:

Jerry: So, Mr. Khan. Some people say you're being a little hard on Europe.

Khan: Well, this is a difficult time, Jerry. It's not easy being the guy that everyone hates. I'm just trying to give it a hundred and ten percent.

Jerry: Do you have any new plans you can share with us, Mr. Khan?

Khan: You know, I'm just trying to take it one continent at a time. But I've got to tell you, I'm tired of hearing about how I play croquet with the heads of my enemies. That's just a vicious rumor being perpetuated by an irresponsible media.

Jerry: And how does that make you feel, Mr. Khan?

Khan: It's tough, Jerry. It's really tough. I mean, a barbarian's got feelings too, right? Sometimes Khan finds it hard to get out of bed, but then he remembers how many people there are left to kill.

Jerry: I understand. Thanks for the interview, Mr. Khan. And good luck this season.

Jerry's second flaw is that any sentence he writes that's longer than five words reads as if it's been transcribed from the instruction manual for a Japanese VCR.

So I wasn't the only person who laughed when my editor pointed to Jerry as a paragon of reportorial prowess. But I was the only one he caught.

"You think that's funny?" he asked, his fat face swelling in anger.

"No, boss."

He wagged his index finger so close to my nose that I could see the black ink on the pad. "I got a story for you, funny man," he said. "I want a profile of that Casey Fox kid. A good one."

"He doesn't speak to the press, boss. How the hell am I supposed to get a story?"

"Not my problem," my editor said. He turned on his heel and

stalked back into his office. The moment his door was safely shut, Eddie called after him.

"Hey, chief. Are we all supposed to be more like Jerry, or just Russell?"

I saw Jerry flush and try to hide behind his monitor, and I strolled over to his desk and rested my hand on his nervous shoulder. "It's not your fault," I said. "And I didn't mean any offense by laughing."

"It's okay," Jerry said.

Casey had a solid if unspectacular return to the lineup, going 1–3 with two hard-hit balls caught for noisy outs. We noted in the press box that the opposing teams were already starting to pitch around him. I didn't pay much attention to the game—I was too worried about what I was going to say to Casey—and when the rest of the reporters went downstairs I dallied behind. By the time I finally reached the locker room, most of the interviews were already in full swing. Casey was dressing by his locker in an eddy of silence. I walked straight over to him and waited for him to look up.

"Yeah," he said when his eyes finally met mine.

"I'm sorry," I said, "but I'm supposed to write a profile of you. My editor assigned it, so I've got to write the thing whether you talk to me or not. Any chance I could get an interview?"

"No," he said. I stared at him for a long beat as he resumed dressing. He eventually looked up again, and I figured he was going to berate me. But instead he wiped his huge hand, which was still covered in strips of white athletic tape, on his towel before offering it to me. I warily took it and we shook. "I'm sorry," he said. "But that's just the way it is." I knew the conversation was over.

I therefore wrote my article directly from the media guide and the Internet. I thought it read like a middle-school term paper— which it was—but my editor liked it. He decided to run the piece on the front page of the sports section next to a picture of Casey

hitting his fifth home run for the Paw Sox. I thought the headline
was a bit over the top, but you can judge for yourself.

A Hero Is Born
Pawtucket welcomes a star of the future
by Russell Bryant

Like many classical heroes, Casey Fox is an orphan. He was
born to parents too young or too destitute to take care of him,
and he therefore ended up in the Rhode Island social service
system before he had even been given a name. Much about
Fox's childhood is unclear, but he must have been adopted and
then abandoned a second time, because he emerged in the foster care system at the age of eight.

He eventually found a permanent home with Sean and Lucy
McDowell, a working-class couple from Providence, but tragedy
would strike the youngster once again at 13 when Lucy died.
Some children might have turned to sports for solace, but Fox,
who had been one of the best Little League players in the country, never played high school baseball. His return to the game
came as a freshman at Rhode Island College when he walked on
to the varsity team. It didn't take his coaches very long to discover exactly how lucky they had been.

The article continues for another fifteen hundred words, but I
think I've embarrassed myself enough.

chapter 4

I WAS AT THE BALLPARK THE DAY THE PROFILE RAN IN THE PA-
per. After the game I was searching the locker room for the
Pawtucket right fielder, who had stolen the first base of his triple-A
career, when Casey accosted me with a folded copy of the sports
section. He banged the paper into my chest, a grin on his face.

"Not so terrible," he said, "considering that you know nothing
about me."

I stared at him, curious and a little bit confused. "It's crap. But
that's your fault."

He laughed, then put his hand on my shoulder. "Can you do
me a favor?" I swallowed a laugh of my own. My pride wanted to
tell him to stick the favor up his arrogant ass, but I knew I would
hate myself later.

"What do you want?"

"My ride got caught up. Can you give me a lift?" I glanced
around the locker room at Casey's twenty-three teammates—who
had rides that ranged from glittering sports cars to merely functional sedans. He read my look perfectly. "I've got to do something I don't want them to see."

"I'll meet you outside," I said, wondering what kind of person would be stupid enough to entrust a secret to a reporter.

I was standing next to my car, a 1986 silver Toyota hatchback, when Casey emerged from the player's entrance. He walked straight past me to the car and ran his hand across the hood, his mouth flopping wide open.

"Damn," he said. "Don't they pay you guys anything?"

"Not like they pay you."

He raised a critical eyebrow. "You know better than that. If I make the bigs, I'll get six figures. Until then . . ." He gestured at his T-shirt and jeans, then looked back at my car. "This is the ugliest vehicle I've ever seen. I can't believe the State of Rhode Island lets you drive it on public roads."

"I keep leaving keys in it and the door unlocked, but nobody will steal it." I opened the door and started the engine as Casey slid in the other side. "Where are we going?"

"Brown University," he said. "Ivy League country." He glanced at me out of the corner of his eye. "Your territory, Yale boy."

"How'd you know that?"

"You think you're the only guy who knows how to use the Internet?"

The drive from McCoy Stadium to Brown takes fifteen minutes during those rare times of day without traffic. After discovering that my radio works only intermittently, Casey amused himself by rummaging through the enormous pile of trash in my backseat. He made a few little grunts of approval—after finding my worn baseball mitt, for example—but mostly seemed appalled to learn that when I'm finished with my morning injection of gas station coffee, I just toss the used Styrofoam cup over my shoulder.

We were passing a long strip of discount liquor stores and

pawnshops when Casey turned back around in his seat and abruptly asked, "So what the hell are you doing here?"

I kept my eyes on the road. "What do you mean?"

"You've got way too much talent to be wasting your time in this place."

"I didn't know you had such a critical eye for writing."

"It's your business," he said. "I was just curious." He rolled down his window, briefly causing a cyclone of cups in the backseat, then rolled it back up. He seemed incapable of sitting still. I watched him as intently as the road would allow, knowing in the back of my mind that I was being indiscreet. But I couldn't help myself; he was simply too interesting. One of the many reasons I imploded at the *New York Times* has to do—vaguely—with the comic strip *Garfield*. My blinding hatred of *Garfield* stems from my belief that it is emblematic of the descent of American culture. A comic strip should be fresh and full of insight, a tiny critique of society that slips under the cultural radar—*Bloom County* and *Pogo* are perfect examples. But the prefabricated *Garfield*, carefully constructed by one hundred lame marketing guys in a Midwest warehouse, is so carefully designed not to upset anyone that it is as funny and topical as the average sitcom.

Most professional athletes are exactly the same way—so afraid to upset the gravy train that they censor any original thought. Getting most athletes to say anything beyond a bland cliché is an exercise in futility, and although I understand why they are so guarded, I also often find myself longing to discover someone who is willing to be real around a reporter. Because how can you write a good story if you can't separate marketing from truth?

From that perspective alone, talking to Casey was refreshing. Everything that he had said to me so far felt real—and he had made absolutely no effort to shine me. But we had also avoided talking about baseball, and I decided to test the limits of his honesty. The Pawtucket coaches had called a meeting immediately after the game, briefly barring reporters from the locker room, and we had heard muffled yelling through the door. I cleared my throat, then warily asked, "How was today's summit?"

Casey paused, perhaps deciding if I had crossed a boundary, then smirked. "The usual crap." He mimicked a rough German accent. "The beatings shall continue until morale improves."

I laughed, maybe a little too loudly, and Casey glanced at me scornfully—he apparently did not suffer sycophants with any grace. Chastened, I kept my mouth shut for the remainder of the drive. We arrived on the main body of the Brown campus shortly after 11 P.M., and Casey expertly directed me down several streets to the red-brick Public Safety building. We pulled in behind a faux police car—rent-a-cops have way too much fancy equipment given their shallow level of training—and Casey rolled down his window. Two Public Safety officers were smoking cigarettes outside the main door.

"Hey," Casey said to the officers. Their heads turned. "You got a kid in there named Nate McDowell?"

"Maybe," one of the officers said. "What's it to you?"

"I'm here to pick him up," Casey said.

The slimmer of the two officers reluctantly dropped his cigarette and ground the tip with the black heel of his boot. He grunted something inaudible to his partner, then disappeared through the front door. Two minutes later he emerged leading a bored-looking kid in jeans and an oversized flannel shirt. Casey reached over his shoulder and popped open the lock on the door to the backseat, and a moment later the kid was perched on top of my pile of trash. The officer rested his meaty arms on the roof of the car and stuck his head in the window.

"You tell that punk that the next time we find him on campus, we're turning him over to the police. Okay?" His gaze flicked back and forth between Casey and me, completely ignoring the recent addition to my backseat.

"No problem," Casey said. "Thank you, Officer."

I started the car. As we pulled out of the spot, the kid's head suddenly appeared next to my shoulder. He punched Casey on his thick arm.

"Why were you thanking those fat bastards?" he asked. "They wouldn't even give me a cup of coffee."

"I'm thanking them for not keeping you," Casey said. "And get your stanky-ass breath out of my face." As Casey spoke, I noticed for the first time that he had a Providence townie accent, which is close to a Boston accent in its reliance on hard As.

The kid flopped against the rubberized plastic of the seat, and I could hear the scrunch of breaking Styrofoam cups. I glanced in the rearview mirror and saw him clearly for the first time. Although he had the wispy goatee of a teenager trying to do too much with too little hair, I nevertheless guessed that he was in his early twenties. Barely. He was dressed in the typical uniform of a white kid from Providence or Omaha who was trying to pretend he was a black kid from Brooklyn or Compton: baggy, oversized jeans, a wife-beater, Timberland boots, one glittering earring, and an overstarched bandanna.

"Those pork-rind bitches copped my stash," the kid said, managing to infuse his voice with an impressive amount of outrage.

"Where's my car, Nate?" Casey asked.

"I got it towed again." Casey made an exasperated sound in the back of his throat. Nate ignored him and gestured at me. "Who the fuck is this honky?"

"Friend of mine," Casey said. "And you better thank him for coming with me to pick up your sorry ass."

"Thanks," Nate said, his tone begrudging. He shifted again, accompanied by a second symphony of cups. "Man, we gots to stop by a liquor store."

"You got any cash?" Casey asked.

"Nope. I'm flat busted. But you know I'm good for it, right?"

"You've never been good for anything in your life," Casey said. He tugged on my sleeve and pointed toward a Denny's on the side of the road. "Pull over here."

The hostess seated us at a table near the back of the restaurant, and Nate wandered off to the bathroom. I pretended to be interested in the menu for as long as possible, but my curiosity finally got the best of me.

"Who is this guy?" I asked.

"He's my brother," Casey said. I stared at him, not sure whether or not he was joking. "Well, foster brother."

"Why does he talk like a gang banger?"

"It's a hobby," Casey said, and stared down at his menu.

Either the loss of his car to a tow truck or my questions had put Casey in a sour mood, because he didn't bother to speak again for the entire meal. I hadn't eaten at the ballpark, so I ordered a full breakfast with bacon—the "Moons Over My Hammie," in Denny's marketing language. With Casey on the conversational sidelines, I spent the meal talking to Nate. We spent a lot of time discussing rap, about which I know absolutely nothing, but as I was enjoying my last cup of coffee, we moved on to his career.

"It's kind of complicated," he said.

"You deal drugs to preppies. That's basically it, right?"

Nate shrugged. "Kind of. I'm not really that into it."

"Why not?"

"It's, you know, unfulfilling. I mean anyone can pass green bud, right?"

"What do you want to do?"

Nate gestured at Casey, who was staring out the front window at the passing traffic. "I want to hit a baseball like this bitch. He's pretty damn good, isn't he?" The pride in his voice caught me off guard, and I smiled.

"Yeah," I said. "He's pretty good."

The check arrived, and Nate carefully pushed it across the table to me. "I want to be famous," he said. "Famous brothers get all the women."

I dropped Nate and Casey off in front of a small row house on the north side of Providence. The yard was neatly kept, but the house itself was one good northeaster away from collapsing into a pile of asbestos and kindling. As Nate stumbled into the building, Casey lingered by the car.

"Nice kid," I said, staring after Nate.

"Sure," Casey said. His mouth made the same disdainful curl it formed whenever a wayward reporter asked him a question. "Tell me straight. When I get to Boston, are the reporters going to find him?"

"If you do well in Boston, everything's going to be in the papers."

"That's what I figured." He stared at the small house, his fingers absentmindedly drumming the door of my car. "He doesn't embarrass me," he finally said. "If that's what you're thinking. I just worry about him."

"You're right to worry," I said. "If the wrong reporter digs him up . . ."

Casey stared at me long enough to make my foot wiggle nervously on the brake pedal. "I hope I picked the right guy."

It took me a long time to fall asleep that night. I knew that Casey had been testing me that evening—and the final test would be whether or not anything showed up in my stories. But his secrets were perfectly safe with me. I don't think the public has the right to know everything about athletes, no matter what the prevailing opinion in this country. If someone like Anna Kournikova chooses to market her personality and social life, then reporters have a right to follow her around and speculate madly on her boyfriends. Aside from those particular cases, however, I don't see how any of those details are our business.

But I know I'm hopelessly behind the curve on that issue. So I lay awake wondering what would happen when the notoriously unpleasant Boston press corps started digging around in Casey's past.

chapter 5

WE LEFT THE NEXT AFTERNOON FOR A TEN-GAME ROAD TRIP to Buffalo, Syracuse, and Ottawa. On the third night of the trip, Eddie and I were in the bar of our Marriott celebrating the Sox's victory over Buffalo. We were arguing over whether the pitch Casey had earlier hit for a home run was a curveball or a slider when Casey himself, who had been playing darts with a big group of players, came across the room and tapped me on the shoulder.

"We're doing some beaver shooting later tonight," he said, flicking his head at the other guys. "You in?"

I had no idea what he was talking about, but I nodded my head authoritatively anyway. "Sure."

Eddie barely managed to wait for Casey to leave before turning on me. "What the hell was that?" he asked.

I couldn't keep the smug scoop smile off my face. "We hung out the other night."

Eddie rolled his eyes and adopted his lecture voice—a tone he had perfected during his years as a mentor at the paper. "You know it's a bad idea to get too close to the players, right?" he asked rhetorically. "That's how you lose your job. Or end up a babbling suck-up like some NBC sideline reporter."

"Don't be jealous," I said. "If you want to write about a team, you've got to understand the players."

"Do you even know what beaver shooting is?" Eddie asked. My eyes must have given me away because he chortled like Ed McMahon. "This is going to be a great story, kid. You'll probably win a Pulitzer."

Two hours later I was dangling four stories off the ground as Jack Tatum, a first baseman, tried to pull me onto the roof. Although Casey had promised me that the fire escape outside his room would be both "safer and more low-profile" than the hotel stairs, what he had neglected to mention was that it ended a floor too low. And while Casey had nonchalantly jumped and pulled himself up the final ten feet, my merely mortal body had balked at the task. My throat contracted as I stared into the stucco wall of the building, my feet waving frantically in the air. I wondered whether the local paper would put my death on page one. A man falling off the roof is probably big news in Buffalo—even if he's only a lowly reporter.

Fortunately, although Jack isn't quick enough to hit an inside fastball out of the infield, he was more than strong enough to pull me over the lip and onto the tarpaper, where I lay gasping like an offensive lineman after a short sprint. I was ready to berate Casey for not helping Jack, but he was crouching with a cluster of players at least 100 yards away across the flat surface. I scraped myself off the roof, and Jack and I ran low like Marines to the group. The Marriott was built around a central courtyard so that every inside edge of the building faced a row of rooms. Casey was gesturing at the far wall with his hand.

"We need to scout," he said. "It'll be more efficient. Put your hand in the air if you see anything and we'll all come running."

Jack, who used to play first base for the Twins, spat a long stream of tobacco juice over the edge and then reached into his camouflage backpack. His hand emerged clutching a pair of night-vision goggles. Casey and I exchanged an incredulous glance.

"Jesus Christ," Casey said. "What the hell do you use that thing for?"

"Deer hunting," Jack said. His large wad of chew bobbed.

Casey shook his head. "Only a hick would confuse stalking Bambi with long patrol in Vietnam."

Casey and I staked out the northern segment of the roof while the rest of the players scattered around the remaining three sides. I stared at the four neat rows of windows across the courtyard. I had never been a Peeping Tom before, not even as a teenager, and I was mortified to be having my first experience with a bunch of ballplayers.

"So we just wait up here until some poor girl forgets to close the shades?" I asked.

"Bingo," Casey said. He reached into the athletic bag he had slung across his broad shoulders and pulled out three cans of Miller Lite. "And we drink."

I stared at a lit window across the way, feeling dirtier than a Louisiana politician, and my embarrassment escaped with an exasperated grunt. "Why are you guys up on this roof when you could be down in the bar picking up real women? I mean, you're frigging professional ballplayers."

Casey patted me on the shoulder, his tone condescending. "This is a long and proud tradition, Russ. Mickey Mantle used to shoot beaver back in the day."

"Do they still do this crap in the majors?"

"I don't know." Casey took a long swig from his beer. "The hotels they stay in are probably too nice."

We sat silently for fifteen or twenty minutes, and I slowly nursed my beer. A few people came into the rooms across the way, but they all swiftly and wisely drew their shades. The night was cold—with the bite that upstate New York air possesses even in the early summer—and I pulled my hands into the sleeves of my flannel shirt. As my eyes slowly adjusted to the dark, I began to see the ghostly outlines of the other ballplayers against the deep blue-black sky. Jack was lying on his stomach, leaning on his elbows while the night-vision goggles swept back and forth in a ceaseless arc. As I watched, his arm abruptly shot up in the air and began to wave frantically. I poked Casey.

"Jack's waving," I said.

Casey grinned broadly. "It's money time."

We ran around the edge of the courtyard, trying to keep our feet light on the roof, and flopped down next to Jack. "Top floor," he whispered when we were all assembled. "Third window from the right."

Only the bedside lamp lit the room, but I could see a shadowy figure lying on one of the two double beds. Her hair was splayed across the pillow like a heavy shadow and no clothes marred her upper body until a faint flush of a red bra around her breasts.

"I don't think she's wearing a shirt," I said, my shock surfacing in inanity.

"No doubt," Jack said. The goggles were suddenly in front of my face, focused on stucco. I panned right and suddenly confronted a glowing green breast. "Pass it on."

I had just handed the goggles to Casey when a second woman, wearing a fluffy white robe, emerged from the bathroom. She flicked a switch and the room exploded with light. The woman on the bed rolled over and sleepily pulled a sheet over her naked shoulders.

"This could get good," one of the players said behind me as the woman in the bathrobe sat on the edge of the bed next to her friend.

"Please kiss," Casey said. "Oh, God. Please kiss."

"This could be a religious experience," Jack said. He elbowed me in the ribs. "And I don't mean no blasphemy by that, reporter man."

The girl in the robe said something and the other girl laughed and sat upright in bed, again exposing her bra and naked shoulders. I watched, utterly mesmerized. Part of my brain, maybe the classier part, wanted to drop back over the edge of the roof and go to sleep. But the voyeur in me, the reporter and writer, was en-

tirely engaged by the spectacle—both the girls and the small audience of traveling baseball players. I come from a background
that preaches private sin: you can do naughty things, but you're
supposed to do them behind locked doors and covered windows.
I even remember getting embarrassed while watching soft-core
pornography on *Showtime* with my friends in college—an experience that is as All-American as chugging cough syrup to get
drunk in high school.

Down in the room the girls were still chatting. One touched
the other on the leg and we all tensed. They laughed. We forgot
to breathe. But then, like a teacher going to call his students in
from recess, the girl in the bathrobe marched over to the window.

"No," Casey said. The girl drew the curtains and his voice rose.
"No! No, *no, no!*"

Jack carefully laid his night-vision goggles on top of his backpack, then rested his head in his forearms. "So close," he mumbled. "That was worse than watching LSU lose to Tulane."

I pulled myself into a crouch. "Cold showers all around," I said.

By the time we sneaked back downstairs, the hotel bar was closed.
The players seemed unusually distraught for a group that had been
cut off on a Wednesday night, and I finally asked Casey why they
couldn't just hold their thunder until the weekend.

"We're on parole," he said. "The coaches are staying in a different hotel and the word around town is that they all went out
for some birthday party. Most nights on the road we've got a cur-
few—Coach even calls our room to make sure we're in bed. And
usually we can't drink in the hotel bar."

"They don't want you shooting beaver?" I asked.

"Something like that." The next words burst out of his mouth
like bottle rockets. "It's none of their goddamned business, you
know. I don't understand why we put up with it."

His tirade might have continued, but Felix Hernandez, a
shockingly obese relief pitcher, wandered over to us and threw his

fat arm over Casey's shoulder. "We're partying in Steve's room," Felix said. "You in, boss?"

"Sure," Casey said. He looked at me. "How about you?"

I briefly weighed the cost of sacrificing sleep and sobriety against missing an opportunity to spend more time with the team. I must have cared more about my job than I usually admit to myself because sleep and sobriety lost by a convincing margin.

The party turned out to be seven or eight players, five women, and a tub filled with ice and Bud Light. Felix had tuned the television to *SportsCenter*, and the room would occasionally fall silent when a baseball highlight came on the screen. The women all immediately lost interest in me when they discovered that I didn't play baseball, and I found myself sitting on the bed next to Casey, who was ignoring the party swirling around him in raucous circles.

"Where'd you find the ladies?" I asked when he finally acknowledged my presence.

Casey glanced around the room as if he were seeing the women for the first time. His disdainful eyes lingered on a brunette wearing just a Yankees jersey and panties, who responded to his stare by pulling the polyester fabric tight against her chest. "Even the sad-ass rookie teams have chicks following them," he said. "You know how it works. They figure that if they catch the right guy it's the big time."

"So why don't you . . ." I let my voice trail off and I gestured at one of the girls.

"I'm a one-girl man," he said.

"Who's the girl?"

He shook his head. "I'm not sure yet."

Casey seemed prepared to spend the rest of the night on the bed wallowing in some sort of self-inflicted misery, so I wandered across the room to Felix, who was tinkering absentmindedly with a large console on the wall.

"Problem with the heat?" I asked. He turned, confused, and I gestured at the panel. "Need help with the thermostat?"

"It's not a thermostat," he said. I peered at him curiously. "I think it's some sort of pleasure device. I just don't know how to turn it on."

At that moment one of the girls slid around us and into the bathroom, her hand carefully brushing Felix's enormous thigh as she passed, and I grinned. "If you're looking for pleasure," I said, "you probably don't need to limit yourself to the heating system."

Felix's lazy eyes wandered the room, pausing on one or two of his more svelte teammates and a few of the more openly flirtatious women. "You think this fat relief pitcher could get lucky tonight?"

"Why not?" I allowed myself a wry smile. "You've certainly got better odds than this skinny reporter."

"That doesn't make me feel any better," Felix said, and we both laughed.

I drank too many beers for the rest of the party to be anything other than a confused swirl of disjointed memories. At some point I felt nauseous enough to wander outside, and I settled on a curb in the parking lot, my head dangling between my legs. The clear air finally slowed the violently spinning pavement, and my shoulders straightened just in time to see Casey settle next to me.

"What are you doing out here?" I asked.

"I saw you leave the party," he said. "Figured I'd check." I was relieved to notice that he was slurring his words—at least this time we were both on the same side of the sobriety spectrum.

"So let me ask you a question," I said after a few minutes. "Why the sudden interest in me?"

Casey flopped back on the sidewalk, his head resting on the lip of a flower bed. "I'm trying to figure out reporters. You seemed okay."

My head was clearing fast in the cool night air, and I took the opportunity to press the issue. "Tell me why you won't be interviewed."

"You reporters ask such stupid questions." He roughly rubbed his palms against his cheeks, and when he spoke again, his words were crisper. "How would you like it if every time you wrote a story a bunch of readers got to stand around and ask why in the third sentence you used a comma instead of a dash. Wouldn't that piss you off?"

"Sure," I said. "But you can find better reasons to hate reporters."

"Such as?"

"You really want to know what's wrong with reporting?" Rather than bothering to answer my question, Casey rolled his head so that he was staring at me. "A couple years ago I'm covering a football team. The Jets. One afternoon the offensive coordinator does me and this other reporter a huge favor. He lets us sit in on a film session—you know, where the coaches break down what happened in the previous game. The whole time me and this other guy are watching the screen, watching players run in random directions, and we're totally fucking lost. We don't have a goddamned clue what's going on. No clue. And the offensive coordinator has this whole foreign language to explain what did or did not happen on any given play. How his team succeeded or failed. We just nod, feeling like the stupidest men in the world. And we walk out of that room and both comment on how the levels of knowledge are different—we know a lot for fans, but we're still hopelessly on the outside when it comes to really knowing anything. So guess what happens next."

"What?"

"Two weeks later that other reporter writes about how the Jets lost a game because they couldn't adjust to the outside linebacker blitzing on third down. And he wrote that story knowing perfectly well that he was full of shit. But he also knew that because he can talk the lingo, most of us won't know the difference. And it doesn't just happen in sports reporting. We have this culture where we worship experts, but most of us don't know enough to tell the bullshit artists from the real thing."

Casey smiled thinly. "So you're blaming society. That's original."

"I'm not blaming anyone," I said. "I'm just tired of it all."

"You know what annoys me the most?" Casey asked. "The opposite problem. I hate it when reporters ask people about things they don't know nothing about. Who gives a shit what Cybill Shepherd thinks about anything? She's paid to be an idiot. I'm paid to hit a baseball. Don't ask me for advice on anything other than how to drive an outside curve the opposite way."

"So can I interview you?" I asked. "If I only ask you how to hit a curve?"

Casey closed his eyes, and for thirty terrifying seconds I knew that he would never speak to me again. I berated myself for having been so daft, wondered what remaining vestige of a reporter buried in my subconscious had asked that idiotic question. Just when I was preparing myself to stand, gather my remaining dignity, and say a graceful good-bye, Casey's eyes popped open and he stared at me, his gaze unwaveringly appraising.

"Are we becoming friends, Russ?" he asked.

"I guess." I shrugged, trying to appear a mixture of noncommittal, indifferent, and cool. "Maybe."

"Then you can write anything you want if you make one promise," Casey said.

"What's that?"

"You promise me that you'll never do one of those 'I'm so frigging sweet because I'm hanging out with an athlete' stories. Promise that you'll never act like you're somehow different than the other thousand reporters who ask me the same goddamned questions as if they're the first person in the world to look at me with deep fucking sympathy and say, 'So, Casey, was it hard to be adopted?' Make me that promise and we can do a hundred interviews."

"I promise."

"Then okay," Casey said. And he closed his eyes and promptly fell asleep on the sidewalk.

chapter 6

EDDIE, PROBABLY TRYING TO PUNISH ME, KNOCKED ON THE door of my room at 7 A.M. I rolled over in bed and conducted a brief damage report. Although my brain was rubbing against my skull like sandpaper and my mouth felt as if I'd licked a beach in New Jersey, the rest of my body seemed none the worse for my trip to the roof. My feet fumbled for the floor, and I slowly made my way across the room. Eddie was grinning as I pulled the door open.

"How was your night of idiocy?" he asked.

I tried not to look smug, but probably failed miserably. "Good," I said. "Casey agreed to let me interview him."

Eddie swore, but there was no anger in his voice. "You little bastard. So there is a method to your madness."

I walked back to my bed and flopped across the mattress like a boxer taking a dive. "I did pay a price for the story," I said. "Where are we going today?"

"Afternoon game in Syracuse," Eddie said. "We've got to hit the road."

· · ·

Even after three hours in the rental car and two quarts of Gatorade, I arrived in Syracuse feeling very grateful that I only had to watch a baseball game, not play in one. Casey and a few of the other guys weren't so lucky—Coach Tubson ignored their sorry state and threw them in the game anyway. He could have been indicted for cruel and unusual punishment. In the top of the second Casey retreated to the clubhouse to throw up, then emerged from the tunnel in time to line a single to right field. It may have been the finest single of all time, and I was the only spectator in the ballpark who fully appreciated it.

Adding to Casey's trouble was Kim Sun Lee, his starting pitcher. The Red Sox had been signing pitchers from the Far East, and Kim had just been assigned to Pawtucket. He had a rubber arm and a great sinker, but spoke only a few words of English. And although the Sox had assigned Kim a "cultural aide" to ease his transition to American baseball, Kim had beaten his translator to the team by a few days.

For the first few innings Casey just let Kim call the pitches. But in the bottom of the fourth, with men on second and third and nobody out, Casey staggered out to the mound. Kim bowed when Casey reached his side. Casey bowed. Kim bowed again.

"Fastball," Casey said. "Inside corner and tight."

"Tight?" the kid repeated, confused.

"Yeah," Casey said. "Fastball."

"Fastball?"

Casey stared at the kid. The kid stared at Casey. Casey blinked. The kid blinked. The confused standoff might have lasted for an hour if the umpire hadn't arrived from home plate to break up the meeting.

"What the hell's going on?" the umpire asked as he waddled up to the mound. The kid bowed low to the umpire, who turned to Casey for an explanation.

"Don't look at me," Casey said, preempting the question. "I don't have a damn clue."

"Where the hell is he from?" the umpire asked.

"I have no fucking idea," Casey said. "I think he played for a team called the Carp."

The umpire scratched his chin. "Is the carp a Chinese fish?"

"I think so," Casey said. "They sometimes have them at Chinese restaurants in big tanks."

"I always thought those were bass," the umpire said.

The kid bowed again and both Casey and the umpire bowed back. Casey turned to the umpire. "I just want him to throw a fastball. That's all."

"I don't know any Chinese," the umpire said. He and Casey were staring blankly at Kim as the Pawtucket pitching coach, his face already a ruby red, trotted from the dugout to the mound.

"Doesn't anyone want to play ball out here?" the coach asked when he reached the little group.

"We've got a problem," the umpire said.

"Is the carp a Korean or Chinese fish?" Casey asked.

The coach's eyes got shifty—no average coach can ever admit that he doesn't know everything. "Japanese," he said. "They have them in sushi bars."

"I just want him to throw a fastball," Casey said. "High and tight. That's all."

The coach threw his hands in the air and rolled his eyes. "Let him throw whatever the hell he wants to throw," he said. "And we'll go get some beers."

"Fine by me," Casey said.

I interviewed Casey after the game in the parking lot so that the other reporters wouldn't see us. The story I e-mailed my editor was about the difficulty of being a catcher in an increasingly multilingual baseball world, and I focused on the exchange on the mound between Casey and Kim. To keep Casey from appearing like a xenophobe, I made sure to mention that he spoke fluent Spanish. Although the newspaper ran the story, early the next morning my editor called my hotel room.

"What the hell was that crap?" he asked when I answered the phone.

"The story?" My voice was still sleepy. "You didn't like it?"

His voice sharpened into an authoritative bark. "Nobody cares what some catcher said to some Chinese kid on the mound."

"Korean," I said. I could hear his sharp intake of breath. "And you should be giving me props. Nobody else has gotten an interview with Casey Fox."

My editor spent the next fifteen minutes explaining to me the basic tenets of journalism as he saw them. His three central points were elegant in their simplicity:

1. Readers want to read quotes from players that either a) insult the opposing team, b) mention how delighted the player is to reside in the wonderful community of Pawtucket, or c) highlight how hard he is working. Quotes about the natural habitat of the carp, which do not fit into any of those categories, are crap.
2. Readers do not want to encounter any difficult or unusual questions in the sports pages. In fact, they read the sports pages to get away from those sorts of questions. My job was to give our readers simply identifiable heroes and villains. Period.
3. I was the biggest idiot he had ever encountered in newspaper writing, and my stories were an insult to my parents, the schools that had educated me, and the *New York Times*.

The conversation was supposed to conclude with me promising to do better, but instead I asked whether he wanted me to bring him anything from Ottawa. He slammed down the phone so hard that I thought a plane had hit the telephone wire. I lay on the bed and laughed for a couple minutes before it occurred to me that I was going to have to write a few stories that made me appear indispensable before I returned to Providence. Otherwise, I realized, he would fire me on the spot.

So the next few articles I wrote were directly out of the *ESPN Magazine* playbook. A few cute quotes, a couple players' favorite video games, and a whole lot of 110 percent. The team made it easier for me by winning nine of the ten games on its swing through the north. Casey's bat was so hot it could have been used to generate electricity. He hit .440 on the trip with eight home runs and 23 RBI, earning himself the AAA Player of the Week award. I began to sneak a few of his postgame quotes in my articles, and when the fact that I was speaking to Casey became public knowledge, my standing in the press corps leapt dramatically. I had never been friends with anyone but Eddie, yet guys suddenly began joking with me in the press box and after the game. Nobody except Brian the Weasel was crass enough to ask me to introduce him to Casey. But I know they all wanted to.

We returned to Providence after a day game in Ottawa, arriving in the early evening. I stopped by the newspaper on my way home and my editor yelled a lot but didn't fire me. My stories must have dragged me far enough out of the hole—and, to be realistic about the depth of his irritation, it's amazingly difficult to fire people these days in America. Even when they're insubordinate enough to deserve it. I took my dressing down with as much grace and dignity as I could muster—not even laughing when my editor again pointed to Jerry as the kind of writer I should aspire toward becoming—then headed for home. I had just settled on my massage chair with a beer when my cell phone rang.

"Hey," Casey said when I answered. "What are you doing?"

"Writing," I said.

"You have any time tonight?"

"Depends. What's up?"

"There's someone I want you to meet," he said. "We'll have dinner."

I thought of telling him that I'd already eaten a sandwich on the way home, but I knew he would consider that fact completely irrelevant. So an hour later I was sitting in a small Italian restaurant next to a miniature statue of Michelangelo's *David* sipping a glass of vinegary red wine. The waiter had brought me a second round of bread when Casey held the front door open for a woman who, despite wearing only jeans, sneakers, and a crew shirt, was jarringly attractive. From her smooth face I guessed that she was roughly Casey's age, and her long legs and toned arms matched his athletic frame. When they reached the table, I stood.

"I'm Russ," I said to the girl, extending my hand. But I felt too flustered to maintain a graceful silence—the last person I had expected to meet was Casey's girlfriend—and my mouth kept flapping. "You two are like an *über*-couple. You should be on the cover of *People* magazine with the rest of the genetic elite."

Casey smiled tightly as the girl suppressed a laugh. "This is Molly," he said grimly. "My sister." As I blanched, he corrected himself. "Well, my foster sister."

"We've lived in the same house," she said. "I know all his dirty little secrets."

As we settled around the small table, I made another effort at chipper conversation. "So what's his darkest secret?" I asked. "The one he hides from the rest of the world."

She glanced at Casey, and he looked away, embarrassed. It was the first time I'd ever seen him embarrassed. "He's a closet slob," she said. "He wants you to think that he's neat, but you look under his bed . . ." She wrinkled her nose. "Just awful."

I had categorized Casey as a beer-and-a-burger kind of guy, but he put on a very credible performance at the restaurant. He ordered a nice bottle of white wine and expertly selected antipasto for the table. I also noticed that he was unusually quiet—in fact, he seemed content to watch Molly speak to me. Molly was, I must admit, utterly engaging. At first glance she appeared to be merely an attractive preppie, her dirty blonde hair dropping just to her shoulder blades, the blue eyes and white teeth, her clean face devoid of makeup and lips glistening with gloss. But there was nothing prim about her mannerisms or her habit of staring you down when you spoke.

As we chatted I learned that she had gone to Williams College, graduating just a few weeks earlier, and that she was still trying to figure out what she was going to do in the fall.

"So I hear you met my brother," she said shortly after the waiter brought us the check.

"Your brother?" I asked. A moment later I finally made the connection. "Jesus. You're related to Nate."

"A lot of people say I must have been switched in the hospital. I don't look or act anything like my brother or my dad. But if you could have met my mom . . ." Her voice trailed off, but I didn't read the warning sign.

"Where's your mom?" I asked brightly. A millisecond later I remembered the research from my own article and wished that I could wrap the tablecloth around my body and disappear into a wormhole.

"It's a long story," she said. "And far too depressing for this dinner."

I awkwardly reached for the check, but Casey slid his hand out and palmed it. "On me," he said.

I reached into my wallet and tossed my corporate credit card on the table. "I can just bill this to the paper. It won't be a problem."

"I don't want to owe your paper nothing," Casey said, disdain curling the edges of his narrow mouth.

We went out for ice cream after dinner, and I began to notice the strange dynamic between Casey and his foster sister. As we flitted from subject to subject, I got the strong impression that Molly was biting her tongue. Casey's behavior also confused me. At the ballpark Casey was brooding and reserved, but also as self-confident as any human being I had ever met. Around Molly, however, he appeared to second-guess every sentence that emerged from his mouth. The stark contrast was so striking that I wanted to film the conversation to be sure that I wasn't imagining the entire thing. And it wasn't that Molly and Casey didn't get along—they listened intently to each other, and were very sweet about little things such as opening doors and splitting an ice cream—but they weren't as relaxed as you would expect two people who had grown up in the same household to be.

We parted on a brilliantly lit street corner and they walked off toward Casey's car at least a foot farther apart than I would have walked from one of my siblings. I spent most of my drive home trying to understand why Casey had invited me to dinner with his foster sister. He seemed to be deliberately showing me the disparate pieces of his life—and I couldn't understand his reasoning. Although I had initially assumed that he was being disingenuous when he said he was spending time with me to figure out reporters, that idea didn't seem quite so ludicrous anymore. If he continued to hit the ball well, he would be in Boston before the end of the year. And if he hit the ball well in Boston, he would soon be in the national news. Maybe I was a test case.

Or perhaps he thought we had something in common. Despite his growing popularity among his teammates, Casey didn't fit well into the homogeneously corporate fiefdom of professional baseball. That was obvious. And it doesn't take stunning powers of observation to realize that I'm not a natural reporter. While we weren't friends yet, every time I spoke to Casey I felt an easy connection. We just seemed to look at the world the same way. And he must have felt the same thing—what other reason could he possibly have had for introducing me to Molly?

chapter 7

THE PAWTUCKET COACHES HAD ABSOLUTELY NO IDEA HOW to handle Casey. He made his utter contempt for them obvious the first day he arrived, and while Casey never made the mistake of breaking the obvious rules—he was universally on time for practices and games—he had a worse attitude toward authority than Timothy Leary. He also had an easy foil in Coach Tubson, the team's glacially witted manager. Sometime in the early 1980s Tubson had been a backup outfielder for the Brewers, and he had kissed enough organizational ass to get a minor-league coaching job when his career as an active player ended. His transparent ambition was to make it back to the majors as an assistant coach.

When Casey first arrived on the team, Tubson probably saw him as an opportunity—plenty of coaches have advanced their own careers by lashing themselves to the coattails of a promising player. But Tubson was far too stupid to realize that Casey had his own agenda. Casey's rebellion began with a few on-field comments. Tubson, like many baseball coaches, second-guessed virtually every decision his players made. In the second game of the Ottawa series, the Pawtucket pitcher threw a curveball on a 2–2 count that the Ottawa batter lined into right field for a base hit. Tubson spiked his Gatorade cup.

"Jesus," he swore loud enough that the pitcher could hear him. "Challenge that guy on a two-two pitch."

In the final game of the same series, a different Pawtucket pitcher, facing an identical 2–2 count, threw an inside fastball that the Ottawa batter muscled over third base for a double. This time, Tubson charged halfway out of the dugout.

"Mary and Joseph," he shouted angrily. "Don't frigging give him the damn fastball."

Most players would have just bit their lips and concentrated on the game, but not Casey. He sprang up from his crouch, tore off his mask, and strode toward the dugout.

"Yesterday, same situation, you said he should have thrown the fastball," Casey yelled, loud enough that we could hear him in the press box. "What is it, Coach?"

Tubson mumbled something and slunk back to the dugout where he fumed for the rest of the game. When I finally finished laughing, Eddie whispered to me, "If that kid stops hitting, they're going to send him to Siberia."

But Casey did keep hitting, and his challenges to Tubson's authority only grew more extreme. On a Monday morning the situation finally came to a head. Pawtucket had won seven games in a row, but was shut out by Syracuse on two hits by some twenty-three-year-old phenom throwing pure smoke. While most managers would have passed off the game as one of those things that sometimes happens over the course of the season, Tubson exploded. Perhaps he felt that some chest pounding would help him reassert his authority. The assistant coaches gathered the team in the locker room the morning after the loss, and Tubson began by storming through the door with a baseball bat and destroying the water cooler. He screamed for a while about wanting more "focus" at the plate—whatever that means—and when he reached the Knute Rockne point in his speech, he spiked the bat and glared around the room.

"You bastards couldn't hit water if you fell out of a boat," he snarled.

Casey's voice floated up from the back of the crowd. "That's a cliché, Coach."

Tubson whirled toward the players. They were all staring at Casey, incredulous, and Tubson immediately spotted his heckler. "You have something to say, Fox?"

Casey smiled just enough to let Tubson know that he wasn't intimidated. "I just think we'd pay more attention if you came up with fresh material."

"Like what, hotshot?"

Casey stood up and began ticking off options on his fingers. "You guys couldn't hit oil if you dug in Kuwait. You couldn't hit pussy if you were dating a porn star. The Top Forty if you were Madonna. That last one's a little obscure, but I think you could make it work." By the time he finished, most of the players were hiding their faces behind hands and towels, although a few stifled giggles nevertheless escaped.

"You've got a crappy attitude, Fox."

"All I'm saying is that we're something like fourteen and goddamned two since I got here. So I don't think we need to listen to one of your tendentious speeches."

Tubson inflated like a frightened blowfish. "What did you just call me?"

"I called your speech tendentious." Casey's voice warbled between annoyed and bored. "Look it up, you ignorant prick."

Several assistant coaches jumped on Tubson before he could charge, and Felix and another pitcher led Casey out of the room. All three of them burst into laughter when they thought the door was closed, but a few peals still reached Tubson's embarrassed ears.

Tubson should have suspended Casey right then, but he didn't. Maybe he possessed enough animal intelligence to intuit the difficulty of his situation. If he had suspended Casey, he might have kept control of the team, but his bosses in Boston certainly would have wondered why he was having so much trouble handling one of their future stars. So Tubson fell back on one of baseball's oldest strategies for dealing with troublemakers—he decided to try and brand Casey as being too smart.

The strategy might have worked if Casey hadn't already integrated himself so well with the team. Tubson didn't know that Casey had been running around shooting beaver, but he should have noticed that a small clique was forming in the back of the travel bus. Casey had a gift for doing running commentary on people the bus passed. For example, when the team drove past a bum pushing a shopping cart in Providence, Casey turned to Felix and said, "Hey, that's what happens when you can't throw the inside fastball." It was stupid stuff, I suppose, and much of it was recycled, but it nevertheless firmly established Casey as one of the beer-drinking boys.

Tubson was able, however, to influence the way the media perceived Casey. My colleagues were already inclined to dislike him for his refusal to do interviews, and Tubson did everything in his power to throw napalm on the fire. In press conferences he took to referring to Casey *sotto voce* as a prima donna, and he would take great pains to avoid admitting that his sole star had played well. After one game, in which Casey had hit two home runs and thrown out three base runners to single-handedly lift the Paw Sox to a 3–1 victory, Tubson actually had the gall to say that the MVP had been third baseman Lonnie Mitchell "for his key diving stop in the third inning." The transparency of his effort amused me on one level, but I was consistently horrified to discover that the other reporters were following his lead and largely ignoring the best player in minor league baseball.

After one string of especially noxious articles, I found the nerve to ask Casey if he was bothered by the way the media covered the team.

"You mean the fact they try to ignore me?" he asked.

"Yeah," I said. "And all the shots Tubson takes at you in the papers."

"It don't bother me at all," Casey said. "Because if I keep playing well, I'll get my chance in the majors. And they'll still be stuck writing ten-cent stories about a two-dollar team." I winced, and he put his hand on my shoulder. "No offense."

chapter 8

IN THE SEVENTH INNING OF AN INSUFFERABLE GAME THAT
was threatening to last four hours, I spotted Molly in the stands
behind first base. When I get really bored in the press box, which
is fairly often, I usually scan the grandstand for attractive
women, so it's not all that surprising that I found her. And, to be
perfectly honest, I had been hoping to see her ever since our
dinner at the Italian restaurant a week before. She was wearing a
polo shirt and tan shorts, her long legs dangling over the back of
the seat in front of her, and for an inning I kept glancing in her
direction while a long line of Pawtucket and Rochester pitchers
stomped angrily around the mound between throwing an endless
stream of bad pitches. She was sitting alone in a row of empty
seats—the other fans had probably been driven away by the poor
quality of play—and judging by her expression she had managed
to remain remarkably interested in the game. She was a better
fan than I.

I finally found the courage to wander from the press box down
to the concourse in the top of the eighth inning. I paced back and
forth between the hot dog kiosks for a while, hoping that she
would leave her seat to get a Coke, but eventually I felt so ridicu-

lous that I had to hide in the bathroom. I stood at the trough for as long as possible, and when I finally forced myself to leave, I walked to her seat quickly enough that I couldn't question what I was doing. For five or ten seconds I stood at the end of her row, but she was too engrossed in the game to notice my presence. I awkwardly cleared my throat. Her head turned, and if she was surprised to see me, she concealed it remarkably well.

"Long game," she said, her blue eyes squinting as she peered upward.

"Horrible," I said. "Baseball is the best sport in the world when the game lasts two and half hours and completely unbearable when it takes four."

"Totally unbearable," she said, smiling.

I shifted nervously on my feet, wondering how to explain my presence without sounding like a stalker. "I saw you from the press box," I eventually said.

She patted the chair next to her. "Do you want to sit?"

The plastic seats in McCoy Stadium are stacked closely together, and I scrunched as far away from her in my seat as possible. We watched quietly as the Pawtucket pitcher threw three balls in a row. Casey stomped to the mound, an expression of extreme displeasure on his face.

"He's been crouching for three and a half hours," I said. "He must be in a foul mood."

"These guys couldn't throw a strike if they were bowling with bumper lanes," she said. Then she laughed. "I'm still working on my baseball smack."

"Not too bad."

"I hated baseball as a kid," she said. "My dad sometimes took us to games. It seemed so boring and slow. But watching Casey play has totally turned me on to the sport. He showed me all the little details that I used to miss."

"It's a beautiful game," I said. "Subtle."

She was staring at Casey, who had returned to his crouch and was flashing signs to the pitcher. "He spent hours teaching me how to notice the positioning of the outfield."

"You find that interesting?" I had gradually relaxed in my seat and our shoulders were almost touching.

"Not really." She watched the pitch—another ball—and then turned to me. "I don't find that stuff too exciting. But watching him hit . . ."

"I know."

"He has a gift," she said, her eyes returning to the field. "It's almost magic."

"I know," I said. "And the nice thing is that he can make a lot of money from his gift."

She looked at me in a way that made me instantly regret my comment—despite its rather obvious truth. "Is that the point of having a gift?"

"It is for some people," I said. "Maybe even most people."

"I think it's stupid to do something that will make you miserable. No matter how much money you can make."

"Do you think Casey will be miserable playing baseball?"

She shrugged, her face expressionless. "I think you're spending enough time with him to figure that out for yourself."

We silently watched the game for five minutes. The Pawtucket pitcher finally threw a strike, which the Rochester batter drilled into the gap in left center for a double. Casey and the pitching coach grimly marched to the mound and after a brief discussion switched pitchers. As the loudspeakers played an unidentifiable Bruce Springsteen song, Casey warmed up the next Pawtucket sacrifice, who appeared to be struggling to put the ball over the plate even in practice. Casey must have been irate because his throws back to the mound were twice as fast as the pitches.

"There's more to him than just baseball," Molly abruptly said. "You know? And I'd hate for his gift to own him."

"What does that mean?"

"I want him to be happy."

"He's happy playing baseball."

"Sure," she said. "He loves playing baseball. He loves the game. But everything else . . ." She waved her hand in the general direction of the press box. "Nothing else about playing baseball fits him. And it's only going to get worse when he gets to Boston."

"Why has he been spending so much time talking to me?" I asked.

She examined me for a long beat, and as her attentive eyes stared into mine, I felt my chest contract and my breath get shallower. Her hand had moved to the armrest between us, a few inches from my forearm. "You need to give yourself some credit," she said. "You're not the worst person to hang out with."

My mouth opened on an impulse that I couldn't stop in time. "Have dinner with me?"

She laughed and pulled her hand back into her lap. "I suppose I deserved that," she said. "Don't you have a game to cover?"

"Sure," I said, fighting to conceal my disappointment and embarrassment behind a rueful smile. I stood and turned to flee. Just as I reached the aisle, she stopped me with her voice.

"Come down again sometime. I'll be at a lot of the games for the next couple weeks."

I looked back just long enough to nod my head, and then ingloriously rushed for the safety of the press box. But for the entire journey up the long set of corrugated iron stairs, her face danced before me.

I couldn't focus for the rest of the game. Something about my conversation with Molly was making me dwell on my failures. I can identify the exact moment my life shifted from an unbroken skein of overachievement into my current status of unblemished mediocrity—I was a senior in college and most of my friends, who were hoping to become stockbrokers, began interviewing for jobs. Before they went to meet with the gatekeepers from Wall Street, they would all carefully don their dark suits, white shirts, and conservative ties. I once asked a friend why he thought the suit was necessary, and he told me with a straight face that "a dark suit is a litmus test. It proves that you're willing to do what it takes to be a team player." During the high season of corporate recruiting a slow trickle of undertakers flowed ceaselessly from the dorms to the Career Services building.

The entire process struck me as being completely ridiculous. The notion of putting on a suit to pass a litmus test of conformity seemed so backward—putting on that suit was a way of saying that if they hire you, you're willing to do exactly what they want. But what those companies really should have been looking for was the kid who wasn't wearing a suit, the kid who was perceptive enough to realize that a college senior in a suit looks like a football player in a dress.

And that was the moment when I realized that I had no interest in playing the little parts of the game that make your professional life much easier. I just couldn't muster the energy. The roots of my failure at the *New York Times* and the reason I was on the verge of getting fired by a crummy newspaper lay in those navy blue and charcoal gray suits. When I'm being honest with myself, of course, I also know that my own laziness and cynicism have held me back. Nevertheless, I think that if I didn't feel such an overpowering revulsion for playing the whole phony game, I wouldn't be trapped somewhat by my own volition in a professional backwater. I just never could think of a reason to swallow my pride.

But maybe Molly was a reason. Perhaps I didn't know her well enough to say that with any authority, but when I got home that night I was feeling heady enough to sit at my computer and write seven pages of my book in one night. And that is proof enough for me.

chapter 9

THE TEAM HAD A DAY OFF ON A MONDAY IN EARLY JUNE. THAT
Sunday night I was lying in my chair watching the highlights of all
the games I'd already seen that afternoon, more annoyed than
you'd think a person could get from eight hours of staring at the
television. But I find it very trying to watch sports these days. The
commentators alone can spoil the purest of athletic moments. The
inanity of the commentary tends to aggravate me less than the
bombast—I think it may be time that we locked John Madden and
Dick Vitale in a box and said, "Look, the world can only support
one of you." I still remember the first time I screamed at a television set. It was one of the U.S. Opens in the early 1990s, and some
smarmy television personality went into the stands to interview
Barbra Streisand as she watched her "good friend" Andre Agassi,
who at that point in his career represented as clear a victory of
long hair over substance as you could ever hope to find, play an
early round match. When asked why she and Andre were friends,
Ms. Streisand replied, "We have a lot in common—he's intelligent
and sensitive. He's like a Zen master on the court." It was two years
before I could bring myself to watch tennis again.

I had just finished my dinner and was preparing for Sunday

Night Baseball when the phone rang. I answered on the off chance that it might be Casey, and I was pleased to hear his voice come through the line.

"We're going out for drinks," he said. "Felix, Nate, and I are going to get it on. You in?"

I forced an exhausted sigh from my lungs. "I'm too old for that crap."

"Come on," he said. "Just a couple beers."

"I've heard that one before," I said. "And it never ends well."

But I went anyway. We met at a dive in downtown Providence, the kind of place where the intoxicated bouncer would have let in a twelve-year-old with a fake library card and where you optimistically refer to the rats and gulag-quality bathrooms as providing "personality." I briefly considered using my lighter to try and sterilize my glass. We sat in the back of the bar, surrounded by neon beer signs and dartboards, and worked our way through pitchers and pitchers of Miller Lite. A couple of skinny women in tank tops and jean shorts talked to us for a while, but Nate chased them away by telling stories about the "Ivy League ho" he'd supposedly "screwed silly" the previous weekend.

Casey and Nate eventually went to play darts, leaving me alone with Felix. He and I had never had a real conversation, and all I knew about him was that he had a nasty forkball and a decent curve.

"Where are you from?" I asked after an awkward minute or two.

"Puerto Rico. But I don't have an accent."

"No," I said. "Not at all."

"Are you really a reporter?"

"Sure." I gestured at his enormous body—I can't call him big boned because it's impossible to see any evidence of bones under his thick layers of muscle and fat. "Are you really a pitcher?"

"Sometimes," he said. "When I feel like throwing the ball over the plate."

"How long have you been in the minors?"

"Ten years. On and off."

The reporter in me was taking over—something that often

happens when I'm talking with strangers—and I instinctively reached into my repertoire of easy questions. "What was your worst moment?"

"That's easy." He leaned back in his seat, and I worried for both the chair and the Hudson Valley fault line. "I was in Japan a couple years ago because the Indians traded me there for a bunch of Big Macs. Something about that country made me pitch like crap. Maybe it was the sushi. Anyway, they were about to release me, I was playing just awful, and the worst thing was that I didn't even have a car. I had to ride a scooter to work. You ever seen a fat man on a little scooter?"

"No," I said. "But it can't be pretty."

"It was the most humiliating damn experience of my life. All these Japanese dudes were laughing at me on the highway every day. I must have looked like a freaking sumo wrestler on a tricycle."

I was still laughing as I asked my next question. "How about your best moment?"

He smiled with such real pathos that my mirth instantly vaporized. "I hope I haven't had it yet. But if I had to pick one . . . The Dodgers called me up two years ago for a cup of coffee. Just seven days. Everything was first class. The hotels, the money, the women." He glanced over at Casey. "He'll see pretty soon."

"Jealous?" I asked.

He shrugged. "Players go up, players come down. You can't worry about anybody else. I just want to get another chance for myself, you know?"

"Good luck," I said. And it wasn't just drunken bar talk or the involuntary signoff at the end of an interview. So many of the star professional athletes I've met take all their success for granted; I think there's room in big-time baseball for a couple more guys like Felix.

The bouncer threw us out when the bar closed promptly at 1 A.M. I was in no condition to drive myself home, and Casey and Felix were in a similar state. Nate, however, claimed to be sober—an assertion I found extremely improbable. But when we made him say the alphabet backward and touch his nose while standing on one foot, he somehow passed with flying colors, so we all piled into Felix's red pickup truck and drove to the nearest 7-Eleven. We bought big buckets of Coke and Mountain Dew, bags of salty chips, hot dogs, and candy bars, and sat in the parking lot and finished the whole insalubrious pile. I was halfway into my food coma when Felix threw his arm around Casey.

"You're a damn fine ballplayer," Felix said.

Casey flushed and tried to wiggle out from under Felix's meaty forearm, but the relief pitcher was too large. "I can smell your pits," Casey said in an atypically shy voice.

Felix ignored him. "I've never seen anyone hit the ball as well as you. You've got to be cheating."

"Nope," Casey said. "No cheating."

I was lying on my back in the bed of the pickup using Casey's sweatshirt as a pillow. "Maybe he's a cyborg," I suggested. "Some sort of baseball super robot designed in a government laboratory."

"Tell them your secret, Casey," Nate said. I propped myself up on my arm and stared at Nate, who was sitting on the curb carefully picking his nose.

"Secret?" I asked.

Nate jerked his head at Casey. "Ask him."

I turned in time to notice Felix's arm tighten around Casey's neck. "Don't make me squeeze it out of you," Felix said.

Casey struggled to shrug under Felix's grip. "It's not a big deal. I can just see the ball hit the bat."

Felix and I both laughed as soon as his words sank in. "Bullshit," I said. "That's complete crap. The human eye can't see things that fast. It's impossible."

"Ted Williams did it, yo," Nate said. "Just like Casey."

"That's a myth," I said. "A bunch of old-school crap."

Felix was nodding his head in agreement. "Nobody sees like that."

I thought that Casey would get mad, but our disbelief appeared to amuse him. He slipped out of Felix's grasp and roughly pulled Nate to his feet. "We're going to the park," he said. "I'll show you."

I wearily shook my head. "I've got to get home."

"Not going to happen," Casey said. "Not after you said you didn't believe me."

We stopped by a liquor store to buy a case of cold beer, then headed up I-95 to the stadium. Felix was sitting in the cab with Nate, and Casey and I were huddled outside in the bed of the truck. As Nate accelerated onto the highway, the sharp wind drove moisture through my thin fleece, and I shivered.

"Cold," Casey shouted over the rush of the air. He waited for me to nod, then cleared his throat and tugged on my shoulder until my ear was next to his mouth. "I saw you talking to Molly in the stands."

"Yeah?"

I must have looked nervous because he waved his hand genially. "It's cool. She needs some new friends in Providence."

The curiosity in my voice carried clearly over the wind. "Is she going to live here?"

"Probably not. She's bunking with me and Nate right now." My eyes swung toward him quickly, too quickly, and the transparency of my interest instantly mortified me. But fortunately Casey was lost in his own embarrassment—his face turned red and he quickly stumbled to explain himself. "I gave her my room and Nate and I are bunking together. She owes me big. That bastard smells worse than an overflowing outhouse."

His weak joke couldn't cover his discomfort, which seemed to be swelling by the moment. I watched him curiously. I had begun to wonder if Casey Fox was even capable of emotions such as embarrassment, and it both relieved and intrigued me to see him display a more human side.

A mile or two later, just when I had started to worry that the awkwardness of the pause might fatally sabotage our burgeoning friendship, Casey finally spoke again. "Can I ask you a favor?"

"Of course."

"It's a big favor."

I shrugged. "If it's too big a favor, I might turn you down. But you're still welcome to ask."

"Can you talk to Molly for me?"

I tried to contain my confused smile, but failed miserably. "That's the favor?"

"We used to have these great open conversations," Casey said, staring at some indeterminate point in the blackness beyond the bed of the truck. "But now it's like she's hiding something, and I can't figure out what the fuck it could be."

"So you want me to scout her out."

Casey looked physically pained and shook his head vehemently. "No. Not like that. It's just that she's a smart girl and you're a smart guy and maybe she'll tell you why she's been acting all weird since she got back from school and I started playing ball."

"Okay," I said. "I can do that." A tiny grin crossed my face as I realized that in his shy request lay the real reason that he had introduced me to Molly—and perhaps even why he had befriended me. It was a motivation as ancient as Genesis; he didn't understand a woman and he needed help. And who better to help than a harmless and somewhat brainy reporter?

We got to McCoy Park at 3 A.M. We parked far enough away from the stadium that no passing security guard would notice the pickup and then slowly walked around the perimeter of the field like generals evaluating a fortress before a siege. Near the right-field fence we found a weakness. Some careless groundskeeper had just wrapped a chain around a gate rather than properly locking it, and a moment later we were striding across the outfield grass, Felix and Casey moving as if they belonged while Nate and I guiltily slunk through the forbidden ground like teenagers in a liquor store.

When we reached the dugout, Casey swung over the iron railing and trotted down the tunnel. A swear and the bang of a sneaker on metal soon emerged. I carefully picked my way down the dugout steps and through the short passageway to Casey's side. In the faint glow of moonlight reflecting off polished concrete, I could dimly make out a hulking door barring our way into the bowels of the stadium. I leaned on the door just hard enough to shake it against its hinges and realized that it was probably dead bolted from the inside—we would have needed either a brilliant locksmith or a block of plastique to get through.

I had returned to the dugout and was lying on the bench while Casey muttered inaudible profanities in the tunnel when a solution suddenly occurred to me. "The press box," I said loudly. "It's got a back staircase down to the locker rooms."

Casey popped out of the tunnel and we trotted back onto the field and gathered around home plate. The press box loomed far above us, empty and foreboding, the dark windows looking like the abandoned bridge of a sunken oceanliner. But on the far left of the structure I saw hope. "Somebody could fit through that window," I said.

Felix and Nate had followed us back onto the field, and we all stared up at the narrow opening in the sliding glass panels. Felix shook his head. "Not me. I'm too fat for that crap."

We all turned to Nate, who waved us off with an elaborately dismissive gesture. "Fuck that," he said, "I ain't Spiderman."

I was praying that nobody would ask me when Casey pulled his sweatshirt over his head, handed it to Nate, and jogged toward the stands. I watched, my breath high in my chest, as an extraordinary athlete with the potential to make mutual funds of money risked his career to shimmy up an access pole, tiptoe across a narrow balcony, and slip through a window. Ten minutes later the huge metal door ground open and Casey emerged, a magician's grin on his face.

"Game's on," he said.

Nate gestured at the dark field. "We've got to wait for the sun to get up. Or turn on the lights."

"No lights," Felix and I said together.

Casey yanked on Felix's elbow. "Let's break into Tubson's office. We'll prank the bastard."

They wandered off with Felix muttering objections to Casey's uncaring back, and Nate and I settled onto the bench for the long wait.

"Are you tired?" I asked.

"Nah. I'm hitting my damn prime," Nate said. He was fiddling with his zipper. I closed my eyes and was on the verge of sleep when his voice rang in my ear. "Hey, are you down with anyone in television?"

I pulled myself closer to upright. "Not really. Why do you ask?"

"I figured out what I want to do now that I'm done with dealing. I'm going to be on one of those reality shows."

"Like *The Real World*?"

"Yeah, that's right. I've been practicing."

"Practicing?"

He must have heard the confusion in my tone because he stood. "Watch." He drew a television screen around his head and shoulders with his fingers and pasted an earnest expression on his face. "It's really hard for me, you know? I come from a different background and stuff than these other guys. So I'm trying to be all, like, understanding. But they gots to give me my space and not be all up in my face."

He stared at me expectantly, and I nodded. "Not bad."

"You see how I pulled that rhyme?"

"Yeah." I fought to keep from smiling. "How are you going to get on the show?"

"I've been spending a lot of time making tapes. You send them in to these producer bitches. I did this thing with my underwear on my head . . ." He ignored my curious look. "But I hear you've got to know somebody."

"That would probably help," I said.

• • •

Nate and I napped until sunrise while Felix and Casey committed unknown acts of mischief in the clubhouse. I awoke to the clatter of wood on cement. As I pulled my sagging eyes open, I saw a large pile of bats scattered across the floor of the dugout like spilled matches. Casey was slinging a laundry bag of balls onto the field.

"The sun up?" I mumbled.

"Almost," he said. I glanced out of the dugout and saw the first red glimmer of light on the horizon. "It's time."

I removed my leather shoes and white socks, leaving them in one of the cubbies in the dugout, and rolled up my khaki pants. I grabbed an old, weathered glove from the ball bag and slowly walked to the outfield. The dew had gathered while I was napping, and the thick grass was cold against my feet. I crouched in center field while Casey warmed up Felix. I wasn't surprised to see that Felix's first few pitches were wild—a night of drinking doesn't usually improve a person's fine motor skills—and Casey let a couple balls fly past him to the backstop. Nate, who had been standing in the infield near where the second-base bag would be, wandered out to me.

"Felix don't look so good," he said.

"A little wild."

"That fat bastard better not hit my boy."

But Felix got a little better his last few throws, and Casey traded his mitt for a helmet and bat. Before Felix threw his first pitch, Casey dipped a rag into a jar of pine tar and carefully rubbed the sticky black pitch over the entire barrel of the bat.

"Who are you?" I yelled. "George Brett?"

"This is for you," he yelled back.

When he finally stepped up to the plate, I was mostly praying that Felix wouldn't hit him. And, I suppose, that Casey wouldn't embarrass himself. Few athletes—with the possible exception of Mickey Mantle—are at their prime after a night of drinking. Felix threw his first pitch, a low fastball over the outside part of the plate, harder than I had hoped. Casey neatly dropped his shoulder and drove the ball into center field 20 feet to my right. I could hear the tight hiss of the seams spinning as it passed, and when it first touched the grass it kicked up a small plume of dew.

"Look at it," Casey shouted to me. "I hit the seam. Right on the tip of the fat part."

Humoring him, I slowly jogged over to the ball, following the thin green line in the silver grass, and I nudged it with my foot. Then I abruptly dropped to my knees. The pine tar had left a small brown smudge on the ball—precisely on the seam. I spun the wet ball in my hand. The mark lay on the top of the curve.

"Am I right?" Casey yelled. "Bitch."

I stood and threw the ball toward the infield. I was embarrassed to see it bounce before it got to Nate. "Do it again."

He did it again. In fact, he did it nine more times before I gave up and admitted that he could indeed see the ball hit the bat. Ophthalmologists should feel welcome to doubt me, but I know what I saw that night. The greatest moments in sports to me are when someone does something that shouldn't be physically possible—scientists studying the human body used to claim that no person would ever be able to pole vault over 20 feet until the Russians found some kid who made it look as simple as hurdling a bike rack. Or the four-minute mile. For centuries scientists crunched the numbers and called the feat physically impossible, but now college freshmen can run that fast. When I was at Yale, I used to go to college track meets just to watch the mile, and every time I saw some kid break the four-minute mark, I would feel as if we had won another victory over people who want to define the limits of human achievement.

chapter 10

THE TEAM TRAVELED TO TOLEDO FOR A SHORT WEEKEND SE-
ries, and my editor asked me to stay in Providence because he
wanted another feature writer to "get his feet wet" on the road. I
didn't perceive the request as boding particularly well for my job
security. He instead sent me to cover a high school sailing regatta
in the harbor, which made for a very long day. I returned to my
apartment early Saturday evening and found myself abruptly
plunged back into my life pre-Casey. I ate a frozen pizza and had
settled into my chair for a long evening of electronic massage and
bad television when I abruptly felt guilty. In all my months in
Providence, I had never made any sort of concerted attempt to
find real friends—or even just entertainment that lay outside a
TV set. My initial efforts to fit in had been limited to searching
personal ads and chat rooms on the Internet, which turned out to
be less than a waste of time. It was a hemorrhaging of time.
Looking back, I suppose that I fit the lonely-guy-at-his-terminal
demographic as well as anyone. I lived in a gated community
where if I knocked on my neighbor's door to ask for a cup of sugar,
she probably would have called the cops. And that little fiber op-
tic cable really was my easiest link to a world outside my walls.

The irony, as I swiftly discovered, was that while I loved the anonymity of making connections on the Internet, how can you ultimately defeat your own loneliness while remaining anonymous? I think that is the Internet's dirtiest secret of all—a secret perfectly captured by the fact that *www.lonely.com* is a porn site. So I quit the Internet cold turkey before I started wishing that people could make the ☺ symbol in off-the-net conversations.

That evening, my guilt eventually swelled to the point where it drove me from my chair. Perhaps the adventures I'd been having with Casey had raised my expectations; perhaps I was just tired of frozen pizza. In either case, I turned off my television, put on a pair of jeans and a polo shirt, and went to the movies at the biggest theater in Providence.

Going to the movies on your own can be one of life's great pleasures. You get to laugh whenever you want without embarrassing anyone other than yourself; you have plenty of space to stretch out; and you can see any movie you choose—movies your friends would mock you mercilessly for renting. But that night I made a huge mistake. Rather than seeing an action flick with all the other lonely single guys, I instead chose a cotton-candy date movie and sat amid the 150 cutest couples in greater Providence. The experience depressed me. I kept glancing around the theater and wondering what the other men had done to earn themselves such loving girlfriends. Could they all be successful and funny and intelligent? Did they all have clean bathrooms and no back hair? Did they floss regularly? How had I dropped the ball so completely?

I was so confused when I left the theater that I almost smacked into Molly. She was standing by the concession stand buying a small popcorn and a large Coke.

"Are you here with someone?" she asked when I had finished apologizing for almost giving her a bath in her own drink.

"Yeah," I said. "You?"

"Yup." We stared at each other and she abruptly laughed. "I don't know why I'm lying. I'm alone. I'm about to go see some terrible action movie with a hundred horny losers."

"I'm lying too," I said. "I'm one of those horny losers."

She gestured down at her sweatshirt and jeans. "I wouldn't wear this on a date. And who goes to a movie at midnight on a date?"

We examined each other again for a long beat. I still couldn't figure out why she wasn't with a large, overprotective preppie. "Alone?" I asked. She nodded. "I mean, how does that happen? Me . . . that I can understand. But you? How hard is it for a pretty girl to get a date in this town?"

She raised an eyebrow. "Apparently it's pretty hard," she said. "What are you seeing?"

"Whatever you're seeing."

Her mouth curled down and she giggled slightly through her nose. "That's not bad," she said. "You're getting better."

We settled into adjoining seats, but I was smart enough to avoid trying any junior-high moves on her. I was pleased to notice that she had a habit of laughing to herself when the movie got especially inane. I walked her to her car afterward, which happily meant that she didn't see my decrepit Toyota, and she paused and rolled down her window before she started the engine.

"When do you think they're going to send him to Boston?" she asked.

"Not too soon. They've got a pretty good catcher, and they probably think Casey needs more seasoning."

"That's good," she said. "He's not ready."

"Nobody's ready," I said. "Not for that. Not for Boston in a pennant race."

Casey called me on Monday morning, twelve hours after the team had returned to town.

"Ask me where I am," he said.

I grunted into the receiver. "I'm not your mother. I don't give a rat's ass where you are."

"I'm in the Shore Mall," he said, ignoring me. "Ask me why."

"Why are you in the Shore Mall at nine in the morning?"

"Come see," he said. And he hung up.

I pushed through the broad glass doors into the mall shortly before ten. The architect who designed the complex must have graduated from the Wal-Mart School of Architecture. The interior looked like a barn with windows, and all the storefronts faced out onto one of those faux indoor squares that represent a cynical attempt to re-create the small town centers that malls have been slowly and inexorably replacing. The square featured both fake deciduous trees and a Roman fountain—which, from a taste standpoint, put it comfortably on the southern Californian side of the standings.

I strolled halfway through the mall before I saw the group. Casey and Felix, wearing their full home uniforms, were standing with the team mascot under a large sign that read: "Support Your Sox! Free Tickets!" The Pawtucket mascot has always made me sick. Walt Disney should be held posthumously responsible for the profluence of hideously cheery and generic figures like Larry the Pawtucket Wonder Bear. Of all sports, baseball should remain mascot free—with the possible exception of the vaguely obscene Philly Phanatic, who sums up Philadelphia better than any article or book ever could.

"How'd you get this gig?" I asked when I got within hailing range.

"We were bad," Casey said.

Felix nodded grimly. "Very bad."

The mascot made a noise that managed to sound disapproving even though it was muffled by twenty pounds of fake white bear hair. I stifled my urge to grab the costume by its smugly smiling mouth, drag it across the polished mall linoleum to the fountain, and throw it into the overchlorinated water. Felix interrupted my fantasy by accosting a passing female shopper.

"Free baseball tickets, ma'am?" he asked, extending an envelope.

The woman paused, far enough away that she could beat a hasty retreat, and carefully examined our little group. Her slacks and blouse were definitely not from the sale rack, and she probably drove a hunter green Ford Explorer with the premium sound package. She could have been my mother circa 1985.

"What team?" she finally asked.

"Pawtucket Red Sox," the mascot yelped through his smiling mouth.

Her nose wrinkled in a way that managed to avoid being either cute or attractive. "Is that a professional team?"

"Oh, we have uniforms and everything," Casey said. As she stared at him, perhaps trying to decide if he was joking, he extended his arms and did a slow pirouette. "See. One hundred percent polyester."

Either Casey or the moronic mascot must have persuaded her, because she took the envelope of tickets from Felix and tucked it in her purse.

"My husband's a fan," she said. "And he's trying to teach my son. We'll try to come, but I can't make any promises."

"I'll be disappointed if I don't see you in the stands," Casey said to her swiftly retreating back. Surprisingly, I didn't hear sarcasm in his tone. I was about to ask him the reason when the two ballplayers and the Wonder Bear turned in unison. I followed their stares to a woman in her twenties, pretty in a bare-midriff-and-heavy-eye-shadow kind of way, who was strutting like a Rockette through the concourse.

"Free tickets?" Felix asked when she came within earshot. "Best seats to the hottest team in town."

"Is it baseball?" she asked, real excitement in her voice.

"Only on Mondays," Casey said. "The rest of the week we play rugby."

The woman paused for a confused second before words began to gush out of her mouth. "I love baseball," she began. "I've been a Sox fan for forever. I thought Roger Clemens was the cutest man I have ever laid eyes on."

"We've got some pretty cute guys too," Casey said. He waved

his hand at Felix and the Wonder Bear. "Felix here is a pitcher like Roger, and under all that white hair is a fine-looking . . ." His voice trailed off. "You're just going to have to trust me."

The woman took the tickets from a preening Felix and slid them into her Victoria's Secret bag, allowing a glimpse of a silken something that sent the group into collective cardiac arrest. She glanced around our little band, a concupiscent smile plastered across her face. Felix and the Wonder Bear clutched each other for support. "Maybe I'll bring my boyfriend," she said. "Thanks for the tickets."

She completely ignored the trauma she had caused—Felix's eyes were the size and shape of footballs and even the artificial fur on the Wonder Bear appeared to have lost its luster—and turned to leave with a self-assured flounce. Casey stared after her as she strutted away, her slender hips swaying even more assertively than before. "She reminds me of my favorite quote," Casey said. His eyebrows narrowed as he tried to recall the exact words. "Baseball is a lot like church. Many attend; few understand."

"Don't be a dick," I said. "People like things for different reasons."

"The wrong reasons," he said. He peered around the sterile mall, disgust crossing his face for the first time. "This sucks. I'm going home."

He leaned down to pick up his bag, but I put my foot on the strap and held it against the shiny floor. He must have been surprised because he just looked up at me, his eyes passive. "You should enjoy this moment," I said quietly. "Today, nobody knows you outside a ballpark. You can say whatever the fuck you want. But in a couple years—or a couple months—if you come to a mall like this, you will be instantly surrounded by a hundred people. And a reporter like me will write down every word out of your mouth."

Casey yanked the strap out from under my feet and slung the bag over his shoulder. "Can't you tell," he said. "I'm enjoying the moment."

chapter 11

MOST PEOPLE—EVEN PROFESSIONAL BASEBALL PEOPLE—SPENT
so much time focusing on the way Casey hit that they missed the
more interesting half of his talent. Even if he were to go 0–4 with
four strikeouts at the plate, his defensive and game management
skills would nevertheless make him an invaluable member of the
team. Catcher is the most demanding defensive position on a
baseball field. Period. Perhaps shortstops and center fielders get
more highlights films on ESPN, but only catchers make several
game-altering decisions every half inning.

Casey had three great strengths behind the plate. First, his
prodigious physical gifts changed the way other teams played the
game. Once scouts passed the word around the league about
Casey, only the boldest and most egotistical base runners at-
tempted to steal on the Paw Sox. He could fire the ball to second
base from his knees harder than most major league catchers can
throw with two steps and a crow hop. He also had a nasty proprietary attitude toward the plate. Even on a deep fly ball, runners
tagging from third base knew that they couldn't go around
Casey—he would force them to go through his elbows and knees
and burly shoulders.

His second gift stemmed from his intellect rather than his physical talents and therefore impressed me even more than his arm or his size. Catchers are often compared to field generals in baseball literature, and the analogy is unusually apt for a cliché. A great catcher owns the field. He knows his pitcher's strengths and weaknesses; he knows his fielders' strengths and weaknesses; he knows the batter's strengths and weaknesses; he knows the dimensions of the park and the condition of the infield dirt; he knows the direction of the prevailing wind and the percentage of moisture in the air. He knows everything. So when a great catcher flashes the sign for an inside curveball, he has crunched enough variables (perhaps consciously, perhaps not) to make even a statistician squirm.

I once forced Casey to watch a tape of a game he caught, and he talked me through his interior monologue during one at bat. I've transcribed his condensed notes below—I won't bore you with the full version, which included details on the shadows in center field.

Tie game, can't afford to give up any runs. Men on second and third, one out. The man on third runs fast enough to score on almost any fly ball that reaches the outfield. The man on second is fast enough to score on any hit other than an infield single. What do I need? A strikeout, a very shallow pop fly, a sharply hit ground ball to the left side of the infield. Who's the batter? John Hunter, hitting .280. I know he has a big swing, Coach says he likes to drive the ball to the gaps. (Who doesn't? Thanks, Coach.) He dove over the plate last time he was up. What does that tell me? He likes his pitches from the middle of the plate out. What does my pitcher throw? He has a live fastball, decent control, and a great slider. Got it.

Pitch one, fastball on the inside corner. Strike, no swing. Pitch two, fastball on the inside corner. Strike, awkward swing.

Pitch three, fastball too far inside to hit. Ball, batter doesn't swing but looks shifty in the batter's box. Pitch four, slider on the outside half of the plate. Batter doesn't dive into the pitch, instead waves weakly with his bat, and I've got my strikeout. Two outs, what next?

As Casey himself is quick to point out, his careful plan is completely irrelevant if the pitcher throws a bad pitch—if, for example, the pitcher had missed his mark on the inside fastball by six inches and tossed it over the heart of the plate, the batter might have driven it for a home run. Baseball fails as a game of intellect every time a pitcher misses his spot, a shortstop boots a ground ball, or a batter bloops a perfect fastball just over the outstretched arm of the second baseman into center field. But even if the mental part of the game doesn't always reign supreme—which, of course, is part of baseball's appeal—the prepared and cerebral catcher always gives his pitcher and his team an advantage.

Casey's final strength stemmed from his player management skills. He had a remarkable ability to relate to pitchers; he could make them listen to him and he kept them continually focused. Most pitchers are annoyed whenever anyone approaches them on the mound, but the Pawtucket pitchers would focus on Casey like a teenage basketball player on Michael Jordan. He always had something valuable to say. If a pitcher was getting hammered in an inning, Casey would stroll to the mound and talk about foot placement or arm rotation—something small enough to make him believe that the problem was minor and mechanical rather than serious and career threatening.

He also possessed a remarkable ability to break the batter's focus, not by telling obscene jokes or insulting his girlfriend, but by making him believe that Casey knew more about what the batter wanted to do at the plate than the batter himself. Casey waged his psychological warfare via persistent, biting comments. "Dropping your front shoulder," he'd say after a swinging strike.

"We're not going to give you a low fastball, you know." One of the next pitches, of course, would be a low fastball. At least once a week Casey and a batter would have to be physically separated after an especially humiliating strikeout.

Casey could also be a genius at cajoling favorable calls out of umpires. He never played to the crowd or argued balls and strikes, which immediately put him on good terms with most of the officials. His treatment of an old umpire named Ray Rickey also aided his reputation. Ray had been calling games since the Paleolithic era of baseball, and during his years behind the plate his skills had gradually eroded. For the last few seasons, the league office had been looking for a way to gracefully let him go, and Ray finally gave them an opportunity by showing up to a game terribly hungover. The fact that his wife had recently died would not have been sufficient excuse for the Lords of Baseball.

Ray was scheduled to work behind the plate, and when he settled behind Casey in the top of the first inning, he exuded a soft groan. Casey raised himself an inch on his haunches and turned his mask slightly.

"You okay, Ray?" he asked.

"Not so good, kid," Ray said. "I'm not seeing these pitches so hot."

"Want me to call them?" Casey asked.

"Yeah," Ray said. "Just twitch your shoulder if it's a strike."

So Casey called the pitches for nine innings and nobody in the ballpark figured it out. In fact, Coach Tubson charged out of the dugout to argue balls and strikes in the sixth inning, and Ray— displaying a beautiful appreciation for the value of irony—threw him out of the game. But the other catcher, whom Ray hadn't asked for help, complained to the league office after the game that Ray had been drunk, and a contingent of triple-A dons interviewed everyone involved. Casey swore on a copy of the *Baseball Encyclopedia* that Ray had been in fine form, and the officials were forced to return to the office with their pink slips still tucked in their black binders. Ray didn't forget the favor, and word travels fast through the umpire world.

All of Casey's skills made a difference to the Pawtucket pitching staff. They had been coughing up almost six runs a game when he arrived from Lowell, but over the next month they cut that number by a third. When combined with what Casey was doing with his bat, the team's midseason surge seemed less surprising. Pawtucket was 17–23 when Casey arrived, six games out of first place. A month and a half later the team was leading second-place Rochester by two games with a sterling 41–29 record.

Red Sox management in Boston missed few of those details, but they probably would have left Casey in Pawtucket for "seasoning" if it weren't for a bizarre accident. On August 3, during a game against Toronto, Boston's starting catcher, Jason Varitek, slipped on a bat laying on the dugout steps and tore the ACL in his knee. Twelve hours later the Sox summoned Casey Fox from Pawtucket.

Casey called me five minutes after they told him. "I'm going up," he said.

I had seen Varitek's injury on *SportsCenter* and wasn't surprised by the news. "Good luck," I said. "You'll have a great career."

"I might be back," he said. "Maybe they'll trade for an experienced catcher."

I laughed into the phone. "You won't be back."

"I'll call sometime," he said. "Take care of yourself."

I made a dismissive little noise into the receiver and hung up. My chair vibrated gently beneath me. "Well, Casey Fox," I mumbled to myself as I stared into the blinking lights of my mute television. "You just crossed the Rubicon."

Part 2

Boston

chapter 12

THREE DAYS AFTER CASEY LEFT FOR BOSTON MY EDITOR CALLED me into his office and fired me. He left the door open, and I could see most of my former colleagues gathering like professional cannibals to hover just within earshot—I've never seen so many people interested in screensavers and paper clips. Eddie, to his credit, stayed at his desk. Being fired didn't upset me as much as the fact that my editor was crisply professional throughout his monologue, never giving me the opportunity to tell him what I thought of him and his crummy paper.

I didn't keep much stuff at the office, and all my files and personal items fit into a spare paper box from the Xerox machine. My coworkers parted like horses before a 300-pound cowboy as I gathered my things, and only Eddie dared to cross the neutral zone.

"He's an ass," Eddie said. "And you're too good for this hellhole anyway."

I shrugged as nonchalantly as I could manage. "I earned it. He had no choice."

"Maybe I can make some calls," Eddie said. "I know a lot of editors."

I shook my head. "I'll be all right. But thanks."

We shook hands, and then I performed the slow march of death through the office and out the front door as people dove behind desks and into closets to avoid me—I must have reeked of dangerous failure. A big part of me felt relieved. The thought of covering a Pawtucket team without Casey hadn't appealed to me, but I didn't know if I would have had the gumption to quit. A security guard walked me to my battered Toyota, probably trying to ensure that I didn't run my keys across my former editor's car. I stuffed my box in the backseat next to my Styrofoam cups and dirty clothes from the gym, dramatically slammed the door for the benefit of the curious security guy, put my head against the steering wheel, and allowed a tear of self-pity to sneak through my closed eyelids. For the second time in six months I had no job. But this time I knew what I wanted to do; I wanted to follow Casey.

I lay in my chair for a week before I finally found the energy to act on that desire. After only five minutes of leafing through the phone book, I found the name: Sean McDowell, 153 Harcourt Road, Providence. 555–1547. For two days I considered calling, but eventually I just got in my car with a map and a vague sense of where I needed to go. Providence is the perfect American postindustrial town, a low-calorie version of a real city. It has a business district with a few thirty-story buildings and a handful of needlessly ornate government offices, an old industrial area that is slowly being either redeveloped or abandoned, a bright new mall that is supposed to convince the surrounding suburbanites to abandon their own malls and return downtown, and an expensive sports arena and international airport, both of which were built in a bout of giddy self-delusion. But Providence also has a kind of gritty character that I've always admired. For starters, the city is pretty much run by organized crime, which means that while the local government might pick your pocket, you don't have to worry about getting mugged. Providence also has a distinct blue-collar edge, perhaps best reflected by the enormous number of large American sedans built in the 1970s and early 1980s that still roam the city's roads.

After half an hour of aimless wandering with my map, I finally stumbled into the right area. Sean McDowell lived in the perfect Providence neighborhood: a collage of clapboard houses, defunct Laundromats, and dingy grocery stores, which had yet to experience New England's economic revival. Harcourt Road stretched away from a rotary surrounded by dueling gas stations. The first house after a large weed-infested field was marked by a mailbox so rusty that I could barely read the 153 painted on its side, and I parked along the curb. I had just slid through the broken gate when the front door inched open.

"What the fuck do you want?" asked a rough voice from inside the house. I saw a glint of metal just inside the door, which my imagination immediately transformed into the stub barrel of a shotgun.

"I'm a friend of Casey and Molly," I said. "I'm looking for Mr. McDowell."

The door didn't move. "What's your name?"

"Russell Bryant."

The door swung open to reveal a stooped man with a gray mustache and an oft-broken nose. The "shotgun" in his hand turned out to be an ancient 3-iron, a fact I found only marginally more comforting. "I'm McDowell," he said. "You write for the paper."

"I used to," I said, carefully eyeing the golf club, which was transcribing tight circles a foot from my chest.

"You wrote some nice things about Casey. Especially when all those other assholes were putting him down." He paused, the golf club dropping to his side, and his caustic blue eyes slowly examined me. I found myself wishing that I had worn work boots and a sweatshirt rather than moccasins and khakis. "What can I do for you?"

"I just wanted to know where Casey grew up," I said.

He smiled humorlessly and waved his vein-riddled hand at the street. "This is it. Twenty years ago it was a real neighborhood." His hand flicked toward the adjacent vacant lot. "The kids played ball there. We used to keep that field good. You know, before the blacks and browns from the islands started moving in. I finally gave up mowing it a couple years back. All they did there was fornicate and smoke their drugs."

I didn't know what to say, so I just mumbled something and pulled out my notebook. I carefully wrote, "mowed" in large block letters and underlined it twice.

"You want to come in?" he asked.

The interior of the house was bachelor clean—every picture and coaster had been stowed with military precision—but the place was in desperate need of a vigorous dusting. Photographs covered most of the spare surfaces. I glanced at one and saw a young Molly and Nate standing in Sunday clothes outside a neat suburban home. It took me a moment to realize that it was the same house. Mr. McDowell wandered over to a brand-new Sony television, the only object in view that looked to be less than twenty years old, and rested his hand on the top. "I bought it two weeks ago," he said, the pride obvious in his voice. "So I can watch Casey up in Boston."

"It's a fine set," I said.

I fidgeted awkwardly, wondering if I was supposed to say more nice things about the Sony, while Mr. McDowell continued to stroke the top of his television. "Why don't you go up to Casey's old room?" he eventually suggested. "I'll fix us a drink or something."

I climbed the narrow staircase, relieved and excited. Mr. McDowell, evidently a neurotic man, had labeled all the rooms at the top of the stair with stenciled blue paint, and I stepped into the one marked with Casey's name and closed the door behind me. The air was stale, but over the dust and nitrogen I could detect the faint trace of leather and linseed oil. It smelled like an old mitt. Baseball memorabilia covered every scrap of wall space in the tiny room—photocopies of old baseball stories, vintage posters, and team pennants. The headlines and pictures featured

Walter Johnson and Sandy Kofax and Ted Williams. I couldn't see anything more recent than a blurry copy of the Willie Mays retirement story from the *San Francisco Chronicle*.

I idly rummaged through the room, trying to avoid the places where Casey might have kept his really illicit stashes, and under the bed I found a shoebox filled with old baseball cards of now-forgotten players from the '50s and '60s. Casey had used paper clips to attach little notes to the front of some of the cards. "Great bunter," he'd written on one. "Got the high fastball down."

I was browsing through the eclectic book collection on the small shelf under the window when Mr. McDowell opened the door. "You doing okay?" he asked.

"Yeah." I pulled a copy of *Crime and Punishment* off the shelf. "I didn't know Casey was so into books."

"Molly made him read those," Mr. McDowell said. "That girl was on him to read a book a week. He did it, too. I never could figure out why he paid any attention to her."

We wandered back downstairs and had grainy black coffee in the gloomy sitting room. Our conversation flickered like a candle in a stiff breeze until I noticed a framed photograph of a Little League team over the mantel.

"What's that?" I asked.

"Best team we ever had around here," Mr. McDowell said. "Casey's first team."

I stood and peered at the picture. Casey was the same size as the other children, but he filled his uniform in the way that most Little Leaguers don't. "How old was he?"

"He'd just moved in with us," Mr. McDowell said. "We put him on the local team. It cost me fifty bucks, but I figured the kid had to make some friends, right? Anyway, the coach came over a couple days later and told me we had something special. I went to every game after that.

"Little League can be real scrappy down here. Coaches cuss all the time and sometimes people get into fights in the stands. I remember this one time Casey decked a kid at home plate and the kid's dad came running out of the crowd and took a swing at him.

Casey hit him in the knee with a bat. That slowed the bastard down.

"Anyway, none of that stuff bothered him until they won the league—that's the picture—and got to this tournament. Winner goes to the Little League World Series. The team won its semifinal game, and afterward Casey comes up to me and tells me he just quit. I thought he was joking. The damn team had a chance to go a wicked long way—maybe even be on ESPN. I called him all sorts of names. You know, quitter, fag, things like that. And I told him that if he didn't play he'd owe me the money I'd paid to get him in the league. He just ignored me. Didn't bother him at all. And a couple weeks later he handed me an envelope with fifty dollars in cash."

"The team win in the final?" I asked.

Mr. McDowell shook his head. "Nah. Not without Casey. They got killed."

I stared at Casey's face in the picture. Something in the deliberate way he had set his jaw made him look like a veteran of Gettysburg and Cold Harbor rather than a young ballplayer. "Why'd he quit?"

"He never told me," Mr. McDowell said. "And I never could figure it out. Damn foolish, I always thought. And he didn't play ball again until college."

On my way out of the house I asked for Molly's number, which Mr. McDowell gave me without hesitating. I called her two days later, my stomach so tight that I had to hunch over in my chair.

"We should bump into one another by accident again," I said when she picked up the phone.

"Same place?" she asked.

"Yeah. How's Saturday around seven?"

"Maybe I'll see you then," she said.

I got my hair cut on Saturday morning, and I deliberately didn't use a razor on Thursday or Friday so that I would get an extra close shave before the date. If that's what it was. In an outrageous fit of optimism, I spent five minutes deciding which pair of boxer shorts I should wear—I have a couple pairs that I save for special occasions. It had been a very long time since I had felt any reason to wear the A-list underwear.

I got to the movie theater twenty minutes early, and I stood under the air-conditioning vents in the lobby to keep myself from sweating. She arrived exactly on time. I tried not to stare as she crossed the room, but she looked so perfectly cute in jeans and a ponytail that I couldn't help myself. When I lie awake in bed and try to imagine what my life should have been like, I always picture myself dating a girl like Molly.

"What are we seeing?" she asked when she got within earshot.

"Something funny." I gestured at her outfit. "I thought you said you wouldn't wear jeans on a date."

"Who said this was a date?" she asked, her sunny eyes blinking with expert innocence.

We picked a broad comedy that turned out to be so generic that I've already forgotten the plot. It starred someone like Ben Stiller or Jim Carrey, and the main male actor spent most of the movie humiliating himself in various ways. I laughed a few times, but mostly I enjoyed the fact that my elbow touched Molly's on the seat rest for at least twenty minutes. Given my long winter of dating discontent, any human contact qualified as a major victory.

We walked from the theater to a nearby mall in search of dinner and found a Thai restaurant that confused poor lighting with a romantic atmosphere. Before the main course arrived, we were arguing over the movie.

"It's emblematic of sexism in society," she said.

"Come on," I said. "It was just bad. That's it. No women were degraded."

She shook her head, frustrated. "That's exactly my point. Reverse the roles. Make the movie about a woman being repeatedly humiliated by a guy. Getting punched in the breasts. Falling out a window. Not funny. Why do you think that is?"

"Maybe men can't stand to see women humiliated because we feel an inherent need to protect them." As I paused, I could feel the small smile creeping across my face. "Or maybe women just aren't funny."

She glared at me, and I didn't know her well enough to tell if her anger was real or for dramatic effect. "Are you trying to provoke me?"

"I'm willing to bet you're cute when you're angry," I said. "Or is that a sexist thing to say?"

"Very." She let a grumpy little sniff sneak through her nose. "But I might forgive you if you pay for dinner."

I did pay for dinner, and after we finished eating I took her to the only coffee shop I knew in Rhode Island that has survived the onslaught from Seattle. We sat at a table in the corner, so close that our knees almost touched, and huddled silently over our coffee. For the first time that night I felt awkward.

"How did you end up in Providence?" she eventually asked.

"I wish I knew," I said. "I was never one of those people who had a plan. The only thing I wanted was to do something useful. Something interesting."

"Is writing interesting?"

"Sometimes. Sometimes not. I spent a horrible two years after college covering sports in Jackson, Mississippi." I involuntarily shuddered. "I hated every moment."

"Why was it so bad?"

"You try interviewing professional bass fishermen without a southern accent."

"I see your point," she said. "So is that why you ended up in Providence? To escape the handicap of talking like a college graduate?"

"It seemed like as good a place as any. I don't really have a home."

"Where's your family?"

"New Hampshire. But that wasn't an option."

"I don't have a physical home either," she said. "Not since my mom died. But I used to have that sense of being home when I was with my brother."

"Nate?" I asked incredulously, wondering if we were discussing the same person.

"No. Not Nate." She smiled in a way that let me know that I wasn't allowed to smile with her. "I have to love Nate because he's family, but I still know that he's an ass. Casey's been my real brother since . . ." Her voice trailed off and she absently stirred the dregs of her coffee. "I guess everything changes, huh?"

"What happened?" I asked, not certain that I really wanted to know the answer.

"It's simple," she said. "I'm not the person Casey thinks I am."

"Meaning what?"

"I'm not perfect."

"Sure you are," I said as I plastered my most flirtatious smile across my face. But my smile slowly faded as Molly stared at me for a long minute.

"Don't even joke about that," she eventually said. "Do you know how exhausting it is to date men who need you to be perfect? I had enough of that crap in college to last me three lifetimes. I have to be with someone who isn't afraid to see the whole me. And once he sees me, he's got to be willing to accept the entire package, warts and all."

"Then I'll see any flaw you want," I said lightly. But even then I knew that I was lying; I needed her to be perfect more desperately than any college senior ever could.

Shortly before midnight I walked Molly to her car. I wish that I could have thought of a suave way to ask her back to my apartment, but that's never been a specialty of mine. She might even have come—she held my nervous hug a moment longer than she had to—and as she drove away, I felt an unexplainable tightness in my chest. So I went home and consoled myself with a shot of Jack Daniel's and the thought that I would see her again soon.

chapter 13

CASEY HAD BEEN PLAYING IN BOSTON FOR THREE WEEKS WHEN
one of the senior editors at *Sports Illustrated* called and invited me
to the New York office. I took the insufferably slow Amtrak train
to Penn Station and walked twenty blocks uptown to the Time-
Life Building near Rockefeller Center. The *Sports Illustrated* offices are a circular honeycomb of small cubbies cramped with file
cabinets, bulky computers, and reporters who, despite not working on a daily deadline, nevertheless manage to appear perpetually harried. In fact, if you were to run through the office at a
quick trot, you might think that you were passing through the regional headquarters of a Big Five accounting firm rather than the
best sports magazine in the business.

Tim Davis, the editor who had called, met me in the lobby and
escorted me into the large office of editor-in-chief John Abbot, Jr.
I had met Abbot once before when I was at the *Times*. He had
made his reputation as a manager and editor of writers, rather
than as a writer, and I felt that under his tenure the magazine had
shifted away from its traditional role as America's literary sports
magazine toward something more corporate. Although, to be fair,
the pressure on Abbot to squeeze every last dollar out of the sole

remaining cash cow in the *Time* magazine empire must have been extreme—the *Sports Illustrated* swimsuit issue makes more money for Time, Inc., than the flagship *Time* magazine makes in an entire fiscal year. My largest objection is as a reader and a fan: I would like my sports magazine to take sports seriously and itself lightly. But most sportswriters and editors have somehow reversed that formula, and while *Sports Illustrated* isn't the most egregious violator of that principle, it's certainly the most visible.

Abbot, wearing a neat black suit he must have bought in the kind of shop that wouldn't let me through the front door, was perched on the edge of his desk when I entered the office. He leapt across the room, his hand extended like the prow of an extremely powerful motorboat. His energy unsettled me.

"Good to see you, Russ," he said. "Can I get you a drink?"

"I'm good," I said.

He waved at a small sitting area at the far end of the office, and I warily settled into the seat closest to the window. Abbot sat across from me, and Davis grabbed a notepad from the desk and perched between us, his pen hovering above the paper. Davis had made his reputation breaking scandals in college athletics, and I could feel his practiced eyes boring into the side of my face.

"Do you have any idea why you're here?" Abbot asked when we were all seated.

"I think so," I said. "It's probably because of Casey Fox."

"Bingo," Abbot said.

I allowed myself a tiny, smug smile. "He won't talk to you."

"He won't talk to anybody. The kid's having the greatest August in history, and he won't talk to a single goddamned reporter." Abbot couldn't keep the frustration from his voice, and his tone made me appreciate Casey even more. Not many people—let alone athletes—buck the wishes of John Abbot, Jr. "We were hoping you could go do some freelance reporting for us. We want to write a feature."

"I'm a reporter," I said, "not a Dictaphone. I'd be happy to write the feature, but I'm not sending you guys interview tapes that you can turn into a story."

Abbot waved his hand as if my request was completely impossible. "We can't let you write the story. For starters, we're already over budget on freelance features."

"Bullshit," I said. "*Sports Illustrated* makes more money than any other magazine in the industry."

"My hands are tied. We're part of a corporation, Russ. I can't even hire the people I want to hire. Otherwise, we could have come after you a couple years ago."

I ignored the transparent lie and stared out the window. "He's even more important than you think," I said after a short and awkward pause. "Casey has a chance to be the guy who rescues baseball. He's incredible on the field, but he's also smart, good looking, and funny. Baseball needs him. Desperately."

"We know that," Abbot said. "That's why we want you to help us."

"Give me a feature."

"No."

"I'll go to ESPN. They'll do it in a second."

For a millisecond my threat transformed Abbot, the composed businessman, into the belligerent editor at any city desk in the country. His face swelled and he leaned forward. Before he spoke, however, he took a deep breath, and his voice, when it emerged, was perfectly composed. "You don't want to do it with ESPN."

"Why not?"

"It's a promo network. They're just one long commercial—no integrity at all. Take Dennis Miller. Monday Night Football hires him, which is a total joke. Right?" I nodded. "They can't criticize Miller on ESPN. Because ABC is a sister network. In fact, they've got to promote him. So they suck his dick on the website."

"Casey has nothing to do with Dennis Miller," I said.

Abbot ignored me and continued. "They don't care about writing over there. They care about entertainment. They've got a bunch of former athletes who can't form a complete sentence working as senior writers. Trust me, a guy from Yale would be much happier with us."

"I didn't like Yale that much," I said. "Feature."

"Fine," he said. But from the expression on his face I could tell that he didn't like it.

The next day I threw caution to the sharks and moved out of my apartment in Providence. I stuffed my chair, my television, and my bed into a small storage locker on I-95 and sold the rest of my furniture to one of my less aggravating neighbors at Rolling Oaks—I have to admit that I won't miss putting that return address on my outgoing mail. When I finished emptying my apartment, I was fully mobile, a fact that both thrilled and terrified me. Part of my mind fretted that in a few weeks I would either be living out of my car or crawling home to my eminently unimpressed parents. But the optimistic part, which had been buried for so long that I had almost forgotten it existed, imagined a Fitzgeraldian new beginning.

I got to Boston on a Friday morning and discovered that *Sports Illustrated* had decided I was the kind of ace reporter who warranted a chain motel overlooking the Massachusetts Turnpike. After only a few minutes of inhaling exhaust in my dreary room, I fled for the sanctuary of Fenway Park. The Sox were playing the Tigers in the early evening, and I watched them take batting practice from the press box. Casey was crushing the ball. When the team retreated to the clubhouse, I slipped downstairs and wandered around the old park. Fenway is a shrine for any true baseball enthusiast, but it is a shrine that seems increasingly out of place in the high-revenue modern game. The press box is new, but most of the park survives as a vestige of a time when people came to watch baseball rather than to eat sushi and cheer for computer-generated images on the Jumbotron. I'm sure they'll tear it down someday soon.

I wandered through the stands and finally settled in a seat just behind the visitor's dugout. The grandstands had been built for antebellum legs, and I had to draw my knees up toward my chest. Even without the crowd, the unmistakable scent of crushed peanut shells and stale beer filled the air. I stared out at the field.

Fenway has a personality that goes far beyond the legendary Green Monster in left. Pesky Pole seems but a short toss from home plate; generations of Red Sox have carved their names into the scorekeepers' room beneath the Monster; and slow grounders bouncing across the infield act more erratic than pinballs in an earthquake. You can't replicate those wonderful little details— just as no photograph could ever fully capture the sprawling majesty of the Polo Grounds.

But part of what makes Fenway great is the unique character of the crowd. I've always thought that Red Sox fans have much in common with the old southern loyalists. Both groups worship a lost cause, believe heavily in the doctrine of original sin, and faithfully subscribe to a romantic view of history. Old triumphs are carefully guarded and immortalized, and old defeats are end-lessly replayed and critiqued. Any southern loyalist can tell you that Stuart was delinquent at Gettysburg; any Red Sox fan can tell you that Bucky Dent made a pact with the devil. The South has Faulkner; Boston has Roger Angell. In many ways Fenway is the epicenter of New England's remaining Calvinist instincts and, by logical extension, the center of its guilt. Calvinism says that God predestines those who shall win and those who shall lose, which means that the failures of the Red Sox can only be explained by the cruel reality that God has chosen us to fail—we are the anti-Israelites. It's hard to argue with that reasoning. After all, four times since 1946 the Red Sox have lost game seven of the World Series. In other words, four times the team has played one game to determine the Major League champion, and four times it has lost. Worse yet, in 1986 Boston came within one pitch of winning the World Series thirteen different times. Thirteen fucking times. Mention those facts to a true New Englander and he will tell you with the apathetic shrug that has typified the region for three hundred years that he isn't surprised. God simply hates us.

When the first fans began to trickle into the grandstand, I re-treated to the press box. The local reports claimed that Casey's ar-rival had helped break the team from its August torpor, and the

Sox were now only six games behind the Yankees—and three games out of the wild card spot. Casey was hitting .432 with six home runs and 17 RBI in his eleven games in Boston. His numbers were so good, in fact, that the press corps was only just beginning to get grumpy that he wouldn't speak with them.

The game started on time at 7:05 and the Fenway crowd gave Casey a standing ovation every time he came to the plate. He again did his part, going 2–4 with another home run, and the Sox won 7–3. I went down to the locker room after the game. Casey spotted me as he emerged from the shower, just a small white towel wrapped around his waist. He practically ran across the room and threw his arm around me.

"Goddamned," he said. "What the hell are you doing here?"

"*Sports Illustrated* wants a story."

His face flickered for a second, but he forced a smile. "That's big time, huh?"

"Won't change anything," I said.

He gestured at the reporters clustering around the other players' lockers. "They're about to get me anyway. The club has passed down a decree: Contract be damned; Casey Fox shall speak."

I felt a tiny pang of proprietary jealousy, which I quickly squelched. "Poor bastards. They don't know what they're getting into."

Casey insisted that we go out to celebrate after the game, and he invited another player, Terrell Jordan. I remembered Jordan mostly from his glory days in the early '90s with the Cubs, and I'd always admired his quiet dignity. This season Jordan needed all the dignity he could muster—his average was hovering around .230 while his salary weighed heavily upon the books at just over $6 million per year. Our little group of three crossed Lansdown Street, which runs along one side of Fenway Park, to one of the district's interchangeable large nightclubs. The bouncer waved us past the long line of eager tourists and overendowed college students standing behind a velvet rope, and a pretty brunette in tight-fitting silver pants led us to a table near the back of the dance floor.

We had a few drinks and chatted quietly, but when the band began to warm up, Terrell excused himself. He is only a few years older than I am, but he had a wife and two children waiting for him at home. Casey and I had just finished a round of tequila shots when a tall woman wearing tight black shorts and a bra out of Madonna's late-'80s collection snuck up behind Casey. Before I could warn him, she wrapped her arms around his chest and stuck her reptilian tongue in his ear. I almost gagged up my tequila. Much to my surprise, he turned and kissed the strange woman on the lips, and she swung her legs over the back of the chair and dropped neatly into his lap. Casey winked across the table at me.

"I've made a new friend," he said.

"I'm Rachel," the girl said, extending her hand like a diva. Her skimpy top was designed to highlight her stunning breasts, and I fought to keep my eyes focused on her too-angular face. She was chewing an enormous wad of gum.

"You don't have to work tonight?" Casey asked the girl.

"Nah. I did this party earlier. Ugly old guys, but they tipped well."

The band had just struck its first chords, and I had to shout over the buzz from the amplifiers. "What do you do?"

"I'm a dancer," she said. "Exotic dancer."

I nodded my head and tried to keep my face perfectly blank. "I'm going to go get Casey a drink," I said. "Do you want anything?"

"I don't drink."

She delivered the line with just a hint of self-righteousness, and I found myself teetering between surprise and annoyance. "That just means you're going to have to go to a lot more funerals than I will," I finally said.

She looked at me, confused, then whispered something in Casey's ear. A moment later she bounced up and pranced across the room to a small group of women.

"Nice girl," I said. Casey just nodded absentmindedly and stared after her. A question burst out of my mouth before I could contain it. "What the hell was that?"

Casey shrugged. "It's a lonely town, bro."

"You don't mind that she dances? For other men?"

"Why would I?" he asked, his voice bored. "She enjoys her work. And it's helping her pay for graduate school."

"Grad school?"

"Physical therapy. She gives a killer backrub."

"I'm sure she does," I said. "I'm sure she does."

The band played until 2 A.M. Their music combined ska, rap, and pop in a disconcerting mixture that spun my head worse than all the alcohol I'd consumed, and by the end of the set I was hiding at a table in the corner while Casey and Rachel danced near the stage. As the final song came to a crashing conclusion, the band disintegrated into a swarming mob of eccentricity. The bassist screamed a long and discordant note into his microphone; the guitarist, wrapped in a pirate flag, did a victory lap around the stage before collapsing like a poleaxed steer into the arms of a groupie; the lead singer wrapped police tape around the instruments and other members of his band; and the drummer slowly and methodically covered his head with whipped cream. If they were trying to simulate the effects of taking acid, they were doing a pretty good job.

As the bass player's lone note finally concluded, the club DJ spun a track with a heavy drumbeat and the crowd began to bob and sway. Casey pulled Rachel up onto a table near the stage and sloppily kissed her. Through the artificial fog and uneven light I could see his hands moving near the middle of her back and suddenly her tight top popped off, exposing her bare chest. She frowned and pushed him, but I couldn't see any real anger in her reaction.

"Dumb-ass," I whispered to myself. I pulled my sluggish body out of my chair and headed toward the stage, but I got trapped in the crowd on the dance floor and the club's bouncers beat me to the scene. By the time I caught the small convoy, they were already at the door. Rachel, now wearing one of the club's promotional T-shirts, was arguing with the largest bouncer.

"But he's a ballplayer," she said, her voice a grating whine.

"I know," the bouncer said. "And we're really sorry. But this establishment has a policy. There's nothing I can do."

As Rachel opened her mouth to argue, I grabbed her by the elbow and dragged her toward the door. I hooked Casey with my other arm as I passed him. "We're cool," I said over my shoulder toward the amused bouncers. "We'll go someplace else."

Rachel slid out of my grasp as soon as we emerged from the club. "That was totally embarrassing," she said. "We should sue or something."

"Or maybe we should chill," I said. "It's time to call it a night." Casey was still slumped against my arm, and I shook him gently. "You ready?"

"You guys are on your own," Rachel said icily. "I'm out of here." She stalked away, her hips swaying rhythmically for Casey's benefit, but he remained oblivious. His breath reeked of alcohol. I warily scanned the street, searching for writers or photographers. Fortunately the crowd appeared uniform in its amateur revelry. I knew that trying to find a cab would be an exercise in futility, so I reluctantly started toward the lot where I'd parked my car. I've always been extremely dumb about drunk driving. When I'm sober I understand that it's one of the stupidest things a person can do, yet after a few drinks that knowledge mysteriously leaks out of my head. Especially when I can't think of any other way to get home.

I decided to drive to Casey's apartment in Newton rather than trying to cram both of us into my motel room—although that might have been amusing. I took Storrow Drive, which on a Saturday night is a few Formula One cars away from being a racetrack, to the Mass Pike. We only had to go three exits on the Pike, and I stayed in the far right lane, concentrating furiously on the road. I thought that I was doing an excellent job until I suddenly noticed flashing lights in my rearview mirror.

"Fuck," I said. Casey straightened slightly in his seat. "No worries. You're in the clear."

I slid over into the breakdown lane and a dark gray State Police cruiser pulled in behind me. The officer, stern looking and old enough to be Casey's father, strolled up to my window at the pace reserved for defenders of the law.

"Evening, son," he said when he finally reached us. "Could I get your license and registration?"

"Sure," I said, doing my best to keep my breath in the car. I reached across Casey, who was trying to turn the color of his seat, and rummaged through my glove compartment. As I slid the registration out the window, I noticed a tiny flicker of amusement in the officer's eye.

"I'm assuming that you boys were out celebrating Mr. Fox's home run," the officer said, speaking in the exaggerated Massachusetts cop voice that is somewhere between a South Boston accent and a drawl.

"Yes, sir," I said. "But whatever I did wrong, he had nothing to do with it."

"Do you know the speed limit here, son?" the officer asked.

"It's fifty-five," I said, guessing.

"That's right," he said. "And how fast do you think you were going?"

"Sixty?" I asked, my tone hopeful.

"Nope."

"Sixty-five?"

"Try again."

I paused, trying to remember exactly how quickly the road signs had been rushing past the car. "Seventy-five?"

The officer shook his head grimly. "You were going exactly forty-one miles an hour."

"Forty-one?" The number caught in the back of my throat as I wondered if forty-one was better or worse than seventy-five. I'm sure it was much worse.

"Maybe you want to follow me home," the officer suggested.

"Maybe that's a good idea," I said.

• • •

The officer left us in front of Casey's apartment building only after Casey had signed a bunch of baseballs for the entire State
Police department—although his signature was so sloppy that
they all looked forged. Casey crawled off to his bathroom for a
long bout of throwing up shortly after we got back, and I wondered how he had gotten so drunk. He must have taken a bunch
of complimentary shots while he was talking with Rachel. But my
brain was having its own trouble keeping the room from spinning,
so I collapsed on the couch and never heard Casey return from his
bout with the toilet.

chapter 14

I WOKE BEFORE TEN AND WAS WATCHING SPORTSCENTER WHEN Casey emerged from his room, his hair rumpled.

"How are you feeling?" I asked.

"Not bad," he said. He sank into the couch next to me and made some vigorous stretching sounds. He probably felt better than I did.

"Must be nice to be young," I muttered.

"So what happened last night?" Casey asked at the first commercial break. "I get kind of hazy around midnight."

"Do you remember dancing on the table?" Casey shook his head. "How about getting stopped by the cop?"

"Oh, no," Casey said. "No cops. Tell me there were no cops."

"There was a cop," I said. "And some public nudity in the club."

Casey moaned softly and his head banged back into the wall behind the sofa. "Stupid." His head hit the wall again. "I don't remember any of that."

"You were pretty far gone," I said, trying to keep from sounding superior. "You've got to be more careful. You never know when a real reporter might be watching."

"I know," Casey said. "Some kid will probably have obscene pictures of me on the Internet by tonight." His expression abruptly shifted from modestly playful into something far more morose. "I hope Molly doesn't hear about this foolishness."

"Why would Molly care?" I asked, trying to keep the strain from my tone.

"She'd be disappointed," he said as if that were the worst thing in the world. "It would confirm her suspicions."

"There are worse things than making an ass of yourself in a club," I said. "This wouldn't even register as a minor tremor on the Dennis Rodman scale of celebrity idiocy."

Casey waved his hand absentmindedly and settled into the sofa. I dragged my aching carcass into the kitchen and smiled to myself when I opened the refrigerator—it contained thirty or forty plastic jugs of Gatorade, half a case of beer, a huge jar of pickles, and absolutely nothing else. I grabbed two Gatorades and returned to the living room. Casey had turned off the television, and I placed the bottle by his head.

"So how's the team?" I asked when I had sunk back into my chair. "I didn't get a chance to ask you last night."

Casey stretched on the couch, and for a moment I thought he was going to ignore the question. Instead, he took a huge swig of his lemon-lime Gatorade and cleared his throat. "It's cool. Different than I expected. Guys are even quirkier here than they were in the minors. Which, by the way, I didn't think was possible."

"For example?"

"Nomar's more superstitious than a Haitian witch doctor. Some of the other guys are the same way. It's like a pagan culture. I keep worrying that if we stop hitting we're going to light a bonfire in the bullpen and sacrifice the fat kid."

"Good thing Felix is down in Providence," I said.

Casey smiled tightly, then abruptly sat up and stared around the room. "What time is it?" he asked. "I've got to get to the park."

"Your car's still in the Sox lot," I said. "I'll give you a lift."

• • •

Casey's first encounter with the Boston media came late that afternoon. He had again helped the Sox win—the team's fifth in a
row—which meant that even the most unpleasant reporters were
in the mood to be charitable. Boston has a surfeit of unpleasant
reporters. New York may be a worse media town in terms of the
number of guys sniffing for a story, but the Boston media closes
the gap by being as mean as a pack of fraternity brothers without
beer. Once you set aside the people who just trudge through their
jobs waiting for the next paycheck—and you get them in every
profession—the remaining sports reporters fall into three general
categories. The first is a fan, still full of oohs and ahhs. In the
business we refer to them as jock sniffers. They spend most of
their time fawning through their interviews and filing stories that
inarticulately state the obvious, and they have been completely
seduced by their proximity to the athletes. Television stations rely
almost exclusively on the jock sniffers.

The second kind of reporter is a far more interesting species.
They are writers who happen to love sports. For some internal reason they see something so interesting in athletics that they're willing to devote much of their time to describing other people's
accomplishments in overgrown playground games. Most of them
love their jobs. When these kinds of reporters are at their best, they
produce the finest sports journalism. I think of John Updike covering Ted Williams, John McPhee on tennis, Roger Angell on the
Miracle Mets, George Will on baseball, Norman Mailer on Ali. As
I examine that list, I realize that only Angell ever concentrated
largely on sports—maybe that explains the lack of cynicism in this
group—and it also occurs to me that it's been a long time since a serious writer wrote about a serious athlete in the way Mailer wrote
about Ali. Instead we learn that Shaq likes Run DMC and Kevin
Garnett is good at video games. I'm not certain if that means we
have fewer serious writers or fewer serious athletes. Or both.

The service performed on behalf of sports by those writers is almost entirely undone by the venom of the final group. For these

men and women, sports eventually turn inexplicably sour. The process starts when they stop being able to buy a hot dog and a beer and enjoy a good game. They become constant critics and insufferable bores—they cannot watch a single play without having to point out all the mistakes to anyone within shouting range. Slowly their wonder and appreciation turns to bitterness and cynicism, and one day their articles stop celebrating the beauty of sports and instead become laundry lists of cynical asides. The obvious explanation for this phenomenon lies in human frailty and weakness, but the broader cause is that most of these reporters trust neither their knowledge nor their audience. After all, if you don't know enough to really understand why a team does well or poorly, you have to reduce everything to a soap opera. And if you think your audience is as cynical as you are, then you can't say anything charitable for fear of appearing soft.

Boston's chief negative as a sports town is that it has far too many of the final category of reporters. Maybe those writers just reflect the bitterness of New England's sporting public, but they certainly don't do anything to improve the atmosphere. I privately refer to four of the best-known columnists—three at the *Globe* and one at the *Herald*—as the Four Horsemen of the Writing Apocalypse: Bitter, Angry, Cynical, and Mean. They write with the predictable and tedious anger of spurned lovers. The Red Sox have burned them so many times that they are unwilling or unable to do anything other than forecast doom and gloom. And when things actually go well for the baseball team, as they occasionally do, they turn their attention to some poor jackass on the Patriots or Celtics who has been caught speeding or carousing with an exotic dancer.

Casey held his impromptu press conference in front of his locker, and every reporter in the room came over to hear him finally speak. One of the beat guys from the *Globe* asked the first question: "How are you finding your first taste of the big leagues?"

"Well, Casey Fox is just trying to fit in," Casey said. "Casey Fox is doing what the team needs. In fact, if the owners want Casey to put on a cocktail dress and entertain the corporate fans, Casey would be happy to do it." He smiled into the whirring cameras. "But they haven't asked."

A television reporter with a bleached smile and plastic hair stuck his microphone in Casey's face. "It seems like you're playing really hard. Is your motor always running?"

"I'm sure that I don't have to tell you guys that you can't give 87 percent in August and hope to give 113 percent in October," Casey said, his eyes large and serious.

"Tell us about the home run in the third inning," said a reporter from the back of the group.

"I'm going to have to thank Jesus for allowing me to hit that curve." Casey cleared his throat authoritatively. " 'I saw the hanging breaking ball and smote it with a thunderous stick.' That's John 5:13."

"Is this guy for real?" the reporter next to me muttered. I suppressed a laugh. Another reporter was already asking the next question.

"So, Casey. Do you think you guys can really catch the Yankees?"

Casey shrugged nonchalantly. "Sure. It's like European culture. Throw enough Americans at anyone and eventually they'll succumb."

A reporter who I couldn't see called from the back. "Are you saying the Yankees aren't American?"

It was the kind of foolishly leading question that professional athletes always ignore, but Casey stood on his tiptoes and looked for his interrogator. "Of course," he said grimly. "They're a bunch of dirty fascists."

At that point the Sox media man leapt in front of his player, his hands waving frantically. "That's going to be it, guys," he said. The group grumbled as Casey feigned massive disappointment. "We'll do it again sometime."

I had dinner that night with Casey and Terrell. We drove downtown in Terrell's enormous SUV—a vehicle just two revolving treads away from a tank—and got caught in the construction traffic near the junction of Storrow Drive and the Southeast Expressway. Casey flipped on the radio and tuned in to one of the sports talk stations. The host and his callers spent the first ten minutes effusively praising Casey, and we all laughed when the flattery turned especially embarrassing. But in the course of just one call, the tone of the program abruptly changed. Freddie Richardson from Malden wanted to talk about Terrell Jordan.

"I don't understand why the Sox are paying this dude six million dollars to suck," Freddie began, his nasally North Shore whine scratched by both the phone line and the radio waves. "This jerk couldn't hit water if he fell out of a boat."

"That's clever," I mumbled.

"Terrell Jordan," the host said, his voice rising. "We've been meaning to talk about this guy. What's he batting, a buck-twenty?" The show's sidekick made an approving noise. "It's been so long since Terrell got on base that he's probably forgotten which way to run."

"If Terrell's as bad with his wife as he is with his bat, it's amazing he's got kids," the sidekick said.

The host laughed the canned, sneering laugh of radio personalities, then dropped his voice into his imitation of Mike Wallace. "So," he said, "is this a hitch in Jordan's swing or the beginning of the end? Caller, you're on the air."

I was bracing myself for the next hot blast of vicious ignorance when Casey snapped the radio off, and I breathed a deep sigh of relief. I felt a bizarre sense of responsibility for the conversation—even if talk radio hosts are the bastard stepchildren of journalism, they're still in the same food chain. A block later Terrell cleared his throat.

"You know what Eddie Mathews used to say? 'It's only a hitch when you're in a slump. When you're hitting the ball, they call it rhythm.' " Casey and I laughed politely, but didn't have anything intelligent to add. Terrell waited a moment, then said softly, "I hope my kids aren't listening."

"Does this stuff get to you?" I asked.

Terrell snorted dismissively. "It don't bother me. Comes with the job, right?" He turned around in his seat and smiled gently at me. "I'm just glad the team's winning. Otherwise they might be really vicious."

Casey and Terrell had chosen a restaurant overlooking the harbor that was well beyond my usual means. The maître d' seated us at a dais that overlooked the room—probably so that the other patrons could see that the Red Sox favored his restaurant—and I nervously opened the menu. The first item that caught my eye was fois gras, and my wallet shuddered.

"Don't worry," Casey said, reading my look perfectly. "It's on us."

"And the restaurant usually picks up the tab anyway," Terrell added.

I nevertheless ordered extremely conservatively—free-range chicken is my usual staple, although the vegetarian option sometimes works well. I enjoyed the food, even if it seemed that the chef had written all the ingredients in his kitchen on index cards, shuffled the stack, randomly picked six items, and called the resulting mixture his entrée. How else could I explain the prunes, Swiss chard, and peanuts on my chicken?

We had just finished our main courses when the maître d' arrived with a bottle of extremely expensive champagne. "It's from the gentlemen in the corner," he said, trying unsuccessfully to keep the sniff from his voice. I followed his gaze to a table of four suits. They were trying to act nonchalant, but one guy smiled and waved. His friends immediately berated him for being so uncool.

"We're supposed to invite them over," Terrell said out of the corner of his mouth. "That's the usual routine."

"What if we don't want to?" Casey asked.

"We send back some autographs or something," Terrell said. "But it's rude."

Casey threw his hands in the air and shook his head. "Send in the clowns."

As soon as the maître d' relayed our message, the suits came bouncing over to our table like a group of hyperactive puppies. One of them, a salesman, had been assigned by his firm to entertain the other three. Judging by the group's level of sobriety, he was doing an excellent job.

"I've been seeing you on *SportsCenter*," one of the suits said to Casey as soon as everyone was settled.

"I hope I look okay," Casey said.

"You look great," the suit said. His face turned bright red. "I mean, your swing and stuff." As we all stared at him, he stammered on. "I'm not gay or anything."

"Good to know," Casey said.

"Are you guys going to catch the Yankees?" the salesman asked.

"We'll do our best," Terrell said.

"Do you hate those guys?"

Terrell held up his hand and displayed his wedding ring. "David Cone was my best man. So I don't really hate him."

"But we hate the rest of them," Casey said.

"Even Derek Jeter?" asked the salesman.

"Especially Derek Jeter."

Casey and Terrell signed a few cocktail napkins, and one of the suits pulled out his cell phone and called his wife. "Guess who I'm hanging out with?" he asked, then didn't bother to pause long enough to get an answer. "Casey Fox. And Terrell Jordan." He paused while she said something. "Yeah, I'll ask him." He turned to Casey and offered him the phone. "It's my wife. Would you mind saying hi?"

"No problem," Casey said, but his face made it clear that he would rather talk to an IRS agent. He took the phone. "Hello?" I could tell the wife said something inane because Casey's face twisted as if he were listening to a Bob Dole commercial for Viagra. He waited for the squeaking to stop and then handed the phone back to the suit, holding it by the mouthpiece as distastefully as if it were a used Kleenex. "She said I was hot," he said, the expression on his face blending confusion and horror.

"Thanks," the suit said. "You just made her week."

"If I ever pose for *Playgirl*, I'll send you a copy," Casey said.

After twenty minutes and a round of expensive champagne, we beat a hasty exit. Terrell wanted to get home to his family and Casey had a date with Rachel, so they dropped me in front of my motel. I stood outside, staring at the stucco façade and wondering if I could bear to go upstairs and sit alone in my generic room. Eventually I turned and walked down to the Charles River. The night air remained warm—although I could feel the beginning of fall in the wind—and I felt spry enough to turn onto the Massachusetts Avenue Bridge. But halfway across I ran out of motivation, and I stopped and rested my hands on the iron railing. I was almost exactly at the center of the bridge, Boston to my right, Cambridge to my left.

On some vague impulse that I can't explain, I climbed over the railing and sat on the thin I-beam on the other side, my legs dangling over the edge. I could feel the rush of traffic to my back, and I sensed rather than saw the dark water swirling beneath the pillars under my feet. Directly in front of me lay the vague outline of the Salt and Pepper Bridge. To its right the golden dome of the State House, illuminated like the Madonna in a Renaissance painting, dominated the skyline. On the other side of the river, much closer to me, was MIT's own dome, which the local fraternity kids used to top with a nipple around Homecoming Week, transforming it into an enormous breast. They hadn't pulled that prank in years—maybe they were finding enough enormous breasts on the Internet to keep them satiated.

The MIT dome made me reflect on the pranks I'd pulled in my own life, which in turn led me to high school. A year or two ago I was stupid enough to go to my ten-year reunion, and I was shocked by how little I had in common with most of my old friends. They had grown up, gotten adult jobs, and were well on their way to forming solid American dysfunctional families. I guess I had always figured that anyone who would help me rent a cow to sneak into the headmaster's office would never get married. Or, God forbid, have children. Since we had nothing in common except old stories, we ended up spending most of our time retelling the tale of the cow—we didn't know when we led the poor thing up to the office on the third floor of the schoolhouse that cows will climb stairs but refuse to go down them. My favorite photograph in the yearbook is of the cow, suspended by a crane, dangling over my science teacher's car. I'm sure the poor beast was terrified, yet it had the composure to launch a grassy missile at his windshield. The cow must have shared my opinion of physics.

It bothers me that I think most of my friends at the reunion would still identify high school—cow included—as the greatest period of their lives. The members of my clique, which consisted largely of athletes good enough to play in high school but not college, peaked before twenty. We had felt like kings. Girls thought we were funny rather than crass, we used beer and drugs for entertainment rather than relief, and we always had something to do on a Saturday night. We acted like the subjects of the chorus in an early Bruce Springsteen song.

The people I chose as friends in college were very different. Less athletic, more intellectual. We had lots of serious conversations and some memorable moments, but none of the pure fun that I remember from high school. I think we were afraid that unbridled laughter would make us appear too plebeian. I avoided my fifth college reunion—I wasn't in the market for a spouse—and my only real contact with my college friends comes via e-mails regarding the results of various Yale sporting events. I'm sure that in a few years they will all be sending Christmas cards bedecked with golden retrievers and golden progeny.

Part of the reason I enjoyed spending time with Casey was that he combined the best attributes of both of those groups. And, to be honest, I hadn't made a lot of new friends since Yale. Sure I had drinking buddies, but I hadn't lived in one place long enough to really know anyone. Or I hadn't cared enough. The net result was that almost a decade after graduating from college I still hadn't found my dream woman, any real friends, or a job I loved. In fact, the only tangible things I had to show for my time were a meaningless degree from Columbia and a bunch of articles that even the most dedicated sports fan would never read again.

When I got tired of feeling sorry for myself, I began to wish that I had someone with whom I could share my morose mood. Even a complete stranger. I stood on the I-beam so that my upper body protruded above the railing of the bridge, but the passing couples and groups of fraternity guys heading to the bars of Kenmore Square were too preoccupied to notice me. I eventually grew tired of being ridiculous, clambered back over the railing, and returned to my motel room. I tried in vain to find soft-core porn on one of the cable channels and finally had to settle for *Saturday Night Live*. I fell asleep to the numbing sound of forced jokes and banter, and my dreams, when they came, all featured a nonsensical laugh track.

chapter 15

THE BOSTON SPORTS SECTIONS THE NEXT MORNING MADE ME laugh. Four different writers used Casey's quote about giving 87 percent utterly without irony, and one guy even cited his line about wearing a dress as an example of Casey's dedication to the Boston Red Sox. When you're hot, you can do no wrong. Most of the articles glowingly praised the team—which had pulled within four games of the Yankees—but Bruce McCall, one of the Four Horsemen, had written a piece about Terrell titled "The End of the Road." He criticized Terrell for his low batting average and poor power numbers, which he had every right to do, but he attributed those statistics to a lack of effort. "Boston fans have a right to expect more from their six-million-dollar bust," he wrote. "It's been so long since Jordan looked like a real man at the plate that his wife has filed a missing person report."

The game that afternoon was a disaster as the Sox collapsed like the French army in every war since Napoleon. Casey played his first bad nine innings as a member of the Sox, going 0–4 and making an error in the field, and Boston lost 9–1 to fall five games behind the Yankees. I could tell that Casey was in full simmer as soon as I got to his locker, but the other reporters either couldn't or wouldn't read the warning signs. Casey answered our inane questions about his first encounter with adversity with monosyllables until Bruce McCall pushed his way through the group, his huge mop of '70s-permed hair leading the way.

"So what went wrong this afternoon?" he asked. "Problem with your swing?"

"Bruce McCall," Casey said flatly.

"That's right." Bruce nodded as if it was only appropriate that Casey should know his name.

"You're a mean old drunk," Casey said. The area around the locker abruptly fell completely silent, and even a few players turned to stare. "If you wrote half as well as Terrell played this game, you'd be a decent writer. But instead you're a broken-down hack."

Bruce's watery eyes turned hard, and I saw a tiny glimpse of the tough investigative reporter he had once been. "Watch your mouth, you little punk," he said, little flecks of spittle flying from his tight mouth.

Rather than retreating, Casey took a step forward and leaned his face toward Bruce. "You think anyone cares what you write? Only the nasty old guys who bitch in barbershops even bother reading you anymore. You should do everyone a favor and quit. Let someone who still cares about the game cover this team."

A few hands touched Bruce to hold him back, but I could tell from his body language that he didn't want to get in a fight. "Don't cross me, kid," he said. The implied threat in his voice was unmistakable. "I've been here for thirty years, and I'll be here after you're gone."

Casey smiled humorlessly. "Your liver won't make it that long."

"I've run better players than you out of this town."

"That's not an admirable thing, you prick," Casey said, his voice rising to a shout. He waved his hand to encompass the entire locker room. "Everyone in here ought to be embarrassed about what happened to Ellis Burks, Mike Greenwell, Mo Vaughn, Roger Clemens. You guys don't know the difference between a curveball and a slider, yet you criticize the mechanics of Terrell's swing. It's a damn disgrace." His shoulders suddenly slumped, the anger gone, and he stared at all of us for a long moment. I shifted uncomfortably when his gaze touched me. "Get away from my locker," he said quietly. "You're all either whores or vultures. But you're not getting a piece of me today."

I was lying on my motel bed, watching clips of the exchange on the local news, when Casey called.

"Did you like my temper tantrum?" he asked after I picked up the phone.

"Your skin is way too thin," I said. "You've got to look after yourself and let the other guys fight their own battles. That's how this system works."

"I thought you'd understand," he said. The disappointment in his voice pained me, but I continued anyway.

"I do understand. It was a nice thing, what you did. But reporters have written nasty stuff about Terrell before. And he can handle it. Because he knows that if he starts hitting the ball, everyone will forget all the awful articles. Today, however, you made an enemy for life. Bruce will never forgive you, and you can't win that fight. He'll repay you every time he writes a story."

"I don't give a rat's ass what that big-hair prick writes," Casey said. We were both silent for a minute, and I fiddled with the remote control. He finally spoke. "Can you do me a favor?"

"Depends," I said.

"Molly's coming into town tomorrow afternoon on the train." I felt something tighten high in my chest. "Can you pick her up and bring her to the park?"

"No problem," I said, doing my best to keep the excitement out of my voice.

I arrived at South Station half an hour early, and I spent most of the wait reading—or rather pretending to read—the front page of the morning's sports section over and over. My stomach was again a mess and my head felt light. In fact, I was so preoccupied that even the articles couldn't annoy me. The *Globe* had ripped Casey in a column that ran under the game story, and the lead picture showed Casey angrily pointing toward the camera. The article in the *Herald* was slightly less rabid, but just as critical.

When Molly's train pulled in to the station, I went outside and stood by the engine, ignoring both the overpowering stench of diesel fuel and the dull roar of the idling motor. She emerged from one of the middle cars wearing a baseball cap, sweatshirt, and jeans, and carrying only a small backpack. She laughed when she saw me.

"What the hell are you doing here?" she asked as we hugged.

"Casey asked me to pick you up."

She shook her head. "I mean what are you doing in Boston?"

"Oh, that. I'm writing a story on Casey for *Sports Illustrated*."

Her eyebrows narrowed slightly. "Isn't that a conflict of interest?"

"Not these days," I said.

I carried her bag to the subway, and we took the Red Line to Park Street where we, along with a thousand Red Sox fans going to the game, switched to the Green Line. The trolley was far too packed for us to talk, and I spent most of the ride trying to keep the drunken guy sharing my personal body space from drooling on my shirt. The rest of the crowd got off at Kenmore Square, but we waited until the first stop after the train burst from the ground. I led us down a paved pedestrian walking trail that ran behind a line of medical buildings. A few years earlier an animal too large and too vicious to be a mere rat had tried to mug me on that path, and I'd been forced to fend him off with a beefy Irish policeman. Today, however, the enormous volume of people streaming toward the park had forced his kind back to the storm sewers. And, I suppose, tougher creatures than mutant rats surface in Boston during a pennant race.

We were crossing a large parking lot, the façade of Fenway rising in front of us, when Molly glanced at me out of the corner of her eye. "I was wondering why you didn't call," she said, her voice too casual to be natural. "I thought we had an okay time on our almost date."

I abruptly felt like an enormous ass—my fear had made me appear uncaring. "So did I."

"Then what happened?" She paused and pointed her finger at my chest, her expression pretending to be playfully threatening, but at the edges I could see something more real that simultaneously thrilled and terrified me. "And none of this I-was-too-busy crap. Guys are never too busy if they really care."

"Would it help if I mentioned that I've been in Boston?" Her aggrieved look answered my question. "I guess I dropped the ball."

She touched me gently on the arm, and I shifted under her warm palm. "You haven't dropped it yet," she said. "But you've sure been fumbling a lot."

Casey had left two tickets at the will-call window, and I decided to ditch the press box and sit in the stands. We passed through the dingy concourse, pausing to buy hot dogs, and emerged from the tunnel near the Sox dugout. I always forget how beautiful Fenway can be on a sunny summer day. Everything is so green—the grass, the scoreboard, the nets above the Monster, the walls—the whole park gleams with a deep, rich Irish green. The contrast with the Sox's bleached white uniforms sometimes hurts your eyes.

As we settled into our seats, Molly gestured at a guy near us reading a *Globe*. "So what's this I hear about our boy bawling out reporters?" she asked.

"He had a little thing yesterday," I said, wondering if I should explain the whole scene. I decided to take a minimalist approach. "He's not real great about backing away from a fight."

She smiled wryly. "He never has been."

Casey had found wonderful seats—I don't know if they came from the team or a friend—and I settled into enjoying the game in a way that is impossible in a press box. I encouraged the batters, instructed the pitchers, and berated the umpires. I even kept a scorecard. That's a neurotic habit, I know, but to fully understand the appeal of baseball you have to be fascinated by the minutia. Baseball is a bureaucrat's dream. The rulebook alone could serve as inspiration for the IRS, and for one rabid subset of fans, numbers rule the game. Understanding a batting average is simple enough, but when you start adding on base percentage, WHIP, slugging percentage, ERA, and the ever-evolving numeral composites designed to rank batters and pitchers against each other, the game makes the tax code seem relatively elementary.

But aside from us statistics geeks, most of the crowd comes to the ballpark because baseball is a wonderfully social game. If the programmers at Microsoft asked a supercomputer to design a sport that would allow spectators the maximum amount of time for idle chat, I think the computer would reinvent baseball. After all, what other game allows its fans seventeen separate breaks to buy beer and snacks? Or pauses three quarters of the way through the contest to allow everyone the chance to stretch?

The gentle rhythm of the game, however, may also explain baseball's gradual evolution from America's pastime to just another popular professional sport. Baseball was designed for a less frantic era—it is, for example, the perfect game for radio. An entire generation of kids grew up listening to tiny shortwaves hidden under their sheets; the words of the announcers and the crack of the bat are all you need to imagine the action. But baseball, especially in contrast to football, looks miserable on television. Football fits perfectly into the era of instant replay, and its unparalleled visual violence leaps from the screen. Baseball, on the other hand, loses all of its magic when confined to a box.

But I am a man designed to hallow an irrevocable age, so as I sat with Molly I took full advantage of baseball's social character. In between filling out my scorecard and yelling at the players, I asked her about her life in Providence. She said that she was doing well, although I sensed that she was getting lonely. I could empathize with that feeling. She also remained cryptic about her plans for future employment, and I didn't press her, figuring that a transient writer would be on very boggy ground if he lectured a friend about her career path.

Our section was filled with corporate ticket holders and their clients, but a few longtime fans also had seats. One older man sitting near us reminded me of a guy named Donny I once met at a game in North Carolina. Donny had attended every Durham Bulls home game for the last eighteen years—despite suffering a stroke midway through his streak that had robbed him of any feeling on the right side of his body. He had literally escaped from the hospital to watch three games. Why, I asked him, had he come to the ballpark? Could some minor league game really be so important? He shook his head, his tired eyes never leaving the field. He probably knew that if he had to explain it to me, I'd never really understand. "I guess I just like watching the stitches spin," he eventually said.

In the eighth inning I left Molly and climbed up to the press box to grab the day's package of statistics, and when the game ended I followed the herd back down to the locker room. The press coordinator told us that Casey wouldn't be taking any questions, so I waited on a wooden bench in the corner until he was done changing. On his way out of the room, he flicked his head at me, and I followed him into the hall.

"You want to come to dinner with me and Molly?" he asked when we were alone.

"Sure," I said, doing my best to sound nonchalant.

"I invited Rachel to come." My head whipped around. "You think that's a good idea?"

"It's a terrible idea," I said. "Just awful." I stared at him, knowing that my face had contorted itself into a mask of disbelief. "In fact, it might be the worst idea I've ever heard."

Casey continued breezily as if I'd given his plan the rubber stamp. "I think they'll hit it off." He paused, and a small and slightly devilish smile pulled at the corners of his mouth. "If Molly can get over the whole exotic dancer thing."

chapter 16

MOLLY DID NOT GET OVER THE WHOLE EXOTIC DANCER THING. Her hackles rose the moment she first saw Rachel, who exacerbated the situation by wearing black satin pants and a shiny red halter top, and the two sparred viciously all night. Casey was stupid enough to get between them and spent the evening slowly sinking into depression. I, on the other hand, kept my mouth firmly shut and passed the uncomfortable time by studying Rachel. You see a lot of Rachels around professional athletes—tough, attractive, and always playing an angle. Although Rachel was smarter and more interesting than most, I could tell that she was working toward something. I just couldn't figure out what she wanted.

But everyone plays an angle around professional athletes—that's the most exhausting part of the job. Ballplayers get complimentary golf clubs, meals at restaurants, women, everything. The price, however, is that everyone wants something in return. Maybe it's a signed ball or a set of tickets. Maybe it's a cut of your salary or a sponsorship deal. I think Molly objected to Rachel so strongly because she could tell that Rachel wanted something from Casey. And perhaps Molly didn't believe that Casey knew how to protect himself. If so, she was probably right.

The worst moment of the evening came at the very end. We had eaten at an elegant Italian place on Hanover Street and were walking back toward Casey's car, which he'd parked in a lot under the Southeast Expressway. Workers from the Big Dig, one of the world's largest public works projects, were pounding pilings into the ground in an adjacent lot, and pulverized dust and dirt filled the air. Casey and Rachel were strolling ahead of Molly and me, Rachel's hand resting prominently and possessively on Casey's left buttock. When they reached the car, she kissed him and turned to us.

"We're going back to our place for a drink," she said, her voice straining over the incessant roar from the nearby machines. "Would you guys like to come by for a little while?"

I could feel Molly bristle next to me, and I instinctively flinched. "Our place?" she asked, her voice dangerous.

"Casey's place," Rachel said. She tried to smile sweetly, but it came out as a leer. "My mistake."

"It's okay," Molly said brusquely. "I've got to get up early. I'll just go crash at a friend's."

Casey, who had been buried in his bunker under a pile of verbal rubble, arched his eyebrows in confusion. "I thought you were going to stay with me."

Molly's expression could have turned Medusa to stone. "I wouldn't want to get in the way." She turned her head in my direction. "Walk me to the train?"

"No problem." I shook hands with Casey, doing my best to look sympathetic, and then led Molly away from the lot as quickly as my feet could carry me.

She was still fuming when we got to the Government Center T stop, and I suggested that she might feel better if we kept walking. She nodded, not bothering to waste any words on me, and we marched up the back side of Beacon Hill to the State House. I led her to a small garden in the eves under the dome, and we perched on a bench beneath a statue of Fighting Joe Hooker. She stared blankly at the traffic rushing down Beacon Street for a long time, and I watched her closely. Her melancholy profile dissuaded me from even attempting conversation.

"He's selling himself short," she said just when I'd given up any hope of hearing her voice. "I've always worried about this happening."

"It's nothing permanent," I said.

She ignored me so completely that I felt as if I hadn't spoken at all. "He had a part of him that wasn't baseball," she said. "A part of him that never would have chased a bimbo."

"Rachel's smarter than you think." Her eyes turned to me, so upset that I tried to swallow my sentence. "It's not that bad."

"Can't you see?" she asked. "He's playing into the whole scene. And the parts of him that I care about are dying and being replaced by this whole jock thing. If this keeps up, he's going to start reading his own press. And then he's going to start thinking he's more than a ballplayer."

"He is more than a ballplayer," I said.

"I know." She said it so loudly that a group of young partygoers on Beacon Street turned to stare at us, and I gazed blankly back at them until they moved along. Molly had shifted on the bench, and a foot of uncomfortable air now lay between us. "I know he's more than a ballplayer," she eventually continued. "That's not what I mean. I'm just saying that he's not some kind of hero because he can hit a leather ball six hundred feet. That kind of thing doesn't make you a superman or a god. It just makes you a great athlete."

"What's wrong with being a great athlete?"

"Nothing," she said. "Unless all the crap that comes with being a great athlete keeps you from developing the other parts of your personality. Casey could hit five hundred home runs and make the Hall of Fame, but if he marries a Rachel and retires to the Caribbean, his life will have been a waste."

"In your opinion," I said.

"That's right," she said. "In my opinion."

We sat silently again until the passing traffic on Beacon Street had slowed from a torrent to a trickle. She eventually stood and extended her palm toward me.

"You ready?" she asked.

I took her hand, so softly that only the tips of our warm fingers touched, and we walked together down to the Park Street Station. I bought two tokens, and when we pushed through the turnstiles I paused and looked back at her, the hot air from the tracks rushing up the stairs behind me and rustling my hair.

"Where are you going?" I asked.

She shrugged. The anger had disappeared from her eyes and she just seemed tired and lost. "I don't know."

"I thought you had a friend," I said, confused.

"I thought you were a friend," she said, taking my hand again.

We didn't speak on the train, or even look at each other, and my pulse was heavy in my ear the entire ride. The guy who worked the night shift at the motel's front desk had come to know me over the past week, and his eyes widened like the hole in the ozone when he saw me waltz in with a beautiful woman on my arm. I'm sure he thought I was paying Molly by the hour. We took the elevator to my floor, and when I opened the door to my room, Molly froze. My laptop computer lay on the desk, several books scattered around the keyboard, and I had filled the small closet with my clothes. She walked to my fake oak dresser and picked up my travel alarm clock, hefting it in her hand.

"This is where you live," she said, a judgment rather than a question in her tone.

I closed the door. "Just for now."

She abruptly crossed the room and hugged me, her soft hand touching the back of my head, her nose buried in my collar. "You must be so lonely," she whispered in my ear.

"It's not so bad." The fuzz on the back of her neck was tickling my nose and I could smell her floral shampoo. "I've got HBO."

She pulled away, her eyes still hazy, and we stared at one another. "Can you do something for me?" she asked.

"Of course."

She took her backpack from my shoulders, tossed it on my bed, and rummaged through an inside pocket. Her hand emerged grasping a battered copy of *Shoeless Joe* by W. P. Kinsella. "Can you read to me?"

I just nodded. She changed before I began, putting on a pair of boxers and a plain white T-shirt, and eventually she settled next to me on the scratchy polyester comforter. She lay still for only a moment before she made me stand up so that she could strip the bed down to a naked sheet.

"Where do you want me to begin?" I asked when we were again settled.

"Anywhere," she said. "I know it almost by heart. Casey and I read it together a thousand times."

My chest tightened and I had to close my eyes for a moment. But I could feel the warmth of her body just a few inches from mine, and the image of her smooth, shiny legs refused to disappear from my brain. I opened my eyes and began to read.

" 'The catcher has been talking to Chick Gandil. He looks at us and smiles, and I can feel my heart shatter. But I do not die. Richard's hand grimly holds my bicep, his knuckles white. "I admire the way you catch a game of baseball," I say, my voice sounding like thunder in the nearly empty park.' "

I continued until I reached the end of the book, which took almost an hour. It had been years since I read aloud, and I could remember the first time I had picked up *Shoeless Joe*. I must have been thirteen or fourteen years old. Baseball had been magical for me back then, and baseball players had been more than just men with fantastic hand-eye coordination and superb fast-twitch muscle fiber. I had no trouble believing that there is a heaven just for ballplayers or that Roy Hobbes, the Natural, could hit a home run and trot through a shower of electrical sparks to his destiny. That was just the way it was supposed to be.

But somewhere in the intervening decade and a half I had lost my ability to believe in such things. As the words of the book came pouring out of my mouth, I wondered how I had let it happen. How had my heart grown so cold that I had lost all interest in baseball until Casey came along? How had I stumbled through the most recent years of my life without assembling anything more permanent than a solid credit history? And lying in the bed of a crummy motel reading a book to a stunning woman, pieces of myself that I had forgotten I possessed gradually awoke until all I felt was a searing pain in my chest and the trickle of tiny tears gathering in the corners of my eyes.

I closed the book when I finished the final paragraph and laid it on the nightstand. I blinked my eyelids a few times to clear the moisture, then rolled my head to the side and looked at Molly. She was asleep. Her chest was rising and falling in an even cadence and the slackened muscles in her cheeks had relaxed her face into a tiny, beatific smile. I slipped out of bed and brushed my teeth. When I was done, I stared at the bed for a beat, and then got the extra comforter out of the closet and folded it in half on the floor. I turned out the light and my back groaned as I settled onto my simple pallet. My head had just touched the flat foam pillow when Molly stirred in bed.

"You don't have to be a perfect gentleman," she whispered softly.

"Nobody's ever accused me of being a gentleman," I said. "Certainly not the perfect kind." I lay still on the floor, wondering what I should do. But midway through my internal monologue I made the mistake of closing my eyes and the image of her legs reappeared in my mind and forced me to my feet. I slid into the bed and she turned to meet me, our mouths pressing together too firmly to properly kiss. Energy flowed between our naked legs. I wanted to be gentle and slow and treat her like a goddess, but she wouldn't let me. We descended into a whirling cascade of legs, arms, and mouths, and when I caught little glimpses of her face in the flat neon light streaming through the window, I saw a mystifying mixture of intensity and fear.

• • •

She was sitting on the edge of the bed when I awoke the next morning, her chin cradled in her hands. I quietly moaned to myself, and then asked the question all men worry about having to ask the morning after.

"You okay?"

"Yeah," she said. Her face turned to me and I could immediately tell that she was certainly not okay. "Will you promise me something?"

"Of course," I said, doing my best to sound as trustworthy as a young George Washington.

"Promise me you'll never tell Casey."

I flipped over on my side and stared at the windows. The drape was parted slightly in the middle, and I could see the outline of a concrete warehouse across the street. I've never been good at hiding disappointment. Her hand touched my thigh, just the thin sheet between us. "What's wrong?"

"This meant nothing to you," I said, my tone flat.

"How can you say that?" When I didn't turn to look at her, she cleared her throat. "I don't sleep with many guys, you know."

"If you thought we'd be together for a while, you wouldn't ask me to never tell Casey. Because eventually he'd have to find out."

I rolled over and sat up. She was staring at me, her head cocked and her face curious. "I thought only girls were this psychotic," she said. I smiled despite myself, and she leaned over and kissed me.

"Don't think you're forgiven," I said when we separated. She just grinned and put her head in my lap. I ran my fingers through her soft hair and let my mind wander. We were quiet for a couple minutes, and the stillness evolved into one of those silences when you know that the other person is thinking just as furiously as you are. I spoke first.

"So why did you spend the night?"

"What do you mean?" she asked.

"I read in GQ once that guys should always be self-confident— I guess self-confidence is supposed to be sexy—but this question has been bothering me all morning: How does a girl like you end up in bed with a guy like me? Was I just in the right place at the right time?"

She stared at me closely, her lips pursed, and my hand froze in the tangles of her blonde hair. "You know," she said, "that's actually an insulting question. You're basically implying that I'm the kind of woman who would sleep with a guy as a distraction."

"I'm sorry. I didn't mean it that way."

"Are you asking so that I can inflate your ego? Or do you really not know?"

"I just want to hear your answer."

She pulled her head out of my lap, sat upright, and crossed her legs. I instinctively touched the warm spot on my thigh where her neck had rested just a moment earlier. "Why did I spend the night? Lots of reasons."

"Give me one," I said, trying to ignore how pathetic my request had become.

"Well, you've been to a lot of places. You've seen stuff."

"I've been to ballparks. I've seen baseball."

"You've seen more than baseball."

I almost said, "Sure, I've seen football and basketball too." But I restrained myself because I knew that she was being unusually honest. The primary thing that I could offer Molly was a glimpse of the world she wanted to see—I was a temporary anecdotal substitute for real experiences. When she started exploring the world on her own, my usefulness would evaporate like sweat in the mountain air. I was still stumbling over that revelation when she asked a question that could have originated in my own subconscious.

"Have you met anyone you could imagine spending the rest of your life with?"

"No," I said. "Not yet. I guess I haven't been looking very hard." I paused, wondering if I should ask the question if I didn't really want to know the answer. "How about you?"

"I don't think so. I'm not sure I'm ready to meet him. You know?"

She looked at me for confirmation, and at that moment I first saw the seven years between us. Because I'm desperate to meet the right person. I've done the alone thing ever since college, and I'm tired of it. Immensely tired. If I'm never alone another day in my life, it will be too soon. I crave company and companionship, long for the stupid arguments over the toilet seat or who has to drive the kids to school. Being alone has to be the most overrated experience in the world. Maybe there are Buddhist monks who can perch on a mountaintop and transform the raw emotion of solitude into a spiritual event, but I tend to hunker in my big vibrating chair, watch television, and pray that the pizza boy will want to hang out for a little while.

But I also knew what she meant. My best friend in college, Pete North, dated a wonderful girl. They were perfect together—she tempered his cynicism and she made him so happy that even his male friends could see it. I always assumed that they would get married, but right before graduation he dumped her. His reasoning at the time was that while he knew they were right for each other, he thought they were too young to get married. He figured that after a couple years of dating other people they would be ready to get back together. But she never forgave him, and she married a doctor from Dallas a couple years ago. The last time I saw Pete he was dating his therapist and doing his best impression of Dustin Hoffman in *Death of a Salesman*.

So I mumbled something inane in response to Molly's question, and an hour later we were standing next to her Amtrak train in South Station.

"Where do we go from here?" she asked.

Since I didn't want to scare her off, I did my best to keep my voice casual. "Whatever fits."

She touched my arm, her eyes warm. "This has been wonderful," she said. "So mature. So much better than anything in college."

A huge part of me wanted to scream "Mature? You think I'm mature? I'm going to devote the next year of my life to following you like a lovesick puppy. I'll call your house late at night and hang up; I'll write long, drunken e-mails. I'll make your college years seem like a goddamned golden age of maturity." But instead I just smiled weakly and kissed her good-bye.

That night I wrote the article for *Sports Illustrated*. It took me five hours to find an opening line. Although I figured when I took the assignment that the story would be tough to write—I was balancing my friendship with Casey against my need to give *Sports Illustrated* enough to justify my price tag—the true difficulty of the task had escaped me. Shortly before midnight I finally discovered a solution. I wrote about what it must be like to go from anonymity to fame in the course of one call from Boston to Pawtucket. I gave details that presented the illusion of intimacy—the color of Casey's sofa, for example—without really giving anything away. I think my best paragraph was the one that explained how Casey sands down the handle of his bat much more than most players because he so rarely gets jammed. I threw in a quick story about how Casey had once stopped in midswing and the bat had shattered in his hands. They love that mythic hero crap at *Sports Illustrated*. I e-mailed the story to John Abbot just as the sun came up and collapsed into my motel bed, lonely again.

chapter 17

THE JINGLE OF THE CHEAP MOTEL PHONE WOKE ME A FEW
hours later. I rolled my tongue in my mouth, trying to raise a
down payment on enough saliva to loosen my vocal chords, and
picked up the receiver.

"Yeah," I grunted.

"Abbot here." Even his voice wore a conservative suit.

"Morning," I said, sitting up.

"I got your story," he said. "This is fucking great stuff. You may
be a pain in the ass, but you can write."

"Thanks." His reaction surprised me—I had thought he would
be smart enough to see through my smoke.

"We want you to stick with the Sox. They're hot, and if they
catch the Yankees we're going to need another story. And you
seem to be the only one who can get anything decent out of Mr.
Fox."

"They're going to the West Coast," I said, staring at the wreck-
age in my motel room.

"I know." Abbot's voice explained that his cerebral cortex contained more information about sports than I could hope to com-

pile on an IBM mainframe. "I'll connect you to our travel people. They'll set you up."

The travel people booked me on a United 757 to Los Angeles that evening. I arrived too late to catch the Sox/Angels game, so I rented a car and drove to my hotel. The magazine had sprung for a room in one of the big resorts that surrounds Disneyland, and I even had a fax machine and a smoggy view of what passes for downtown Anaheim. I ordered a $12 burger from room service, which I washed down with a $6 beer from the minibar, and watched the last few innings of the game on the 25-inch Panasonic television. Boston lost 2–1, but the game wasn't a total washout because their fourth starter pitched into the eighth inning for his first decent showing in almost two months. Still, I knew Casey would be upset since the loss dropped the team four games behind the idle Yankees.

After the game I searched through the complimentary room guide trying to find something to do the next morning. I had no interest in going to Disneyland, and I didn't know where Casey and the team were staying. The room guide, as usual, contained a wealth of information. I'm often fascinated by the ads in those publications—they always seem to say something about the city where you're staying. In Houston, for example, half the ads are for strip clubs. In Manhattan you get Broadway shows. New Orleans features Cajun restaurants and private dancers named Lace. And in Anaheim, California, the special appeared to be cosmetic surgery. You could get your nose shortened, hair lengthened, breasts enlarged, butt reduced, tummy tucked, face lifted, skin bronzed, and teeth straightened—all with an extra 15 percent of your body fat liposuctioned for free.

So the next morning, just for the hell of it, I went in for a complimentary consultation at the office of a local plastic surgeon. I emerged even more demoralized than I had expected. By the standards of southern California, my body was a wasteland. The doctor recommended a package that he was crass enough to call the

Hollywood Actress (minus the silicone option), but he cautioned me that I would also need a personal trainer and a nutritionist if I wanted to see serious results. I spent my lunch naked in the hotel bathroom, poking and prodding my body in an effort to discover if it was really as shopworn as the doctor had intimated. I fucking hate southern California.

The game began in the late afternoon, and I arrived—along with most of the crowd—in the third inning. Traffic was my excuse. The Sox pounded the Angels' starter, a kid recently up from the minors, and most of the crowd had disappeared by the top of the eighth. I guess four innings is a long time to be separated from your shrink and personal nutritionist. The jubilant atmosphere in the Boston locker room after the game had even Casey in an ebullient mood. He spotted me the moment I walked through the door and shouted to me through cupped hands.

"You talk someone into paying you to get a tan?"

The cluster of reporters surrounding Casey turned and stared at me, and I instinctively glanced down at my notebook. I knew that they hated me. They probably justified it to themselves by griping that I was a sycophant, but I knew they were mostly jealous of my access. I'm sure that most of the reporters at the *Washington Post* in the 1970s secretly hated Woodward and Bernstein. When I had composed myself, I strolled across the room to Casey's locker. A television news crew grudgingly parted to let me through.

"I'm having trouble with my English," Casey said when I reached his side. "Would you translate for me?"

I stared at him as he began to spout gibberish. From the back of the group I heard the voice of one of the Four Horsemen. "This is some juvenile shit," he said. "Who the fuck does this kid think he is?"

And suddenly some internal governor in my brain snapped. When Casey finished blathering, I turned to the reporters. "Questions?" I asked firmly. The Four Horsemen stalked away, but the beat reporters, who needed a story, just shifted nervously. One of them finally spoke.

"So how did you hit the ball so hard, Casey?"

Casey stared at me, and I launched into a sentence that combined my high school Spanish, college German, and a bad Brooklyn accent. Casey replied in something even less comprehensible, and I turned back to the reporter.

"He'd like to thank his proctologist," I said. "He told him to sit on the outside fastball."

"The proctologist?" the reporter asked.

"That's right," I said. "And Casey says that kids who want to be ballplayers should eat a lot of broccoli. Any other questions?"

"Can we really quote him on this stuff?" someone else asked.

I glanced at the reporter's worried face and abruptly felt guilty. The guy was just trying to do his job, working on a tight West Coast deadline, and I was toying with him solely for my own amusement. My shoulders slumped; my internal governor returned.

"He doesn't want to talk," I said. "I'm sorry. And I wouldn't use any of that stuff. Just say that he was looking for the outside fastball."

Casey gave me a nasty look, probably annoyed that I was taking liberties with his joke, but I didn't care. I walked out the door and sat on a bench outside the locker room, waiting for my own Godot.

"You didn't think that was funny?" he asked when he finally emerged.

"It was very funny," I said. "But I don't have any right to mess with them. I'm supposed to be a reporter too."

Casey examined me closely, his face peculiar. "I hope you weren't this serious when you wrote your article."

"What if I was? It's my damn job."

"You're not good at your job." He paused, probably waiting for a reaction, but I kept my face as passive as possible. "It's the reason I trusted you," he continued when he realized I wasn't going to say anything. "Baseball doesn't mean that much to you—it would never occur to you to kiss my ass to get a story. You just don't care."

"That's not true," I said, but my voice held no conviction.

"A kid comes to a park, excited to see his heroes," Casey said, his voice rising. A few writers exiting the locker room stopped to listen, and I felt myself flush. "The great baseball writers can cap- ture that excitement. Because on some level they're still those kids. And every time they write a story they're grateful that they get to cover baseball for a living. But most of you . . ." Casey paused and waved at the other writers. "Most of you forget that you owe your readers that passion. You owe them more than venom." Casey turned back to me, and his eyes burned away what remained of my ego. "You owe them your love of the game."

"You tell me what's left to love about this game," I said. And because I knew he couldn't, I turned on my heel and strode down the long concrete corridor toward my waiting American rental car.

I skipped the game the next afternoon and was lying in my bed watching cartoons when my cell phone rang. I didn't recognize the number in the caller ID box.

"Hello," I said cautiously as I flipped open the phone.

"How's it going?" I heard Casey's voice, which my brain imme- diately registered as being logically impossible, and I flipped the television to the game. The Sox were in the field.

"Where the hell are you?" I asked.

"Coach gave me a day off," he said. "I'm calling from the bullpen phone."

"That phone works?" I asked. "I thought it was just plugged into the dugout."

Casey snorted. "Do you have any idea how boring it is to sit in a bullpen? We just had a competition to see who could spit his gum the farthest. And these damn relief pitchers prank everyone. We just called and ordered Coach a home enema kit."

"That's funny," I said dryly. "Is there a point to this call?"

"I'm sorry about yesterday." Casey's tone had abruptly shifted to what sounded like real remorse. "I'd like to make it up to you. Terrell and I are having dinner with someone I think you'd like to meet. Are you free?"

My curiosity overwhelmed my pride in the millisecond it took for me to open my mouth. "Sure," I said. "Just give me directions."

I pulled up to the house in Beverly Hills just as the sun was setting across the ocean, its oblique rays glittering off the whole human mess that is the Valley. Casey had given me an address but no name, and I double-checked the sheet when I saw the enormous mansion that lurked beyond the bronze security gate. A small sign warned me that a specially trained team from SecureTec would shoot any unwanted intruders with special reporter-shredding bullets. I rang the buzzer next to the gate, fully expecting to be interrogated by the intercom, but the enormous bronze doors opened without comment and I drove my car a hundred yards into a setting that would have made Louis XIV feel inadequate. To describe the trees and shrubs that surrounded the mansion as landscaping would be to miss the point. The owner of the estate had constructed a private world for himself—a world on par with Oz or everything behind the looking glass.

I parked behind a Lexus SUV and had just stepped out of the car when Casey emerged from the front door, followed by Terrell and a tall man I immediately recognized. After all, the whole world knows Gary Smith. Even if you've never seen him play for the Lakers, it would be impossible to miss the Gatorade advertisements, rap videos, overblown movies, and never-ending stream of televised interviews. He moved with a grace that belied his size—a hallmark of all NBA greats—and I instinctively straightened my back and tried to appear a little taller. I had dressed well for a reporter and was wearing Dockers khakis and a long-sleeve polo shirt. Casey's outfit matched mine, but Terrell and Gary were sporting the kind of suits that would make even an Italian tailor drool.

"Hey, dude," Casey said. "This is Gary Smith."

"I got that." I offered my hand to Gary and he took it, his fingers completely encircling my palm. "Good to meet you."

"Welcome to my chateau," he said. His voice, which sounded deep on television, was so unnaturally low in person that he must have been doing stretching exercises to lengthen his vocal chords. "We're just doing the tour," he continued. "You want to have a look around?"

"Sure." I gestured at the garden. "Your place is tight." I flinched, realizing that I had instinctively slipped into the white man's habit of using Spike Lee lines around black people we think are cool. Gary had the grace—or the practice—to just smile.

"Thanks," he said.

The interior of the house matched the opulence of the garden. Gary had installed a full sound studio in his basement, complete with a mixing board, and he could have held a Lakers practice in the master bedroom. He had also hired a premium interior decorator. Every room supposedly possessed a unique mood, which Gary repeated when we entered: productive, cool, serene, functional. I did my best not to laugh. To accentuate the work of the decorator, Gary had also commissioned a large amount of artwork, the highlight of which was a set of six gold panels he had mounted on the wall of his living room. Each panel displayed a relief meant to symbolize an important period of Gary's life—from birth to the Lakers' ascension as NBA champions. The set looked like the Gates of Heaven in Florence, except that it was dedicated to the glory of Smith rather than the glory of God.

Casey and I lagged behind to ogle the panels while Gary and Terrell went into the kitchen. We stood silently for a few minutes, just staring in mute disbelief.

"It's the same in every sport," Casey eventually said, his voice soft. "Money changes some guys, other guys ignore that stuff and play as hard as Bill Russell."

"So what has a hundred million done to Gary Smith?" I asked.

Casey stifled a loud laugh. "Are you kidding? The guy's a corporation. He's the Microsoft of basketball. He doesn't make one move on or off the court that doesn't improve his net worth."

Casey reached out and touched a golden sneaker, the gesture more reverent than he probably intended. "Do you know that when Smith is on the road he demands a grand piano in his suite? If it isn't there, he throws a temper tantrum."

"Bullshit," I said. Casey just shrugged. "Does he play?"

"Nope. But a few years ago he was hosting a party in his suite after a game against Chicago. That suite happened to have a piano, and a couple jazz guys got up and banged out some tunes. I guess he had a good time because he put it in his next contract."

"Athletes." I muttered it under my breath, but Casey's young ears heard me anyway.

"Hell," he said. "We're no worse than bands. Or actors. In fact, we've got to be better than actors. Those bastards ask for toast without wheat and beds filled only with the shampooed feathers of Norwegian geese."

"So tell me, Casey Fox," I said. "Are you going to be the Microsoft of baseball?"

Casey, still staring at the golden panels, shook his head. "I don't have that kind of patience."

When the tour concluded, we sat in the sunroom and watched the lights in the Valley spread and sparkle. The other guys drank gin and tonics and I nursed a beer that Gary said came from a sect of monks in Belgium that had been brewing lager for a thousand years. Although I would have been just as happy with a Sam Adams, I was duly impressed. Gary spent most of the time lecturing Terrell and Casey on finding ways to make money off the field. "It's all about diversifying," he said at some point. "Basketball don't last forever, you know. Or baseball."

"Especially if they outlaw the designated hitter," Casey said.

I ignored the rest of the conversation and my mind wandered to other questions. In my life as a reporter I had never really seen firsthand the things that a star athlete can buy. Sure, I've noticed the fancy cars and presidential hotel suites, but Gary was operating in the kind of rare air reserved for serious financial players. I

wondered if the original multimillionaires who founded basketball and baseball could ever have predicted that they would eventually be sharing the locker rooms at their exclusive country clubs
with a mere employee—and an uncouth athlete at that.

But I didn't begrudge Gary his wealth. Or Casey. I plugged in
my calculator once and figured out that the Boston Red Sox were
paying Casey $1,300 a game his rookie season—or four cents per
spectator at Fenway Park. Would you watch Casey play for four
cents? The same rule applies to the high-end players. Enough people have decided that they're willing to pay to watch baseball
games—and would you rather see athletes getting compensated
well or owners making enormous profits? Sure, $8 million a year
is a lot of money for playing baseball. But we don't pay people
based on their worth to society. After all, is some Silicon Valley
billionaire who badly executed a derivative idea really more deserving of vast wealth than a baseball player? At least the player
brings joy to someone other than his accountant. And when it
comes to entertainment value, I'd much rather overpay a guy who
can hit a curve ball than some actor who's making a million bucks
for being cute.

My primary objection to professional athletes is the attitude
that so often accompanies the money. The salary isn't the crux of
the problem; it's the boorishness. No human being should ever
complain about being paid a mere $10 million, and when an ath-
lete signs a big contract, he should understand that with the cash
comes the responsibility to be respectful and patient toward fans
and to support local charities. And most fans, unlike reporters,
don't demand perfection from athletes. We realize that men like
Lou Gehrig and Ray Bourque come along only once in a generation; we understand that our heroes are human—and we wish
that they knew that too. The seed of destruction for all professional athletics lies in the increasing sense of disassociation that
the regular fan feels from his heroes. The problem is worse for
some sports than others. Professional basketball, for example, is
increasingly a game played before an exclusively corporate audience, largely because only corporations can afford the outrageous

ticket prices. If baseball joins basketball in becoming too expensive for the average family, it will incinerate its only remaining argument for being considered America's game.

When we finished our drinks, the other guys decided that they wanted to go hit some trendy clubs in Santa Monica. I didn't feel like being the civilian in a group of three athletes—as amusing as that might have been—so I excused myself and drove back to the hotel. I think Casey wanted me to stay, but I wasn't in the mood to do him any favors after his speech the day before. I lay in bed for a long time. While I wanted to call Molly, it was far too late on the East Coast. And I was too scared anyway.

chapter 18

THE SOX ROLLED THROUGH OAKLAND, WINNING THREE OUT
of four, arrived in Minnesota at midnight, and won another game
before the sun went down the next day. Baseball is a mental sport,
a rhythm sport, and the team had acquired the attitude of a winner. The Boston players believed before they took the field that
they were virtually guaranteed a victory—they knew they would
get the key hits, make the big defensive plays. So when they went
down a couple runs early in the game, they relaxed, believing that
they would score before the nine innings ended, which often became a self-fulfilling prophesy. On paper, the Red Sox didn't come
close to having the most talent in the league. But baseball, more
than practically any other game, values intangibles such as team
chemistry, confidence, and hustle.

After the first game against Minnesota, I had dinner with
Terrell and Casey at a barbecue place in Minneapolis that Terrell
knew. We had to drive to the outskirts of the city, where the sterile apartment complexes and office buildings faded into railway
tracks and abandoned warehouses, to find the restaurant. When
we arrived, I wasn't sure I wanted to go inside—any sanitation
commissioner who saw the exterior of the building would have

demanded either a large bribe or a firebomb. But Terrell dragged me through the door and ordered for all of us because, as he had said in the car with a meaningful glance in my direction, the large black woman who worked behind the counter had a short fuse when it came to stammering or incompetence. We got a huge pile of barbecue beef slathered in sauce, a loaf of bright white bread, a bowl of coleslaw, and a pitcher of Miller Lite to wash the whole thing down.

We ate quietly and happily until the loaf of bread had shrunk to just a crust. Casey was the first to push himself away from the table, and he leaned far back in his chair. He watched us for a moment, an expression of discontent on his face that didn't match the meal we'd just consumed.

"What's wrong?" I asked through a mixture of beef and bread.

Casey's sudden annoyance tumbled out of his mouth like popcorn overflowing a hopper. "What am I supposed to do about all these goddamned agents?"

"Ignore them," I said, shrugging.

Casey made a noise in the back of his throat that explained that ignoring them was not an option. "They're getting unbearable," he said. "They've always been around, but now they've spun out of control. They call all the time, send me crap. I'm thinking about picking one just to drive the others away."

"You should get one," Terrell said. "Everyone has an agent. They'll make you a lot of money you wouldn't otherwise get. Endorsements and stuff."

"I just don't want to deal with them," Casey said. "Everything about that side of the game is so dirty."

"You could have worse problems," Terrell said.

Casey ignored the gentle rebuke in Terrell's tone and snorted. "Name one."

"You could be hitting the ball worse than when you played in high school."

Casey and I exchanged a quick, worried glance. Terrell's eyes had dropped to the table, his dark face a blend of sullen shadows. When I couldn't bear the silence anymore, I said the only thing that popped into my head. "I'm hitting the ball worse than when I played in high school." No one laughed.

"It's going to turn around," Casey finally said.

Terrell wearily looked across the table, his eyes too tired. "But what if it doesn't? I bring tapes back to my hotel room and study opposing pitchers. I take batting practice until my hands are raw. Nothing works. I just can't hit the fucking ball anymore."

"All you need is a hot streak," Casey said, his tone uncharacteristically full of pep. "It'll happen. Everyone goes through streaks."

"A slump that lasts the whole season isn't a bad streak. It's the way things are." Terrell's voice was so empty that I knew he wasn't being melodramatic; he was speaking his version of the truth. "I don't have it anymore. But I've got to finish this contract. My wife and I have plans for that money."

"How many years do you have left?" I asked, my idiotic reporter's instinct taking over.

"Two. And I'm going to be in Boston unless they release me. Because no team is going to be stupid enough to trade for a washed-up right fielder with no bat speed."

Casey drained his beer and stood. His right hand grabbed the collar of Terrell's leather jacket and pulled him upright. "You're coming with me," he said. His other hand reached out and grabbed my arm, too rough to be a joke. "You too."

Casey drove us to a sporting goods store, where we bought a wiffle bat and a can of tennis balls, and then continued on to a nearby softball field. Two teams from local bars had just finished their game, and Casey waited until the players were drifting off to their pickup trucks before he approached the maintenance man raking the infield and picking up the bases. Terrell and I, feeling foolish, waited near the dugout. Casey and the man chatted casually for a few minutes. I watched as a signed baseball and a couple of bills changed hands, and then Casey turned and gestured us onto the field. We went reluctantly.

"Home run derby," Casey said to Terrell. "You and me." Casey tossed the ball into my unwilling palm. "And you're pitching."

"But I can't pitch," I said. I wasn't exaggerating—I have the arm of a twelve-year-old designated hitter. Casey ignored me and trotted back to the car to fetch the bat and the rest of the tennis balls. I sighed and wandered out to the mound. The rubber seemed far too close to home plate—especially since bona fide major league hitters would be smacking the ball back at me—and I remembered that the dimensions of a softball diamond are considerably smaller than a baseball field. I wandered as far toward second base as I figured I could get away with, then crouched on my haunches in the burned-out grass. Casey was standing at home plate, wrapping the barrel of the wiffle ball bat with duct tape.

"Why are you doing that?" I asked, impatience putting an edge on my question.

Casey didn't bother to look up from his work. "So the barrel doesn't crack when we hit the ball. Don't you know that?"

I sniffed. "I haven't even seen a wiffle bat in ten years."

"You're letting the best in life pass you by," he said.

When Casey had covered the bat in so much tape that it looked like a hot water pipe, he trotted out to the mound and gestured for Terrell to join us. Terrell came slowly, his face indicating that he was far too old for this kind of foolishness.

"Simple rules," Casey said when Terrell finally arrived. "Anything that isn't a home run is an out. And we don't have to swing at Russell's crappy pitches."

Casey walked to the plate, swinging the bat behind his head to loosen his wrists, and Terrell trotted out toward center field. While we waited for Terrell to get into position, Casey took a few practice swings.

"Who am I?" he asked just as Terrell slowed to a stop. He swung from his heels, but his stroke was as smooth as silk.

"Don't know."

"Griffey, Jr." His stance abruptly shifted. This time he stood tall and made the barrel of his bat point toward the sky. "How about now?"

"Fisk?"

He shrugged and dropped into his normal stance. "Close enough."

I held the tennis ball over my head and Terrell waved to say that he was ready. My first pitch was a pathetic lob, and it hit Casey on the bounce. I threw my second pitch much harder, but at the last second I again let my aim wander toward Casey and the ball drilled him squarely on the shoulder.

Casey raised his bat threateningly. "Hit me one more time and I'll come out there and beat you senseless."

"That thing would tickle," I muttered.

I paused before my next pitch to compose myself, taking the time to wrap my fingers around the ball in a cross-seam grip the way my Little League coach had taught me long ago. I made the mistake of glancing in at Casey as I started my windup. I'd never seen him hit from this angle before, and suddenly the look of stark terror I'd noticed on the faces of opposing pitchers made much more sense. He looked like a cheetah in his natural stance—a ball of kinetic energy waiting to explode into violence. His elbow hung over the plate and his legs remained as solid as a skyscraper's foundations until, with the slightest of steps, his body snapped forward. I heard the hiss of the unaerodynamic bat against the cool air followed by a dull thump, and the ball soared over the scoreboard in left field, a streak of yellow fuzz against the night sky. The groundskeeper, who was leaning against the backstop, whistled softly.

"One," Casey said.

He hit five more before he got three outs, and then jogged to center field to trade places with Terrell. I could tell that Terrell was reluctant to hit by the deliberate way he swung the bat during his practice swings, but he knocked home runs on my first two pitches and his body language abruptly changed. By the second inning he and Casey were exchanging idle smack, and by the third they were wagering a hundred bucks a swing. And although Casey was averaging one or two more home runs an inning than Terrell, the contest certainly hadn't disintegrated into the blowout I would have predicted.

I spent my time between pitches watching Casey. Whenever I saw him play professionally, he was composed, focused, and businesslike. Those are all good attributes, I suppose, but the very best and most popular baseball players project a sense of how much they enjoy playing the game. That's the difference between Albert Belle and Sammy Sosa. I'd never gotten that feeling of unbridled pleasure from Casey—with the possible exception of the night we broke into the field in Pawtucket. But playing a game of home run derby, his expression had turned magical, and I realized that he didn't just play baseball because he was good at it; he played because it gave him joy.

Everyone was animated on the drive back downtown. Casey dropped Terrell at the Four Seasons and then gave me a ride to my hotel near the stadium. I expected Casey to mention offhand during the trip that he hadn't been trying his hardest during the home run derby, but he just said a few nice things about how well Terrell had hit the ball and left it at that. I lay in bed for a long time, still flushed with an unexplainable sense of victory, and it never occurred to me to turn on *SportsCenter*. My last thought before I fell asleep was that I hoped I would get to see Molly when we returned to Boston.

chapter 19

THE FIRST TIME TERRELL CAME UP TO BAT THE NEXT NIGHT, I could see a difference just in the way he walked to the plate. His body language, which had been defeatist for at least a month, had new life, and he swung the bat during warm-ups with authority. The change was so noticeable that one of the guys in the press box even commented upon it. But apparently there is a large difference between a batting practice change-up thrown by Russell Bryant and a looping curveball thrown by a real Major League pitcher, and Terrell grounded out weakly to second base. By the time the game ended he was again 0–4, which he took with his usual quiet dignity. Jimy Williams, the Sox manager, benched him for the final game of the series.

We flew back to Boston on a Thursday. The team had chartered a plane, and *Sports Illustrated* had somehow gotten me on the flight. The players, coaches, trainers, and equipment guys were scattered in first class and the forward section of coach, and I was sitting in the back with a couple other reporters. At least I had the whole row to myself. The in-flight movie was something rancid about love in a small town, so I flipped to the map in the airline's magazine and tried to figure out our position by using the landmarks and lights far below. I had just decided that we must be somewhere south of Albany when Casey slid into the seat next to me.

"You navigating?" he asked, gesturing at the map.

"I figure the pilot needs some help," I said. "I think we're over Moscow."

Casey yawned. "I'm bored out of my mind. Terrell's too upset to talk and the rest of the guys are either playing cards or sleeping."

"I'm glad to know I'm your last choice," I said.

Casey just grunted and pushed his chair into full recline. He appeared to be settling in for the duration, so I closed the magazine and slid it back into the pocket of the seat in front of me.

"Tell me something about your life, Russ." Casey, speaking with his eyes closed, looked like a kid requesting a bedtime story. "I don't know anything about you. Not the important stuff."

"What do you want to know?"

"What was your favorite team when you were a kid?"

"Red Sox," I said, not sure that I really wanted to answer that question—or any question about my life outside reporting.

"Really?"

"Yeah, I grew up in New Hampshire." Despite my initial reluctance, I felt myself warming to the subject—I rarely get an opportunity to share my autobiographical details with anyone. "One of the events that changed my life was when Bill Buckner let that ball slip through his legs in 1986. Until that moment I still believed that good things happen to good people. But watching that team of New York crackheads get break after break and win . . ." I suddenly noticed the anger in my tone, and I let my voice trail off. Reporters get accused of bias often enough—even without admitting to hating particular teams. "I sometimes wonder if the way I see the world comes partially from those Sox. It's funny how viciously a baseball team can break a young boy's heart."

"You're telling me a fucking baseball team made you cynical?"

"Maybe." I let my head flop to the side and I stared at Casey, realizing that he had never known what it meant to be a true fan, to live and die with a team. That fact explained more about his approach to Major League Baseball than all the other details I had so painstakingly assembled. "I think a team can make you cynical. Especially a team like Red Sox. The way this team loses . . . An editor at the *Globe* said this perfect thing about them a couple years ago: 'They killed my father, and now they're coming after me.' I don't think he was entirely kidding. You probably won't believe me, but really following a team can be kind of like falling in love. It's a big deal. And not just for kids."

"I didn't mean to crap on you," Casey said after a minute, his tone as close to apologetic as it could get. "I just didn't know you ever cared so much."

"I knew everything about those Sox," I said. "Every reliever out of the bullpen, every statistic. No team has ever mattered half that much to me ever since."

"If you weren't a reporter, would you still be a Sox fan?"

"If I wasn't a reporter, I wouldn't watch baseball."

"That's pathetic," Casey said. "You've got the wrong job."

"Maybe you're right." I intended for my response to be patronizing, but it ended up sounding real. My brain had just begun exploring that paradox when Casey pulled me back into the conversation.

"When was the first time you went to Fenway?" he asked.

I knew instantly, but I made a show of scrunching my eyebrows and rubbing my right sideburn. "I was nine," I slowly began. "My dad drove me down I-95 on a Sunday morning in his big, blue Ford truck. He's a lawyer, but he always buys trucks to remind him where he came from. Anyway, we got to the park early enough to watch the players take batting practice. I remember Jim Rice—he looked like a god."

"Still does," Casey said, nodding toward the front of the plane where Jim Rice, coach, lay snoozing in his chair.

"Everything looked so different than on television," I continued, not really caring if Casey was listening. "So much bigger. I don't think I said a word the whole game. My dad and I went down every year until I got to college. But the more I got to know about the team—the contracts and the prostitutes and the fights—the less magical it seemed. And when the players became just people, it wasn't worth the three-hour drive any more."

"That's a good story," Casey said. He paused, and then let a small, critical smile creep across his face. "Is any of it true?"

"It's all true," I said. "Except for the part about the truck. My dad drove a BMW."

Casey nodded, and I could hear him take a deep breath. "Ask me a question," he said quickly. "Anything."

I knew what he was offering—and how important it was—so I took a second to ponder. I could only think of one appropriate subject. "What happened to your parents?" And then, as if the question needed clarifying, "Real parents."

"My biological father was killed in the Pam Am crash over Scotland," Casey said, his tone flat.

"Really?" I didn't want to be morbid, so I tried to keep the curiosity out of my tone. I'm sure I failed miserably.

Casey snorted so loudly that I saw a bald head turn a few rows in front of us. I hoped the reporter didn't have good ears. "Of course not," he said. "But that's how I like to imagine it. Cold, sterile. Maybe it was more anonymous than a plane crash. He ate bad fish at a sushi bar in Omaha and died of worms. How do you like that?"

"I don't like it," I said. "And I don't believe it. Nobody's that cold. Not even you, Casey Fox."

I thought for a moment that he was going to tell me to fuck myself—and he would have been perfectly justified—but he just sighed and settled further into his seat. I was on the verge of apologizing when he spoke. "I don't want to know my parents," he said quietly. "No bullshit. They'd be a hassle right now. And they'd never seem real. The only people who ever really felt like family were Molly and Nate. Mr. McDowell was okay, but he got real mean when Mrs. McDowell died."

I felt something sink inside of me when he mentioned Molly's name, and my desire to have an honest conversation dissipated like vapor from a jet engine. "I've got to go to the bathroom," I said.

By the time I finally returned from the tiny lavatory, my ears still ringing from the vacuum flush of the toilet, I expected Casey to have retreated to the safety of first class. But he had instead slid next to the window and was crammed into the economy seat like Houdini into a particularly devious trap. I sat down, leaving a cushion between us. Casey was staring out the dark window at the flashing bright light at the tip of our wing, his expression so vacant that he overwhelmed my reserve.

"Are you all right?" I asked.

"Fine," he said. "Just thinking." He took a deep breath, and in the reflection from the window I could see his jaw tighten. "Have you talked to Molly yet?"

"About what?"

Casey turned toward me, his expression strangely disappointed. "You know, the thing I asked you to do."

"Oh, that." Somehow in the emotional confusion of the preceding weeks I had forgotten my original mission—the ostensible reason, at least in Casey's mind, for why I was spending so much time with Molly. "No," I said. "Nothing yet." As soon as the words left my mouth I felt the first pangs of an unusual guilt. It had been a long time since I had betrayed anyone other than myself, and the feeling so annoyed and upset me that I asked the question that had been bothering me ever since I met Casey Fox.

"Why do you hate this game?"

"You don't know me at all, do you?" Casey peered at me strangely. "Or do you? That's a weird question to ask, Russ."

"I just can't figure out where your anger comes from."

"Do you remember what Mark McGuire said when he hit seventy home runs?" I shook my head, even though I knew the answer. "He said, 'I'm in awe of myself.' That's a direct quote. And that's fucking foolishness. He didn't discover penicillin. He didn't write *War and Peace*. He didn't invent the telephone. He just hit a ball seventy goddamned times."

"Come on, Casey. You know it's more than that."

"It is and it isn't," Casey said. "And my problem with baseball is that everyone can see how it is and nobody can see how it isn't."

A patronizing smile slipped onto my lips. "Except you."

I expected Casey to explode, but instead he leaned back into his seat, only his fierce eyes betraying his anger. "Russ," he said, carefully enunciating every syllable, "you spend every waking hour pretending you're not a reporter. So I really don't need your shit. Not on this issue."

"Fair enough," I said. And then I crossed my arms across my chest and pretended to fall asleep.

Boston had a full-blown case of pennant fever when we returned. Our plane landed after midnight, and five hundred people were standing outside the gate cheering as we emerged. I could understand their passion. With three weeks left in the regular season, the Sox were playing wonderful ball, catching the Yankees, and looking like World Series contenders. New England, already giddy, was ready to go wild. Boston fans have long been seeking a reason for optimism. The region is utterly mad for sports, yet the baseball team hasn't won a World Series in eighty-one years; the hockey team hasn't won a Stanley Cup since Orr retired; and the Celtics, once the dominant franchise in professional basketball, have fallen further than an alcoholic angel. So when the Red Sox are actually doing well, the crooked streets of downtown Boston practically vibrate with the volatile combination of ecstasy and stark terror. Many people have speculated about what would happen if the Sox were ever to win a World Series, and my own belief is that New England would explode in a kind of Calvinist Mardi Gras, a typically schizophrenic celebration for a region that somehow inexorably binds happiness with guilt.

It took Casey only twenty hours after he landed at Logan Airport to complicate things. The evening after we returned, the league had scheduled a one-game makeup against Toronto. In the bottom of the second inning, when Terrell came up to bat for the first time, a cascade of boos came pouring from the stands. Perhaps the Fenway crowd was reacting to the fact that he had ten strikeouts and only two hits on the trip; perhaps the fans wanted the team to play someone else in right field. Terrell accepted the boos with the dignity I had come to expect from him—he just bowed his head slightly and dug in at the plate, patiently awaiting the pitch.

Casey, however, exploded like Billy Martin protesting an umpire's call. He sprinted out of the dugout, stopping short on the patch of grass adjacent to the on-deck circle, and tore off his Red Sox jersey. The whole park stopped. Everyone. The opposing pitcher stepped off the rubber to stare, hot dog vendors turned in the aisles, fat guys in the bleachers lowered their beers. Terrell took a few steps toward Casey, his hand up and his lips moving, but he was too late. With one sweeping, disdainful glance at the crowd, Casey spiked his jersey onto the ground and deliberately stepped on it. And before the boos could begin again, he jogged off the field and down the tunnel to the locker room. He never reappeared.

The Sox media coordinator announced in the seventh inning that Casey would be holding a press conference immediately after the game. The last three innings seemed to take forever, and when the third out of the top of the ninth finally settled into the center fielder's glove, all the reporters who didn't have to write game stories practically ran down to Fenway's largest conference room. The newspaper and magazine writers scattered themselves across the neat rows of folding chairs while the television crews set up a barricade of cameras along the back wall. We all stared at the empty table on the small dais near the front of the room. The number of microphones and tape recorders on the table made it look like a hedgerow, and I knew that Nike, which had sponsored the banner hanging behind the dais, would get plenty of free advertising that evening.

Casey finally stalked into the room about fifteen minutes later, wearing just a white T-shirt and his baseball pants. A Sox media guy, looking like one of Leonidas's shield carriers at Thermopylae, stepped into the room behind him and closed the door.

"Casey has a short statement," the media guy said. "And then he might take a couple questions."

"He better," muttered a reporter beside me.

Casey settled into the chair behind the table, his face almost disappearing behind the microphones. He stared at the small yet rabid crowd, his eyes blinking quickly in the unwavering light from the cameras.

"I've apologized to the team for leaving the game," he said slowly. "I'm just glad that we won. That's my statement. Questions?"

We all shifted nervously—nobody wanted to become a target if Casey was as annoyed as he appeared. A guy from the *Herald*, whose name among local reporters is synonymous with stupidity, took the first shot. "What do you have to say to a guy who paid fifty bucks for a box seat and had to watch that?"

Casey let an expression of complete disdain, too perfect to be unpracticed, torque his face. "You're saying that since they pay they have a right to boo. Correct?"

The reporter, too stupid to know he was in the crosshairs, smiled brightly. "Yeah, that's right."

"That's a dumb-ass way of looking at things," Casey said. "You can boo a lack of effort. I have no problem with that. You can boo a guy who beats his wife or throws baseballs at kids. You can boo the Yankees or Baltimore. But don't boo a guy who's busting his butt for this team." He paused. "I know he's trying a lot harder than I am."

We laughed nervously. Casey glanced around the room, and we all ducked again. One of the Four Horsemen finally stood.

"What about the kids in the park, Casey?" he asked.

"Terrell's wife and kids were in the stands," Casey said quietly. "Did you guys know that? Can you imagine what it feels like to be twelve years old and listen to your father get booed by thirty thousand people? I mean, what are they booing? Huh? The fact that his bat is a little slower this year? That the little pops to the outfield, the dying quails and Texas Leaguers, haven't been falling in?"

The words were tumbling out of Casey's mouth, propelled by real passion, and I could feel the whole room begin to listen more closely. Even the clicking and the whirring of the photographers' cameras begin to slow. "We all deserve better," Casey continued, staring at some fixed point in the back of the room. "Fans deserve less obnoxious behavior from baseball players. I shouldn't be stepping on my uniform. Other guys shouldn't be charging little kids for autographs or making asses of themselves off the field. But we also deserve less critical treatment. Just because a guy makes a lot of money doesn't make him an open target for whatever pent-up frustrations people want to unload."

He paused again and then rubbed his eyes, giving the photographers the picture that would appear on the front page of every sports section in New England. "If some dad in the stands today had to explain to his little kid why Casey Fox was stamping on his uniform, I'm sorry. And I hope a lot of fans come back tomorrow and root for this team. We need your help. But if you're going to cheer for us, cheer for all of us. That's all I'm trying to say."

The media guy led Casey off the stage and the other reporters ran off to get interviews with the players. But I remained in my hard aluminum seat, all alone, thinking about the evening. Casey can be infuriatingly self-righteous. Sometimes I forget exactly how young he is, but that night his immaturity had been unmistakable. I liked his reason, liked the fact that he would stick up for a friend in front of thirty thousand people. But his tactics left a lot to be desired. I'd suspected from the moment I met him that Casey had a self-destructive streak, and as we had spent more time together, I had come to understand that he was perpetually seeking bastions to charge. And although that instinct appeared noble at times, it was also a sign that he wasn't ready for a stage as large as Major League Baseball.

I was just about to leave when my cell phone rang. I recognized the number immediately.

"Hey, Eddie," I said. "How's Providence?"

"I'd be twiddling my thumbs if I didn't have one up my ass," he said. He waited for me to finish laughing. "I see our old friend had another little incident today."

I wandered over to the room's small window and stared out at the cars jockeying to fight through the tight knot of traffic surrounding the park. "He snapped like Mike Tyson without happy pills," I said quietly.

"I read your article last week." Eddie paused, long enough to let me know that criticism was on the way. "Not bad, but you're much too close to the guy."

"I know," I said.

Eddie cleared his throat with a hacking cough and I wondered if he was alone in a bar sucking smoke. "You're better than that, kid," he said when he got his breath. "A lot of reporters use athletes to help drag them up, but that don't mean it's right. I've been watching these reporters doing beer ads with big stars—the ones where they kiss the athlete's ass."

"Coors beer," I said. "I've seen those."

"Disgraceful." Eddie spat out the word and I was surprised to hear the vehemence in his tone. He had never struck me as a crusader for purity in journalism. "You think Dan Rather would do a beer ad and talk about how great Richard Nixon was? How he was an original?"

"I'm not doing beer ads," I said. "I'm just getting a story."

I didn't fool Eddie one iota. "I know you don't believe that," he said. "You can be friends with this guy Casey. You can hang out with him if you find him interesting. But either hold yourself to the standard of a real reporter, or don't write about him. Because you were wasting your time writing that last article."

"Thanks, Eddie," I said, and clicked the phone shut.

chapter 20

MY CELL PHONE RANG EARLY SUNDAY MORNING. I IGNORED IT for the first dozen rings, but finally rolled over in bed and picked it up.

"Morning," Molly said. "Did I wake you?"

"No," I said, struggling to clear the sleep out of my throat without sounding too obvious. "I just got back from a run."

"Right." She may not have known me intimately, but she knew me well enough. "What are you doing today?"

I dragged myself roughly upright and glanced at the clock. It was 7:10. "I hadn't thought past breakfast," I said. "And the Sox are playing this afternoon."

Her voice, too cheery for such an ungodly hour, skipped through my receiver. "How about you ditch that boring baseball stuff and come meet me on the Cape?"

I didn't even bother to pretend to pause and consider the invitation. "Give me directions."

I left early enough to avoid any church traffic, and by the time I crossed the Sagamore Bridge onto Cape Cod, my eyes were staying open almost normally—although my mouth remained unnaturally dry. I do not reach my pinnacle as a sentient human being on Sunday mornings. Yet despite being woken early, my spirits were soaring. Not only had Molly cared enough to call me, but the flexibility of my job had allowed me to drop everything and drive south to the Cape. That alone made up for both the instability of my career and the fact I was living in a hotel room.

I stopped to wash and vacuum my car at a Shell station off of Route 6, and as I lathered my rusted hood I couldn't help smiling at myself. It's interesting the little things we try to conceal from women. Did I really suspect that Molly would like or respect me any less if she discovered that I drove a dirty car? But the more interesting implication of my visit to the Shell station was what it said about my growing feelings for Molly. I remember a roommate of mine in college who spent several hours scrubbing three months of male slime from the tiles of our shower the morning before his high school girlfriend arrived for the weekend. He never told me that he loved her, and he never needed to—the act of getting on his knees with a sponge spoke volumes. In the same way, even though I couldn't be totally honest with myself about the way I felt about Molly, I could roughly gauge the depth of my emotions by the lengths I was taking to conceal my superficial flaws.

I suppose my life would be easier if I could have just freely confessed my feelings. And I suppose life would be easier for all of us if we could admit that we soil our showers and dirty our cars. It would save us so much time. But in my experience, honesty in relationships comes in tiny steps. For most of us it begins with showers and cars and only gradually evolves into emotions and goals and dreams. Some people probably remain stuck cleaning showers for their entire lives—which, I suppose, is one of my great fears. I've long believed that my best chance at true happiness lies in finding a woman with whom I can be completely honest, completely myself. I had only recently realized that the roots of such honesty might rest within me rather than a woman, and that realization made it even more ironic that I took the time to vacuum

not one but both sides of my floor mats before I left the Shell station.

Molly's directions led me to the southern elbow of the Cape,
my tires rolling from highway to pavement to crushed gravel and
finally to sand. I stopped in front of a gray clapboard house with a
large porch that overlooked rolling dunes and the ocean. A red
Jeep was parked in the driveway. I got out of the car, not sure if I
was in the right place, and awkwardly climbed up onto the porch.
I was searching for a doorbell when the sliding door opened and
Molly bounced out.

"Nice place," I said.

Molly, rather than answering me, gestured to a girl emerging
from the house behind her. "This is Annie," she said. "My college
roommate."

Annie, shorter than Molly and almost as pretty, plastered a
properly disarming old-money smile across her face. "It's my parents' summer house," she said.

We stood awkwardly for a moment, only the sound of distant
wind chimes breaking the silence. I was on the verge of saying
something idiotic when Molly fortunately cut me off. "Annie's
leaving," she said.

"Goodbye, Annie," I said.

Annie stuck out her hand, which I primly shook. "Nice meeting you, Russ." She turned and kissed Molly on the cheek. "Play
safe, kiddo."

"I'll see you tomorrow," Molly said, and my heart leapt. Annie
grabbed a bag from behind the door and got into the red Jeep. As
she backed out of the driveway, I noticed that Molly was staring
wistfully after her.

"Something wrong?" I asked.

Molly shrugged, her narrow shoulders moving under her gray
sweatshirt. "She's going to her boyfriend's house in Malden. He's
a bit of an ass. But that's a long story." She whirled toward me,
suddenly on her tiptoes, and kissed me on the cheek. "I'm glad
you're here," she said as I clutched her. "I was worried I was going
to get lonely."

We walked the wandering streets of Annie's neighborhood before lunch. The summer crowds had left with the start of school, and the only sign of life we saw was a golden retriever jogging down a sandy tire track. Although the leaves had yet to turn, signs that September is a fall month in Massachusetts surrounded us. In midsummer the air in the narrow back alleys of the Cape is laden with the rich scent of the honeysuckle that drapes every fence. By September, however, the pollen has disappeared and the air is as sharp as Vermont cheddar. I can't precisely describe the smell, but I know it reminds me of pumpkins. And while the sun may remain warm, the shade has a bite that clenches your fists and makes you walk a little faster.

"So how's Casey?" Molly asked as we turned down a meandering lane.

"Good," I said. "You haven't talked to him?"

"Not since that night in Boston." Although she smiled, her eyes were worried and sad. "I keep expecting him to call. But he hasn't."

"We were on the road." I paused, then squeezed her fingers a little tighter. "I didn't call either."

"That's right." She carefully withdrew her hand from mine. "You didn't."

"I'm an idiot," I said, doing my best to staple a dumb-guy expression on my face. She frowned, but couldn't hold it, and a moment later we were again walking hand in hand.

We bought sandwiches at a general store for lunch and ate them on Annie's porch. When I asked Molly what she wanted to do that afternoon, she smiled enigmatically and stood. I followed her around the house to a large garage and watched as she wheeled open the door.

"We're sailing," she finally said over her shoulder. "Annie told me that we could use the Sunfish."

I peered into the garage and saw the vague outline of a white

hull hanging over a beat-up Ford station wagon. I felt a small ball
forming in the pit of my stomach—I've been afraid of the ocean
for as long as I can remember. "I didn't know you could sail," I
said, stalling for time.

"I went to Williams," she said. "It's like Yale. They don't let you
graduate unless you can play a decent set of tennis, make a quality martini, and sail small boats." She turned and kissed my smile
so passionately that my resistance to all things aquatic quickly
slipped away.

We lowered the Sunfish from the garage rafters onto a small
trailer and dragged it down to the beach. As we splashed in the
shallow water, struggling to set the mast and raise the sail, my fear
of the ocean resurfaced. The conditions seemed just a little too
perfect—the air so clear that it seemed as if we were in an Omni
film and the sky a vibrant, menacing blue from horizon to horizon. I became increasingly certain that a squall was hiding behind
the moon, just waiting for us to get far enough away from shore
that it could viciously strike. It would be hypothermia that would
kill us—the cool water, which had begun to lose its summer
warmth, conjured up images in my mind of *The Perfect Storm*.
And the Sunfish was much smaller than a fishing boat.

Molly, perhaps sensing my discomfort, made me sit in the cockpit while she pushed us deep enough that I could drop the rudder
and dagger board. The intermittent east wind was rippling the
water in fits and starts, and as soon as I tightened the main sheet,
we accelerated. Molly dragged herself into the boat a moment
too late, her Patagonia shorts wet to the top of her thighs. She
swore under her breath, but she was smiling as she took the tiller.
We slowly beat up the coast, tacking often enough to keep the
shore within a comfortable distance. I was still nervous, but Molly
seemed so happy that I tried to ignore it. The perfect preppiness
of the afternoon also amused me. Molly and I matched: red
cheeks, gray sweatshirts, tousled hair, and aviator sunglasses. I
felt like a Kennedy, and I realized that we were strangers in a
strange land. My mind flashed back to Mr. McDowell's house in

Providence, the place where Molly had grown up, and once again I was struck by her remarkable adaptability. The ease with which she was able to move in two such contrary worlds amazed me.

We eventually sailed into a dead spot in the wind and drifted to a sluggish stop. Molly took the main sheet from me and fiddled with it, but there was hardly enough breeze for the sail to even luff.

"Look at this silliness," Molly said. "Totally becalmed." She stood, bracing herself against the aluminum mast, her feet fighting for traction on the slippery floor of the cockpit. "Come on, wind!"

I stared up at her intense expression, more than a little enraptured. "They taught you to sail at Williams?"

"Not really." She plopped down across from me and began violently moving the tiller back and forth. Driven by the raw power of the rudder, we lurched forward at a rate of roughly six feet an hour. "I learned at Girl Scout camp. I was too busy at Williams for that kind of stuff."

"What was your thing in college?" I asked.

She abandoned the tiller and I offered her my arm. We sank to the bottom of the cockpit, ignoring the quarter inch of sloshing seawater. "Soccer got me my scholarship," she said when we were settled.

I turned my head, surprised. "I didn't know you were an athlete."

"Yup," she said. "Four years for the Ephs. Our team was great for Division III, but I gradually lost interest in the sport."

I imagined Molly sprinting for a long ball in a soccer uniform, and the image made me press my naked leg into hers a little firmer than before. "Why'd you lose interest?"

"Sports helped me get where I wanted to go—which was a good college. And once I got there I had other things to do."

"Such as?"

"Strategies for sustainable growth in the developing world." I stared at her, trying to see if she was kidding, but her eyes were tracing the horizon. "It's my thing," she said. "I know it's kind of dorky. But the more I learned, the more interested I got."

"That's pretty heavy," I said. She possessed the dignity to ignore me, and I chattered blithely onward. "So do you think I'm wasting my life by covering sports instead of developing the Third World?"

She squirmed away from me and reached back for the tiller. "Honestly?" I nodded and swung around to face her. "It's your life," she said, her tone already answering my question. "Like I said, sports can help you get where you want to go. But maybe sports shouldn't be your final destination. You know what I'm saying?"

"Sure," I said. "You're telling me that Casey and I are wasting our time."

"No." Her face was perfectly neutral, her eyes focusing on a point over my head. "There's a difference. Casey is wasting his time. You're wasting your talent."

Neither of us spoke during the long run back down the coastline. We stripped the boat quickly and struggled to drag it through the soft sand to the garage. I walked back up onto the porch when we were done, Molly following me, and when I bent down and put my hand on my backpack, she gently touched the top of my head.

"Are you going to leave?" she asked.

I smiled as softly as I could manage. "Why would I want to leave?"

"Why wouldn't you want to leave? It was a terrible thing I said." She sounded more curious than apologetic, and I glanced up at her face and instantly noticed that her usual sunshine had vanished. The transformation so startled me that my own lingering grumpiness fled like a rodeo clown before an onrushing bull.

"I'm sorry I didn't listen better in the boat," I said.

She stared at me, still transparently curious. "Why are you apologizing, Russ?"

"Because I'm Hamlet."

"What does that mean?"

I paused, unsure of how to answer her question. I had used that phrase to describe myself only in my most incriminating internal monologues. And although I knew exactly what I meant, I couldn't think of a way to explain it to her without making myself sound either conceited or pathetic. "Can I let my ego run for a minute?" I eventually asked.

"I think you'd be much better off if you let your ego run a lot," she said. Again I looked at her, and I noticed that her usual softness and sweetness had yet to return. This was the side of her personality that she hid from Casey—and, perhaps, the world. She had more iron than I had suspected, which was both a good and a bad thing. Good because sweetness without backbone is a prescription for Prozac. Bad because she was picking a completely unnecessary fight. I had the feeling that she was testing me—was she trying to ensure that I wouldn't leave her at the first provocation? Or did she just want to confirm that I cared about her enough to fight? Whatever her motivation, I refused to allow myself to rise to her challenge, and I instead concentrated on the original question.

"I call myself Hamlet because I think you're right," I said. "I waste my talent. I'm arrogant enough to believe that I could do almost anything I want, but the problem is that I don't know what I want. So I've been wandering through a bunch of crappy jobs and shallow relationships and killing time until I find something that lights a fire in me. But lately I've started to worry. I mean, what if I spend my whole life like this? What if I never find something that I really want to chase? And that's a real possibility. Because the truth is that I don't have any passions. Any compelling reason for existing." I paused to take a breath, exhausted and more than a little scared. I had never said any of those thoughts out loud, and I could almost feel them hanging in the air like hydrogen-filled balloons. When I could no longer stand the silence, I asked, "Do you have any idea what I'm talking about?"

Our eyes met long enough for me to read an emotion that

seemed closer to frustration than sympathy, and her eyes dropped to the floor of the weathered oak porch before she answered my question. "No," she said. "I have passions. Several of them."

"What are they?"

"Stick around and I might tell you," she said. And she walked into the house before I could ask the idiotic question of whether she meant stick around the Cape or stick around the relationship.

We made dinner and then watched an old Cary Grant movie from Annie's collection. Late that night, when we were cuddled like spoons under a pile of crocheted blankets, Molly reached back and rubbed her hand down my rough face.

"I've got something to tell you," she whispered.

"You can't already be pregnant," I said.

She pinched my ear, then slid her arm back across her chest. "No jokes. Have you been wondering why I've been out of college for four months and still don't have a job?"

"It has crossed my mind," I said. "This is the best economy of the last millennium."

"I have an offer from a foundation in Chicago," she said slowly. "They do a lot of cool stuff with children's nutrition. But I'm waiting to hear back from this other place." I nudged her naked back, my hand lingering on her sharp hip a moment longer than it needed to. "It's an orphanage in Honduras."

I stiffened. "Chicago I can do," I said wryly. "But Honduras is going to be kind of a problem."

"I figured," she said in a voice that carried all the intonation of a dial tone.

"I do have to admit I'm curious," I said. "Explain to me how a girl from working-class Providence goes to Williams, a training ground for preppies, and ends up a hippie. That's a story that makes no sense to me."

"Aren't you dodging the real issue?" she asked.

"I don't think so," I said. "Because until I understand why you'd want to work at an orphanage in Honduras, I won't know anything about you. And if I don't know anything about you, then any conversation we have about you and me is just two people pretending to be bit players in a daytime soap."

She rolled her head far enough that our eyes met, and I got the feeling she was evaluating me. After a long moment, her head turned back toward the far wall. "My sophomore year in college I went to a U.N. youth conference in New York," she began. "I was there to do a documentary for a film class, and I spent the first day worrying about lighting and sound quality and chasing the celebrity speakers. But the morning of the second day, I started to notice the people on the other side of my camera." She abruptly stopped speaking, and I felt her stiffen in my arms. "This sounds really dumb when I say it out loud. Like some goddamned infomercial for a stupid cult. Am I boring you?"

"No," I said. "Not at all."

"Okay." She took a deep breath, and I let my chest rise and fall in unison with hers. "At the conference there were all these amazing speakers from places like Honduras and Bolivia and Zaire and Vietnam. And they talked in a really clear way about the things their countries needed. Simple things. Water. Food. Medicine. As they spoke, I thought about the things I had thought that I needed. A car. Tickets to see Dave Matthews. A laptop computer to replace my desktop. And something in my mind just broke. I can't deal with living in a culture where we spend a majority of our time wondering if Justin kissed Britney. I mean, don't you find it ridiculous that the people we hear from the most in this country are athletes and actors? It all makes me want to set fire to Jay Leno's big, stupid hair."

She stopped, and then my hand felt the muscles of her firm stomach tighten and she laughed a laugh too genuine to be mere embarrassment. I joined her, but gingerly enough that I could stop if her mood suddenly turned serious. I buried my face in the soft fuzz between her ponytail and neck. She still tasted slightly of salt. "Well, you're a subversive little thing, aren't you?" I mumbled.

"Maybe. At least by the standards of your middle-class mind."

"And where did you learn these egalitarian ideas? At an elite liberal arts college and a conference in the Four Seasons–New York?"

"You know," she said, "the fastest way to a girl's heart is to patronize her."

We laughed again, but that didn't conceal the enormous gap between us. I had listened patiently to her entire monologue without really absorbing any of it—largely because I was more than happy to listen if the price of lying in bed with her was listening. But I was also struggling to find a way to categorize her speech as being either hopelessly idealistic or naively self-righteous. When it comes to those sorts of issues, I wade in the shallow end with most of my fellow Americans. Sure, I donate my used clothes to the Salvation Army; I buy cookies from kids raising money for UNICEF; I send an occasional check to the Red Cross or another international aid organization. I have no stomach, however, for the unpleasant details of suffering. When the *New York Times* occasionally runs a piece on conditions in Somalia or the Sudan, I skip it. When an in-depth report on the mushrooming AIDS crisis in Africa comes on the Discovery Channel, I flip to a baseball game. It's not that I don't care. But I am simply unwilling to confront the contradictions inherent in my own lifestyle and priorities that would become inevitable if I asked the kind of questions Molly had asked. Perhaps that makes me a bad person—or perhaps that is exactly the kind of emotional shield an average human being has to construct in order to keep his head from exploding. In either case, I knew that I had nothing intelligent to say in the wake of Molly's honesty.

She lay still for a long time, and just when I thought that she had fallen asleep, she abruptly flipped over so that our noses were almost touching. "Casey doesn't know about Honduras," she said. "And you can't tell him."

"Okay," I said, doing my best not to gloat. "I won't say a word."

We lay quietly for a long time, and my mind continued to pore over every detail of our conversation. Was she really going to go to Central America? Did our priorities and view of the world really have so little in common? I tried to imagine returning to my life before Molly, the emptiness I had known so intimately for so long, and my mind recoiled at the thought. But I knew I was being dramatic. What I loved most about Molly was that she had proved to me that my heart isn't as calcified as I feared. I had long worried that my great romances—at least in terms of feeling great waves of passion toward another person—had all occurred while I was still a teenager. Molly had proved that I was still capable of getting nervous before a date or spending long hours daydreaming about a woman I loved. And the relief I found in that realization was powerful enough to bury my disappointment.

chapter 21

CASEY CALLED ME IN THE PRESS BOX DURING THE SEVENTH IN-
ning of Monday's game. He needed a ride home. Apparently Nate
had decided to move into Casey's apartment in Boston, and
Casey—in a fit of complete irrationality—had let Nate borrow his
car. We met in the parking lot, and during the drive back to
Newton, Casey asked me if I thought he'd made a mistake by letting
Nate live with him. I mumbled something noncommittal. I had absolutely no interest in getting myself banished from Casey's inner
circle over Nate—only an idiot steps between old friends, even if
one of those old friends happens to be a walking magnetic mine.

When we got to Casey's apartment, Nate was lying on the
couch watching Monday Night Football and drinking a beer. The
controversy over ABC's choice of Dennis Miller as a football
color man had been raging for several months, which I thought
was perfectly emblematic of the problem with sports journalism.
When ABC had first decided to generate headlines by adding a
controversial person to the crew in the early 1970s, it had chosen
Howard Cosell—a man whose notoriety was based entirely on his
contentious opinions. But in the year 2000, with ratings plum-

meting, the network had reached for a guy who relies upon being outrageous, cynical, and a little silly.

Casey and I joined Nate on the couch and popped open a few beers. The game had evolved into a blowout by the middle of the third quarter, and Casey picked up the remote and flipped through the channels. He stopped on the Sydney Olympics. Women's gymnastics was on, as always, and I waited for the inevitable round of jokes. Yet Casey and Nate sat as quietly as a pair of librarians and watched as the American team performed its rotation on the uneven bars. One of the girls, a fragile-looking thing who had spent most of the night listening with a trembling lip to the shouted instructions of her mustached coach, stumbled badly on her landing.

"Oh, that's going to cost her," the male announcer said. "And the American team isn't going to medal if they keep making these mistakes. I know Bella won't be happy with that step."

He might have continued, but Nate stood and threw his pillow at the television. "Shut up, you fag!" Nate shouted at the screen. I turned, startled. Nate had never struck me as the kind of guy to get passionate about women's gymnastics.

"What did he do?" I asked, gesturing at the television.

"Those gay pricks can't do anything but criticize," he said angrily. "That little chick does the swinging crap better than he's ever done anything. And all the little homo can talk about is her mistakes."

"He's a catty bastard," Casey said. "Those fourteen-year-old girls have tortured themselves for half their lives to be in Australia. Can't he think of one goddamned nice thing to say?"

"I agree with you," I said. I leaned back into the couch, still surprised. We watched for ten minutes in silence as NBC cut away from gymnastics to show a feature story about another young woman who had fought a repressive political system to achieve her Olympic dream. I kept waiting for the tearjerker about the suburban white swimmer from Connecticut who didn't get asked to her junior high prom, but I guess the right girl hasn't come along. Maybe next Olympics. We had made it through half the feature—on-screen the girl was hugging several of her family's farm animals—when Nate again lost it.

"Enough with the dumb-ass stories on a Romanian girl and her goat!" He peered around for something to throw, but his pillow was still on the floor. "We don't give a flying fuck!"

Casey put his hand on Nate's shoulder to calm him, and then turned to me. "Is NBC trying to piss America off?" he asked. "I didn't think the coverage could get any worse after Atlanta, but . . ." His voice trailed off and he sighed the sigh of a disenfranchised television watcher. "What's the problem, Russ?"

"With the Olympics?" I asked. Casey nodded, and I felt flattered that he was seeking my opinion. "The coverage is being produced by people who don't love sports. It's that simple. Because if they really loved sports, they would know that they don't need to cover every story in this prefabricated syrup."

"So you really think Americans have the patience to watch unedited water polo games?" Casey asked. "We have trouble sitting through a whole baseball game, not to mention some sport we don't understand."

"Maybe," I said. "But NBC isn't even giving us the choice. In 1980 everyone in America suddenly became a hockey fan. Not because we saw a string of sappy stories on the players, but because we all watched those games in Lake Placid. But these days we're replacing real emotions and real stories with trumped-up miniature soap operas."

Casey shrugged and waved his hand, dismissive. "We do that in everything. Not just sports. Watch the nightly news—it's tears and Jesus."

I took a swig of my beer and kept my eyes on the television, a tiny grin pulling at my mouth. "Let's see if you're so calm when they do the first soft feature on your life."

"Do you think that's coming?" His tone was so innocent that I had to chuckle.

"Of course."

"I hate publicity," Casey said distastefully. "Especially here."

"Why here?"

"This is Boston. The city of Larry Bird."

I shook my head, still confused. "I don't get it."

"Really?" He stared at me for a long moment. "It's kind of hard to ignore the fact that a big reason so many people want to interview me is that I'm a successful white athlete in an increasingly black and Hispanic world."

"Okay," I said. "I understand that. But let's also not ignore the fact that you're hitting the crap out of the ball."

I decided to leave shortly before midnight, and Casey walked me out. We were standing in his narrow alcove, the door behind me, and I offered him my hand. He took it, and then pulled me so close that I could smell the beer on his breath.

"I've got to ask you a question."

"Anything," I said, praying that he wasn't going to mention Molly.

He frowned, concern showing through his usually guarded expression. "I'm worried about Terrell. He's getting real down and I don't know what to say anymore."

I knew I didn't have any good advice, but I decided to say something anyway—I figured Casey was just trying to get his worries off his chest. "It's baseball," I said. "Slumps happen."

Casey stared at me as if I were trying to sell him a business-to-consumer Internet company. "You know this isn't a normal slump."

I shrugged. "Well, try the normal stuff anyway. Take him out and show him a good time. Hire him a stripper. Get his mind off things."

"Yeah," Casey said, unconvinced. He leaned back against the row of mailboxes lining the wall and examined me, closely enough that I shifted uncomfortably, then abruptly dropped his eyes. "We're having a little party on Wednesday night after the game. You in?"

"Sure," I said. "I'll be your designated driver."

Casey smiled and I relaxed. "No cops this time."

• • •

But Casey ended up getting his own ride, and I drove alone. The party was at one of the player's houses, an enormous mansion in the affluent suburb of Wellesley. Although parking spots abounded in the surrounding neighborhood, the host had hired a valet parking service. I pulled in behind a Mercedes sedan and watched four women, dressed like either high-end professionals or low-end royalty, primp before getting out of the car. They were the kind of expensive, glamorous women that guys like me only see in the windows of stores and restaurants that we can't afford. Both my car and I felt firmly out of place. I almost drove around the block and parked myself, but at the last moment I decided that I had nothing to be ashamed of—1986 was a fine year for Toyota hatchbacks.

The expression on the valet attendant's face, however, changed my mind; he looked embarrassed just to touch my keys. I did my best to ignore his distress and followed the group of tittering women up the driveway, muttering the whole way about how I was too old for this kind of crap. The women made it through the front door without incident, but an enormous black man in a tuxedo stepped out of the shadows and intercepted me.

"You looking for somebody?" he asked in a tone that told me I had come to the wrong house.

"I'm Russ Bryant," I said. "A friend of Casey's."

"Could you turn around, Mr. Bryant?" Confused, I followed the instructions and found myself being expertly patted down. As the man's firm hands probed every crevice of my body, he recited a monologue in my ear. "No cameras," he began, "no tape recorders, no guns, no knives, no ninja shit. Start any fights and I'll break your arm. And then throw you out on the street."

He finished, and I turned back to face him. I flashed my best disarming smile, which he met with a completely impassive look. "Got it," I said. "Does everyone get this lecture?"

His head moved incrementally from side to side. "Only Mr. Fox's punk-ass white friends who look like they're begging to be the problem."

I gave up on the conversation and wandered into the foyer. A waiter offered me a glass of champagne, and as I took it, I couldn't help laughing. "I guess he met Nate," I mumbled to myself.

I found Casey upstairs in the billiards room, Rachel draped over him like a tacky fur coat. Nate was sitting in the corner, talking to a stunning woman in a tight blue dress who was going to be distraught when she discovered that Nate didn't match the profile of the average guest. I didn't feel like interrupting either conversation, so I wandered through the open rooms until I came to the library. It was empty. I'm always curious to see what other people have in their collections, so I browsed through the shelves, running my hand across the spines of the books. The collection was so eclectic that I found myself laughing—I discovered a first-edition copy of *Moby Dick* sandwiched between Rick Pitino's screed on how to be a winner and *Chicken Soup for the Soul*. I'm sure that Herman Melville would have rather been eaten by a white whale.

I was so engrossed in the books that I didn't realize I had company until a chin settled on my shoulder. I leapt as high in the air as I can leap—maybe a foot and a half—and the chin yelped. When I landed, I whirled to confront my spy, but when I saw her, my mouth snapped shut with a case of male brain lock. She was wearing tight black pants and a blouse strategically parted to attract men's eyes.

"Looking at books," she said, her voice betraying her amusement at my stunned expression. "Either you own the team or you're a reporter."

"Reporter," I said. I awkwardly stuck out my hand. "Russ Bryant."

She ignored my hand and walked over to the shelves, the muscles in her legs contorting beneath the thin layer of fabric. I waited for a wave of desire to sweep over me and was delighted when it didn't come. Molly must have been affecting my libido. When she got to the shelf, she looked back at me over her imperious shoulder. "How are the books?"

"It's the best collection too much money and poor taste can buy," I said.

She smiled, but it didn't reach her eyes. "His art is the same way. It looks like a collection by a guy who started buying art to impress other people."

"You don't seem like the flavor of the night," I said.

She raised an elegant eyebrow. "I'm not a hooker," she said. "If that's what you're asking. And I'm no baseball groupie."

My question didn't appear to have offended her in the slightest, which made me suspicious. A wife or a girlfriend of one of the players would have gone for my throat. "Then why are you here?" I asked when I could no longer contain my curiosity.

"I'm in your line of work," she said. "My name's Jessica Young. I'm a freelance photographer." She gestured down at her pants and precariously placed blouse. "I dress like this to get in the door."

I let my eyes wander her outfit, not sure whether or not I believed her. "Where's your camera?" I asked suspiciously. "I hear they're confiscating them."

"I can get it if I need it," she said. And the perfectly confident expression on her face made me believe her. She examined me for a moment, and I thought I saw a flicker of quiet amusement in her expression. "So are you a writer or a reporter?" she asked when our eyes met.

I instinctively knew what she meant. "Writer."

She nodded. "Good. Reporters bore me." She turned and strode across the room to the door, her sandals light on the heavy Persian rug. As her hand touched the doorknob, she turned back to me. "But you and I might talk again."

By the time I returned downstairs, the demure cocktail party had evolved into a full-blown bacchanal bash. The staff had cleared all the furniture out of the enormous living room, and a disc jockey I dimly recognized from one of Boston's premier clubs had set up shop in the corner. A whirling group of dancers, mostly women auditioning for the players on the sidelines, filled the center of the room. In the eye of the storm I saw Terrell. He was standing with his hands in his pockets, eyes closed, bobbing his head to the heavy bass beat of the music. I cut through the crowd, ignoring the flattering glances from women who thought I might be a utility infielder, and tapped Terrell on the shoulder. His eyes popped open.

"You doing okay?" I shouted in his ear.

He smiled the lugubrious smile of the truly intoxicated. "I'm spinning like a top, man. I'm a big old king pimp jungle god."

I had absolutely no idea what he was talking about—and wasn't even sure that I'd heard him correctly over the thumping music—but I nodded my head anyway. "That's cool," I said. "Have a good time."

I walked over to a chair by the window and sat alone. When a waiter passed me, I intercepted him and ordered a martini. I sipped it slowly when it came, my eyes scanning the crowd, and noticed that the room contained several distinct factions. That didn't surprise me—all baseball teams split into cliques, and the Red Sox were certainly no exception. The 1980s cliché about the team said that when the games ended the Sox were a syndicate of "twenty-four players, twenty-four cabs." In defiance of that long-standing tradition the Red Sox had become known over the previous few years as being a team with good chemistry, which basically meant they had been winning games at a rate greater than the sum of their parts.

Having chemistry on a baseball team, however, doesn't mean that everyone hangs out in one happy family. It just means that the factions can coexist in relative peace. The new expression could have been "twenty-four players, six SUVs." I could identify at least four distinct groups: the Latin players surrounding Pedro, superstar Nomar and his low-key friends, the old veterans hovering uncomfortably at the fringes of the festivities, and the rookies partying like a group of fraternity kids. Casey appeared to be a free agent. While the various factions weren't exclusively defined by race, it certainly played a major role. And even if the groups weren't mingling, the fact that almost the whole Red Sox team had come to the party was a good sign.

I was so involved in my observations that I didn't notice Nate until he sat on the arm of my chair.

"What's up?" he asked.

"Not much. Where's the girl?"

"That skanky bitch blew me off," he said, his tone indignant. "I guess she's stalking some homo ballplayer."

We were quiet for a minute while I racked my mind for something to say. "How's the *Real World* thing going?" I finally asked.

Nate exhaled through his mouth, his lips smacking together like a flag flapping in the breeze. "I gave that shit up. I got better things to do with my time, yo."

"So what's the new plan?"

"I'm going to be in a boy band." I tried to keep the smirk off my face, but wasn't successful. Nate glared at me. "Not a gay one. One of those cool ones that gets mad chicks."

I turned in my chair and examined his outfit—finally understanding why his clothes had evolved from ghetto casual into hip-hop wannabe: baggy jeans, football jersey, and a cap on backward. "So how do you get into a boy band?" I asked when I could straighten my mouth.

"You got to try out and shit," Nate said. "But I got it covered." He examined me, and I could see something flicker in his eyes. "Hey, you're a writer. You got any song ideas, bro?"

"For a boy band?" I thought for a moment. "How about 'GAP love'? Or 'I may not be as cute as Leo, but I have his heart'?"

I realized halfway through my suggestions that Nate was ignoring me and staring across the room. I followed his eyes to a tall brunette. "That's tight," he said absentmindedly. "I'm going to go chase that chick." He stood and tapped me on the shoulder, eyes still locked across the room like a missile guidance system. "Later, dog."

• • •

Nate marched off, and I sat alone for another five minutes before I got bored. I wandered again through the house, wondering idly the whole time why I had agreed to come to the party in the first place, and I eventually found myself back in the library. I picked a copy of *Catch-22* off the shelves and sank into a thick leather chair. After I had read only a few pages, I heard what sounded like a shriek from the other end of the hall, and I stuck my head out the door just in time to hear another scream—too piercing to be anything other than a cry of terror. I sprinted down the long corridor, and at the top of the staircase I slammed into Casey, who was swinging himself around the corner. We ran together to the end of the hall and stopped in front of a white wooden door.

"This it?" he asked.

Uncertain, I put my hand on the knob, but another unearthly scream answered our question. I cautiously pushed the door open, Casey right behind me, and saw two women huddled over a prone body in a large bathroom. One of the women stared up at me, her eyes large and scared.

"Help us," she whispered.

I took two steps into the bathroom before I recognized the body—Terrell. I felt my throat close, and I had to gather myself before kneeling down on the marble floor. The woman started speaking, the words coming in a rush.

"He had a thing and we tried to calm him down and he just stopped." I couldn't understand her words; all I could hear was the fear and confusion. She clutched my arm like the safety bar on a roller coaster. "It's not our fault, I promise. I don't know what happened."

I gently moved her out of the way and saw Terrell's face for the first time. His eyes were wide open, unblinking, and a thin stream of frothy white drool was running from the near corner of his mouth.

"What did you give him?" I asked, trying to keep my voice calm. I rested the tips of my fingers on Terrell's neck and couldn't feel a pulse—although my hands were shaking too much for me to be certain.

"Nothing," she said, more scared than defensive.

"What the fuck did you give him?"

She broke, and half a sob emerged from her mouth before her answer. "Cocaine. But that's it."

"Coke?" Casey's voice was fuzzy. "But he's been clean since Chicago . . ." The words died in a confused mumble, and he abruptly spun on the two girls. "Was it your shit?" he asked angrily. "Did you give a ripped man bad shit?"

"Calm down, Casey," I said as sharply as I could manage. Two men had appeared in the door and I glanced at them. "Could you call an ambulance?"

The two men disappeared, and Casey, his face pale, touched my shoulder. "Do you know medicine?"

"I'm a reporter," I said. Casey gazed at me blankly, then leaned against the wall. It was the first time I'd ever seen him not in complete command of a situation—and suddenly I was utterly terrified. I reached over one of the sobbing girls and grabbed a hand towel from the rack next to the sink. I carefully swabbed Terrell's mouth, tilted his neck back slightly, and began CPR—mostly because that was the only thing I knew how to do. Terrell's lips were cold and his body felt as lifeless as a training dummy. As I worked, I could feel people gathering around me, but I kept my eyes focused only on Terrell until a scared backup shortstop knelt across from me.

"I learned this in college," he said. "Want me to take a turn?"

"Yeah," I said, wiping my mouth. Eight or nine people were now crowded into the bathroom, and I could feel an utterly inappropriate emotion—embarrassment—rising in my chest. Casey was still leaning against the sink.

"Is he going to be all right?" he asked.

"I'm not a doctor," I said curtly. Casey's head dropped, concern etched into his features, and I felt guilty. I tapped him on the knee. "No. I'm sorry."

Casey shuddered, his eyes closed, then took a deep breath. When his heavy lids flicked open, I could see a hint of his usual complete self-control. "What do we do?"

I thought for a moment, and as I surveyed the situation I realized that a perverse part of me liked being in this position. Reporters don't get to take charge of situations very often—we are the ones on the sidelines when decisions are made. And I also knew that I had a choice to make. A true reporter would be in the background of this scene, taking notes and getting ready to write the story of his life. I had to decide whose side I was on. Did I want to break this story and flatten Casey, Terrell, and the rest of the team, or did I instead want to bury it? In a millisecond I had made that decision.

I looked up. At the fringes of the group I saw Jessica Young, her camera steadily clicking and whirring. I gestured to several players by the door. "Get her out of here," I said. "And close that door until the ambulance comes."

The door slammed shut and I heard an outraged squeal from the hallway. There were seven of us in the room: me, Casey, Terrell, the two women, the scared shortstop, and Mike Fletcher, the party's host. I waited until everyone was looking at me and then started giving directions, my voice slow and deliberate. "Everyone in this room is going to stay and talk to the police," I began. "We need to get the other guests out of here right now. Especially the players." I glanced at Fletcher. "You should keep the security guys and have them hold the reporters at the foot of the driveway. And if you can find that chick with the camera, you should expose her film." I smiled a private, humorless smile. "But she's probably at a photo lab by now."

I waited for a moment and nobody moved. "Go," I said impatiently.

The room emptied, leaving Casey and me alone with the scared shortstop and the lifeless body that my mind refused to identify as Terrell. I was watching the shortstop force air into the body's unwilling chest when Casey spoke, his voice barely a whisper. "Are they going to test him?"

"For drugs?" I knew the answer, so I continued without waiting for a response. "They'll check for everything. This is going to be big."

"They're going to find a lot of crap in his blood."

"More than cocaine?"

"Steroids, uppers." As I whirled on my knees to face Casey, he stretched his hands out to his sides. "It's all baseball related. He's been taking 'roids the last two seasons. And uppers for at least a couple weeks to keep him focused at the plate."

"You don't know that."

Casey's distraught face tightened. "He told me," he said, annoyed that I was challenging him.

"You don't understand." I could taste the condescension in my tone, but I didn't care. "Listen to me. From now on you don't know that. No matter who asks you. Period."

The paramedics burst through the door a few minutes later and the next half hour was a blur of hurried questions and frantic activity. They disappeared as quickly as they had arrived, leaving only black boot marks on the marble floor of the bathroom and a tiny piece of Terrell's shirt that they had cut away. A long line of confused partygoers followed them down the driveway. I pulled our little group together in the living room. We had only five minutes before the police would arrive and begin asking questions, and I pulled everyone into a tight huddle.

"This is a horrible situation," I said. "And I know we're all worried about Terrell. But you guys have to watch out for yourselves too. So this is the story. It was a quiet party, just a bunch of guys from the team. Everyone knows Terrell has been going through a slump, and he's started slipping back into his old coke habit—"

Casey cut me off. "That's not true."

I stared at him, trying to make my eyes hard. "Terrell had been slipping back into drugs," I repeated. "At some point he went upstairs alone. I discovered him on the bathroom floor."

Casey grabbed my arm, tight enough that I could feel my muscles grinding against my bone. "Why does he have to be an addict?"

I took a deep breath, partially for dramatic effect and partially to keep myself from yelling. "Because it explains how he got the drugs," I said. "It explains why he would use the drugs alone. And because it makes this tragedy the sad act of a disappointed man rather than an indictment of you and the whole fucking team. Okay?"

"Okay," Casey said.

The police were gentler than I would have expected, and they accepted our version of the events without question. When they finished taking our statements, Casey told me that Nate had borrowed his car and asked if I would give him a ride. I reluctantly accepted—I was ready to leave the evening far behind—and peeked out the front window. A crowd of reporters was already clustered around the bottom of the driveway.

"You wait here," I said. "I'll get the car. You don't want to walk through those guys."

I ambled down the paved drive, trying to look like a plain-clothes detective or forensic specialist, but I didn't fool anyone. Ten flashbulbs went off as soon as I got within range of the media herd, and reporters began shouting questions. I ignored them and pushed through the group, my shoves more violent than they needed to be. I recognized a few reporters from the ballpark, and the jealous expressions inscribed on all their faces sickened me.

The valet attendants had parked my car as far away from the house as possible—probably trying to conceal the fact that someone at the party was so gauche as to drive an '86 Toyota—and I took my time on the walk. The other houses in the neighborhood all appeared perfectly peaceful; the investment bankers and lawyers were tucked all snug in their beds. When I got to the car, I flirted with the idea of driving straight home. Casey could get a cab or a mule or something. But after a short internal debate, I drove back to Fletcher's house and waited while the security guards cleared enough space so that I could pull up the driveway.

Casey jogged out of the front door as soon as I stopped the car, and I backed out as quickly as I dared. I don't have tinted windows, but Casey pulled his jacket over his head and all the pho-tographers got was a blue blob with hands. We had driven two blocks when Casey finally straightened.

"Thank you," he said.

"Sure." I glanced at him out of the corner of my eye and saw, much to my surprise, that he appeared perfectly composed. For some reason that bothered me. "I have a question," I said. "And I'm only going to ask once. Where was he getting the drugs?"

"How would I know?" Casey's innocent face seemed too prac-ticed to be honest. I slammed on the brakes, and my Toyota slid to a stop with a reluctant groan. I turned in my seat.

"Tell me, Casey."

I stared at him, and I was shocked to see his expression collapse under my gaze into unguarded panic. The words came a moment later with the speed of a confession. "I don't know where he scored the coke, but I was getting him the uppers. Nate still has some connections. I didn't think it would be a big deal. Lots of guys use greenies at the plate. I was just trying to help."

"Oh, you were very helpful." The sarcasm felt cheap even to me, but Casey nevertheless sank even deeper into his seat. His voice, when it emerged, sounded as thin and forlorn as an aban-doned calf.

"What do you think Molly will say?"

My anger, which had been simmering along in its usual passive-aggressive form, exploded like a badly tapped oil well. "Jesus, that's the last thing in the goddamned world you should be think-ing about. I mean, could you be more fucking self-centered?"

"Why are you so pissed at me?"

"Because Terrell is supposed to be your friend, Casey. And you let me stand up and lie about him. You pretend not to care about reporters and good press and the whole bullshit game, but the one time it really mattered, you sold out your friend to save your own ass."

"Is it my fault he's dead?"

I knew the real answer to that question, and if I were a better man I would have instantly relieved Casey of a burden he didn't need to carry. But I was too tired and angry. "That's a question you're going to have to ask yourself," I said.

We didn't speak for the remaining twenty minutes of the drive. After I dropped Casey off at his apartment, I sped to my hotel as quickly as my four-valve engine would take me. I felt as dirty as I've felt in a long time. Maybe my duplicity hadn't really hurt anyone—and maybe I'd helped a friend—but I didn't feel as if I'd presented a real profile in courage that evening. Furthermore, the final act of my performance had been perhaps the least honest. The real source of my anger at Casey had nothing to do with Terrell or the drugs or the party. In a moment of crisis, when his brain could have been occupied with either concern for his friend or selfish questions about his own future, the issue that had bothered Casey the most was how Molly would view the evening. And, even worse, I was fully aware that until that moment Molly had never entered my own thoughts.

I took a long, hot shower, then lay in bed and turned on ESPN. They were showing replays of the World's Strongest Man competition from a Club Med on one of the Caribbean Islands. I had been watching for about ten minutes when they abruptly cut away from a keg toss and transferred us to the studio in Connecticut. A sleepy anchor, who, like most ESPN anchors, has made a career out of being glib, told me what I already suspected: Terrell Jordan, thirty-four, had been pronounced dead upon his arrival at Deaconess-Glover Hospital. The anchor added that an "unnamed source" had mentioned drugs as a possible cause of death.

I watched as ESPN ran a hastily produced tribute segment—mostly shots and clips from his glory days in Chicago with the Cubs. The Terrell on the television looked like the larger-than-life superstar he had once been, and when the contrast between the image on screen and my memory of his prone body became too great, I hit the power button on the remote control. I rolled over and stared at the clock and was relieved when Molly called at 3 A.M.

"Hey," she said when I picked up the phone. "Did I wake you?"

"No," I said.

"Are you okay? A girlfriend called and gave me the scoop."

"Long night."

She waited for me to continue, but I had no interest in reliving anything that had happened. When she spoke, her tone was cautious. "Is Casey okay?"

"Oh, he's just peachy," I said.

Somewhere buried in my sarcasm she must have heard my distress because she didn't snap at me. "What's the matter?" she asked.

"We weren't exactly heroes tonight."

"It's okay," she said. "You don't have to be a hero all the time."

"Maybe not." I paused, and a tiny crocodile tear seared its way down my cheek. "But it would be nice to be one every now and then."

Part 3

Chasing the Pennant

chapter 22

I AWOKE THE NEXT MORNING TO THE UNPLEASANT SOUND OF both the motel phone and my cellular ringing at the same time. Choosing blindly, I grabbed the cell. I had picked poorly—John Abbot's voice came pounding through the line.

"Tell me you were there," he said. "That's all I want to hear."

"I found him in the bathroom."

Abbot made a noise that sounded like a reserve fullback celebrating his third touchdown of the game. "You beautiful bastard. When can you get me the story?"

"I'm not writing it."

Abbot didn't say anything for a minute, and in my imagination I could see him ripping the legs off a voodoo doll dressed like me. "I'm sorry it happened this way, kid," he eventually said. "But this is the opportunity of a lifetime. Most reporters would drool at this chance. We've got a once-great player falling apart on the field and then blasting his brain to shreds at a team party. That's Shakespearean, buddy."

I lay back on my bed. "Then get one of the jock poets you've got sniffing around the office to write it."

Abbot's tone sharpened like one of his articles after editing. "I'll pass that off because I woke you so early. But—"

"I'm not writing the story. Period."

I snapped the phone shut and glanced at the clock. It was before eight—far too early for me to face the world. I unplugged the motel phone from the wall, shut my cell in the minibar, and went back to bed and slept until noon. When I finally awoke, I ordered a pizza from Domino's. I ate half the pie for lunch, watched soaps all afternoon, and finished the other half for dinner. On my way to the soda machine to buy a third Coke to flush the cheesy grease down my recoiling esophagus, I saw the cover of the *Boston Globe*. Jessica Young's photo covered half the front page, Terrell's inert face in perfect focus. Although my knee was in the picture, they'd cropped out the rest of my body. My knee was famous.

The next morning I decided that the time had come for me to emerge from my room, so I walked down to a local coffee shop to read the morning papers. The first in-depth articles about Terrell dominated the sports section. The coroner had already determined that the combination of uppers, steroids, and cocaine had basically exploded his heart, and I felt a tiny glimmer of guilty satisfaction as I noticed that the reporters had all pitched their articles exactly the way I'd anticipated—a tragic story of a guy who felt the pressure of Major League Baseball too acutely. And no one incriminated Casey or any other member of the Red Sox.

I went to the ballpark that afternoon and watched most of the game from the press box without taking a single note. The Sox had draped black bunting over the home dugout and across the back of the bullpen wall, and before the game they held a moment of silence. Casey didn't play. I was spinning my pencil up and down my knuckles, my eyes idly running over the box score, when someone tapped me on the shoulder. I slowly turned my head, expecting to confront a reporter with a fishing pole, but instead saw Jessica. She was wearing sweatpants and a T-shirt and had strapped two cameras around her neck and a film pack around her waist. She remained striking.

"Hey," I said, trying to sound disinterested and a little annoyed.

She appraised me for a long moment, her expression far more curious than it had been the night of the party. "You were impressive in that bathroom."

I swung around on my chair and glanced meaningfully at the phalanx of reporters surrounding us. "Can we talk about this somewhere else?"

We stepped out of the press box and walked down the long, institutional hallway to an empty broadcast booth. The team had hung a photograph of Yaz standing in left field on the sound-proofed wall, and as my eyes flashed from the picture to the window, I realized that the only real change in the landscape since the 1960s was the obscene inflatable bottles that the Sox had recently allowed Coca-Cola to lash to the top of the Monster.

I was still gazing out the large window when Jessica impatiently interrupted me. "You wanted something?" she asked. "I have to work, you know."

I slowly turned, and I could feel a little red ball of anger building behind my eyes. I enjoyed the feeling—anger is one of the few things that manages to effectively focus me—and when I spoke I clipped my words. "Tell me, Jessica. Did you make a lot of money off that picture?"

She batted her eyes expertly. "Which picture?"

She was almost irresistible enough to get away with it, but the blustery energy of my anger kept me primed. "The one in every paper in the country," I said. "I think you've seen it. I'm sure that's exactly the way Mrs. Jordan wanted her husband remembered."

"Don't get snippy with me," she said, cocking her head. "You're writing a story on it."

"No, I'm not."

We stared at each other, and I could see both amusement and confusion on her face. She was still examining me when she spoke. "I didn't take you for a player pimp."

"What the hell does that mean?"

"I thought you and I were at the party for the same reason," she said. "To do a job."

"Do you remember our conversation in the library?" I asked, still annoyed. "I told you I was a writer, not a reporter."

"Maybe you don't understand the difference." I could feel my-self bristle, but she spoke before I could cut her off. "Sure, a re-porter would write a dumb-ass article about what happened and hurt people for no reason. But a real writer would also do the ar-ticle. Instead of dodging his responsibility, he'd ask the real ques-tions. And maybe something worthwhile would come from a horrible night."

I walked out of the booth without saying good-bye, and later in the press box I felt myself growing more and more irritated. I knew that there must be some flaw in her logic, but I couldn't find it. And since I couldn't find it, her indictment of me became in-creasingly damning. I left the game in the seventh inning, and rather than going back to my dirty motel room, I took the T downtown and strolled along the wharves. Although the cold, damp wind coming off Boston Harbor tore viciously through my flimsy windbreaker, the intense chill made me feel better. I had walked all the way out to the tip of Pier Four when my cell phone rang. It was Casey.

"You weren't in the locker room after the game," he said, his tone frosty.

I held the receiver tight against my numb ear. "I didn't feel like it."

"What?"

I cupped my hand over the microphone to shield it from the wind. "I'm getting tired of seeing you guys naked."

"Terrell's funeral is tomorrow," he said, his tone admonishing me for having the gall to make a joke.

"When and where?"

"South End at noon. There's a big cathedral." He paused and all I could hear was rushing air and static. "Will you go with me?"

Something in his voice was so tentative, so frightened, that I temporarily forgot my anger. "Of course," I said. "I'll pick you up in the morning."

chapter 23

FOUR THOUSAND FRIENDS OF THE FAMILY CAME TO THE FU-
neral at the large brick cathedral in the South End. Only the presence of Casey ensured that I was one of the lucky eight hundred
the police let inside. We sat in a section near the front reserved
for the team, and while I silently fretted that one of the players
would protest my presence, nobody gave me a second glance.
Perhaps my actions at the party had earned me a spot.

The cathedral was Catholic, but the ceremony was Baptist—
apparently no Baptist church in Boston was big enough for the
expected crowd. Since I only enter churches to attend weddings
and funerals, I never quite know how to behave. I stand when
other people stand, sing when other people sing, but mostly just
feel uncomfortable. Terrell's funeral, however, was one of those
moments when I truly saw a purpose for religion. André Dawson,
whom I knew only as a guy who could pound a baseball, gave a
moving eulogy for his dead friend. The priest was funny when it
was appropriate to be funny, strict when taking a collection for
Terrell's family, and somber when wishing Terrell a safe passage
into heaven. The service concluded with a long rendition of

"Amazing Grace," and if tears hold the key to catharsis, everyone came out of the church a little healed.

Since it was a public funeral, the press was waiting outside when we stepped into the bright September sun. I began leading Casey through the crowd, dodging reporters, but he pulled away from me. Without uttering a single explanatory word, he walked to one of the top steps of the cathedral and stood in front of an enormous door. The cameras swiftly clustered around him, the reporters following their instincts. Casey reached into the inside pocket of his dark suit and pulled out a neatly folded piece of yellow paper.

"I have a statement," he said. A reporter in the back got out the first few words of a question, but someone wisely nudged him in the ribs. Casey unfolded the paper and began reading.

"Baseball, the American game, is a game of failure. Even the best hitters fail twice as often as they succeed. Maybe that's why the talk radio people love baseball so much, because everyone fails sometime. Nobody is immune.

"In this game of failure, Terrell beat the odds for a long time. And when things went badly—and they went badly this whole season—he took his failures with a grace that I will never forget.

"I am trying to avoid blaming anyone for what happened. Terrell made his own choices, and one of those choices cost me my friend. But I think we would all be better off if we could remember the way we used to act in ballparks. The way we used to feel about baseball. Because if baseball is just a game that eighteen rich guys play in front of a bunch of drunk fans so that owners and television announcers and talk radio guys can make money, then I don't know why I play. And I don't know why you watch."

As Casey had gained momentum in his speech, the piece of paper had drooped and his eyes had become fixed on the center camera. But when he paused, his face contorting in a vain attempt to stifle tears, he shoved the paper into his pants pocket and his gaze dropped to the ground. I thought he had finished and was stepping forward to lead him to the car when he swallowed hard and refocused his eyes on the cameras.

"There was no magic left in baseball for Terrell. It was just a job. And no job, no matter how much money they pay you, is worth what he went through."

Casey again dropped his head and carefully picked his way down the steps. The shouted questions from the line of reporters were more respectful than usual, and I had no trouble cutting through the crowd to his side. When we slammed the doors of my car, Casey slumped against the window and closed his eyes.

"You okay?" I asked.

"I was friends with the guy for a month," Casey said. "One month. But this is fucking killing me." He took a deep breath and opened his eyes. "Let's find a bar, okay?"

We drove into Boston's financial district and found a pub covered with lawyers taking a liquid lunch break. We sat in a booth, Casey's back to the room so nobody would recognize him, and drank quietly for a while. The silence felt pleasant rather than onerous—I think we both needed some companionship—and my shoulders were just beginning to relax for the first time in several days when Casey began to talk.

"Can I tell you a story I read in a book?" I nodded, curious. "It's by this Harvard anthropologist who went down to the rain forests. Anyway, he's studying these aboriginal people—a really cool tribe that believes in using this particular kind of hallucinogen for religious purposes—and after a year or two of studying them, he decides that to really understand their culture he needs to try the drug. So he licks a frog or something and goes on this deep trip. Much worse than LSD. And in the middle of the trip, he meets these superintelligent aliens. They come out of this enormous ship and tell him that they're planning on taking over the world. They've got a secret plan and sometime in the next few years they're going to start shooting. And at the very end they tell him that if he mentions a single word about their plan to anyone, they'll kill him.

"Anyway, the Harvard guy wakes up in this little hut in the rain forest, covered in sweat, the shaman standing over him. And he decides that if he tells the shaman really quickly about the alien's plan, they won't have time to kill him. So he spills the story as fast as he can get it out of his mouth, just tripping over the words in his rush. And when he's done, the shaman looks at him very seriously, puts his hand on his shoulder, and says, 'Don't worry. They always say that. But they lie.' "

I laughed when Casey finished, but he was staring at me, his face completely earnest. "Cool story," I said, swallowing hard.

"Yeah," Casey said. "And the more you think about it, the cooler it gets."

We were quiet again for half a beer as my alcohol-addled mind wondered why Casey had suddenly decided to share the obscure work of a Harvard anthropologist with me. Casey must have sensed my confusion because he eventually smiled for the first time in several days. "You want to know what aliens and aborigines have to do with Terrell."

"It's not an obvious connection. But I think I get it."

"Analyze me," he said.

I paused, reluctant for two reasons. For starters, I've never had a good conversation that began with critiquing a friend's life. Second, it seemed as if Casey needed to spend some time rambling. And I was perfectly willing to listen. So instead of answering his question directly, I decided to prompt him. "It has something to do with expanding your interests."

Casey shrugged. "Kind of." He drank heavily from his beer, and then the words came in a rush. "I don't want to be the man I can feel myself becoming."

"You're becoming the best baseball player of the last twenty years," I said.

"Do you think there's more to me than baseball?" I stared at him, trying to think of the perfect response, but he must have taken my silence as a negative because his eyes fell to the table. "Molly thinks so," he said quietly. "And when I'm around her, I believe it. She makes me want to be more."

At that moment I saw the depths of Casey's feelings toward Molly for the first time. He had just said that he loved her in terms so clear that even I could understand. He loved her because she was the only person in the world who saw him the way he wanted to be seen—as more than a phenomenal athlete, more than an endorsement opportunity or a can't-miss segment on the evening news. Casey desperately needed to believe that his gifts went beyond the ability to hit a white leather ball, and Molly, ever since she'd begun handing him books in junior high, had been the one person who had treated his athletic abilities as just one of his talents rather than the whole package. For that reason alone he loved her fully, completely. Because she gave him the space to be the person he wanted to be.

I wish that I had reacted to my revelation in a way that reflected well on my essential decency; I would prefer to lie and say that my friendship with Casey made it possible for me to see him as more than just a threat. But the first emotions that engulfed my chest were fear and jealousy. I wasn't even comforted by Casey's ineloquence—just the fact that his love existed was like knowing that the Russians have somehow managed to "lose" enough nuclear material to make several atomic weapons.

"I don't think you're going to get much sympathy with the self-pity act, Casey," I eventually said. "Almost every man in this country would give up a testicle to be in your position."

"Is that the point?" Casey asked, his tone suggesting that I ought to know better. "A lot of people would love to be highly paid lawyers or Wall Street guys. Well, you went to Yale. You could be making a lot of money and having people kiss your ass. But you're not. You're a writer."

"I'm an idiot. Don't use me as an example of anything."

"All I'm saying is that just because you're good at something doesn't mean that you have to do it," Casey said. "I'm good at baseball, which means I have the option to play baseball. But maybe I'd be happier as an anthropologist or police officer or forest ranger."

"Getting to play a game for a ton of money . . . Listening to thirty thousand people cheer for you . . . These aren't such bad things."

Casey's chin dropped to the table and his eyes got vacant as if his brain had checked out for an extended stay at a health spa. "No," he said slowly. "Maybe not." He banged his chin against the table several times, hard enough that I could feel the wood vibrate beneath my palm. "I've got to get my head on straight."

"You should take a couple days away," I said. "Go to Maine or something."

Casey looked at me as if I'd just suggested he play naked. "During a pennant race?" he asked, incredulous. "In Boston? They'd burn an effigy of me in the Public Garden. Trust me, my ass will be on the field tomorrow."

That afternoon Casey drove to Terrell's house to give Ayana Jordan an enormous amphora filled with roses that he'd bought at the most expensive flower shop in Boston. Casey had only met Ayana twice—Terrell had believed in keeping his baseball and private lives separate. When Casey got to the brick mansion, he was too scared to go inside, so he sat in his car for half an hour and watched the long line of delivery men and well-wishers trickle in and out the front door. He might have sat in the car all day, but a cop eventually wandered over to investigate the strange man staking out the Jordan's property, and Casey had to sign another round of autographs for a police department.

When he finally entered the house, holding the amphora and flowers in front of his body like a hoplite's shield, he discovered that an impromptu wake had sprouted. Men and women dressed in their Sunday finest filled the rooms, and Terrell's older brother was hosting a cookout in the backyard. Casey fled for the bathroom. He splashed some water on his face, trying to collect himself, and when he finally emerged, he was on a strict mission to find Ayana, give her the flowers, and beat a hasty retreat. He searched the entire house before finally discovering her upstairs in a guest bedroom with an auditioning group of slick lawyers. Casey stood in the door and listened for ten minutes. The lawyers were trying to convince Ayana to sue both the Red Sox and Fletcher for damages, and Casey could tell from the rapt expression on her face that they weren't wasting their time.

At a pause in the pitch, Casey stepped forward and offered the flowers to Ayana. "These are for you," he said. "I'm really sorry."

The lawyers all hovered uncomfortably in the background while Ayana kissed Casey on the cheek and gave him a long hug. When they separated, Casey waved his arm at the rest of the room. "Why are they here already?"

One of the lawyers, a man who runs personal injury advertisements during the local news, stepped forward. "We're just here to make sure that Mrs. Jordan gets what she is owed," he said. "She has suffered a terrible loss."

Casey turned and glared at him so intensely that even the practiced lawyer—battle hardened by a thousand belligerent expressions on the stand—recoiled slightly. "I didn't ask the pimp," Casey said, every word crisp. "I asked the grieving widow if the legal parasites were taking advantage of her."

Ayana stepped forward, regal and composed, and gently rested her hand on Casey's arm. "It's okay. These men are here to help me. They're real professional—some of the best-paid lawyers in Boston."

"Just because they earn a thousand dollars an hour doesn't mean they aren't sleazy," Casey said. "They shouldn't be here."

Ayana's hand snapped back to her side, and she drew her head so erect that the tendons in her neck showed. "Get out of my house," she said, her tone tinged with the beginning of hysteria. "What the hell do you know about what my family needs?"

"You're right," Casey said quietly. And he turned on his heel and left.

Casey drove from Terrell's house to the gravesite. Mourners had been filing past the fresh earth and temporary stone all afternoon, and Casey stood at the end of the long line and waited his turn. Since he was wearing a ski cap and sunglasses, nobody recognized him—or at least nobody was insensitive enough to ask for an autograph. When his turn to shuffle past the grave finally came, he knelt amid the pasture of fresh flowers and lowered his lips as close to the ground as possible. He whispered something for at least thirty seconds until one of the police officers eventually wandered over from his post and put his hand on Casey's shoulder.

"Keep moving," the officer said.

Casey peered up at him, and the officer flinched as he abruptly realized that he hadn't interrupted just another anonymous mourner. "I'm doing my best," Casey said softly.

Later that afternoon Casey drove to a park in Brookline with a view of the distant, huddled skyscrapers of downtown Boston. He stayed in his car—the engine off but the power on—and tuned the radio to one of the ubiquitous local pop stations that play interchangeable songs. Eventually the radio began to fade, and he had to start the engine to keep the battery from dying. He watched as the edges of the great glass buildings turned red with the setting sun, the windows flashing and then fading one after another. On his way out of the park he tossed a crumpled piece of paper into a trashcan, which was promptly retrieved by a local schoolteacher who had noticed him on top of the hill. Most of the paper is covered with random scribbles, but a few items are clear enough to read: the word *warning* written in ornamental script, a crude sketch of a baseball, and a rough imitation of the back of a baseball card.

CASEY FOX	Fox, Casey—6' 2" 220 lbs.
CATCHER	B. Unknown, Providence, RI
	D. Unknown

	G	AB	H	HR	RBI	BA	SA
2000 BOS	Are these goddamned numbers my life?						

chapter 24

TO SETTLE MY OWN MIND AFTER THE FUNERAL, I DECIDED TO drive down to Providence. Although I toyed with the idea of going to see Eddie, even the chance of having to listen to another lecture on my lack of ethics was unbearable. I really wanted to see Molly, but I had no idea where to begin looking. I knew she wouldn't be at her father's house, and I distantly remembered her mentioning that she was going to stay with a friend from high school. So I took a long tour of the places I'd spent time with her: the Thai restaurant, the movie theater, the coffee shop. Pathetic, I know, but just seeing those spots reminded me of a feeling I desperately needed—companionship.

I was perched outside the movie theater on a bench, watching junior-high couples snap bras and sneak off to make out behind parked minivans, when my cell phone rang. It was Molly.

"I want to come up to Boston," she said as soon as I answered. "You worried me on the phone the other day."

"You're too late." I paused long enough for her imagination to tie the noose and launch me off a stool. "I'm already in Providence."

"When do I get to see you?" she asked.

"Who said I wanted to see you?" She faked a whimper and I felt myself grinning like an idiot. "Tell me where you are."

It turned out that Molly was staying at a small house on a beach north of Providence. She brought an overnight bag to the car, which I celebrated without comment, and we drove to a local lobster shack. I bought two bowls of clam chowder in Styrofoam containers and a lobster for us to share, and we carried our food out on a long breakwater and sat on the rocks. The lobster had been raised on a farm—the meat had the texture of a wet sponge—but we ate it without complaint. The clear air was cold enough that we huddled together for warmth, and when we finished eating we slid into the lee of a large boulder to escape the steady north wind.

"So what brought you to Providence?" she asked when we were settled.

"You did." I still didn't have the self-confidence to leave it there. "And I had to do some research."

Her hand was playing with the hair on the back of my head, her chin resting on my shoulder. "What kind of research?"

I tilted her head toward mine, kissed her gently, and then smiled. "I wanted to see what it was like to hit a home run."

She laughed just enough to let me know that I was pressing my luck. "I think you came to the wrong town," she said with the slightest of smirks. She settled back into me, and I wiggled my cold hand up to the far side of her face and ran my fingers back and forth across the crest of her ear. When she spoke, the soft wool of my sweater muffled her voice. "What are we doing?"

I brought my nose to her forehead, so close that I instinctively held my breath. "I don't know," I said as I softly exhaled. "But it's good, I think."

"Me too." And she said it quickly enough that I knew I hadn't forced it out of her. I suddenly wanted to tell her something personal—something so intimate that she would begin to understand exactly how important she had become to me.

"I used to drink a lot," I said after a moment. She shifted so that her eyes were on my face. "Sometimes alone. I don't think I was a real alcoholic—I think I just liked the image of being a tortured writer."

"That's the stupidest thing I've ever heard," she said.

"Maybe. But the worst thing is that I never even got any words on the page. I've been trying to write this book for six years and I could never get past the first couple chapters." I was staring across the water at the ghostly masts of the boats in the small harbor, too embarrassed to look at her. "Everything changed when I met you. I don't drink alone anymore. And I'm writing faster than Jack Kerouac."

"I'm your muse," she said, her tone light but not mocking.

"Perhaps." I paused, wondering if I should continue. "You do the same thing for Casey."

As soon as I said his name I realized that I'd made the wrong decision. She stiffened under my arm, the coiled muscles of her shoulder and chest tensing against my side, and her leg moved a fraction of an inch away from mine. Casey's name sat in the air like the *Hindenburg*, an enormous, flaming mistake.

"What do I do for Casey?" she asked, clipping her words.

"You make him want to be more than a ballplayer." I was again staring at the thick forest of masts, but my brain was locked on the one thing I'd been meaning to say to her for weeks. "You make him want to be a man."

Her body melded back into mine, and when I turned to her in surprise, she kissed me hard on the mouth. I closed my eyes and kissed her back, but when I peeked I saw that her eyes were wide open. And somewhere in her dark pupils I saw, or imagined I saw, love.

We checked into a chain motel on I-95 north of Providence because going back to Molly's friend's house wasn't an option and we didn't feel like driving back to Boston. And, I suppose, only a motel awaited us in Boston anyway. When I opened the door to the bland room, an entirely unfamiliar feeling rose in my chest. I wanted to be opening the door to my home. Not a place where I ate and slept. A real home. During my years since college I had grown used to telling myself that I enjoyed my itinerant life—and maybe that was true. But I also knew that I had become jealous of my classmates who had found lives for themselves, who were beginning to have children and coach Little League teams and collect things such as commemorative spoons and single malt scotches—all the useless crap that adds up to roots.

We didn't quite know what to do with ourselves when the door closed, so we bustled around the room. She unpacked while I used my Swiss Army knife to uncork a bottle of decent white wine that I had brought from Boston. Since I had forgotten wineglasses, I had to use the Dixie cups from the bathroom. Molly smiled when I handed her the paper cup, perhaps charmed by my inelegance. We perched on the edge of the bed, a few feet between our bodies, and sipped the wine until the bottle was almost empty. I noticed her eyes tracing the worn edges of the curtains and the cigarette burns on the rug, and I felt increasingly guilty as the tiny lines between her eyebrows deepened.

"I feel a little like a prostitute in this motel," she finally said.

"I can understand why." Her nostrils flared like an infield tarp billowing in the wind, and I quickly explained myself. "Guys who look like me generally only end up with girls who look like you if they pay for it."

"You have a very backhand way of making compliments," she said. But I could tell she was mollified because she tossed her Dixie cup onto the floor and lay back on the bed. I mimicked her motions, and when my head was touching the comforter, our hands met, our faces still pointed at the stucco ceiling.

"This is different than the last time we were in a motel," she said.

My mind flashed back to the evening with Molly, Casey, and Rachel in Boston, and blood began pouring to my groin. "The first night."

"That's right." I felt her warm hand stiffen beneath mine. "Don't take this personally, but that night I just wanted to be with someone."

"It's okay," I said. "Just promise that tonight is something different."

"It is," she said. "Tonight I want to be with you."

"Just not in a motel."

She giggled. "That's right. The Four Seasons would be okay, though. You're going to have to sell that book."

"I don't know if it's best-seller material," I said. "It doesn't have any vampires. Nobody's bodice gets ripped. The Russians don't have an evil plan. The main character doesn't drown at sea . . ." I might have continued, but she rolled on top of me, pinning my arms by my side, and kissed me passionately. We began to remove our clothes, but stopped halfway and lay in T-shirts and underwear, our naked legs intertwined like snakes under a heat lamp. We lay still for at least an hour, sometimes kissing, but mostly just examining each other's faces, fingertips running across closed eyes and lips, and sometimes resting cheek to cheek. Although my desire grew like a mushroom cloud at first, I forced myself to relax and enjoy the kinetic connection between our bodies. The wine had made our skin warm, and I felt as if our overlapping heat was melting the space between us into common ground.

At some point an idle part of my subconscious noticed that Terrell and Casey and the Red Sox and the party had all vanished from my mind, vaporized in the time it takes a neuron to fire. I had forgotten—or never known—what it means to lose yourself in someone. To have your problems fall away for a moment; to see the whole world shrink down to a distant mosquito buzzing at the fringes of your consciousness. Molly had given me a gift. And even if her gift wasn't deliberate, an overarching feeling of gratitude nevertheless surged through my body. I briefly wondered why this particular girl was affecting me so deeply, then I realized that I didn't care. I was just grateful that she was lying in bed with me.

• • •

Late that night, when the restless sounds of the motel had faded into a loose cacophony of static, snoring, and the endless footsteps of the overvigilant security guard, Molly got up to go to the bathroom. I was sitting on the edge of the bed when she returned, and she came and stood between my knees. I ran my hand up her smooth, bare leg, and my fingers caught the top of her silk panties. I carefully drew them downward, just enough to expose the slight swell of her hipbone, and I pulled her to me and kissed the tiny canyon between the rise and her lower abdominals.

"I thought you were asexual tonight," she said, teasing.

I ignored her and locked my hand behind her narrow waist. She giggled as I swung her into bed. I kissed upward from her bellybutton to her smiling mouth, pausing briefly in the trough of her breasts, and then back down again to her hip to her bellybutton to her hip, my hand sliding farther down and then up again, my mouth back to her tense abdominals, now loose, the mirth abruptly vanishing from her sounds as she desperately pulled my face upward. We ravenously tore off T-shirts and underwear, my fingers so impatient that her bra came free with a loud snap. She sighed when we joined, one hand in my hair and the other fiercely rubbing my ear and cheek, our eyes unwaveringly locked. Our breath became syncopated, first intense and deep, then short and panting, until finally parting in a pair of long, tremulous sighs.

She went to the bathroom again, and when she returned I lay on my back with her chin resting on my chest. She had to clear her throat before she could speak.

"I don't have a good word to use for sex." I lifted my head off the pillow to look at her, surprised. The comments that emerge from people's mouths after intimate moments never cease to amaze me. "Most of the terms are so crass," she continued, ignoring my curious gaze. "And I always thought that 'making love' was the most ridiculous expression in the world. I dated a sensitive guy in college who was always trying to 'make love' to me. I got so frustrated that I had to dump him—otherwise, I might have had to seduce the lacrosse team or something. Those guys were fuckers. In both senses of the word."

She took a deep breath, and I could feel her firm breast swell against my side. "But this was really nice. I don't know exactly how to say it, but I want you to know that it was nice in a way that means something."

"I understand," I said. And I really did. The previous hour had made me realize exactly how my love for Molly had evolved. I had initially loved the idea of her—her intelligence, her beauty, her wit. Now, however, I loved the reality. The difference had manifested itself even in the way we had sex. I usually perform in bed with the voice of the *Cosmo* woman shouting instructions in my ear: "Do This! Touch That!" The inevitable result is that something that should be pure intimacy instead becomes merely physical. Perhaps this comment demonstrates my lack of expertise, but I've always thought that sex was something like learning to play golf: much frustration, occasional blissful satisfaction.

So the first two times we had been together, I had been so terrified of rocking her pedestal that I had tried to "make love" to her—and she had responded by trying to turn it into an act of pure athleticism. But in a crummy motel north of Providence, we had somehow managed to meet each other halfway.

The next morning began and ended poorly. Molly was in the shower when I awoke, and I crept into the bathroom to surprise her, only to be driven out by a horrified squawk and several muffled but unmistakably obscene comments about stupid boys who fail to properly understand boundaries. I returned to the bedroom and was sulking on the bed watching *SportsCenter* when Molly finally emerged from the bathroom. She ignored my mood and swiftly dressed, pausing only when a snippet of Casey's speech from the church steps appeared on the television. She gestured at the screen. "I can't believe he's famous."

"And soon to be rich," I said a little bitterly.

"That means nothing."

"It means something."

She sat on the corner of the bed, far enough away that I would have had to roll over to touch her, and I could tell from the inconstant expression on her face that she was thinking hard. "You know," she said after a long minute, "one thing used to make baseball beautiful. It was the way a kid could look at Joe DiMaggio or Hank Aaron. But now it's all about getting the money and the episode on MTV about your ridiculous mansion. It's exactly the same bullshit that drives me crazy about America. Tell me, Russ, when did we get so far past comfortable that we destroyed the beauty of things like baseball?"

"It's easy to be cynical," I said. "But don't get so caught up in how much fun it is to knock baseball and America that you ignore the whole story."

"What is the whole story, Russ?"

"I have no idea. All I'm saying—and I don't mean this in a condescending way—is that there may be more to life than you've seen at age twenty-two."

I wasn't sure that I had insulted her until I saw the swath of fiery red burn upward from her cheekbones until the tips of her ears could have ignited a pile of wet leaves. "I don't mean this in a condescending way," she said before she possibly could have counted to ten, "but I'm pretty sure you're missing my fucking point. Let me try to find an analogy that you'll be able to understand." I felt my expression change slightly at her cheap shot, but I just waited, mute, as she thought. "How about this? Don't spend so much time scouting that you never play the game. Not in baseball, not in life, and certainly not in this relationship."

An hour later, as I was driving north to Boston, I finally thought of a witty reply to her comment. But at that moment all I could do was turn away and begin to pack my things.

chapter 25

THE MEDIA PRESSURE IN BOSTON OVER THE NEXT WEEK DE-
fied belief. Not only did all the usual outlets send their teams to
do features, but the story also had enough crossover appeal that
shows and magazines that don't traditionally cover sports sent in-
vestigators: *Nightline* and *Entertainment Tonight* and *People* magazine. Even the tabloids managed to divert resources from the
latest alien abduction case. As the week progressed, Casey gradually became the focal point at the center of the whirlpool—and it
doesn't take a James Carville to figure out why. Nightly news pro-
grams across the country had played excerpts from Casey's eulogy
on the cathedral steps, and the image of a handsome young athlete saying something other than "I'm going to give it 110 percent" resonated with a huge number of people.

Casey responded to the pressure with one of the greatest weeks
a baseball star has ever played. He would stride to the plate for
every at bat with thousands of flashbulbs popping in the stands, a
raucous mixture of cheers and boos rolling over the field, professional photographers clambering over one another to get the best
angle. Opposing pitchers, knowing that his bat was scorching,
threw him nothing but breaking balls in the dirt and fastballs a

foot off the outside corner. Nothing mattered. He hit .650 in the six games after Terrell's funeral, scoring eleven times and hitting five home runs. The Yankees won four of six that week, but the Red Sox swept the Royals and Rangers to pull within two games of the division lead and four games of the wild card slot.

The press box was bursting from all the extra media people in town, and I took to wandering down into the stands when Casey came up to bat. The seats at Fenway are so close together that when the crowd rose to its feet the atmosphere felt like one of the banned terraces at an old English soccer stadium—a mob formed into a single sentient unit that swayed and chanted for reasons beyond any one individual's control. Even in the first inning we would shout Casey's name, our hands clapping, our feet pounding the crumbling gray cement so hard that our knees would ache. And then, when Casey swung at a mediocre pitch and drove it on a line toward some distant corner of the ballpark, we would leap as one beast. If the ball fell into the glove of a lucky fielder, we would sigh and return to our seats, but if it instead skipped on the ground or landed in the stands, we would roar with a single mouth, our shout reverberating off the distant glass of the John Hancock tower, letting the entire city of Boston know that the Red Sox were still charging toward the goddamn Yankees. It was intoxicating.

I didn't see Casey outside the ballpark until Thursday night. He called when the afternoon game ended and asked if I wanted to have dinner. Taking Casey to a restaurant would have been like taking Elvis to a girl's summer camp in 1956, so I bought several bags of Taco Bell and brought them to his apartment. Felix was there—the Sox had promoted him earlier in the week from Pawtucket, probably to keep Casey company—and we slapped hands when I walked in the door.

"Welcome back to the show," I said. I turned to Casey. "You're having a hell of a week."

Casey shrugged, his face blank. "It's okay."

"He's upset because nobody talks to him," Felix said.

My voice squawked with indignation. "Every reporter in America would burn his Rolodex to talk to Casey Fox."

"No, no," Felix said impatiently. "Nobody on the team. I tell him that nobody talks to me either, but he doesn't care."

"I understand why nobody talks to Casey," I said. "Not only has he become a star in a month, which probably pisses everyone off, but he's also an asshole." I looked at Felix. "But why won't anyone talk to you?"

"Remember the strike a couple years ago?" he asked. I nodded—the strike, in fact, had been one of the great blows against my faith in the game. "I was a replacement player."

"You were a scab?" I asked, surprised.

If Felix was offended by my characterization of him, he concealed it well. "I was in the Dodgers' system," he said. "I thought I had a shot at making it someday, but I was just a fat Hispanic kid with a decent forkball. They gave me a choice: be a replacement player, or they'd release me. I wasn't drafted. I didn't have a guaranteed contract. I didn't figure that any other team would even bother picking me up." His eyes rolled toward the ceiling, his mouth twisted in a slight frown. "I think I'd probably do it again."

Casey, who was lying on his back on the couch, spoke with the anger that should have been in Felix's voice. "He says it doesn't piss him off when the millionaires in the clubhouse won't even look at him. But I know he wants to pop a couple guys in the head during batting practice."

Felix appeared embarrassed, but didn't say anything, and the room was silent for a few minutes. A few weeks earlier I'd heard a story in the Red Sox clubhouse that had sickened me. The Sox had a right fielder who had been a replacement player, and during a pigpile in an on-field brawl, several members of the other team had kicked him in the back. I idly wondered at the time why none of his teammates had come to his defense, and I decided that it must have been because none of the other Sox players had seen the incident. But a clubhouse attendant, speaking in a hushed voice, had told me that I was mistaken. Nobody had come to his aid for the simple reason that he had once been a scab—and the players' union does not forgive scabs.

When Casey got tired of the silence, he picked up the remote control and began flipping through channels while I moved the Taco Bell tacos and enchiladas from the bags to the table. He stopped on a sports quiz show. We watched silently for several minutes until one of the contestants selected American League Rookies.

"Which current player holds the Major League record for most home runs by a rookie in the month of August?" the host asked.

"Mark McGuire?" guessed a pale man in an ill-fitting suit who was probably going to owe the show money by the end of the half hour.

"It's me, you asshole," Casey said. His anger swelled exponentially over the next few seconds as the other two contestants stared blankly at the camera. "Jesus, don't any of these monkeys read the goddamned newspaper?"

"This is surreal," I said.

"Not as surreal as it's going to be in five minutes," Casey said, his sudden anger swiftly receding.

"What happens in five minutes?"

"Just wait."

Four minutes and fifty-six seconds later Casey flipped to one of those news magazine shows where they always use a soft camera. I thought his choice was curious until Casey's face suddenly appeared on the screen. I picked up a taco and covered it in hot sauce, but I couldn't eat it because I was laughing too hard to put anything in my mouth. The show had somehow acquired home videos of Casey playing Little League, and the narrator, speaking softly in the background, was doing his best impression of Kathie Lee. "When Casey Fox was thirteen," the voice said, "he began living at the home of Sean and Mary McDowell. The McDowells were impoverished—financially, not spiritually—but they somehow managed to find a way to feed another mouth."

"What kind of crap is this?" Casey asked in the background. "Old man McDowell is about as spiritual as Karl Marx."

The profile continued, carefully shaping the rough details of Casey's life into the fairy-tale redemption of a lonely orphan. But before the program broke for a commercial, the music abruptly changed, the camera darkened, and the narrator promised in a grim voice that "Casey would meet a new series of challenges in the big city of Boston."

We were all laughing as an advertisement for women's hygiene products played on the screen. "I wonder what they've got on me," Casey said. He didn't appear particularly apprehensive, and I tried to imagine how I would feel if I were in his position, my life being dissected on screen for the entertainment of millions of Americans. A title for my profile flickered through my brain: Russell Bryant, a portrait of mediocrity. I wondered if my relationship with Molly would redeem or condemn me in the eyes of my countrymen.

When the show returned from commercial, Casey turned up the volume. A few shots of Casey hitting home runs for the Sox ran across the screen until the last one—a still photograph—abruptly negatized.

"Cheap effect," I mumbled, low enough that my voice wouldn't carry over the narrator. His tone had shifted into a rough imitation of the host of America's Most Wanted.

"But Casey would fall in with the wrong crowd when he got to Boston," the narrator continued. "And big-city temptations would prove to be too much for this small-town kid. His closest friend on the team became Terrell Jordan, a former party animal who was trying to reform but still privately fighting his own demons. And, making matters worse, Casey started dating Rachel Brown, an exotic dancer with known links to superagent Howard Reich, a man known for getting his clients anything they want."

I was leaning closer to the screen, my mouth no longer chewing the taco, when Casey slammed the remote control. The image disappeared.

"What the fuck was that?" I asked, trying to act as if I were surprised. Nothing about Rachel had ever seemed authentic to me.

Casey stood, his cell phone appearing in his hand. "I'm going to find out," he said. He stalked across the room toward the kitchen, the deliberate set of his jaw indicating that Ms. Rachel Brown was about to receive a merciless grilling.

"Give her a chance," I called after him. "Maybe it's not true." His pace didn't slow. "Maybe she just needs the money." The door slammed, authoritatively enough to let me know that I had been wasting my breath. When I turned back to Felix, he was eating a soft taco and examining me closely.

"Defending a dirty ho," he said. "You're worse than Johnnie Cochran." And his gaze was so accusing that I wondered if he could see my real motivation—that with Casey dating Rachel, I would never need to worry about his influence on Molly.

We had torn through the pile of food on the table and were watching the Mets-Braves game when Casey finally emerged from his room. I flipped the television off.

"It's over," he said, his voice flat. "The report was pretty much right. She's an agent whore."

"I'm sorry," I said. Felix mumbled his support.

"Not a big deal," Casey said. "I didn't really care about her. But it's still a crappy thing to do to someone."

"You wear your little hat every time you were with her?" Felix asked.

"Yeah."

Felix shrugged. "Then no worries, boss."

Casey grunted something incoherent, lay back on the couch, and stared at the ceiling. Felix and I, meanwhile, focused on the blank television screen as if *Playboy* were holding a huge Playmate sleepover and pillow fight. I desperately wanted to say something to relieve the brooding atmosphere in the room, but I couldn't think of any appropriate topics.

"Was the agent really Howard Reich?" I eventually asked, figuring that any conversation would be better than none.

"Yeah," Casey said in a tone that explained he didn't want to talk about it. I had met Reich when I was working for the *Times*.

He fit the mold of what I consider a typical agent, which meant that he had nothing in common with Jerry McGuire. The new breed of agents drips with cell phones and laptops and Palm Pilots—the newer the better—and seems locked in an escalating arms race to see who can average the most incoming calls per day. Reich, for example, told me three sentences into our conversation that his "daily ring average" hovered near four hundred even in the off-season. But I always thought that Reich's true identifying feature was his hair, which looked as if it had been lopped off a particularly greasy beaver.

I was half-smiling when Casey abruptly straightened on the couch. "What the hell's happening in that Braves game?" he asked.

Felix leapt for the remote control faster than I thought his big body could move—he must have been bored beyond reason—and the television flashed to the right channel.

"Since when have you started watching the National League?" I asked.

"Since I started thinking about the World Series," Casey said, his voice so matter-of-fact that I never thought to laugh.

chapter 26

Looking back, I think one of the bonds between Casey and me was that we both perceived a decline in our respective disciplines. Writing may be a continually evolving art form, but over the last thirty or so years the quality of writing has not simply evolved. It's gotten worse. The impoverishment of our language stems largely from the idea that the average American reader wants bells and whistles and one-line jokes rather than substance. What other explanation exists for why the average length of feature stories in national magazines has dropped 50 percent since 1970? Or why those same magazines hire "writers" who think a semicolon is an unpleasant medical procedure?

The real source of the problem is that fewer children read extensively these days, which means that America is developing fewer competent writers—and readers. Our cultural environment also doesn't help. Every sports fan knows the face of the crappiest ESPN anchor, but Frank Deford can walk through the grandstand at Yankee Stadium without drawing many long looks. I don't want to limit my criticism to sports writing—after all, no writer of fiction these days draws the attention of a Fitzgerald or a Salinger—and I don't mean to imply that the lack of famous writers necessarily implies a decline in the discipline. But when you combine modern magazine culture, a less-discriminating audience, and a country unable to fully celebrate the gifts of its best writers, then perhaps the transparent flaws in my profession become easier to understand.

Casey also felt that his discipline had waned, but for vastly different reasons. For all the phenomenal athletes and home runs and 100-mile-an-hour pitches, the quality of baseball hasn't necessarily improved since the Second World War. While the average modern ballplayer may be faster and stronger than the ballplayer of the 1950s, he doesn't have the same fundamentals. He might drive the ball farther, but he bunts worse and is a grossly inferior situational hitter. Striking out a hundred times in a season used to be one of the most humiliating things that could happen to a player; now it's commonplace. Too many teams play big ball—coaches sit around and wait for some guy jacked on a combination of legal supplements and illegal steroids to hit a home run—rather than trying to carefully work a runner around the bases.

The truth is that even on the field Casey secretly longed to be playing in a different era. He took far less satisfaction from hitting a home run than from advancing a runner or blocking the plate. And I think he had the temperament to have succeeded in an age when pitchers would throw at your head because they didn't like the way you were standing in the batter's box. Casey played catcher with the same fire Bob Gibson used to bring to the mound, and he had the injuries to prove it. He'd broken his fingers at least a dozen times in the previous five seasons—once so badly that bone ripped through the skin. A batter in Rochester had hit him in the head with the barrel of the bat during an elongated follow-through, an injury that required five stitches, and he had sprained his knee in Toronto. His worst accident in a Red Sox uniform came when he was catching a pitcher who needed a little extra break on his slider, and therefore always asked Casey to scratch the cover of the ball on the buckle of his kneepad. Casey had whetted the iron until it was as sharp as a dirk, and during a collision at the plate with a

Twin outfielder, the kneepad had twisted around and cut a four-inch gash in Casey's calf. But none of those injuries ever forced him to miss a game.

Casey also felt that money was ruining baseball. When he arrived in Boston in the fall of 2000, the average baseball player made almost $2 million a year in salary alone. Just a few months later, several players signed deals that would net them $20 million per season. Casey thought that money had spoiled the game in two ways. First, he felt that players were putting individual statistics above the success of the team because individual success is what earns big contracts. Second, he believed that money was one of the primary reasons for the poisonous atmosphere between players and the fans—a guy earning forty thousand a year who has to fork over two hundred bucks to take his family to the ballpark is far more likely to resent the millionaires on the field.

Casey's solution to this problem was so childish and so beautiful that I smile every time I think of it. He knew that capping players' salaries would just redistribute wealth from the players to the owners, so he instead derived a complex plan. Ticket prices would be set by the commissioner's office at exactly the rate that would keep the stands full, and every team would have to abide by a strict salary cap. The television and gate money would go into a common pool. A certain percentage would be allocated to the players, a certain percentage to the owners, a certain percentage to promoting baseball, a certain percentage to youth development, and a substantial percentage would be returned to the community through a variety of charities. It was a plan that would make baseball truly America's game.

Of course, Casey's ideas would be harder to implement than a sensible national tax code, and they also wouldn't solve the problem that Casey took the most personally—the fact that baseball players are celebrities (which, as Joe DiMaggio or Babe Ruth would have told him, isn't exactly a new phenomenon). Casey hated every aspect of being a celebrity. He hated being recognized in public; he hated hearing his name on the radio and seeing his face on television; he hated the reality that his life had changed when he arrived in Boston. And with a week and a half remaining in the regular season, all his fear and mistrust of the public life was justified.

That afternoon I was walking from Fenway to my car when my cell phone rang. The game had just ended, and I barely heard the electronic chime over the buzz from the jubilant crowd. When I answered, I was surprised to hear Casey on the other end of the line—I had figured he would have been surrounded by reporters.

"I need your help," he said.

I paused, just long enough to serve him notice that I still hadn't recovered from the last time I'd helped him. "What do you need?"

"A guy who says he's my dad is waiting outside the locker room."

"I'll be right there," I said. Before I snapped the phone shut, I was already pushing against the spilling mass of fans, a rat fighting to get back on a sinking ship. By the time I reached the locker room, my legs were tired and my shirt was splattered with beer and mustard. Casey wasn't at his locker, and I paced restlessly until one of his kinder teammates told me in a whisper that he was probably in the trainer's room. I pushed through the bright red door, ignoring the sign that read "Members of the Media Not Allowed Past This Point," and found Casey sitting alone on a padded trainer's table. He was carefully wrapping and unwrapping his wrist with white athletic tape.

"Is it really him?" I asked.

"Beats the hell out of me," Casey said. "Anything's possible."

"Have you ever met him?"

"I don't even know his name. But he's got a camera crew with him. That's not a great sign, is it?"

"No," I said because there was nothing else to say.

Casey sent me out to negotiate with the camera crew—a team from one of the tabloid shows—and they insisted that the reunion between Casey and his "father" needed to occur on camera. I pushed for a private meeting until the producer, a man with a thinning ponytail and bad skin, waved a thick contract in front of my nose, and I abruptly changed tactics.

"Do you have proof that this guy is the real deal?" I asked. I could see the subject of our conversation, a paunchy white man only a few years older than me, lurking at the far end of the hall.

"We got a copy of the birth certificate and he's willing to take a blood test," the producer said.

I didn't like having to rely on the research of a sleazy show, but I didn't have much choice. "What's his name?"

The producer checked his clipboard. "Buck Stiener."

"And how much are you guys paying him for the story?"

"I can't tell you that," the producer said, annoyed. I couldn't quite suppress my smile—he had already answered my real question. I turned and walked back into the trainer's room. Casey was lying on the table, the white athletic tape abandoned by his side.

"Real deal?" he asked when I came through the door.

"Maybe," I said. "No way of knowing."

Casey sat up. "How old is he?"

"Young. He must have been a teenager when you were born."

"That's what I always figured," Casey said. He stood and started toward the door, his face frozen into a welcoming smile that was eerie around the edges. He stopped on the threshold and looked back at me, the smile disappearing. "If you're a reporter, you'll want to see this," he said. "If you're a friend . . ." He shrugged nonchalantly. "Maybe not."

"They don't pay me the big bucks for nothing," I said. But I could tell from Casey's expression that my joke hadn't concealed my eagerness, and I felt guilty as I trailed him into the hall.

The camera crew reacted like metal shavings to a magnet the moment we opened the door, although they carefully left a small aisle to allow Casey's "father" his dramatic walk. Casey didn't see the man until he was ten feet away, and when he did, he twitched. The camera crew panned from one startled face to the other.

"Dad?" Casey asked, his choreographed smile never wavering. "Is that really you?"

"Son?" The man opened his arms, and the two men stepped into a hug too awkward for Hollywood.

"It is my dad!" Casey held the man away from his body as the camera jostled to get a tight shot of the tearful reunion. Casey smiled wistfully. "I can't believe you're here," he said, his voice as soft as a drag bunt. "Last I heard you were filming gay porn in Thailand."

The man abruptly stiffened and extracted himself from the embrace. "Excuse me?"

"Or were you pimping twelve-year-old girls to support your crack habit? I can never keep them straight."

The man threw a worried glance in the direction of the producer, who just twitched his greasy head. "I don't know what you're talking about, son."

"Oh," Casey said, real surprise in his voice. "Then you must not be my dad. Because he's a real bastard."

The camera crew carefully filmed Casey's dramatic exit, which came complete with a slamming door, and then the red light flickered out. The producer sighed deeply; he'd wasted his trip from Los Angeles. I smiled at him, my expression as friendly as I could manage without my mouth filling with ashes.

"I guess you're going to have to find another father if you want that Emmy." I turned my head and examined the paunchy man, who still seemed stunned. "But you should get a taller one next time. It'll look better when Casey hugs him."

I was halfway through the door to the trainer's room when I heard the producer mutter behind me. "Prick."

I turned on my heel, fast enough that he flinched. "Hey," I said. "I'm sorry you film enemas for a living. But don't take it out on me."

Casey was soaking his feet in one of the hot whirlpool baths, the headphones on his ears blaring hard rock so loud that I could hear it across the room. During a momentary pause in the music, he slid the earpiece down to his neck. I walked over to the whirlpool and dipped my hand in the water. It was so warm that the tendons in my forearm liquefied.

"Are you sure you won't regret that?" I eventually asked.

Casey shrugged. "He's a bastard either way, right? Either he's my dad and had the lack of class to show up with a film crew, or he's some guy grubbing for a moment in the spotlight. Either way, he comes out a loser."

Despite all the bravado in Casey's speech, I could tell he was shaken. I wondered if he could possibly be telling the truth. Although my relationship with my own father constantly teeters between begrudging acceptance and outright antipathy, I would never pretend that his existence doesn't matter to me. Casey could claim that his father was irrelevant until his lungs collapsed, but I found it impossible to believe that somewhere in the hidden depths of his soul he wasn't at least curious. I was going to press the issue, but one of the rookies on the team, John Larson-Dwight, stuck his head in the door.

"You seen the trainer?" John asked.

Casey shook his head. "You could check the coach's room."

John closed the door and Casey stared after him, amused. "He's in here every damn day." He thought for a moment. "Of course, if you've got a hyphenated last name, you're probably hurt a lot."

"Yeah," I said. "If I got in a fight, I'm not sure I'd want him with me." I paused and smiled at the irony of my critiquing a professional athlete's manhood. "Not that I'd want me with me." Casey laughed a real laugh, and I felt marginally better. "Let me buy you a beer tonight," I offered. "You've had a long couple of days."

"No thanks," he said. "I'm going to head home and get some sleep. But I'm taking Molly and Nate to dinner tomorrow night. Are you in?"

I should have refused, but discretion has never been one of my strengths. "Sure. It will be good to see them."

I started toward the door and had my hand on the knob when Casey loudly cleared his throat. Amused by the transparency of the device, I turned. The analytic part of my brain, however, wondered what kind of subject would make Casey abandon his usual directness. A moment later I found out.

"You and Molly are becoming good friends." I wasn't sure if it was a question or a statement, and I shifted nervously, feeling as if I were back in seventh grade.

"Yes."

"That's nice." He kept his tone as bland as his words, and the only evidence I could see of his discomfiture was his right hand, which was gripping the edge of the whirlpool bath so tightly that his bicep was stretching his thin white T-shirt. I knew at that moment that if I were smart and brave, I would take the opportunity and tell him everything. But I'm only occasionally smart and never brave, so I just stood dumbly in the doorway and waited for him to either dismiss me or keep talking. He finally gestured at the water swirling beneath his knees.

"Put your feet in this," he said. "It'll relax you. I promise."

"Do I need to be relaxed?" The expression on his face answered my question. "I don't think your teammates would be thrilled to see a reporter bathing his feet in their whirlpool."

"Screw them," he said.

I crossed the room and removed my shoes and socks next to the huge plastic tank. As I bent over, I could feel the warmth of the moist, chlorinated air bubbling up from the whirlpool. I rolled up the cuff of my khaki pants and casually swung myself onto the narrow ledge overhanging the pool—so casually that my butt slipped across the slick plastic and I slid into the water. I hopped out immediately, but my carefully rolled pants were soaked to mid-thigh.

"Clusterfuck," I swore to myself. Casey smiled slightly, his expression so reserved that I knew his mind must be elsewhere. As I waited for the inevitable question, I tried to wring the warm water from my cotton pants. I was relieved to discover that my wallet had remained dry.

"Is Molly really pissed at me?" Casey asked when I had finally finished fiddling. "It's just that she's coming over to my place be-fore dinner and I really want to make it up to her. Whatever I did."

I rolled my eyes dramatically. "I'm sorry, I lost my secret de-coder ring. But maybe one of the other kids will bring it for show-and-tell."

"That was beneath you," Casey said, his tone empty rather than judgmental. I instantly regretted having been so flippant.

"You're okay," I said. "Molly just thought you were selling your-self short with Rachel. That's all."

"She was right," Casey said. "She's always right."

Either the heat of the whirlpool or the conversation was mak-ing me uncomfortable, and I wiggled on the seat until I was sitting roughly opposite Casey, five feet of murky green water between us.

"Do you know why I quit Little League?" Casey asked when I was settled.

"No," I said, not sure if I really wanted an explanation.

"Because she told me to." Casey smiled wryly. "She said that if I played in high school I'd turn into a dumb jock and she'd never be able to love me. She was twelve years old. Can you believe that?" I shook my head, more in sympathy than agreement—I knew Molly's capacity for insight more intimately than Casey could possibly imagine.

"So why did she let you play in college?" I was joking, but Casey took me completely seriously.

"Because she knew I loved the game," he said, his voice barely audible over the stifled buzzing of the whirlpool.

I tried to stifle the tight feeling that instantly rose in my chest. I pulled my flushed legs from the hot water and carefully used one of the trainer's towels to dry my calves and feet, paying special at-tention to the cracks between my toes. But my mutinous imagi-nation, which seemed determined to drive me insane, refused to be distracted. It painted me a vivid picture of Casey as a thirteen-year-old kid, abandoned, only one person in the world upon whom he could truly rely. I felt as churlish as I have felt in my life. I pulled on my socks and slipped into my shoes.

"You want my advice?" I finally asked. He nodded, mute. "Tell her that you were overwhelmed when you got to Boston. You didn't know anyone, the whole sob story. Now you've got your feet back on the ground, and you're ready to be the man she thinks you can be."

"You think I should kiss her ass?" he asked, and once again I was reminded of exactly how young he could act.

"Don't say it if you're kissing ass," I said. "Say it if it's true."

chapter 27

CASEY, MOLLY, AND NATE PICKED ME UP AT THE MOTEL IN Casey's car, and we drove to a Japanese restaurant near Harvard Square. Graduate students and professors, who probably wouldn't have recognized Casey if they were holding copies of his baseball card, filled the tables, but Casey nevertheless had booked a private room in the back. We removed our shoes at the sliding door and padded across the reed mat in stocking feet. I waited for everyone to sit, then took the spot next to Nate across the table from Molly and Casey. Molly and I hadn't spoken since I left the motel in Providence, and in the hours before dinner I had carefully constructed a juvenile plan for the evening. I was going to be surly and annoyed and preoccupied until Molly noticed my discomfort, at which point she would submit a tearful apology, I would graciously forgive her, and the Boston Pops would play the closing song from *An Officer and a Gentleman* in the background as we embraced.

The plan failed for two reasons beyond its transparent idiocy. First, the moment I saw Molly in the car, I smiled like an utter idiot. I simply couldn't help myself—just seeing her made me as

happy as I had been in a week. Second, when I recovered my equi-
librium and began acting properly surly, Molly didn't even appear
to notice. The conversation in the car had been filled with jokes
and laughter as I grew ever more annoyed. The idea that Molly
would simply ignore my bad mood had never occurred to me. I
had the moral high ground; I deserved to be appeased—in fact, it
was my inalienable right.

We ordered a round of sake, which arrived in a chilled ceramic
flask. As we bartered over the menu, Molly teased Casey and Nate
over how dirty their apartment had been when she arrived. Nate
shrugged her criticism away with a brother's casual indifference,
but Casey vigorously defended himself.

"It's not my fault," he said. "Companies have been sending me
a ton of crap."

"Why?" I asked, briefly emerging from my funk. "They want
you to endorse them or something?"

Casey nodded. "Since I don't have an agent, they're coming
straight for me. Free gloves, free bats, free shoes, free cars, free
cookies, free suits, free underwear—"

"Free women?" Molly asked softly.

"Women are never free." Casey's arm slid across Molly's shoulders and he squeezed her tightly, his face curling in a broad imitation of a lecherous John. "Right, babe?"

Molly shrugged his thick arm off her shoulders. "Your last
bimbo certainly got her pint of blood." I was just beginning to feel
a warm, secure glow spread upward from my stomach when Molly
abruptly giggled. "God, I'm glad that bitch is gone."

"I still don't understand why you two didn't get along," Casey
said.

Molly dramatically raised her hands and began counting on
her fingers. "Because she was a money-grabbing ho. Because she
sold you out on national television. Because she thinks ordering a
five-hundred-dollar bottle of wine makes a person sophisticated.
Because she dresses like a Thai transvestite."

"And what are you?" Casey asked, smiling slightly.

She set her head at a jaunty angle. "I'm the kind of woman who can kick your ass all day and all night and then make you banana nut pancakes the next morning."

"You better find a guy who likes banana nut pancakes," I said.

"Bullshit," Casey said, the strange smile still on his lips. "Any guy who couldn't love banana nut pancakes for Molly isn't worth her time."

"Boys are ridiculous," Molly said, shaking her head. "It's always about sex or baked goods."

"No, no," Casey said. "It's about sex *and* baked goods. That's love's magic formula."

They were silent for a moment, then simultaneously burst into an unrestrained fit of laughter. When the laughter finally abated, the conversation continued in the same tone, although I was no longer a participant. I knew them both well enough to understand the importance of the moment. Molly had been joking and not joking, making conversation and testing the water at the same time. This Molly with us at dinner was not the demure, brainy, sweet girl that Casey knew. She was something else. And Casey had accepted her abrupt metamorphosis without bothering to blink—which was a miracle that Molly must have noticed.

I eventually summoned the strength to chat casually with Nate, exchanging inanities about popular music and the food on the table, but I soon felt an overwhelming, burning jealousy storming previously sane parts of my mind. I hadn't experienced an emotion that gripping since college. In an attempt to break the spell, I excused myself and went to the bathroom. As I splashed water on my face, I wondered why I was being so irrational. If any-one had a right to feel jealous and upset over being betrayed, it was Casey. But deep down I knew the source of my envy. Every moment I spent with Molly I felt like an impostor—I still hadn't gotten over the idea that she was somehow too good for a guy like me. She and Casey, however, looked right together. I had never envied Casey his swing or his good looks or his assured future. But I bitterly envied him for that.

So when I returned to the table I pounded several quick shots of sake and asked Nate how his quest to become the next Backstreet Boy had been coming. His usual fake scowl descended into a genuine frown.

"It's hard to break in," he said. "I got to get my face up on the TV."

The combination of sake and jealousy in my system finally overwhelmed me, and words started to spill from my mouth like football players fleeing a furious coach. "I've got an idea you can borrow," I began. "It's an invention. You come out with a CD that's filled with little complimentary sounds. Things like 'You're right! Mmm . . . Interesting point. Tell me more!' So when people are driving alone in their cars, they pop your CD in the stereo and when they start talking to themselves they'll have some support. You could sell it on late-night television. Call it the Personal Appreciation CD."

He had stopped listening halfway through my pitch, and when I finished, he waved his hand unenthusiastically. "Sounds like a lot of work, dog."

"Basically you want to be famous without really doing anything," I said.

"Yeah. That's right."

I smiled so grimly that even Molly noticed, and her foot touched mine under the squat table. I refused to be mollified. "Well, you live in the right era," I said.

I hunkered in the backseat on the way back to my motel, once again trying to be just sulky enough that Molly would get the point without Casey or Nate noticing that anything was wrong. But everyone else was talking and joking, still rolling from the sake, and my silence went unnoticed. When we got to the motel, Casey and Nate shook my hand and Molly waved from the front seat. I watched them drive off, the stereo so loud that the car was practically bouncing, and I wondered where Molly would be sleeping that night. Even my knowledge that she had long shared a roof with Casey didn't allay my fears.

I went upstairs and had a slug of whiskey from the flask I keep in my laptop case. I stared at *SportsCenter* for a while, not really watching, and eventually turned on my computer. Instinctively, I opened Microsoft Word. Although I intended to work on my book, for some reason I created a new document and stared at the empty page for several minutes. And suddenly I wanted to write the Terrell article. I started typing blindly, just throwing words and images on the screen as they occurred to me, and after an hour or so I had several pages of material. I went to the bathroom and chugged two glasses of water, cursing the haze clogging my brain, then returned to the computer. If I was going to make the article as good as I wanted it to be, I needed a plan.

The most important thing was to write something that *Sports Illustrated* would print. Despite my hot material, that criterion was more difficult to meet than it initially appeared. Although the magazine likes the kind of controversy that moves copies at news-stands, the editors are wary of picking on rising stars—a fear I always thought stemmed from the incident when *Sports Illustrated* was critical of Michael Jordan, who retaliated by never speaking to the magazine's reporters again. Whatever the motivation, I knew that I had to largely limit my criticisms to poor Terrell, who wasn't going to be able to give them any more quotes anyway.

And I wanted to focus on Terrell. His story fascinated me, and by a stroke of odd coincidence I had been in exactly the right position to get the right information—close enough that I had good material, far enough that the details weren't choking me. Any guilt I felt at exploiting his family's tragedy to write a magazine article dissipated in my belief that I was finally writing something important.

American Tragedy
The sad story behind Terrell Jordan's overdose

It was his heart that finally went. The doctors and forensic guys might talk about how this valve popped or that circuit jumped, but Terrell Jordan's heart stopped long before the night he mixed cocaine, steroids, and uppers into a lethal cocktail. Because Terrell Jordan's heart was baseball, the game that made him famous and rich, the game that finally killed him. We all had a hand in his murder. You, me, *Sports Illustrated*, the Boston Red Sox, the little boy who stopped buying baseball cards and started listening to Jim Rome on talk radio.

To understand what happened to Terrell, you had to see him on a chilly night in Minnesota, playing home run derby with Casey Fox. You had to see the joy with which he swung a wiffle ball bat covered in duct tape at a tennis ball. You had to see the way he pumped his fist when he drove that tennis ball over the chain-link fence in right field. And you had to see the shadow that crossed his face as we walked back to the car when he remembered that real baseball, the game he played in front of thousands of fans, was no longer so easy.

The article continued in roughly the same tone for almost three thousand words, describing the intimate details of Terrell's last few weeks. I initially resisted using any metaphors, but the story ultimately slipped into the cadence of a classic tragedy set in modern times. I wrote at a furious pace for me, almost five hundred words per hour, and I read the complete piece only once before sending it via e-mail to John Abbot at six in the morning. I had no idea whether or not he would run it—and at that point I didn't care. I took another shot or two of whiskey before collapsing into bed. Despite my exhaustion, which was making my brain buzz incoherently like a television with a busted tube, I still had trouble falling asleep. I was lying on my side, staring at the brightening shadows beneath my curtain, when Abbot called.

"You're up early," I said.

"And you're up late." His tone was brusque. "I'm bumping space. I want to try and run your story in the issue that closes today."

"That's cool." I didn't feel any joy at the news, and I wondered if it was because I was tired or because my feelings about the story were even more ambiguous than I had suspected. I wracked my brain for something intelligent to say. "I wrote down the phone numbers of some sources at the end of the article. Maybe they'll help your fact checkers."

"They will," Abbot said. "And I might have to call you again for some details. Mrs. Jordan seems intent on suing everyone, and I don't want to be on her list."

I stifled a yawn. "Makes sense."

The line was silent for so long that I thought for a moment that my phone had dropped the call. I rolled over and glanced at the clock—8:06, just two hours after I had sent the story. I wondered if Abbot was calling me from home or the *Sports Illustrated* office. It seemed impossible that a guy like Abbot would allow himself the luxury of actually having a bed.

Abbot's voice finally snapped me out of my reverie. "You would have saved us a lot of hassle if you'd told us that you were writing the article. I'm only running it because it's the story of the year. And one more day and you would have been too late—it was this issue or bust."

I knew exactly what he was looking for, and I was just too tired to avoid dropping to my knees and kissing the ring. "Thanks."

"Nice work," he said. "It isn't often that you come out ten days after a story breaks and still scoop everybody."

chapter 28

A LOUD KNOCK ON MY DOOR AWOKE ME FROM MY NAP AT FOUR
that afternoon. I staggered across the room, peered through the
peephole, and saw Molly, cute even through the eye of a fish. I
swore softly to myself—I needed much more time to cull through
my leftover angst from the previous night. But I couldn't leave her
standing in the hall, so I pulled on a T-shirt, ran my fingers
through the wiry jungle atop my head, and opened the door.

She wrinkled her nose at the stale air that followed me out of
my room. "Were you asleep?"

"Yeah. Taking a nap." I thought I saw judgment in her eyes, so
I quickly explained myself. "I was up to all hours last night."

"Why? Have you found another girlfriend already?"

"Not yet," I said.

"Good." She smiled, and then her breath caught. "I'm sorry
I've been so hard on you. I really can't explain my behavior."

I stared at her, and as she shifted nervously under my gaze, I realized that she was once again all sweetness and vulnerability. Her
other, tougher qualities, which had been so prominently on display the previous evening, had vanished in her concern like
Cinderella's livery. Part of me wanted to berate her, to explain

how terrible she had made me feel until her cheery smile faded into the quick tears of a girl with a good heart. Five years ago that part of me might have won. But in my travels I have acquired a shred of wisdom, and I knew that making her feel bad would only make me feel worse. So I smiled weakly and touched her hand. "It's okay," I said. "It's really okay."

"I'm glad because last night you seemed upset and I was worried." As she spoke, I could feel my fake smile spreading into something far more real, and my vision got blurry around the edges. It had been so long since anyone had cared enough to monitor my moods. Her hand gently squeezed mine. "Are you free tonight? I want to take you somewhere."

"Somewhere? I think I've been there before. Maybe we should go someplace instead."

She giggled softly at my effort rather than my joke. "Maybe you should take another nap," she suggested.

"Maybe we should," I said, gently drawing her into my dark room.

Later that night she took me to a club that neither of us could really afford on the fifty-sixth floor of the Prudential Building. We sat at a window overlooking the Charles River, nursing our $10 gin and tonics slowly enough that we would be able to stay for more than an hour, and every now and then we got up to dance to the geriatric rhythm of the brass band in the center of the room. Yuppies flush with dot-com money were just starting to replace the post-theater crowd when my leftover emotions from the previous night burst from a part of my brain that I wish I could kill.

"Why are you with me?"

She glanced up from her drink, tiny smile lines running away from her right eye. "That's a romantic question." She paused. "Are you serious or are you just looking for compliments?"

"I'm serious."

She shifted in her chair so that she was gazing out the window.

I examined her face in the glass, the dark reflection deepening her eyes into crevices and molding her face into a dirge. She spoke quietly but intensely. "Because before I read a word you wrote, I knew you had an amazing ability. Last week when I said that I was your muse, I wasn't entirely joking. My real talent is spotting the greatness in other people. Greatness that they sometimes don't even know they have." She turned to look at me. "Like Casey."

I smiled. "It didn't take a muse to see Casey's talent."

She shook her head, frustrated. "After all the time you've spent with him, I would think you'd be starting to get it," she said. "Baseball isn't why I see greatness in him."

"You want him to change the world." Although it wasn't a question, she nodded anyway. "Well," I continued, "maybe the way he can change the world is different than the way you can change the world. Maybe he can be a star who actually talks about something real. Being a famous athlete is one hell of a platform, you know."

She allowed me my entire speech, which was generous, but I could tell from her flat eyes that she didn't agree with anything I said. When I finished, she took a deep breath and let her carved chin rest in the palm of her hand. "No."

"No?" I was completely confused—I hadn't even realized that I'd asked a question.

"No," she said again. "It's simple, Russ. You have to change yourself before you can change anyone else. You have to heal yourself before you can heal anyone else. You have to save yourself before you can save anyone else."

It took me months before I could distill the wisdom in her words—in fact, it took me weeks before I had even an inkling of what she meant. At the time I remember being just vaguely confused, and a moment later she was speaking again. "In some ways your situation is more interesting than Casey's," she said, her tone reflective. "Because while Casey hasn't discovered that he has certain things, you already know that you're a good writer. And yet you ignore that gift. I can't figure it out."

I wanted to mention the Terrell article—to defend myself from her quietly withering charge—but I was too scared. So I escaped with a dumb question. "How do you know I'm a good writer?"

Her hands were holding mine on the table, our drinks forgotten. "Because of the way you read to me that night."

"That's not a good reason."

"Define irony," she said.

"What?"

"It's a simple question. Define irony."

I carefully removed my hands from her warm grasp and made a list with my fingers. "Irony is Alanis Morissette writing a popular song in which every example she gives of irony isn't ironic. Irony is naming the airport in Washington, D.C., after the president who fired all the air traffic controllers. Irony is Regis Philbin hosting a game show based on intelligence."

"Why is that ironic?" she asked.

"Because the only bright thing about Regis Philbin is his shiny tie."

"See," she said, laughing. "You're a writer."

"No." I tried to keep the frustration from my voice, but her shoulders tightened and I knew that I had failed. "Too many people confuse one-liners with writing. And that's not writing; it's bad stand-up comedy. I've always thought that humility is having something clever to say and not needing to say it. Well, good writing is the same way. There's an enormous difference between being clever and being a writer—because a writer sees things deeply enough to understand that cleverness is just a way of concealing ignorance."

Her hands covered mine again. "I'm not talking about what you said. I'm talking about the way you said it. You have passion. And, to answer your original question, passion is attractive."

I paused. "So you're saying you're with me because I have an undiscovered passion for writing that might someday make me great."

"Kind of."

"I was really just hoping you were going to tell me I had a cute butt," I said.

We danced again and then settled into a booth, hidden from the predatory glances of passing waitresses hoping to sell us more $10 drinks. My arm encircled Molly's waist, my hand resting on her far hip, and she allowed her forehead to sink to my shoulder. I closed my eyes and let myself revel in the warmth of her body.

"I have something else to tell you," she said.

I buried my nose in her smooth hair. "Is it about my butt?"

"No. The foundation offered me that job at the orphanage in Honduras."

"Oh." My eyes popped open, but I refused to allow myself any reaction. "Are you going to do it?"

"Yes," she said. "It's what I want to do." Her eyes avoided mine so artfully that I knew she must have more bad news. "I'm leaving at the end of the week."

"So soon?" I asked, fighting to keep the panic from my voice.

"They needed someone yesterday," she said softly. "That's how these places work. As soon as the funding goes through, they want to get you out there."

"Well, congratulations." I took a deep breath and tried to relax, tried to think of anything that might keep my natural reaction from spilling out and ruining everything. A group of overage fraternity guys passed our table, and two of them stopped to ogle Molly, their eyes lingering on her long legs. I stared at them, a smile twitching at the corner of my mouth. I was far too proud of the way she looked to care. The men turned and were strutting off in search of unguarded prey when Molly poked me in the ribs.

"You okay?" she asked.

"Sure."

She pulled away from me, and my arm slunk back to my side, driven by her fierce gaze. "Don't you dare do one of those male zombie acts on me," she said, her voice crackling. "I want to know what you think."

I shrugged as neutrally as I could manage. "I think it's a great opportunity. And if you want to do it, you should definitely go."

"Fine," she said. She settled back under my arm, but her body was as stiff as a mannequin. I wondered what I had done to upset her—I had thought that my reaction to her news had been wonderfully restrained and mature.

"Everything all right?" I asked when it had long been obvious that everything was certainly not classifiable as all right.

"Of course," she said.

She remained distant the rest of the night, and when I put her on the train to Providence the next morning, I felt alone for the first time in several months. Casey had left with the rest of the team twelve hours earlier. The Sox had six games remaining—three in Kansas City and three in Fenway against Tampa Bay—and remained stuck one game behind the Yankees. The wild card slot appeared out of reach unless both Seattle and Cleveland completely collapsed. Although I believed that the Sox would need to win five of their six remaining games to catch the Yankees, I figured that the playoffs were still a legitimate possibility. After all, baseball represents capitalism, not socialism, and Kansas City and Tampa Bay were both small-market teams struggling merely to convince their season ticket holders to reinvest the following spring.

That night, however, the Sox lost in a way that would have devastated most teams and towns. But for Boston, which has suffered through Bill Buckner and Bucky Dent and the undying pain of the summer of '49, it was just a run-of-the-mill disappointment. The game began well, with the Sox jumping out to a 6–0 lead. The forecast in Kansas City had predicted rain, and in the bottom of the fourth inning it started falling across the field in great sheets, driving the few fans remaining in the stadium under the ledges and into the concourse. Everyone on the Sox knew that if they could just get through the fifth inning, the umpires would call the game—after five innings a game becomes official and doesn't have to be replayed. Yet in the bottom of the fifth, with victory seemingly just a three-out formality, the Royals scored six excruciating runs on a bizarre series of broken bats, infield hits, and Sox errors. And since the umpires knew that it would be immensely difficult to make up the game before the end of the regular season, the soggy contest continued.

The rain slowed through the sixth and seventh, but picked up again in the eighth until it reached the point where it could accurately be described as a monsoon. In the top of the inning, Casey got to third with one out, but the Sox couldn't get him home. In the top of the ninth, Nomar hit a leadoff double, but died at second on two pop-ups and a muddy grounder. The Royals came to bat in the bottom of the ninth, facing Boston's second-best relief pitcher, a tough veteran from the Mets. The Sox rookie on third started yelling inane encouragement—stuff like "let's get this guy at the plate" and "give us a strike, pitch"—probably to impress the coaches. The pitcher, cold and itching in his wet uniform, yelled at the rookie to shut the fuck up, and Casey, water streaming off the top of his helmet and down his back, his chest protector feeling like a lead vest, called a fastball so they could get in out of the goddamned rain, and the batter slapped it through the driving storm into the right-field stands for a game-ending home run.

The Sox players retreated slowly from the field and scattered themselves around the clubhouse, too stunned to take the hot showers they sorely needed. The reporters and photographers were smart enough to give them a few minutes to compose themselves before launching the usual barrage of questions, but after only thirty seconds of chilly silence a man strolled across the room to Casey's locker. His name was Chuck Norwood and he owned a bunch of car dealerships in the Kansas City area. Rich guys often get access to locker rooms after games, and Chuck possessed the additional advantage of having been a college roommate of the Sox general manager.

Casey's head was drooping toward his locker, his hand cradling his eyebrows, when Chuck reached his side. Chuck cleared his throat with the authority of a man who had once sold cars on the floor.

"I was wondering if you could do me a favor?" Chuck asked in a tone as respectful as his voice box was capable of producing.

The reporters and players in the room dove behind tables and lockers, hoping to shield themselves from the thermonuclear explosion certain to come, but Casey just turned his somber eyes upward. "Yeah?"

"I'm sorry to ask, but . . ." Chuck's voice trailed off as Casey's expression turned impatient. "It's my little girl's birthday and she's up in the stands and I was wondering if you could maybe—"

"Sing to her?" Casey asked.

"If that would be all right," Chuck said. "I don't mean to be causing no problems or nothing but she sure would—"

He might have prattled all day, but Casey cut him short. "No problem."

Casey stripped off his soaking uniform top, replacing it with a Red Sox sweatshirt, and wandered over to Carl Everett's locker. "Come sing with me," he said.

Everett, who was born cool, shook his head. "Hell no."

"It's a little girl," Casey said. Everett didn't even bother to blink. "If you come and sing to her, I'll run out to the waterfall in center field wearing only my jock."

Everett's intensity is legendary, and for the second time in two minutes the bystanders in the locker room ducked and covered. And for the second time it turned out that they had overreacted because a slow smile spread across Everett's face. "Now that I would pay to see," he said.

So Casey, Everett, and at least ten other players went upstairs and sang "Happy Birthday" to the little girl in the concourse as the few fans remaining in the stadium gathered around the group. Practically the whole team was huddling under the overhang in the dugout when the singers returned to the field. Casey trudged out into the rain and then performed a comically begrudging strip tease while the dugout whistled and cheered. He removed his pants last, flung them in the general direction of Felix, and then took off at a dead sprint for the decorative waterfall behind the center field fence. He was halfway there when a couple of other guys, wearing only baseball pants, burst out of the dugout and followed him, their feet kicking up little plumes of water on the soggy green grass. When Casey reached the blue fence, he pulled himself up in one smooth motion, and a moment later was taking a shower in the antiseptic spray of the fake waterfall.

The other players stopped at the wall, suddenly wavering, until Casey dropped back into their midst. He shouted, a rebel yell that echoed off the metal bleachers, and then the little group was charging like Stuart's troopers toward the infield. Casey aimed directly for the bright blue tarp that the groundskeepers use to cover the dirt, and when he reached the edge he launched himself into the air as if he were leaping onto a slip-and-slide. Miraculously, it worked. He slid on his belly for thirty or forty feet on the wet plastic, a line of players following him like attack planes on a bombing run. When Casey finally stopped, he pulled the edge of the tarp away from the infield and suddenly he was rolling in the dirt. And before the coaches could say a word all the players who weren't too old or too cool were wrestling frantically in a little mud pit near the third-base bag. The coaches walked back into the clubhouse, washing their hands of the whole affair, and someone told me that the Sox GM watched the entire scene from his luxury box. I bet he was saying Hail Marys the entire time as he watched his millionaires cavort on the eve of the playoffs.

The entire incident went almost completely unreported. A few blurry pictures of Casey's naked butt appeared on the Internet, and a few anonymous veterans complained to the Boston papers that Casey wasn't treating the game of baseball with an appropriately serious attitude, but most reporters—and the entire coaching staff—decided that the team had just been blowing off steam. And since the Sox destroyed the Royals the next two games, they were probably right. The team received a hero's welcome upon its return to Boston—five thousand fans were waiting at Logan Airport when the charter arrived—and half the conversations I overheard on the street were discussions about whether or not the Sox could catch the hated Yankees. Pennant fever had begun in earnest.

I'm not sure how to describe the tremendous energy and mass hysteria of pennant fever to the uninitiated other than by telling the story of a childhood friend of mine named Evan McTavish, who was the biggest Red Sox fan in my high school class. When I went away to college, Evan stayed behind in New Hampshire and started a lawn mowing business called Green Monster Mowing. The fall of my senior year I called him to say hello and got his answering machine, which related the following message: "Hello, this is Evan. The Red Sox were swept at Fenway this weekend by the Angels despite giving up only five goddamned runs in the series. I will be unable to return your call or mow your lawn until the world is a better place, but feel free to leave a message. The Yankees suck."

So imagine walking through downtown Boston and seeing the same glint that Evan would get when the Red Sox were on a winning streak reflected in the eyes of a thousand businessmen and barbers and policemen. That is the energy of a pennant race.

The issue of *Sports Illustrated* containing my article arrived on the newsstands the morning after the Sox returned to Boston. It caused quite a stir. I first became aware of the controversy I had generated while listening to the morning sports show on one of the local radio stations. The host referred to my article with a slew of words that had to be covered with long, high-pitched beeps—never a good sign—and he called me "another reporter with Clinton's ethics and Pat Buchanan's love for making trouble." I thought that was kind of clever. By midday, however, I was ready for all my critics, clever or not, to take an intermission. The allegations that bothered me the most were the claims that I had fabricated large parts of the article. Several local sports reporters, including two of the Four Horsemen, went on the radio and said that various players were disputing parts of my story.

The only criticism I really feared arrived in the midafternoon. I was lying in my bed watching a European soccer match when someone banged furiously on my door, and I didn't have to stretch my imagination very far to guess who it was. Sure enough, Casey was standing outside, snorting as hard as an offensive lineman in the fourth quarter.

"You're a bitch," he said when I opened the door.

"I always warned you that someday I was going to do my job," I said.

He pointed at my chest, his finger pumping like an engine valve. "Your job is a waste of your fucking time. What could possibly be so important about a game that would make you want to embarrass a dead man?"

"The story said something about America. I thought you might understand that."

Casey turned his trademark look of disdain and disgust on me, and I felt myself shrink two shirt sizes. "I understand what it says. It says that you're starting to become one of them."

"One of who?"

He put his hand on the frame of the door and allowed his body to relax a tiny bit. "Let me tell you what I hate most in sports," he said, spitting the words like sunflower seeds. "I hate the anchors of popular sports shows. Why? It's not just because they're smug and cynical and self-assured. It's not because they're thirty-year-old white guys trying to talk like black teenagers or because they think sarcasm is always funny. I hate those guys because they confuse their fame and their worth. And you . . ." His eyes narrowed. "You might get famous from this article, but you still won't be worth anything."

As he spoke I felt myself growing increasingly angry, and I barely allowed him to finish before I began my own tirade. "Let me tell you what I hate about sports, Casey Fox. I hate that those anchors don't use their fame to ask the tough questions. Like why baseball has abandoned the small-market towns. Or why there are no openly gay athletes in the major male sports. Or how we've allowed the atmosphere between players and fans to become so poisonous." I cleared my constricting throat. "But now I know why they're so afraid to ask those kind of hard questions. Because Terrell's death said something important about sports. And when

I wrote about it, really wrote about it, it cost me my one great source."

We stared at each other for a long beat, and when I spoke again my voice was tired. "So, Casey Fox, fuck it. I don't need to listen to your sanctimonious speeches."

I firmly closed the door and took a deep breath before peeking out through the peephole. Casey, his shoulders slumped, stood motionless for a moment and then turned and trudged down the hall toward the elevator. The anger poured out of my body, leaving as smoothly as sweat in a sauna, and I reemerged from my room.

"Will you let me ask one more question?" I called after him.

He turned, slowly. "One," he said begrudgingly. "One question for the one time you saved my ass."

I knew my question, but not how to phrase it, so I ended up sounding like an awestruck child. "How are you so good?"

"You want an honest answer or some 'gift from God' bullshit?"

"Honest answer."

He shrugged a shrug of complete bafflement. "I was given a gift from God. I can't explain it. I see the ball. I hit the ball. It's the purest, easiest thing in the world." He paused, and an expression of remembered rapture flashed across his face so fast that I almost missed it. "I love that feeling," he said. "I hate everything else. Everything. But I love that feeling."

chapter 29

SPORTS ILLUSTRATED FLEW ME TO NEW YORK THE NEXT MORNING.
I spent a couple hours with a Time-Warner lawyer compiling a re-
buttal to the people contesting various parts of my story, and then
Abbot took me out to lunch. We ate at a trendy spot in midtown,
complete with starched linen napkins and insufferable waiters,
and I spent most of the meal wondering why Abbot was spending
a couple hundred bucks and two hours of his time on a freelancer
like me. We chatted idly about various topical issues in sports until dessert came and he abruptly answered my unspoken question.

"We want you to come work for *Sports Illustrated*," he said.

I couldn't contain my grin. "I thought you were overbudget."

Abbot shrugged. "We always have room for young talent." If he
was hoping to flatter me, it certainly worked. I could feel the tips
of my ears flushing.

"What would I be doing?"

"You'd be a reporter. We'd assign you in-depth features. And I
can guarantee that you'd move up the masthead fairly quickly."

Abbot watched me closely, waiting for the inevitable yes that
he always got when he asked a wayward reporter this question. It
was one of those moments when life needs a pause button. If I

could have stopped time, I would have paid George Will and Robert Reich to argue the merits of Abbot's proposal on *Crossfire*. But unfortunately I was stuck with ten seconds of stall time and my own mediocre mind. The rough details of my potential life at *Sports Illustrated* flashed through my brain: the long road trips, the weeks of trailing professional athletes from a reporter's usual distance, the hours of interviewing background sources on the telephone. I would be much higher up the totem pole than I had been at the *Times*, but the subject matter of my job would remain the same.

"That's a wonderful offer," I said when I could stall no longer. I swallowed hard. "But I'm going to have to say no."

Abbot's only reaction was to carefully wipe his mouth with the edge of his dazzling napkin. "You're making a career out of rejecting me," he said when he was finished.

"It's nothing personal."

Abbot smiled the assassin's smile of a successful businessman. "I'm sitting here because I think everything is personal," he said. "And maybe I'm just confused. You're a sports reporter without a job. We're the best sports magazine in the business. That seems like a match to me."

"I'm sorry." My ribcage was squeezing me, constricting my breath, probably because I knew I was blowing my best chance to become an elite sports reporter—which had been my ostensible goal when I chose the profession. Abbot was staring at me like a doctor incredulously examining a patient who has rejected life-saving surgery.

"Can I offer you some advice?" he finally asked.

I didn't have to think very hard—when a man like Abbot offers you free advice, you at least listen to what he has to say. "Sure."

"I see a lot of writers," he said. "And I'll tell you one thing I notice. Most of the stars at my magazine are solid reporters who understand the rest of the business. They're not brilliant. They just work hard, do their jobs, and earn the respect of our readers. The brilliant writers we sometimes get are usually head cases. They could be superstars, but they flame out. Maybe they spend too much time inhaling their own exhaust; maybe they just think people will put up with their crap if they write well enough. Being brilliant isn't the best thing in life."

I felt myself start to preen, but he stopped me with a judgmental glance. "You're not brilliant," he said. "But you're very good. And if you come to my magazine and work hard, you'll be happy with the results."

The waiter arrived with the check, and I waited until we were again alone. I knew that Abbot hated weakness, so I made my tone far firmer than I felt. "I understand what you're telling me," I said. "And I really appreciate it. But every now and then in life, if you're really lucky, you get a chance to bet on yourself. I think I have that chance. So thank you for the offer and for lunch. But I have some other things I need to do."

I think Abbot knew what I was trying to say—he couldn't have gotten his job without taking a few chances—and he nodded his head slowly. "Good luck," he said. "And if you ever make friends with another athlete like Casey Fox, give me a call."

I smiled wryly. "We both know that there will never be another athlete like Casey Fox." I stood and shook his hand, and as I left the restaurant I knew that we would never speak again.

I took the train from Penn Station to Providence, and Molly met me at a little kiosk that sells newspapers and chewing gum. We walked in silence all the way down the platform to a cement bench that overlooked the train yard, and I sensed that something from our night of dancing was still bothering her. As we sat, I noticed the crispness of the air for the first time, and I turned up the collar of my blue blazer and buttoned the front against the wind.

"How long do we have?" she asked when we were settled, and from her tone I could tell that she wasn't entirely delighted to see me.

"Another train leaves in a half hour," I said. "But I don't have any real reason to go back to Boston."

"You're not covering the team anymore?" she asked, her curiosity overcoming her diffidence.

"No."

She shifted on the bench, and I couldn't tell if it was the cold or the conversation that was making her uncomfortable. "Casey called," she said. "He was really upset about the Terrell story."

"I know," I said. "Did you read it?"

"Yeah." She shifted again, and as I turned my head to look at her, I realized that I cared more about her reaction to the story than I had admitted to myself. "I thought it was really good," she said. "I think it's the kind of story you should be writing."

We were quiet again for several minutes, and I shivered in the wind. She moved slightly toward me, as if she wanted to put her arm around my shoulders to keep me warm, but she stopped herself. I wanted to say something, anything, that might break us from our strange impasse. "I turned down a job with *Sports Illustrated* at lunch today."

She turned, startled. "Why?"

"It wasn't what I wanted to be doing."

"What do you want to be doing?" she asked.

I took a while to consider her question. It wasn't that I hadn't thought about it—I had spent much of the train ride staring out the window at the passing urban landscape and wondering where I was going to go next—but I hadn't found an answer that I could articulate. I knew roughly what I wanted to do. I wanted to keep writing, but after turning down a job at *Sports Illustrated*, accepting a position at another magazine or newspaper would have been foolish. What I wanted to do was write something worthwhile. Maybe even a book. My resources, however, were limited. Although I had a small reserve of cash sitting in a Rhode Island bank account, I didn't have close to enough money to live on for the six months or a year it would take me to write enough material to interest a publisher.

Suddenly a solution popped into my head, so simple and so perfect that I couldn't believe I hadn't thought of it any sooner. "I want to go with you to Honduras."

"What?" Her eyebrows furrowed together and cute lines appeared on her forehead. From her reaction I knew instantly that I had made a mistake—she was too young, we were too new, I was too unstable, she was too . . . And then, just as my mind was on the verge of collapsing under the weight of my doleful doubts, she pulled me into a hug so tight that I could feel the small buttons of her shirt pressing against my chest. The warmth of her body enveloped me like a thermal blanket. "The other day I thought you didn't care that I was leaving," she said in my ear.

I took a deep breath and tried to find the most honest words. "I cared a lot. I just didn't want to get in your way."

We relaxed our embrace so that our noses were six inches apart, and when I could see her eyes I realized that she needed more convincing. "Why do you want to come?" she asked after a few seconds. "Because I can't be the only reason."

I froze, momentarily baffled. Of course she was the only reason I was going. I wanted to be with her, and I was willing to subscribe to any cause she espoused for that privilege. But I could also understand her discomfort with that kind of commitment—and I was far too scared to be that kind of honest anyway—so I stalled for time. "Tell me again why you're going."

She looked at me strangely. "That's an obvious way of avoiding the question."

"I don't mean it that way," I said. "You've never explained it to me in a way that I can understand. I need something solid. Something real. Something that makes sense to me. Otherwise, my own answer will be nothing more than an idle guess."

"Fine," she said. She untangled her arms from my torso and leaned back against the bench, her eyes locked on the roof of a warehouse across the tracks. "Everything comes from this feeling I get sometimes. When we were in that club on top of the Prudential, for example, I felt like throwing up. I mean, ten-dollar drinks? Or this one time I went to South Beach when I was in Miami on spring break. My girlfriend wanted to get in this club, so we were standing outside with two hundred and fifty people trying to get the attention of this asshole working the door. And the only thing that would turn his head was either a lot of money or big tits. You should have seen what those people were willing to do and willing to pay. Just to get in some stupid club. So the answer is that I don't want to live in a place where people can get their priorities that fucked up. Because I can feel my own center getting sucked away. I need to go someplace where I'm forced to be the person I want to be—where my better side has to come out. Then, maybe someday when I'm strong enough, I'll be able to come back and keep my core."

"I understand what you mean," I said.

"Really?"

"Yeah." And I did. Kind of. I understood the less-interesting part of her story; I shared her aggravation, but not her passion. Being offended by a club in South Beach made perfect sense to me—and I could even empathize with her ability to turn that annoyance into an indictment of an entire society. My empathy ended, however, at the point where her irritation evolved into something more than mere grousing. She was realistic and grounded enough to see the ugly side of life that most people ignore, yet somehow could still summon the idealism to take a job at an orphanage in Honduras. And I envied her that ability. In fact, on a deep level, that envy explained why I wanted to follow her. I wanted to be a parasite on her passion—I was so desperate to abandon my cynicism and care deeply about something, anything, that I was willing to attach myself to a venture that was entirely foreign to me.

I was still lost in thought when she shifted impatiently on the bench, her hand, which had been resting on my leg, withdrawing onto her own lap. "You still haven't answered my original question."

"Why am I going?"

"That's right."

"I have to get away from opinions." She peered at me, trying to get the joke. "I'm serious," I said. "They're making me crazy. This country is dripping with uneducated opinions. Radio, movies, television, magazines . . . every time we have a national crisis you turn on CNN and see idiotic people screaming at the top of their lungs. The reason we can't have a real debate on anything—even the designated hitter—is because we give stupid people equal time. And we let other people tell us what to think on politics, sports, fashion, culture—"

"You're being a snob," she said, but her tone was affectionate.

"I'm just not being clear. I do think everyone should have opinions. That was the original genius of baseball—you listened to the game on the radio and went to the stadium and you talked about what happened with your friends. You made up your own mind. But now we've got a thousand people who don't know anything about the game telling us what to think twenty-four hours a day. I turn on the news and some guy who's never read the *Federalist Papers* is criticizing the electoral college. All opinions aren't equally worthwhile, yet we give ignorant opinions equal time. We give all opinions time. And that constant buzz make me want to vomit."

At some point in my speech she had started laughing, and when I finished she kissed me on the cheek, so sweetly that it didn't feel condescending. "So your opinion is that this country needs fewer opinions?" she asked when she got her breath.

"That's right," I said, doing my best to look grumpy. "I can't take it anymore. Honduras will be perfect. If people are shouting their stupid opinions, I won't be able to understand them anyway."

"You don't speak Spanish?" she asked, surprised.

"Not a word."

She smiled. "Maybe you should take a class before you come down."

"I'm leaving when you leave. In three days."

"How?"

"I'll do whatever I have to do," I said. "Trade in frequent flier miles or something. If I'm going to come along, I'm not doing it half-assed."

She moved toward me like a wrestler going for a takedown, and she bowled me over before I could defend myself. Her body covered mine, the unyielding cement bench pressing firmly against my back, my hand helpless over my head, and she kissed me so fervently that my brain filled with helium. When we parted, I moved my mouth to ask the logical question, but her fingers gently covered my lips.

"Thank you," she said. And I saw the beginnings of tears catching in her lower eyelashes. "Thank you. That feels so good. Nobody's ever taken a leap of faith for me."

chapter 30

I MISSED MY TRAIN BUT WAS BACK IN BOSTON BEFORE MID-night. The next morning I got out of bed early and spent the day working on the logistics of fulfilling my promise to Molly. The process began at the American Airlines office, where I traded in three years of frequent flier miles for an open round-trip ticket to Honduras. Next I phoned the owner of the greyhound racetrack in Wonderland—who is a client of my dad's—and got his permission to park my car at the track for a few months. I sent a form e-mail to a few of my college and newspaper friends, explaining that I would be out of touch for a while, called a few people, and found my pass-port in my laptop case. Packing took less than an hour—my furni-ture would be okay in the storage bin in Providence, and I was taking most of the stuff in my motel room. And then I was done. The portability of my life shocked me. Had I really done such a ter-rible job of putting down roots over the thirty years of my existence that I could be ready to transplant myself in a matter of hours?

So that night I had time to go watch the biggest regular season game in recent Red Sox history. Boston was one game behind the Yankees with only that evening's contest against Tampa Bay re-maining. If the Sox won and the Yankees lost to the Rangers in

New York, Boston would meet the Yankees in a one-game playoff at Fenway to decide which team would go to the Divisional Series. But if either the Sox lost or the Yankees won, the season would be over and New England fans would have to suffer through another bitter winter.

I knew that getting tickets to the game would be almost impossible, but I figured that I would just use my press pass one more time—certainly no one at *Sports Illustrated* would argue that I hadn't earned that perk. I arrived almost an hour before the game was scheduled to begin and strode through the press entrance, imperiously waving my pass in the general direction of Charlie, the security guard. He always passed me through with a gentle wave and a benign comment about the team, but this time he stepped forward and put his hand on my chest.

"I'm sorry," he said. "I can't let you in."

"What?" As my voice squawked, I flinched, embarrassed.

"Orders from up top," Charlie said. He appeared mortified to be stopping me. "They're checking on your press pass."

I knew that I was guilty—if I wasn't writing another article for *Sports Illustrated*, I shouldn't really be using the pass—but I felt outraged anyway. After all, the Sox couldn't possibly know that I was bending the rules. I let my voice rise. "I write one critical article and suddenly you won't let me in the park? What is this? Russia?" I stared at Charlie, who wilted under my glare, and I fought to suppress my sympathy. "That's some real juvenile shit."

Someone spoke behind me. "Don't be a drama queen." I turned and saw Bruce McCall, a smug smirk making his caustic features even more unpleasant than usual.

I wanted to punch him, but settled for being ugly. "How about I'll stop being a drama queen when you get a little class."

"At least I'm not a player whore." Bruce smiled a victorious smile. "But the word in the locker room is that your John isn't going to be putting out anymore. So welcome back to the real world with the rest of us." Bruce brushed past me and started down the hallway toward the field.

"Angry hack," I muttered as he passed.

"Rookie burnout," he said over his shoulder just as he disappeared around the corner.

I stood still for a long beat, my arms dangling limply at my sides like dead tentacles. It annoyed me that Bruce McCall had been able to get under my skin—and it annoyed me that I was still annoyed. If the guy was really beneath contempt, I should have been able to ignore him. If I really didn't care about the "game" of reporting, I should have been able to ignore him. But I couldn't and that irked me.

"That guy's a dick," Charlie said softly when we were alone.

"Yeah," I said, still staring down the empty hallway. "Sorry about yelling at you. I know this whole thing isn't your fault."

I turned to leave and almost smacked into Jessica Young. She was smiling so broadly that I knew she must have heard the entire exchange.

"You keep catching me at my best moments," I said.

Her smile got even wider—if that was possible. "I sure hope not," she said. "Are you writing another article for *Sports Illustrated?*"

I shook my head. "Nope. I think my time as a sports writer is over."

"Good choice." She glanced from me to Charlie and then back to me. "So why do you want to get in?"

At that point my real answer probably had something to do with my injured pride, but I couldn't admit that to her. I shifted awkwardly for a minute before I found something else. "I feel like I started this journey for a reason and I want to see it finished."

Jessica stared at me closely, and for the first time I saw a flicker of something softer in her eyes. "I've got a spare pass," she said. "If you carry some equipment, I'll let you come in with me."

She dug in her lens bag and pulled out two passes. Charlie gave them a cursory glance and then clapped me on the shoulder. "I can let you through on that," he said.

But I could hear the concern at the fringes of his voice—security guards and office personnel who buck management around Fenway, to use the prevailing local expression, get canned faster than tuna. I shook his hand and gave him my most reassuring gaze. "I won't get you in trouble, Charlie. I promise."

The game was tense, noisy, and not particularly dramatic. Jessica and I were confined to the tiny photographers' pen down the third-base line, and I spent most of the game repaying her favor by handing her lenses and film. The game essentially ended in the third inning when Casey hit a three-run homer to put the Sox ahead 6–0. With the incomparable Pedro Martinez on the mound, the chance of the Devil Rays scoring six runs approached the odds given to things like meaningful tax reform or finding quality prime-time programming on CBS. So 35,432 fans, forty-six Red Sox players, coaches, and trainers, and several hundred reporters and photographers spent the last six innings watching the huge, anachronistic out-of-town scoreboard in center field. The Rangers were leading the Yankees 4–3 going into the bottom of the ninth inning, and we were waiting, praying for the score-keeper to replace the "9" with an "F." Minutes felt like eons as we waited and waited for the scorekeeper. And when he wouldn't put that letter up and wouldn't put that letter up we booed him—I think we all believed that he had the power to decide that game, and that if we could just cheer hard enough the events happening several hundred miles away would actually be decided in Boston.

In the top of the eighth, with the Sox leading 8–0, the score-keeper finally slipped the "F" into its slot and the park exploded like the headquarters of a winning campaign on election night. A tsunami of red and blue tore through the stands. I could feel the floor of our tiny green box shaking under the rhythmic stomping of thousands of feet, and Jessica was shooting pictures as fast as she could reload film. I could see a quiet celebration in the Boston dugout, but the Sox players on the field did their best to ignore the madness around them. The final inning and a half were the roots of the party that would spill onto Landsdown Street after the game. I remain convinced that only two facts prevented a full-blown Los Angeles–style celebration riot. First, the crowd knew that the Sox still had to play the Yankees—and enough Boston teams have lost enough big games to New York to temper any local fan's enthusiasm. Second, and perhaps more importantly, they don't sell beer in the Fenway stands after the seventh inning.

When the Boston-Tampa game ended, the Sox players marched onto the field and quietly celebrated in a restrained way that seemed intended to demonstrate that they knew they hadn't won anything yet. But I could tell they were happy because Casey hugged several members of the team whom he liked even less than reporters. When the players had all disappeared into the dugout, Jessica carefully packed her camera and the film into her bags and then looked over at me.

"Thanks for the hand," she said.

I made a dismissive gesture with my arm, trying to indicate that I knew I had almost certainly created more problems than I'd solved. "No worries. And thank you."

I helped her step over the padded green barrier that separated the box from the field, and as her foot touched the grass she slipped a little and I had to clutch her with both arms. When she caught her balance, we stepped apart, awkward. She tucked a stray ringlet of brown hair behind her ear, a tiny hint of a smile circling her green eyes. "You're graceful for a writer," she said. "And now I know you're a writer."

"What do you mean?"

"I read your article," she said. "I admire people who are observant enough to see more than their own biases. That's what I try to do with my camera. It's nice to find someone on the same mission. I mean, we're almost partners, right?"

In that instant I realized that if I asked her to dinner, she would probably say yes. I always think it's remarkable when another person is willing to give you that kind of chance, but when a woman as attractive as Jessica feels that way . . . it's certainly flattering. I tried to savor the moment—after all, it hadn't been so long ago that I had embarrassed myself in a bar in Rochester. And when the moment ended, I remembered Molly and carefully offered Jessica my hand.

"Thanks again," I said. "I'll see you around."

• • •

I strode into the Sox locker room, bold as a base stealer, but my confidence evaporated when I saw Casey chatting casually with a group of cameras and pens. I froze and stood alone in the middle of the room. Perhaps it was my imagination, but I thought I could feel the triumphant glances of the other reporters—I knew how deeply they had resented the out-of-towner with unlimited access to the new star. But now they had won. I felt like the new kid looking for a place to sit in a high school cafeteria, and I was slinking toward the door when Casey called to me from across the room.

"Russ," he shouted.

I turned, surprised and a little bit grateful. And when I saw the jealous looks on the faces of the reporters surrounding Casey, my gratitude turned into smug elation. "Yeah?"

Casey had jogged across the room, and he draped his arm around me. "We've got to talk. Dugout okay?"

"Sure," I said.

We walked down the long red and blue hall, and before we reached the entrance to the dugout, I already knew that Casey's friendliness in the locker room had been an act. He ripped open the door at the top of steps so hard that I feared it might fly off its cast-iron hinges, and as soon as we were in the dugout he whirled on me. His finger drilled my chest, and I took two steps backward and awkwardly leaned against the concrete wall.

"*Hard Copy*'s doing a special report on me tomorrow night," he said, his eyes as hard as titanium. "I've been seeing the trailers the last two days. You wouldn't know anything about it, would you?"

"Nope." I considered adding a smart-ass comment, but his body language was so aggressive that I decided not to provoke him.

"You see, they claim they've got someone really close to me talking on camera. And I was just wondering . . ." His voice trailed off, his insinuation clear.

"You were wondering if I was the source."

"Not the source," he said. "The snitch. The sellout. The little bitch who took advantage of me."

"You got the wrong guy," I said.

"Do I?" He leaned against the field side of the dugout and folded his arms across his massive chest. I felt as if I were being interrogated by the SS. "Last I heard you were writing an article about a dead friend of mine."

"I'm not having this argument with you again." I stood to leave, knowing that no good could possibly come from this conversation.

Casey slid over to block my path to the door. "That's because you're a pussy." I knew he was deliberately provoking me, but I could feel the gorge rise in the reptilian part of my brain anyway. "Just another pussy reporter too scared to be a real man."

"I'm going to Honduras in two days," I said. "With Molly." I don't know how or why it popped out of my mouth—I'd blame my anger and resentment, except that I'm usually fairly good at controlling those emotions. Casey was staring at me, stunned, and I felt a tiny twinge of dirty joy when I realized that I had deeply hurt him. "She hasn't told you?"

"Why the fuck are *you* going?" he asked.

"Because I love her." His face registered shock and then— maybe—panic. "And I think she loves me."

"She can't be in love. Not with you." He had slumped back against the dugout railing, his usual confidence and self-assurance forgotten. "You were supposed to be safe. I mean, how does someone like Molly . . ." He stared at me blankly. "What a ridiculous fucking world."

"You thought a guy like me couldn't get a girl like her, huh?" I tried to be offended, but a big piece of me still agreed with him. "I guess you were wrong."

"I can't be wrong," Casey said.

"Why is it so impossible that she could love me?"

"Because she's supposed to love me," he shouted, his words echoing from the weathered green wall of the Monster. His voice, when he spoke again, was barely a whisper. "That's the way it's supposed to be."

"You picked baseball," I said, shocked and a little scared that he'd finally articulated his feelings. "So don't pretend to have regrets. Molly could never love a guy who yelled at a reporter for doing his job. A guy who watched his friend die and then hid from the responsibility. If you can't be the man she wants, have some goddamned grace and let someone else make her happy."

He allowed me my lecture, but he was swelling the whole time and he rose to his feet when I was finished. I smiled at him, feeling unnaturally calm. I needed to hate him—needed it so badly that I deliberately tossed napalm onto the fires of his anger. "You're the real coward," I said.

His heavy fist hit me flush on the right side of my jaw, just low enough that his knuckle avoided my cheekbone. My knees weakened with pain, and I folded onto the dusty floor of the dugout, the smoke of a wet campfire in my mouth. The warm rush of blood came a moment later, and I let the first ounce run onto the dirty cement floor where it formed a little pool of moral superiority. Casey knelt beside me, his hand resting gently on my shoulder.

"If you're going to be with Molly," he said quietly, "I know I'll have to see you again. And the only thing that will keep me from kicking your ass every time we meet is if I see that she's happier than she's ever been in her life. You understand me?"

"Yeah." I spat again. Something wasn't right with my jaw because when I opened it to talk, I felt a click and a sharp needle jab just beneath my ear. But I had something I needed to say, so I mumbled through the pain. "I was her second choice, Casey. Don't blame me for your mistakes."

His hand flinched away from my arm as if I'd just told him that I had Ebola, and his mouth snapped open and shut for a minute before he composed himself enough to speak. "Do you really think that you can be everything that Molly needs?" I just stared at him, and he stood. "Fuck it. You can figure it out for yourself."

I closed my eyes and soon heard the metallic slam of the dugout door. I began to slowly poke and prod at the right side of my jaw, trying to ensure that Casey hadn't caused any major damage. Honduras isn't the kind of country where you want to undergo major oral surgery. As I finished my investigation and determined that I was bruised but not broken, I heard the skip of quick steps down the dugout stairs. When I opened my eyes, I saw Jessica standing over me.

"You okay?" she asked.

I smiled weakly enough to point out the inanity of her question—after all, I was bleeding on the floor of a dugout—and then struggled to pull myself upright. "Just dandy. You see that?"

She triumphantly held up her camera. "Everything. You got that son of a bitch nailed. That's an easy million-dollar lawsuit."

"No," I said.

She was petting her camera like a prize poodle. "This is a ten-thousand-dollar picture. At least."

"Jessica." I grunted as loudly as I could through my sluggish jaw. "If you sell that picture, I'll claim that Casey and I were play fighting."

She looked away from her camera, shocked and a little annoyed. "Are you serious?"

"Completely," I said. "I deserved to be hit."

"Because of your story?"

I shook my head, ignoring the judgment in her tone. "Because of a girl. I stole the most important thing in his life."

She examined me carefully, one of the dimples next to her mouth disappearing and reappearing like evidence in the Los Angles Police Department. "A girl chose you over Casey Fox?"

"Are you surprised?"

"Not really," she said. "I'd go out with you long before I'd go out with a ballplayer." With one last long glance at me, she popped open the back of her camera, slowly unwrapped the film from the reel, and tossed the exposed roll in the dugout trash. When she was finished, she offered me her hand. "I'm doing this as a favor to you," she said. "Not to him."

I waved away her hand—I needed to sit for another couple minutes. "Any chance you could find me some ice?"

chapter 31

LATE THAT NIGHT I CALLED MOLLY AND TOLD HER THAT I HAD managed to get a ticket on her flight to Honduras. A happy little noise that made everything worthwhile burst through the line, and I had to hold the phone away from my ear. I told her that I would meet her at Logan before six o'clock, and she asked if I was going to the playoff game earlier that afternoon against the Yankees. I said I didn't know, which was the truth. As much as I felt that I needed the closure of watching Casey play in a game that seemed destined to make a hero of someone, I also knew that my bizarre ride needed to end eventually. I was tired of living vicariously though the success of other people.

The following morning I took care of a couple little details that I had forgotten during the rush of the previous day. I overpaid my credit cards and health insurance, threw my savings into my checking account, and switched all my billing addresses to my parents' house in Vermont. I would need them to occasionally send out checks and fill out forms—just another example of how modern life conspires to keep you in one place by making mobility impossible without either a secretary or an understanding mother. The best news of the morning was that my jaw had responded well to a steady diet of ice and Advil, and although I had a heavy bruise that would slowly fade from blue to green like a seasick chameleon, I seemed to have avoided any long-term injury that would require a doctor.

I bought a travel guide to Honduras at lunch and spent the afternoon in a café leafing through it. Since I didn't even know what region of the country Molly would be working in, I browsed through every section. In the late afternoon I napped in a patch of grass near the Charles River and dreamed of coffee plantations and rural farms and mystical, fog-enshrouded mountains. I ate dinner in a sandwich shop in Kenmore Square and then packed all my belongings into a duffel bag, two suitcases, and a laptop case. I wondered briefly if my laptop would return safely from Central America and decided that it would probably be stolen in the first week—if the bizarrely intermittent power grid didn't kill it.

I tried to avoid watching the *Hard Copy* special on Casey, but my finger was drawn to the remote control like a politician to PAC money. I had a morbid curiosity about the identity of the source—my best guess was that they had paid Mr. McDowell for old photographs and a couple of vague rumors. When the show's trademark overdramatic music began playing, I found myself leaning closer to the television. The host took what felt like an hour to introduce the story, and I was on the verge of throwing my shoe at the screen when they finally cut to the interview. I blanched as the soft camera peered up into Nate's face. He finally had his moment on television.

The interview itself consisted of an embarrassing series of revelations vaguely supported by grainy pictures and interviews with kids with bad hair and thick accents. Nate told the typical story of a kid growing up poor in Providence—bushels of pot, cheap vodka, chugging cough syrup when they couldn't find pot or cheap vodka, breaking windows, avoiding cops, fighting anyone and everyone. The way *Hard Copy* put the material together managed to make Casey's life sound clichéd and sordid at the same time. And when Nate finally revealed that Casey had been supplying Terrell with his uppers, the producers ran a "dramatic re-creation" that made it seem as if Casey had been rooting for his death.

I turned off the television at the end of the interview and lay still on my bed. Even my aching jaw couldn't prevent me from feeling sorry for Casey—most people aren't betrayed on national television. The show had been over for an hour when I heard a tentative knock from the hall. I considered ignoring it, but eventually rolled out of bed and padded across the dingy carpet in my bare feet. I opened the door a half inch and saw Casey standing outside, his face ashen. Two Buds dangled from his right hand.

"Share a beer?" he asked, his voice unsteady.

"Sure."

I put on a pair of jeans and a sweatshirt, and we walked to the concrete bridge that connects Fenway to Kenmore Square. Fall drizzle was leaking from the hazy yellow sky in uneven clumps, and a wet rush of cars ran beneath us on the Mass Pike in a steady and unending stream. We opened our beers on the chain-link fence that was supposed to prevent Casey from jumping off the bridge, and hid them every time a cop came rushing past us en route to saving downtown Boston from yuppies and rich college kids. I stared up at the bright neon Citgo sign.

"So it was Nate," I said.

"Yeah." Casey took a long swig from his beer. "You can't trust many people in this world, can you?"

"He wanted to be on TV."

"I've only had one person I could trust in my whole life," he said. "Just one."

"Nothing's changed," I said. "She'll always be there."

He slowly turned to face me, and I could feel his heavy gaze on my cheek. "Look at me, Russ," he said. I took a careful breath, and then turned to face him. Our eyes locked, and I was reminded of my fear the night I was pitching tennis balls to him and Terrell. "Do you love her?"

My eyes shifted to his shirt, and I let my upper body lean against the chain-link fence. "I guess."

"Oh, no," he said, his tone as lethal as an adder. "Don't guess. Either you love her and will make her happy, or you disappear from her life and get on the next bus back to nowhere. Because you owe me that. And, more importantly, you owe her that."

I took another deep breath, and as my lungs expanded and my heart came free in my chest, I found the strength and honesty to look him again in the eye. "I will do everything that I can do, for as long as she'll let me stick around, to make her happy. And that's the first real promise I've ever made in my life."

Casey abruptly reached up and touched my jaw, turning my head so that the bruise was facing him. "Let me look at that," he said, peering at the mark he had made.

I slapped his hand away. "I haven't forgiven you, Casey. And you haven't forgiven me. So let's cut through all the smoke." I paused and then spoke as slowly and deliberately as my terror would allow. "Knowing you for the last four months has saved me, so I'm going to give you one chance. You can have my ticket and go to Honduras instead of me."

His eyes exploded for a fraction of a second with the most brilliantly ecstatic glow I've ever seen outside a Rubens painting, then faded quickly, crushed by reality. I kept talking so he would know that I was completely serious. "Plane leaves tomorrow after the game. All you need is a passport and a swimsuit."

I had made the offer because I knew that he couldn't possibly accept—and because I knew that it would relieve some of my guilt. But as I watched his face struggle tortuously with the consequences of saying no, I realized how cruel I was being. And when he finally spoke, I could practically see his heart fall out of his mouth. "I can't."

"I know," I said quietly. I tossed my beer bottle over the chain-link fence and watched it fall in a flat arc until it finally shattered on the train tracks far beneath us. "Good luck with the game."

I lay in bed for most of the next morning, trying to decide if I wanted to go watch the Yankees play the Red Sox. I was wasting my time. Perhaps I could give you a hundred reasons why the healthy thing for me to do would have been to go to the Museum of Fine Arts and then drive directly to the airport, but none of those reasons would ever outweigh the fact that Boston was meeting New York in a one-game playoff just a mile from my motel. No force in the world could have kept me from that park—not even my knowledge that I would have to spend one more afternoon staring at Casey.

Two hours before the game I began pacing the block of cement on Massachusetts Avenue where you can usually find a pack of scalpers. Since I knew the game would be a tough ticket, I brought an envelope stuffed with $20 bills. After a brief search I found my man. He was wearing the standard Boston scalper uniform of a jeans jacket and a blue Sox cap, and we ducked into the shadow of a brick staircase to conduct our business. When I said that I only wanted one seat, he shuffled through his small stack and offered me a bleacher ticket. I carefully checked the water seal.

"How much?" I asked.

"Two hundred, pal."

I didn't have to fake my incredulous laughter. "That's ridiculous. This isn't New York."

His shrug eloquently suggested that he knew he was working in a seller's market. "It's the game of the millennium, buddy."

"The damn millennium's only ten months old," I muttered.

"Actually," he said, "the real millennium doesn't switch until this year. You see—"

I cut him off. "I know. I'll take the damn ticket."

My seat was nestled above the bullpens in the left-field corner, just a dozen feet from the worst grandstand section in the stadium. The bleachers are a good place for a baseball purist because they're always filled with real fans—no corporation in its right mind would send its clients into the cheap seats at Fenway—and you hear the full range of New England accents.

Guys from Worcester and Revere and Southie all expounding on the same central point: the Yankees represent the purest form of evil in the known universe. An hour before the game, when the position players were jogging in center field and the pitchers were long tossing along the third-base line, the first rhythmic "Yankees suck" chant began. And a small cadre of New York fans sitting near me who had foolishly chosen to wear Yankee apparel were dodging flying $7 beers from the moment the concession kiosks opened.

Usually the endless and tiresome juvenilia of a game in the stands wears on my patience after a few innings—perhaps that stems from my trained reporter's feeling of superiority to the common fan. And life in the bleachers can be pretty stupid. There are two great rules of fan behavior. First, something about being on television sparks a chemical imbalance in the brain that causes an otherwise rational human being to make a complete ass of himself. I used to know a guy who worked the Fox camera at Mets games, and he had less respect for *Homo sapiens* as a species than Larry Flynt. Second, the number of beach balls that are knocked onto the field, waves that roll around the stands, and batteries thrown at outfielders rises in direct proportion to the per-capita beer consumption of the home fans. On a warm afternoon in the Fenway bleachers, when smuggled cans of Coors have been rolling through the crowd like dollar dogs, the entire intoxicated human mass seems liable to slide onto the field in an overheated avalanche of foolish humanity.

On this particular afternoon, however, I reveled in the entire scene. I had been in a press box for so long—a place where you can't root for a team, where you can't show emotion. Baseball feels so antiseptic from up there; the game becomes a box score and a repetitive interview and which player threw the fastball when he should have thrown the curve. I suppose I might have remained in that mode even in the bleachers, but a group of five firemen from Malden broke me from my routine the moment I sat down next to them. They were drunk and passionate, thrilled to discover that I knew something about the team, and quick to accept me as a member of their group. By the time the game began, my voice was already hoarse from yelling a mixture of clever and pedestrian jeers at the Yankees in the bullpen.

The first inning did not go well. Jimy Williams, riding one of his legendary hunches, started the enigmatic knuckleballer Tim Wakefield. To be fair to Jimy, he didn't really have a choice—his two best starters were both too tired to pitch, and he didn't want to rely on a rookie. But the decision proved disastrous as the Yankees scored six runs in the top of the first on a mixture of walks and sharply hit ground balls that nimbly avoided the Boston infielders. Although as a baseball writer I often used the cliché "the air went out of the park" to describe the fans' reaction to something horrible happening to the home team, until that afternoon I'd never known exactly what it meant. But when the Yankees scored those six runs, it felt as if someone had lowered a vacuum cleaner over the stands. We still cheered, but our voices had no depth, no air. We were all throat and no lungs.

In the bottom of the second Nomar hit a home run that soared over the Monster like a phosphorus mortar round, and the crowd ignited once again. A string of Boston relief pitchers did a wonderful job, and when Everett hit a two-run single in the fifth to bring the Sox within a run, the park became a screaming madhouse. We stood to yell every time a Sox pitcher got two strikes on a Yankee batter, every time a Yankee pitcher got three balls on a Sox hitter, every time a Boston player reached base. We swore and muttered when the Yankees scored another run in the top of the sixth to make the score 7–5, but our voices otherwise rose uninterrupted to the clear New England sky.

Our little group, however, got a little panicky as the sixth turned into the seventh and the Sox still couldn't score. We all knew that the strength of the Yankees, the real reason for New York's phenomenal postseason success, was its airtight bullpen. In addition to having two ace setup men, the Yankees were blessed with Mariano Rivera, a closer who essentially shortens the game by one inning. Scoring even one run against Rivera is kind of like predicting that the United States will someday field a championship men's soccer team—it could happen, but you aren't likely to make money betting on it.

So although we cheered avidly when the Sox bullpen held in the top of the eighth, we swallowed hard when Boston didn't even make a whimper in the bottom of the inning. And when Rivera began warming up in front of us in the top of the ninth, our jeers were almost pathetically desperate—telling Mariano Rivera that he sucks is a bit like telling Joe Montana that he can't win the big game. The Sox pitchers made us all nervous in the top of the ninth by loading the bases, but didn't give up any runs, and as the team trotted to the dugout I glanced at my scorecard for the first time in several innings. Casey was scheduled to come to the plate fifth—we needed to get at least two men on base.

Trot Nixon was the first batter of the inning, and he appeared horribly overmatched on the first two pitches, missing the first by a foot and barely fouling the second one off. Rivera wasted a pitch in the dirt and then threw a perfect 100-mile-an-hour fastball on the outside corner. Nixon reached out with his bat, the kind of excuse-me swing that makes you wonder if "swing" is really an action verb, and rolled the ball weakly down the third-base line. He sprinted to first as fast as a burly doctor's kid from North Carolina can run, flying on the strength of our cheers, and beat the throw by half a step. Rivera, however, tempered our enthusiasm by striking out Sadler and Offerman on a combined seven pitches.

The season therefore came down to Troy O'Leary, who had struggled at the plate all year long. Just from the tentative way he dug his back foot into the box, I knew that he expected his disastrous season to end on an appropriately dismal note. I could tell that Casey shared my fears because instead of swinging his bat in the on-deck circle, he was just staring at the mound. And then, on the very first pitch, a miracle occurred. Rivera threw a cut fastball inside that must have slipped off one of his fingers the wrong way, and he drilled O'Leary in the small of the back. I've never seen a man so happy to be hit. O'Leary skipped down the first-base line, a condemned man who had somehow received an eleventh-hour reprieve.

As Casey slowly strode to the plate, the entire park rhythmically chanted his name. His night, so far, had been uneventful. He had two walks and a quiet single that he had looped to right field on a pitch far outside the strike zone. Perhaps the Yankees had decided that they weren't going to let Casey beat them, but in this situation they had no choice—up two runs they couldn't risk loading the bases for Nomar. I was so caught up in the moment that my anger at Casey temporarily vaporized, my mind focusing exclusively on how much I wanted him to crush the ball. I was a fan. Nothing more. My notebook lay unused in my lap, and I let myself feed on the energy surrounding me rather than trying to remove myself from the emotion of the moment. Rarely in life do you find a large group of people who want exactly the same thing that you do, and in my connection to the fans jumping and swaying around me, I felt the purest sense of community that I had experienced since college.

Casey was an eddy in the torrent of noise and motion. Rivera had to step off the rubber three times before he could throw the first pitch, and each time Casey carefully tapped the dirt from his cleats before resetting himself in the batter's box. It seemed as if he was seeking calm by performing the mundane ritual. And then it suddenly occurred to me that Casey probably was calm—in fact, he was almost certainly the calmest person in the park. Because he was the only person who had any control over what was about to happen. Casey once told me that it is impossible to hit a home run on demand. Simply impossible. You can't just swing harder or concentrate more intensely or wish the ball any faster into the air. Baseball is a game of averages, not willpower. Yet I somehow knew that at this particular moment Casey could choose. He could hit a home run if he wanted . . . or he could strike out or hit it to the first baseman or pop out to the shortstop. And he just might be obstinate enough to strike out. But I needed him to hit a home run; I needed him to prove that he was something different. Not just another ballplayer, which would make our entire story merely another sideshow in the strange world of professional sports, but a true force of nature. An athlete beyond rational explanation.

Rivera finally started his abbreviated windup, and Casey's name caught in the back of my throat. From my distant seat I saw the blur of Rivera's arm and then the tiny white streak heading toward the plate. Casey's swing was so controlled, so balanced, that it seemed impossible that the pitch could do anything but meet the bat. I lost sight of the ball as it changed direction, and it was already rising swiftly toward me when I heard the electric crack of wood meeting leather. For a millisecond the park was virtually silent as thousands of brains calculated speed and azimuth and wind and fate. But I had seen Casey hit enough home runs to know from the way he jogged toward first base, his head down and fist gently pumping, that the game was over.

The ball landed in the crowd thirty yards from me, and Rivera was already walking off the field as the jubilant mob from the Boston dugout stormed toward the infield. The crowd, however, remained frozen for a moment in a state of shock and confusion—we were Red Sox fans, trained to accept failure, utterly unaccustomed to dramatic victories in high-pressure situations. Especially against the Yankees. And then, like an avalanche breaking from an overloaded cornice, we shattered with a noise that I have never heard at any sporting event before or since, a great cathartic roar that must have rolled like a shock wave to the farthest reaches of New England. As I joined the mosh pit around me, jumping and hugging and slapping hands, an image suddenly came to me of a Sox fan watching the game on the airport television in Bali—the only place on the island where they get ESPN—leaping and crying with lonely yet irrepressible joy as a hundred confused tourists and locals watched him curiously.

Casey had barely made it to third base when the first fans broke onto the field. A long cordon of Sox security guards and Massachusetts State Troopers on horseback had lined the first- and third-base line to keep the field clear, but it would have been easier for them to stop the rotation of the earth than control the crowd. The fans in the bleachers around me flowed from my section onto the field as one organism, and I had to clutch my seat to keep from being dragged with the churning mass. Casey had disappeared in the mob around home plate, and the only Boston player I could see clearly was Nomar, perched nervously on a horse above his adoring fans. I turned my back to the field, slowly trudged up to the top of the bleachers, and sat under the enormous Jumbotron. I was the only solitary figure I could see in the park—no one, not even an usher, was within 100 yards of me.

I quietly watched the giddy scene unfold, happy and drained. The back of my throat felt as if I'd swallowed a barrel of coarse sand. I was once again an observer rather than a participant, but that fact didn't upset me. I am an observer. That's the real reason I was originally drawn to reporting, and even though over the previous few months I had begun to learn how to participate fully in life, in my heart I knew that I would always be more interested in watching other people succeed. Perhaps that quality will make me a good father someday. I was still lost in that thought when Casey abruptly appeared on top of the Boston dugout, waving his hands over his head, the crowd erupting into cheers like Romans saluting a victorious general. I smiled to myself, knowing that he would never have a better moment in professional baseball.

And suddenly I felt tremendously guilty. While Casey might be standing on top of the dugout dutifully playing the role of hero, he was probably no happier than after hitting a home run in Pawtucket or for his Providence Little League team. Casey loved to play baseball, and he certainly was good at it, but he didn't need to be a Major League player to feed his love of the game. He would have been perfectly happy on one of those old barnstorming teams that used to bus across the Midwest living on $5 a day in meal money, and he could be ecstatic playing on some local team in Central America—just so long as he got to swing a bat and run the bases. In fact, all the trappings of Major League Baseball were just keeping him from the things he really wanted: real friends, space to create a life, Molly.

My chin dropped to my knees as the real reason Casey had befriended me became obvious. He had seen long before me exactly how much we had in common. Casey understood that my life was missing all the pieces that I needed to make me happy, and he related to that perfectly. In the course of our short friendship, Casey had shown me all those missing things, which made him a better friend to me than anyone I had ever known. And in return I had stolen the most important part of Casey's life—the part that could have made him happy. Because what's important to Casey Fox isn't professional baseball or money or all the other crap. What's important to Casey Fox is Molly, the only person he knows who can help him the way he helped me.

An instant later, sparked by those realizations, I had my first true epiphany. The real source of my own feelings toward Molly was the way she made me feel about myself. I had believed that my life, which had so far been largely a waste, could be redeemed by the love of a woman as complete and perfect as Molly. Why I felt that I needed a woman to redeem me is probably a conversation best left to me and my psychotherapist—if I can ever afford one. But the more important issue is how horrible it is to be the person placed upon a pedestal. Molly had asked me to try to see the real her, yet I still needed her to be perfect, which is the most limiting and stifling thing one person can ask of another. I wanted Molly to fit my own idealized image so that I could feel better about me. Casey, however, needed the true Molly. And that was something special.

So the solution was painful but obvious. I don't have many friends—I've lived too lonely a life. But Casey Fox was my friend in the truest sense of the word. He had saved me by showing me what I wanted to become, which meant I owed him even more than my friendship. I owed him the opportunity to change everything.

I allowed myself one more minute to enjoy the wild celebration covering the field below me, then carefully picked my way down the bleachers and onto the grass. I had barely gone ten steps across the outfield when I saw Jessica standing on a front-row seat in the grandstand, balancing a huge lens on the Pesky Pole. I jogged over to her and tugged on her pant leg.

"I need an enormous favor," I said.

She didn't bother glancing away from the viewfinder on her camera. "This is kind of a bad time."

"It's really important." I must have sounded desperate because she stared at me, her eyes wide. "Do you have a cell phone?"

"Of course," she said.

She stepped down from the seat, ignoring my proffered hand, and slung her camera around her neck. "I have to talk to Casey," I said, "but I can't get through the crowd without a press pass." I handed her one of my old business cards from the *Times*. "Get Casey to call this number. Tell him that if he calls right now, he'll never have to speak to me again."

She carefully tucked the card in her front pocket, then smiled mischievously. "You owe me huge," she said.

I sat on the edge of the wall and watched as Jessica walked over to a pair of enormous State Troopers impassively watching the mild riot occurring on the field around them. She spoke for ten or fifteen seconds, her hand fiddling with her hair and her chest occasionally bouncing to accentuate a particularly important point. Whatever she said must have worked because they escorted her into the swirling mass near home plate. I chuckled softly. I admired Jessica's gift for getting men to do what she wanted—my life as a reporter would have been much easier if I could have flirted my way into a police escort.

My phone rang five minutes later, and I took several deep breaths before I answered. Casey's voice, garbled by the shouts and yelps in the background, was waiting. "Yeah?"

I shouted into the speaker to make certain that he could hear me. "You've changed your mind, haven't you?"

"Maybe," he said. "I don't know. I have my stuff in the car."

"Passport and everything?"

He paused for a moment, and the background noise got so muffled that I thought a rabid fan might have swallowed the phone. "I want to see her at least before she goes," he eventually said.

"How fast can you get out of here?"

He paused again, this time to let me know exactly how stupid my question was. "It's kind of tough right now," he said dryly.

"Take a horse," I suggested, only half-joking. I heard what could have been a laugh but what was probably some jackass embarrassing himself in the background. "I'll meet you by the players' entrance in half an hour."

chapter 32

IT TOOK ME TWENTY MINUTES TO GO FOUR BLOCKS IN MY CAR, and when I finally stopped in front of the players' entrance, I was hemmed in on all sides by several hundred screaming fans. The first sign of Casey was a riot squad of ten cops that bullied through the amorphous mass and formed a rough line from the door to my car. The crowd pressed in as Casey, still wearing his dirty uniform, sprinted through the line like a skittish running back hitting a hole against Pittsburgh's Steel Curtain, his bags bouncing wildly behind him. He slid in the car and locked the door.

"Drive," he said.

I gestured at the unbroken crowd in front of my hood. "How?"

People were banging on the roof, pounding on the windows, and the car was rocking so much that I had to squeeze the steering wheel just to keep my balance. Toyota didn't design its economy line for urban riots. "Just drive," Casey said. "Now."

I hit the accelerator and the crowd miraculously parted just enough to allow my little car out toward Landsdown Street. I don't think I took more than four breaths until we were safely on Storrow Drive. Casey dug in his bags until he found a pair of shorts and a T-shirt, and he changed while I waited in traffic at the beginning of the Sullivan tunnel. We were in the middle of the dirty yellow tube, exhaust clogging our lungs, when Casey finally spoke.

"Should I go?" I could tell he wasn't being dramatic—he wanted a real answer.

"Yeah," I said. "But you don't have to go today. You could wait until the playoffs are over."

He shook his head firmly. "If I'm going to go, I have to go today. Because when you make a decision about the rest of your life, you should want the rest of your life to start as soon as possible. Right?"

"Sure," I said. And then the one question that had been burning in the back of my mind finally pressed so far forward that I couldn't ignore it any longer. "What the hell are you going to do in Honduras? Because it's going to be pretty damn dull if you're just sitting around waiting for her to get home from work."

"Spoken like a man from the Ivy League." I refused to rise to the bait and waited for Casey to explain himself. The car burst out of the tunnel, Boston to our back, the looming concrete monoliths of Logan Airport rising in my windshield. We passed the sports complex of a local high school, and out of the corner of my eye I could see Casey staring at the baseball field. As he spoke again, his jaw muscles were working so furiously that his temples were flexing with the strain.

"I think that life is about finding out what's important to you and then doing it. And sometimes that means you've got to stop and figure out what matters. Maybe I'll play on a semipro team in Honduras. Maybe I'll work at the orphanage or at a school or on a farm. And no, I won't be contributing as much to the global economy as if I were playing Major League Baseball. But that's not the point." He paused, and then looked at me for the first time in our conversation. "You know what I'm talking about, Russ. It's why we spent so much time together and why we could have been good friends."

"Could have been?"

"I don't think I want to see you again," he said quietly.

My quad tightened and my foot involuntarily pulled away from the accelerator. I wasn't entirely surprised, but to hear him say it so plainly tore a hole out of my chest. "I understand."

I parked in Logan's brand-new central garage, and Casey left his dirty uniform in my car—he said that I could sell it if I wanted. As we walked down the long glass corridor to the International Terminal, I fought to control my staccato breath.

"Let me talk to her first," I said. "I think it will make things easier."

He just nodded, and we took a long escalator down into the main departure hall. Across the room I saw the American Airlines booth where Molly and I were supposed to meet. She wasn't there, so I scanned the hall and found her standing next to a travel kiosk a 100 yards away. "Wait here," I said to Casey. "I'll be back in a minute."

I turned to leave, but Casey grabbed my arm and I spun back toward him. I could tell from his expression that he was as lost as the night Terrell died—and seeing him so obviously floundering made me feel a tiny bit better. I expected him to say something roughly conciliatory, but when his mouth opened his expression had evolved into intense anger. "Today against the Yankees," he said. "That was a nice moment. But don't get confused—there's no magic left in professional sports. I suspected it before I got to Boston, I know it now. And you know it too. So don't let me ever catch you becoming part of the shit. Because you're better than that."

When he finished he stood frozen, his hands balled into fists, the fierce set of his jaw telling me that he would feel a lot better if we got in another fight. I just smiled. "Do you really think I'd let you run off to Honduras with Molly if I didn't plan on doing something worthwhile with my life here?"

I left before Casey could say anything else and slowly walked toward Molly. She saw me when I was halfway across the atrium, and she gave me a bright smile that made me move even slower.

When I finally reached her side, she kissed me on the cheek. "Hey," she said. "I was starting to worry that you weren't going to show."

I had been on autopilot ever since I had made my decision in the Fenway bleachers, carefully avoiding giving myself the luxury of considering the full consequences of my choice, but standing in front of Molly I felt the first pangs of what would become an exquisite pain. Her eyes bothered me the most—so happy and open and full of faith. All my life I've dreamed of having a woman look at me that way, even for a moment.

"Did you check in?" I asked, my voice hollow.

"Yeah. Where are your bags?"

"I've got something to tell you," I said slowly. She must have thought that I didn't want to go with her because her face collapsed under a critical load of disappointment. "Casey came with me from the park. He wants to go to Honduras with you."

I tried not to watch as the full range of emotions played across her face, but I saw enough happiness to know that I had made the right decision. I had to clear my throat before I could speak again. "I think he should be the one who goes."

"Why?" she asked so softly that I had to read her trembling lips.

I drew as deep a breath as my tight chest would allow. "It's not that I don't really care about you, because you know I do. In fact, I . . ." Although I viciously snapped my mouth shut before I could use the word love, I know she could tell what I meant because she stepped forward and gently rested her hand on my arm. "I think you like having me around," I said, avoiding her soft gaze. "We're okay. But we'll never be the way that you and Casey could be."

"Don't I have a say in this?" she asked, her voice blurry.

"Of course you do." I gathered myself and stared directly into her hazy eyes. "Casey and I both want to come to Honduras. Who are you going to pick?"

I waited for a full ten seconds, hoping against all reason that she would say the perfect thing, but she just dropped her head, and I smiled sadly. I pulled her droopy body into a loose hug, her warm tears searing my neck, and I twisted my head so that my mouth was next to her flushed ear. "Make it work," I whispered. "Make it so great that I'll know I did the right thing."

We parted and she pulled herself together with a violent sniff. "You take care of yourself. Go find another muse."

I smiled again, this time for real. "There's no such thing as a muse," I said. "You made me write because I wanted to be a better man for you. But that's cheating. I should want to be a better man for myself."

I turned and walked away as quickly as my dignity would allow. I stopped by the huge windows that overlook the terminal's loading zone, and some masochistic instinct made me turn and watch Casey warily approach Molly. She was frozen, her arms limp at her sides, and I felt a tiny flicker of irrational hope. They stood awkwardly for a moment, and then Casey dropped his bags and they embraced, clinging to each other like reunited refugees, so right that I had to spin back toward the window and close my eyes.

When a decent enough amount of time had passed, I waved to Casey, and he met me at the American Airlines service counter. I tried to convince an unbearably perky agent that he should let me switch the name on the ticket, and after he had exerted a large indignity on my credit card, he finally acquiesced. Casey checked his bags and then we walked together to meet Molly by the news kiosk. She looked at me, and I bristled at the pity in her eyes.

"Are you going to take us to the gate?" she asked.

"No," I said. "This is the end of the line."

I carefully shook Casey's hand, and Molly leaned toward me. Our cheeks gently brushed. Then they were walking away through the terminal, inches apart but not touching. I was about to leave when Casey abruptly stopped and turned back to me. He looked like a college student in his T-shirt and shorts, and for an instant I saw him not as a famous ballplayer, but as a confused kid still trying to figure out what he wanted in this life. He would need Molly. I had just begun to wonder why he had stopped when he waved to make sure he had my attention. I waved back.

"You can write about me," he shouted. "Anything. As long as you have a point." I gestured to let him know that I had heard him, and then he and Molly walked away again. A few steps later the crowd of restless travelers swallowed them, and the last thing I saw was Molly slowly but firmly taking his hand.

"I admire the way you catch a game of baseball," I whispered.

For over an hour I wandered through the sterile rabbit warren of theme restaurants and security guards and white halogen lights. I passed businesspeople bustling toward never-ending connections with an intensity that left me spinning in their wakes; tourists with white Boston thighs peeking from under too-small cruise shorts. The moment I collapsed on a bench to regroup, I was immediately swallowed by a gaggle of honeymooners in transparent love and grandparents en route to visiting cherubic children in the Midwest. I couldn't breathe. When my loneliness made me desperate to find someone else with a transparently empty life, I strapped myself to a heartless-looking suit, the kind of guy who could have been an extra in *Wall Street*, only to watch him walk straight into the arms of a Hollywood family.

As I absorbed the people around me, watched the couples talking and hugging and living lives, I briefly wondered what idiocy had driven me to sacrifice true intimacy on behalf of someone who could no longer stand my company. Yet even in the searing sadness of that moment, I knew that I had made the decision not for Casey or Molly, but for myself. I couldn't spend my life not being someone. Especially now that I was starting to learn a little bit about the person I wanted to become: the kind of man who is comfortable enough in his own skin to just live.

Or maybe that is just the best lie I have constructed yet.

Eventually I stumbled out of the terminal and into the parking lot. When I found my car, I lay on the hood and rested my head on the smooth windshield, the edge of the cool wiper tickling the back of my neck. The lights of Boston had blotted the stars into an indistinct charcoal mass. I could neither see nor hear another human being, but evidence of our presence overwhelmed my senses. Light towers, glowing runways, and indistinguishable concrete edifices concealed the last remains of the old virgin shore, while over my head the great rolling roars of planes heading for the scattered corners of an ever-expanding civilization thundered in the empty night.

As my body slowly stiffened in the cold sea air, I carefully tried to memorize the shattered feeling in my chest. I could see the difference between the cynical reporter in Providence and the forlorn man lying on the hood of his rundown car, and that vision liberated me. I was no longer numb. Perhaps I would fail a thousand times in the coming years as I pursued love and meaning, yet every failure would be a welcome reminder of the emptiness I had left behind. For the first time since my childhood I knew that someday I would have a home, a place warm enough to reach the solitude of my heart, and it was that knowledge that eventually gave me the strength to get in my car, turn on the radio, and start my life.

epilogue

ON OCTOBER 4 I STOOD IN FRONT OF A ROOM FILLED WITH reporters and camera crews and read the following statement: "Yesterday afternoon Casey Fox decided to retire from Major League Baseball. He has given me a check for five thousand dollars, which is half of his signing bonus, and he has asked me to return that money to the team. He also renounces any rights to a playoff share. Mr. Fox would like to thank the city of Boston for the time he spent here, and he deeply regrets any inconvenience his actions may cause to Red Sox management." At that point I followed Casey's stage directions and glanced up at the rolling cameras. "Since he knows that we won't respect his request for privacy, he has decided not to tell us where he is going. But he wants everyone to know that he plans on being very happy. Thank you for your time."

I made it out of the room alive—just barely—and I had to hide at my parents' house for a week until my cell phone started logging fewer than three hundred calls per day. The city of Boston's reaction to Casey's abrupt departure could kindly be described as irate or accurately described as apoplectic. The columnists, in particular, were very vexed. Their basic argument was that Casey owed the fans and the players (and, of course, them) his presence on the field. My favorite moment came when one of the Four Horsemen, during an interview on ESPN, became so angry that all he could sputter was "I mean, you just *can't* do that." He paused and glanced weakly at the camera. "Can you?"

As I and every other true native New Englander fully expected, the Red Sox were eliminated in the wild card round of the play-offs. Some team must have won the World Series, but I neither noticed nor cared. I quit *SportsCenter* cold turkey in mid-October and the only time I now open the sports section is when the comics are buried inside the fold. With the continuing exception of the rancid *Garfield*, I do like the comics. I got a modest advance from a publisher to write this book and decided to stay in Boston while I hammered out a first draft. I rented an apartment in Charlestown, and I teach a reporting class at North Shore Community College to pass the time when I'm not sitting in front of my computer. I do enjoy the irony of my lecturing anyone on the ethics and values of reporting.

Jessica and I have been fitfully grinding toward intimacy at a pace usually reserved for things like glaciers and world peace. Some days I think she hates me, but so far she has remained for-giving enough to wait until her feelings return to something ap-proaching bewildered love. I loathe the word *nice*, but in this particular situation it's perfect. We have something nice. I think we have survived for the simple reason that we enjoy spending time together, and to this point she has proved remarkably resis-tant to the feminine need to mold boyfriends and husbands—not that I couldn't stand to be changed. She does, however, encour-age me to make new friends. Partially to appease her and partially because I think she's right, I've been bowling with a bunch of guys from a bar near my apartment. And sometimes I go to plays and concerts with some of the younger professors from the college.

My only real contact with baseball these days, outside of my book, comes once a week when I go to a batting cage out on Route 128. I bring a handful of quarters, and usually I arrive late enough that I'm the only person using the machines. My swing is

mediocre, but my eye is getting better, and I'm starting to entertain the idea of someday playing in a senior league. The kid who
works at the cage on Tuesdays and Thursday is pretty good—he
stars for his high school team—and sometimes I buy him a couple
dollars of balls. He always tries the Superfast! machine, which is
too quick for him, and nine times out of ten he either grounds it
weakly into the foam-rubber turf or pops it into the ratty mesh
covering the cage. But every now and then his weight will shift
just right, and his bat will streak through the zone straight and
true and pure, and for an instant I'll be reminded of Casey.

Actually, I often find myself reminded of Casey—and Molly—
although I hope that when I finish this book those memories will
gradually dim. Over the last few months, one particular quote of
Casey's has echoed through my brain. He once said, "There is no
magic left in Major League Baseball." I remember that he spoke
with such authority that he initially overwhelmed my usual intol-
erance for absolute statements, but as time has passed I've grown
to question whether or not he was right. In high school I read a
line by Blaise Pascal that has been with me ever since: "The eter-
nal silence of these infinite spaces terrifies me." For most of my life
those words described my existence on a level more powerful than
I could ever hope to articulate. I felt the overwhelming emptiness
of those infinite spaces; I drowned in a void I imagined myself
powerless to escape. Perhaps I would have floundered forever if
Casey hadn't proved to me that there is another way. In the most
unlikely place, under the most unlikely set of circumstances, he
showed me that I was not alone. And that is the truest kind of
magic that humans can make.

A few weeks ago I came across the work of another great
philosopher, Leroy "Satchel" Paige, who would have been the
Bob Gibson of the 1930s and 1940s if black athletes had been allowed to play Major League Baseball. "Don't look back," Paige
wrote in his autobiography. "Something may be gaining on you."
America has taken his advice to heart. I'm always amused when
other countries accuse us of myopia, for that charge ignores how
steadily we gallop toward the future, arms giddily extended, sel-

dom pausing to wonder if we are even charging down the right path. We like to think that our passion for the promise of tomorrow is our greatest strength; we seldom have the wisdom to reflect on whether that focus might also explain our weaknesses.

Sometimes when I'm sitting alone at the desk in my little study, my computer turned on but idle, I think about how clearly Casey could see what was gaining on him and baseball and America. At those moments I shudder for my friend. But then I remember where he is, and where he will be, and where I am, and where I will be, and I smile the tiniest smile and get back to my work.